"In December 1941, FDR and Churchill are marked for death by a Nazi assassin. A remarkable story that will keep you reading late into the night. Be prepared to be shocked to your feet by the unexpected climax. Don't miss this one."

—Catherine Coulter, #1 *New York Times* bestselling author of *Vortex*

"Another masterpiece from a master, and that's exactly what William Martin is. A reader will never be in more capable hands."

—Steve Berry, *New York Times* bestselling author of *The Kaiser's Web*

"This pedal-to-the-floor historical spy thriller is a knockout!"

—Karen Robards, *New York Times* bestselling author of *The Black Swan of Paris*

"William Martin's thriller *December '41* is a well-written, well-researched, and utterly engrossing work of historical fiction. . . . A great piece of writing that was a blast to read."

—Mark Greaney, #1 *New York Times* bestselling author of *The Gray Man*

"*December '41* is absolutely splendid, a cinematic thriller that takes us across the United States in the first days after Pearl Harbor. It places sharply observed heroes and an unforgettable villain at a unique moment in history, and reminded me of the great wartime movies. Bravo."

—Joseph Finder, *New York Times* bestselling author of *House on Fire*

"This thrilling read grips you by the throat and doesn't let go!"

—Andrew Mayne, #1 Amazon bestselling author of *The Naturalist* and *The Girl Beneath the Sea*

"In William Martin's highly suspenseful historical thriller, America is reeling after the bombing of Pearl Harbor, and U.S. law enforcement at all levels understand that the Nazi threat is not just overseas. *December '41* is the ultimate page-turner. I loved it!"

—Jane Healey, bestselling author of *The Beantown Girls* and *The Secret Stealers*

BOOKS BY WILLIAM MARTIN

December '41

Bound for Gold

The Lincoln Letter

City of Dreams

The Lost Constitution

Harvard Yard

Citizen Washington

Annapolis

Cape Cod

The Rising of the Moon

Nerve Endings

Back Bay

DECEMBER '41

WILLIAM MARTIN

TOR PUBLISHING GROUP

NEW YORK

DECEMBER '41

Copyright © 2022 by William Martin

Map by Jon Lansberg

A Forge Book
Published by Tom Doherty Associates / Tor Publishing Group
120 Broadway
New York, NY 10271

www.tor-forge.com

Forge® is a registered trademark of Macmillan Publishing Group, LLC.

The Library of Congress has cataloged the hardcover edition as follows:

Names: Martin, William, 1950– author.
Title: December '41 / William Martin.
Description: First edition. | New York : Forge, a Tom Doherty Associates
    Book, 2022. | Series: A World War II Thriller
Identifiers: LCCN 2022007996 (print) | LCCN 2022007997 (ebook) |
    ISBN 9780765384249 (hardcover) | ISBN 9780765384263 (ebook)
Classification: LCC PS3563.A7297 D43 2022 (print) |
    LCC PS3563.A7297 (ebook) | DDC 813/.54—dc23
LC record available at https://lccn.loc.gov/2022007996
LC ebook record available at https://lccn.loc.gov/2022007997

ISBN 978-1-250-83975-6 (trade paperback)

Our books may be purchased in bulk for promotional, educational, or business use. Please contact your local bookseller or the Macmillan Corporate and Premium Sales Department at 1-800-221-7945, extension 5442, or by email at MacmillanSpecialMarkets@macmillan.com.

First Forge Paperback Edition: 2023

Printed in the United States of America

0 9 8 7 6 5 4 3 2 1

For Chris
in the boat or on the trail,
in crowded rooms or quarantine,
after half a century
the center that always holds

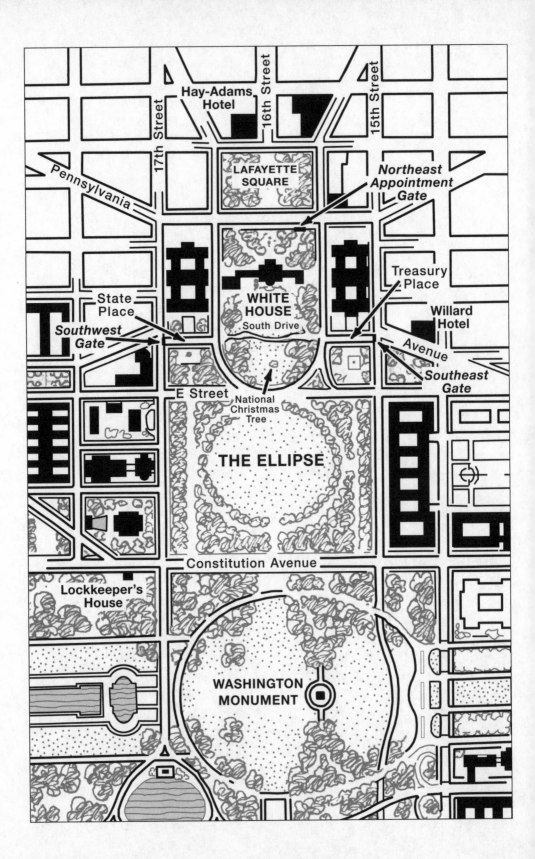

PART ONE

LOS ANGELES

MONDAY,
DECEMBER 8, 1941

It was the largest radio audience in history.

On the cold coast of Maine, they were listening. Down on Wall Street, trading stopped so they could listen. On assembly lines in Detroit, they were taking long lunches so the autoworkers could listen. In Chicago, the butchers stopped slaughtering in the stockyards to listen. In Kansas and Nebraska and Iowa, where they grew corn and wheat enough to feed the world, now that the rains had returned and the dust had stopped blowing, the farmers were listening there, too.

In all the places where the muscle and sinew of America bound one state or town or family to another, they were listening for the warm baritone and patrician inflections that somehow never sounded too upper-crusty coming out of the radio . . .

. . . because America had awakened that morning to the cold reality of war, war in every time zone, war encircling the earth, war once more as the original human fact.

In Hawaii, U.S. Navy battleships burned beneath great funerary clouds of black oil smoke. In the far Pacific, Japanese troops attacked along every line of latitude and longitude. In swirling blizzards of blood and snow, Russians and Germans slaughtered each other before Moscow. Across Europe, jackboots echoed and resistance guttered, while U-boats stalked freighters on the roiling gray Atlantic. But Americans were listening because Franklin Roosevelt was about to make sense of it all.

In Washington, the CBS radio announcer was describing the packed House chamber, the tense atmosphere . . . when suddenly his voice rose: "Now, ladies and gentlemen, the president is appearing and moving toward the podium."

And from out of deep-bass consoles and tinny tabletop radios in every corner of the country, a roar exploded, something between a cheer and an angry shout, the harsh, hard, ferocious cry of Americans lifting themselves from shock and drawing strength from the president who'd lifted himself from a wheelchair and by remarkable force of will was appearing upright before them.

When the roar receded, the Speaker announced, "Senators and Representatives, I have the distinguished honor of presenting the president of the United States."

More cheers and shouts, then Franklin Roosevelt's voice rang out, firm, confident, indignant: "Mr. Vice President, Mr. Speaker, members of the Senate and the House of Representatives: Yesterday, December 7, 1941—a date which will live in infamy—the United States of America was suddenly and deliberately attacked by naval and air forces of the Empire of Japan. . . .”

In the West, radio stations had gone off the air the night before so that Japanese bombers couldn't home in on the broadcasts.

But now, Roosevelt's voice rolled across deserts, up and over mountain ranges, and down into the warm green dream of Southern California, down along boulevards laid like gridwork atop lettuce fields and orange groves, down onto long, straight, relentless thoroughfares that ended where scrub-covered hillsides leaped up to define and divide the expanse of Los Angeles, down into offices and coffee shops and cars where people were listening, unaware that as Roosevelt spoke, a Nazi assassin was shooting at targets in a local canyon and planning the most daring act of the age, unaware also that before it was over, he would draw many of them into his dark orbit.

ONE OF THEM, a young man named Kevin Cusack, was listening in the Warner Bros. story department. He and his friends should have been working. They were the gang who read the plays and novels sent out from New York, then synopsized them and offered opinions. A pile of books and manuscripts lay on the table. But Jack L. Warner himself was probably listening, so why shouldn't they?

Kevin's next assignment: a play called *Everybody Comes to Rick's*. He didn't hold much hope for it. All he needed to read was the story editor's one-liner: “A love triangle set in wartime Casablanca.” He hated love triangles. But when you worked on the bottom rung in the story department for a buck twelve an hour, you took what they gave you.

And the job was good cover, along with his Irish surname and dark Irish brow. His friends in the German American Bund loved that he worked by day in a “nest of Hollywood Jews,” then went down to Deutsches Haus, the Bund hall, to drink German beer and deliver the gossip every night. If they'd known that he was really a spy who passed information to the Los Angeles Jewish Community Committee, who then passed it to the FBI, those jolly Germans might have killed him.

But he felt safe at the studio. When Roosevelt said, “No matter how long it may take us to overcome this premeditated invasion, the American people in their righteous might will win through to absolute victory,” Kevin cheered right along with those congressmen and senators back in Washington.

So did all the others around the conference table. Jerry Sloane, an emotional kind of guy, wiped away a tear. Sally Drake, the only female in the room, the girl with the Vassar accent and Katharine Hepburn slacks, put her fingers in her mouth and gave out with a big ballpark whistle. Pretty good for a college girl.

Kevin liked Sally. He liked her a lot. So did Jerry. And Jerry seemed to be winning. Maybe that was why Kevin hated love triangles.

OVER ON WEST OLIVE, Big Time Breakfast of Burbank was pumping out the all-American aromas of bacon and coffee. In some small ways, life went on as usual on the day after Pearl Harbor. People got hungry. People got thirsty. People dreamed of better days. But in the booths and at the counter, conversation and plate-scraping stopped as soon as the president's voice came out of the radio. Now all the day players and studio hands were listening, except for one young woman in a yellow dress who sat at the end of the counter, sipped her coffee, and stared into space.

Vivian Hopewell didn't have money for breakfast, not in a restaurant anyway. She barely had money for a bowl of cornflakes at home, if that's what you could call a single in a crummy Glendale rooming house.

Rattling around in her purse were three nickels, two dimes, and an envelope containing one glossy headshot. She always carried a headshot. A girl had to be ready. Now that there was a war on, maybe she'd catch a break. Folks back home always said she looked like a young Marlene Dietrich. Maybe that Germanic bone structure might appeal to some casting director who needed a Nazi villainess.

But in the brown paper bag at her feet she carried a pair of white, rubber-soled flats and a gray uniform dress, to show that she knew how to wait tables, too, from back when she was just plain Kathy Schortmann of Annapolis, Maryland.

The owner had already given her the bad news: he'd hired somebody else. "She ain't quite so pretty as you, so she ain't likely to go runnin' across the street if she gets a walk-on in some cheapo serial."

"Across the street" was Gate 4, a breach in the wall surrounding the Warner Bros. soundstages that were more beautiful to Vivian than the Taj Mahal . . . and just as remote. And it was true. If she ever got a role—good girl, bad girl, or background-broad bit part—she'd be gone from that breakfast counter before she untied her apron.

So she finished her coffee and stepped out into the sunshine. At least there was always sunshine. It made the disappointment easier to take. She glanced again at Gate 4, then checked the bus schedule back to Glendale. Maybe she'd hitch a ride and save a nickel. Or maybe she'd walk. It was only six miles, and she had her waitress shoes.

FBI SPECIAL AGENT FRANK Carter was listening, too, until he heard a gunshot. He told his driver to turn down the radio. He was riding in the back seat of a government-issue Ford sedan with three other agents, all in dark Hoover-approved suits.

They'd traveled out Sunset and taken the right opposite the Riviera Country Club, a high-hat address in an up-and-coming part of town. But in L.A., even the best street could dead-end against a scrubby hillside or lead into some wild canyon. So at the top, they'd headed onto the Sullivan Ridge Fire Road, with an LAPD patrol wagon close behind. This was a raid.

To the left, the land dropped three hundred feet through gray-green chaparral and bay bush, down to a stream called Rustic Creek. Then it jumped up again, up into the sunshine, up to that ridgeline running away to the west and down to the sea.

Carter told the driver to pull over.

"Why here?" asked Agent Mike McDonald, who also sat in the back seat with a map on his knees. "This shows all the Nazi stuff down at the bottom."

"It also shows a fence and two flights of stairs. Cut the engine." Carter got out, looked at the paddy wagon, and made a gesture with his hand. *Turn it off.* Then he stood for a moment and listened.

No more gunshots. No shouts of alarm. Only the hum of a generator somewhere below and FDR's voice riding the updraft like a whisper.

So . . . down in their compound, the Nazis were listening, too.

Carter studied the chain-link fence. One side descended into the canyon, and the other ran along the road on fresh concrete footings, cordoning off a property purchased from the enormous estate of cowboy comedian Will Rogers in 1933.

"They fenced it all," said McDonald. "Fifty-five acres. That's a lot of fence. And the road. They paved the road. Who the hell paves a fire road on a ridgeline?"

Carter didn't answer. No need to answer. Not worth answering. In general, he followed the rule of the New York street: Never write when you can speak, never speak when you can nod, never nod when you can wink. It had served him well in the FBI, so well that he'd climbed all the way to second-in-command at the L.A. field office, which overnight had become the busiest place in town.

Before the bombs had stopped falling in Hawaii, the teletype had begun clattering out the names of Japanese and German nationals, along with American citizens who displayed certain disloyal "tendencies." Some were dangerous, some merely victims of their heritage. But by dawn, twenty-five FBI agents, supported by the LAPD, had fanned out across the city and grabbed two hundred and fifty Japanese. Now they were turning to the Germans, and there were a lot of Germans down in that canyon.

The property was called the Murphy Ranch, but the real owners were named Stephens, mining millionaires and Nazi sympathizers, of which L.A. had more than its share: the German American Bund, the Silver Legion, the America Firsters, the Ku Klux Klan, and a lot more.

And they'd all spent the last eight years warming up for *der Tag*, the day when they'd rise up, get rid of all the Jews, and give Hitler a great big happy-days-are-here-again Hollywood welcome. A true fifth column, right in the town where they brought the American dream to life on the silver screen . . . and a lot of folks lived it, too.

That's what Carter believed, anyway, thanks to a bunch of amateur spies known as the Los Angeles Jewish Community Committee, or LAJCC for short. While the FBI spent its time chasing Commies, these Jews and their friends had placed some pretty bold operatives in those pro-Nazi gangs. And Carter was glad of it.

He took off his hat and wiped the sweat from his forehead. Most people loved the perpetual springtime of Southern California. But Carter was an East Coast guy. To him, seventy degrees in December was just . . . strange. Every morning, he told himself that if he did his job, he'd get back to New York or Washington, and sooner rather than later.

On the other side of the fence, a long flight of concrete steps dropped past a massive steel tank and disappeared into tree cover below.

How well these Nazi lovers were building, he thought. They'd even hired a big L.A. architecture firm to design a forty-room mansion, supposedly as Hitler's California hideaway. There wasn't any sign of it yet, but the owners had spent millions on the roads, the fences, a power station, terraced gardens for food, a motor pool, even a stable.

"That's some tank," said McDonald.

"That's for water," said Carter. "Gas for the generators is farther down."

Two guards in shiny silver-gray shirts, blue jodhpurs, and blue field caps—privates in the Silver Legion—came huffing and puffing up the long flight of concrete steps, rifles at the ready.

Before they caught their breath, Carter ordered them to open the gate.

"We can't do that, sir. Private property," said one of them.

Carter flipped his badge. "FBI. Put down the guns and open the goddamn gate." When they hesitated, he gestured to Agent Doane, who raised his tommy gun.

A moment later, the lock popped. The chain-link swung open.

Carter told the cops to arrest the Silver Legion lackeys. Then he told Doane, "Cover the steps, shoot anything that moves, and no smoking." Then he headed back to the car.

McDonald hustled after him, saying, "Doanie gets the jitters without a smoke. And he's trigger-happy enough already."

"Today, we're all trigger-happy. Trigger-happy is good." Carter turned to the paddy wagon and spun his finger in the air. *Start the siren.*

DEEP IN THE CANYON, German agent Martin Browning had been tracking the engine noise. When it stopped, he'd told the others that target practice was over. Then he'd begun detaching his Mauser C96 pistol from its shoulder stock.

But Fritz Kessler had squeezed off one last round, just to show who was boss of their little cell. At least skinny Tom Stengle did as he was told.

Martin Browning had been reluctant to join them that morning, but Kessler had insisted, because doing things out of the ordinary attracted attention. And on Mondays they shot targets at the Murphy Ranch. Martin knew that this Monday would be different. But agents hiding in plain sight should keep to routines. Besides, there might be news from Berlin, picked up on the short-wave in the powerhouse. This might be his last chance to practice the killing shot. So here he was.

Martin Browning preferred to work alone. But he needed a target range, and he needed money, because money let him maintain multiple identities, go by many names, keep numerous addresses.

As far as his family knew, he was still studying in Germany. But Martin Browning—born Martin Bruning, 1911, in Koblenz am Rhein, raised from the age of eleven in Flatbush, Brooklyn, educated at Heidelberg, recruited into Section 6, the foreign intelligence division of the Reich Security Office—had slipped back into the States two years earlier aboard a German ship that docked at Long Beach, a favorite Nazi port of entry, since the FBI paid a lot less attention to Germans in California than in New York, and certain elements of the LAPD were downright friendly.

Martin Browning had connected with L.A. Bund leader Hermann Schwinn, who met every German ship, conferred with Gestapo agents who were always aboard, and returned to Deutsches Haus with orders, propaganda, and American cash to fund operations on the West Coast. When Schwinn asked Martin to join the Bund, Martin decided it would be the best way to stay in Schwinn's good graces, which would be the best way to maintain his flow of Nazi cash, which he needed more than anyone's good graces.

The sirens were moving now, down the fire road toward the compound gate. Martin Browning slipped his Mauser into its wooden holster and slipped the holster into a leather satchel. Then he told the others it was time to go.

"Let's run for the stables," said Stengle. "Get horses and ride out to the north . . . up Mandeville Canyon, up to Mulholland—"

"The feds are too close," said Martin Browning. "You'll never get past."

Stengle's voice quavered. "I . . . I don't want to get caught."

Browning shifted his eyes to Kessler. "Do you have a plan?"

"We parked out on the street for the quick escape." Kessler tapped his temple, the brains of the operation. "So we go up the concrete stairs. We go up while the FBI is down here arresting Silver Shirts. We go up, get in our car, and get away."

A dozen or more members of the Silver Legion were always patrolling the property, drilling, practicing street-fighting tactics, pretending to be real soldiers. Martin Browning didn't give them much thought, although pretending was the first step to becoming. Hitler and his Brownshirts had proven that.

Kessler wiped sweat from his hairline and fumbled for a cigarette.

Martin Browning knew that the big German blowhard, a waiter and bouncer at the Gaststube, the Bund hall restaurant, was doing his best to keep calm. Martin considered Kessler a fool, and the worst kind, who believed he understood life in all its small details and grand strategies, all because he'd spent time in a trench on the Western Front in 1918.

Stengle was younger, quieter, an American-born tradesman who'd migrated from Maine in search of a steady job. He hadn't found it, which remained the fate of many Americans, even after eight years of FDR's New Deal, which made them prime targets for Nazi recruiters. Martin Browning didn't think much of Stengle's brainpower, either. At least he was more likable than Kessler.

But neither would be with Martin Browning when he headed for Washington, so he didn't care what happened to them now, as long as they didn't incriminate him.

He watched Kessler scratch a match and fail. Then another. He pulled out his lighter, flipped, and held it under Kessler's nose.

Kessler took a few puffs and said, "Thanks, Ash."

They called him "Ash" because they said he looked like Ashley Wilkes in *Gone With the Wind:* slender and wiry, with blondish hair and a professorial air.

A mild appearance and a tone of reserved condescension made for a good persona. But did they know that Leslie Howard, the English actor who played the Southern aristocrat, was really a Jew? Now was not the time to discuss it.

Instead, Martin Browning knelt and ran his fingers through the grass.

"What are you doing?" asked Stengle.

"Cleaning up." He'd fired ten shots. He needed to pick up ten cartridges. He'd leave no trails.

"Forget the brass," said Kessler. "Up the stairs."

"But Fritz," said Stengle, "what if they're guarding the stairs?" He turned to Martin. "What if they're guarding the stairs, Ash?"

Martin Browning didn't answer. He was feeling, reaching, searching for that last cartridge. Had he only fired nine shots? No. Ten. Ten in the magazine, ten at the target.

He'd counted. He always counted. He was always careful. But it was time to go.

The G-men might not notice a single stubby cartridge among the longer casings. They might not bother to look. But he could only find nine cartridges.

And now, blue lights were flashing through the trees. The feds had reached the bottom of the canyon.

One of the Silver Shirts came splashing across the creek. "Herr Kessler! They're here. You must run."

Kessler turned to Browning, and said, "Come on, Ash, forget the—"

But Martin Browning was already gone, disappeared, as if into thin air.

IN THE CLEARING AT the powerhouse, Frank Carter was holding up his badge. "Federal agents. You're all under arrest!"

"Do not run," said the head Silver Shirt, a young guy with blond hair and a sharp prairie accent. "Obey their orders."

"That's right," said Carter. "Just line up like good Nazis."

The leader said, "We're good *Americans,* sir."

"Sure you are," said Carter.

And from the powerhouse came a German accent. "Please note, *mein Herr,* that we are obliging peacefully."

Carter jerked his head to McDonald. "See what's in there."

The German asked, "Do you have a warrant?"

"We have orders," answered Carter. "We have custodial detention memos. We have probable cause. What's your name?"

"Hans Schmidt." He raised his chin and affected the arrogant air of a Prussian officer, a neat trick for a man in a rumpled brown suit and squashed fedora.

"What do you do here?"

"I am the caretaker, *mein Herr.*"

"I'm not your '*Herr.*'" Carter told a cop, "Cuff him."

Suddenly the air thrummed with the sound of the tommy gun.

McDonald said, "I told you to let Doanie have a smoke."

MARTIN BROWNING STOPPED RUNNING and located the sound of the firing. Had some trigger-happy G-man shot Kessler and Stengle on the long flight of concrete steps out of the canyon? Good, especially if they were both dead. Better dead than blabbing.

He'd taken an escape route, scouted alone, to be followed alone. He was now pounding through the bushes and brush, straight down the line of Rustic Creek, ducking here, leaping there, running wherever he could, ignoring the wet when he couldn't, flying headlong and fast, rock to rock, downhill but controlled. Always controlled.

He wore good shoes, a blue wool suit, a white shirt. He carried his leather satchel over his shoulder and resembled nothing so much as a businessman on the way to work, even if that way went down a creek that bordered scrubby woodlots and big-time mansions harkening back to the days of Spanish California or Colonial Virginia.

SILVER SHIRTS NOW FILLED the LAPD patrol wagon. Most appeared sullen and angry, but a few went shamefaced, as if they realized that parading in silly uniforms made them look more like movie extras than soldiers, especially now that the real war had started.

Carter told the caretaker, "Next stop, Terminal Island."

"I do not like the sound of this word . . . 'terminal.'"

"You'll have plenty of company. Of course if you help us—"

"How?"

"Tell me what else we've missed . . . and who else."

"I could not say. The owners open this property to many groups. They are good friends of Germany."

"Good friends of Hitler, you mean."

"Hitler and Germany are one and the same, holding the same hopes for friendship with America."

Carter almost laughed in his face.

Then Agent McDonald came out of the powerhouse, shouting. "Hey, boss! They got a shortwave radio!"

"Did you find codebooks?" Carter turned to Schmidt. "Are there codebooks?"

"Codebooks? Why would we need codebooks?" asked the German.

MARTIN BROWNING STOPPED IN the concrete culvert that ran under Sunset Boulevard. He put on his necktie, dried his shoes with a towel he carried in his satchel, and splashed some Old Spice on his face. It would never do for a Burbank haberdasher to come to work smelling like a man who'd just run two miles down a canyon. His last gesture to good grooming: he scooped some water from the stream flowing through the culvert, wet his hair, and combed it straight back.

Thus he became James Costner, a man who cared about his looks and his scent, a man who knew the difference between Egyptian cotton and the cheap stuff, a man to trust when he offered opinions on the length of a cuff or a nip at the waist. The final touch: a pair of horn-rimmed glasses with clear lenses to make him look more civilized, even as he climbed an embankment into the dappled sunshine of Dead Man's Curve.

That's what they called this hairpin turn on Sunset, the famous thoroughfare that ran from downtown L.A., through Hollywood, across Beverly Hills, and ended with this twisty five-mile downhill run to the Pacific. Dead Man's

Curve was the perfect spot for speeders to spin off into the trees or swerve into the other lane. But from here, any G-men stationed at the corner couldn't see him. And just downhill, a turnout led to a dirt road, a good place for a car to stop.

The dirt road climbed through the trees to the Will Rogers Polo Field, where all the Hollywood big shots had their helmet-and-saddle fun on the weekends. Some of them, like Darryl F. Zanuck and Hal Wallis, actually put on the helmets, took to the saddles, and played. At least, that was how it was written up in the gossip pages.

Kessler had often said that they could kill "a lot of big Jews" if they sneaked up the far side of Rustic Canyon and started shooting on a Sunday afternoon. He wanted to kill Zanuck, who was probably a Communist, too, since he'd made that *Grapes of Wrath* movie. When Browning pointed out that Zanuck wasn't a Jew, Kessler said he looked like one and acted like one, which was even worse.

Martin Browning wanted no part of that. Now that *der Tag* had come, he'd have bigger fish to fry than some know-it-all movie producer, Jew or Gentile. Hating Jews had never been part of his profile, despite the indoctrination of his Reich Security training. If he hated anyone, it was the French who occupied Koblenz after the Great War and caused his parents to pack up and move to America.

He walked down to the turnout and stuck out his thumb. He didn't care how he got a ride. He'd even take one from some Hollywood Jew.

FRANK CARTER WAS SITTING in the car with the German caretaker. He knew the guy was lying—about everything—but he still had questions. He held out a handful of cartridges. "Can you explain these? I found these in the grass."

"Shell casings on a target range? Such a surprise."

Carter picked out one that was stubbier than the others. "Looks like 7.63-by-25-millimeter, probably a pistol cartridge, mixed in with rifle casings."

The German stared out the window, as if it were none of his concern.

"All right," said Carter. "I hear Terminal Island is lovely this time of year."

AFTER TEN MINUTES OF thumbing, Martin Browning wished that Claudette Colbert were with him. She got Clark Gable a ride in *It Happened One Night*, just by sticking her leg out. But this was no movie, and nobody was stopping. And the longer he stayed, the more likely the cops would drive by and stop to question a well-dressed guy hitchhiking on a deserted stretch of Sunset on the day after Pearl Harbor.

Then down the hill came a '39 Lincoln-Zephyr convertible, all maroon and chrome, top down, slowing down, pulling into the turnout. The driver was about sixty, gazing up through expensive sunglasses, looking prosperous and looking for company, too.

Martin Browning considered himself an expert analyst of faces, attitudes, and the environments that people built to express themselves. Americans, he had concluded, were far too friendly and much too trusting. But he liked the environment this man had created. He liked the car. So he plugged in the electric grin that he could flash like a beer sign and said, "Dead battery. I could use a lift to the trolley stop at Temescal."

Without a moment's thought—maybe he considered himself an expert at the size-up, too—the driver said, "Hop in."

Martin Browning slid onto the red leather seat and put his satchel on the floor.

The big Lincoln rolled back onto Sunset. Traffic was light. On the radio, they were playing "Chattanooga Choo Choo."

Martin offered his alias: "I'm James."

"I'm Arthur. You like that song?"

"Doesn't everyone?"

"Just topped the charts yesterday. Goddamn bad luck, if you ask me."

"How so?"

"How so?" The man gave the kind of dismissive laugh that a pro gives when an amateur asks a dumb question. "On the day you get to number one on *Billboard*, the Japs go and bomb Pearl Harbor?"

"Takes all the fun out of it, I guess."

Arthur adjusted the tuning knob. "The only station playing music. The rest are still yapping about Roosevelt's speech. We're at war with the Japs. They started it. We'll finish it. What the hell else do you need to know?"

"Are we . . . are we also at war with Germany?" asked Martin Browning.

"Nah. We'll deal with them later."

Martin relaxed. Until Germany and the United States were officially at war, his task was to keep his head down and wait.

Arthur said, "You mark my words, friend. Music will get us through this. The Japs and the Germans, they don't have Glenn Miller or Tommy Dorsey."

Another thing about Americans that Martin Browning found both amusing and encouraging: they had no sense of proportion. They thought their silly songs were as potent as the arsenals of the warrior nations they were about to fight.

Also silly were the man's clothes—blue jersey, tweed knickers, stockings matching the jersey. A golf bag lay across the back seat with a tag reading HILLCREST COUNTRY CLUB, ARTHUR KOPPEL. So, a Jew. Only rich Jews played at Hillcrest.

Martin said, "Golf today?"

"Why retire in L.A. if you can't hit the links whenever you feel like it?"

"Golf I like very much." Martin Browning spoke with no accent and a good knowledge of American slang. But he'd spent so many years in Germany that sometimes his syntax was slightly off, especially when he was lying. And he knew nothing about golf.

The driver didn't seem to notice. He said, "Where do you play?"

"Griffith Park." Martin knew of a course there, named for Warren G. Harding, a bad president. He often wondered how this nation could have survived so long, considering the low quality of some of the men elected to lead it. But perhaps this "experiment in democracy" wouldn't last much longer.

"What's your handicap?" asked Arthur Koppel.

"The clubs," said Martin, hoping to conceal his ignorance with a joke.

Mission accomplished. Arthur laughed, then asked, "So . . . where are you headed?"

"Burbank. I'm a haberdasher."

"You're in luck. On Mondays, I play at the Encino Country Club. I'll take you over Topanga and drop you on Sherman Way. You can catch the trolley straight to Burbank. Much faster than starting at Temescal."

The Pacific Electric trolleys linked all the cities and towns of greater Los Angeles. It might take you half a day, but you could go from Reseda to San Bernardino, Pasadena to San Pedro, all on what Angelenos called "the Big Red Cars." Martin Browning—as James Costner—knew the system well.

"But . . . a haberdasher, you say? A glorified suit salesman?" Arthur Koppel raised an eyebrow. "From Burbank? Way out here on a Monday morning?"

Martin offered an innocent smile. He had an array of smiles. Innocent was one of the best.

Koppel patted his knee. "Don't worry, pal. Your secret's safe with me. But you missed a few spots."

"Missed?" Martin looked out the window so that Koppel didn't see the color drain from his face. Some people blushed when caught out. Martin went white, and his eyes—according to certain women—lost all luster, like a snake's.

"With that towel sticking out of your bag. You missed a few spots on your trousers."

Yes, Martin Browning had missed a few spots. He would have to be more careful. He pushed the corner of the towel back into the leather satchel.

Arthur Koppel kept talking. "So . . . let me guess. You came down Rustic Creek and popped out on Sunset because—"

Martin feared what he would have to do if this guy said the wrong thing.

But Koppel just waved a hand. "Ah, never mind. I was young myself once. I nailed a few rich wives. So . . . did the husband come home early? Did the wife shove you out the back, tell you to go down the creek and not let anyone see you?"

Martin forced out a laugh and added a wink.

Arthur Koppel laughed, too, and drove for a time with his fingers tapping out the beat of the music. Then he said, "Or was it the *husband* shoving you out the door because the *wife* came home early?"

So, thought Martin, was that what Arthur Koppel was fishing for? Had he picked up this well-dressed hitchhiker on a dangerous bend of Sunset . . . for sex?

Arthur Koppel must have seen the look in Martin's eyes, because he said, "Hey, no offense, pal. In this town, you never know. Some of the toughest guys in the movies are just poofs when they pull their pants down. Not like us."

"No. Not like us." Martin decided to let that go . . . or use it. Information of any kind, about anyone, was meant to be stored . . . and used.

As Glenn Miller played them through sleepy Palisades Village, Arthur Koppel talked. Lonely men who picked up hitchhikers were usually talkers. He talked about lawyering for ASCAP, the American Society of Composers, Authors and Publishers. They'd been in a big royalty fight with CBS and NBC. "We didn't let them play any ASCAP songs for six months. All they had was hillbilly stuff—say, you're not a guy who goes for that shitkicker baloney, are you?"

Martin shook his head.

"What about jazz and blues? You know, jigaboo music?"

Another thing about Americans, thought Martin, they preached that their strength was many cultures mixing and thriving. *E pluribus unum.* Out of the many, one. But in private, or when offering unbidden opinions, it was usually the opposite that they embraced. Germans paid no such lip service to false ideals. Germans embraced the truth.

Sunset Boulevard ended at the Pacific Coast Highway in a splash of green palm trees, golden-brown beachscape, and the boundless blues of sea and sky. Martin allowed himself to be transported by the color, by the thrum of the big twelve-cylinder engine, by the breeze blowing over the open top.

Who could know a day like this, he thought, so warm and bright when the rest of the world lay in December gloom, and not believe that all man's troubles might be soothed, even solved, by a little California sunshine, especially when Tommy Dorsey was playing "Blue Skies" on the radio, with Frank Sinatra doing the vocal?

Arthur Koppel said, "My wife loved that Sinatra kid."

"The voice of an angel," said Martin.

"Yeah, well, when the docs told her she'd be singin' with the angels soon, I retired. I wanted more time with her, but—"

Grief was a universal emotion, like greed or joy. Even the assassin understood. When he said, "I'm sorry for you," he meant it. But a few minutes later, he decided that he would have to kill Arthur Koppel.

At Topanga Canyon, Koppel took the turn without slowing, as if to show off the fine cornering of his car. The force caused the satchel at Martin's feet to fall on its side. The flap dropped open, and the towel flopped out, revealing the Mauser shoulder-stock holster.

Did Koppel see it? Would he even know what it was?

As the Lincoln-Zephyr climbed into the canyon, Koppel said, "Do you know, right near where I picked you up, there's supposed to be some kind of Nazi hangout?"

"Nazis?" Martin Browning kept his voice calm.

"Yep. Kraut-fartin', Hitler-heilin', Hebrew-hatin' Nazi son-of-a-bitches. People say they have a place back in Rustic Canyon, and they train and march and shoot and, well, we have to be careful now . . . about a lot of things."

"Yes," said Martin. "Very careful."

"So . . . is that why you go armed? Afraid of Nazis?"

"Armed?" asked Martin.

"I do a little shooting myself, right up ahead, at the Topanga Gun Club. I know my pistols. And the Mauser C96? Helluva gun. Churchill carried one in the Boer War."

"Churchill? Very interesting." Those were Martin's words, bland and blandly offered. But his thoughts were harsh: Arthur Koppel had entered the danger zone.

"Of course," Koppel went on, "if you attach the pistol to the shoulder-stock holster, it becomes a short-barreled rifle. Carrying one of those is a felony under the National Firearms Act of 1934. But you knew that, right?"

"Of course," said Martin.

The radio announcer said, "And now, Glenn Miller and His Orchestra on the RCA recording of 'A String of Pearls.'"

"One of my wife's favorites," said Arthur Koppel.

The road took a bend, ran through the little village, and kept climbing.

As they passed the gun club entrance, Arthur Koppel said, "Sure you don't want to strip a few clips? I have some pals, they'd just shit to see one of those pistols."

"No, no," said Martin gently, although his resolve hardened with Koppel's every word. "I should get to work. The best we can do for our country is get to work."

"I suppose you're right. . . . Say, what's a starched-collar salesman from Burbank doing with a gun like that anyway? Seems a little suspicious, don't you think?"

"I like to shoot." For a moment, Martin Browning held his gaze on Koppel, who'd sealed his fate with words like "felony" and "suspicious." Then he turned to the radio and said, "A song about a man giving his wife a beautiful string of pearls. Did you ever give one to *your* wife?"

"Oh, yeah. She always wore it with a blue cashmere sweater. Matched her eyes."

"You miss her a great deal, no?" Martin patted Arthur Koppel's knee. He knew just how to do this to signal his intentions or allow them to be ignored. "You miss her voice. You miss her touch."

Koppel looked at Martin's hand. "I miss her a lot."

"A man can get lonely." Martin glanced in the side mirror. No one behind them. And up ahead was the turnout for Top of Topanga, the overlook into the San Fernando Valley. He told Arthur Koppel to take it.

"But—"

"I need to piss," said Martin.

Arthur looked at his watch and wavered.

"Come on, pull over," said Martin, inviting rather than ordering.

And Arthur Koppel made the worst decision of his life. He turned into the huge unpaved parking lot with the famous view.

Just as Martin had hoped, the lot was deserted. On the morning after Pearl Harbor, no one was interested in scenery.

Arthur Koppel pulled up and put the car in neutral, but he left the engine running. Then he pointed toward the bushes. "Go ahead."

"It can wait," said Martin. "There are other things we need, I think."

Arthur Koppel answered as if he sensed danger. "Like what?"

"We're both men of the world. You picked me up because you're lonely, like me. I just have one question."

"What?"

"Are you a giver or a taker?"

Arthur Koppel said, "Put up the top and find out."

Martin studied this retired lawyer and wondered: Did he really want it? Or was he just trying to get Martin out of the car before speeding off? So Martin leaned over and turned off the engine. Then he took the key.

Arthur Koppel's eyes filled with panic. "Hey, hey, what are you doing."

Martin opened the door and got out. "I'll show you in a sec."

Quickly, before anyone else came into the lot, Martin undid the flaps and latches on the stowaway top, then lifted. The canopy rose smoothly and dropped with perfect American precision onto the frame of the windshield.

Martin got back into the car and said, "I'm a giver."

For a moment, there was silence . . . and heat, the heat of the sun baking through the canvas top, the heat of anticipation for both men. Arthur Koppel had clearly decided that he wanted whatever comfort this well-dressed stranger was offering. What Martin Browning wanted was a kind of comfort, too, the comfort of a clean kill.

Martin put his left hand on Arthur's neck . . . like a lover, caressing.

Arthur Koppel whispered, "I'm so damn lonely."

Martin drew Koppel's head gently toward him, then tightened his grip, held the head in place.

Arthur Koppel's eyes opened wide in panic. He tried to pull away.

But Martin Browning had arms like steel cables, and Koppel didn't move. Browning looped his right middle finger into the ring on the punching knife that he kept in a scabbard on the side of his shoe. Then his fist flashed upward, driving the four-inch blade into Koppel's throat, just above the Adam's apple. He felt it slice through the back of the mouth, severing the tongue, piercing the soft palate and delicate sinus bones, and digging deep into the brain.

Arthur Koppel was dead before he realized he'd been stabbed.

The heart stopped pumping. The knife missed the major arteries. There would be little blood. So . . . a clean kill . . . and no witnesses.

WHEN IT GOT DARK, thought Vivian Hopewell, it was supposed to get cold. That was how it worked in Maryland. And it made sense. But everything made sense in Maryland. Nothing did in L.A. At least it was warm.

She was wearing just a light sweater over her sleeveless yellow dress, and still she was sweating . . . or radiating, as her mother used to say.

Lord, but she missed her mother. She missed her mother's opinions. She missed her mother's Monday-night meat loaf. And she missed December's cold with Christmas coming on.

She dragged herself up the front steps of the rooming house and heard the landlady scurrying. One of the blinds flipped up, and old Mrs. Murray peered out. House Rule No. 1: No male visitors. . . . Not that Vivian was interested.

Her room looked across San Fernando Road to the train yards. The girls in the back had a better view—the Verdugo Hills, tinted purple in the fading light. Much quieter back there, too, but another buck a week. So Vivian had one of the front rooms.

She'd taken all day to get home from Big Time Breakfast of Burbank, pounding the pavement like a traveling salesman. But she didn't have a sample case. She had legs. Back when she was plain old Kathy Schortmann, people used to say she had the best legs in town. And the pumps showed them off. So for a while, she'd worn them, no matter how much they hurt.

She'd even put some snap in her step when she walked by the new Disney studio, because you never knew who might be driving onto the lot or looking out a window. Not much work for real girls at Disney, unless they could type or take dictation, but maybe some animator might need a model to give Snow

White a few nice curves or . . . nah. In Hollywood, nice curves were as common as cars, and the girls were so pretty, they made Vivian look more like Ma Joad than Marlene Dietrich.

She'd even taken a side trip into the Burbank business district and tried three more restaurants. No, no, and no, thanks. Then, in the window of Mr. Fountain's Men's Shop, she'd seen a sign: TAILOR WANTED. . . .

The little bell above the door rang. A mannequin in a blue suit smiled at her. In the corner a salesman and a customer talked.

The customer was saying, "I sure am glad you're open today, Costner."

The salesman flicked his eyes at her. "Someone will be right with you, miss."

She thanked him and looked around. She ran her hand over the fabric on the mannequin. She inspected the case of men's furnishings—cuff links, tie clips, collar tabs, and a little sign, MADE EXCLUSIVELY FOR MR. FOUNTAIN. PERFECT ACCESSORIES FOR A SPECIAL GENT ON CHRISTMAS MORNING.

She overheard the salesman saying, "An executive visiting Washington must wear a tie that projects confidence. Whimsy won't win a war . . . or a defense contract."

"People like me are going to be flocking to Washington," said the customer. "Airplane contractors to the Defense Department, bankers to Treasury, farmers to the Agriculture Department . . . we'll all have a part to play."

The salesman placed a tie on the man's shoulder to appraise fabric and color. Then he said, "Will you be talking about the new plane in Washington, sir?"

"New plane?" asked the customer.

"The twin-engine fighter? I've seen them in the sky all afternoon."

"The P-38s? We're flying them out. Some we're sending east to safety. Some we're sending to coastal air stations. We'll give the Japs a taste of their own medicine if they try anything in California."

Yes, Vivian had noticed a lot of planes in the sky.

The salesman said, "The long-range fuel tanks you're developing, will they allow the planes to reach Germany?"

The customer winked. "Don't tell Hitler," and they both laughed.

Then a smaller, older man—hair slicked, mustache polished—slid up to Vivian and said, "I'm Mr. Fountain. May I help you?"

She gestured to the sign in the window. "You need a tailor."

"Do you know one?"

"I can cuff trousers, mend holes, take in a jacket like the one on that dummy—"

"It's called a mannequin," said Mr. Fountain. "And I'm afraid I prefer to have men measuring men. A beautiful girl like you, sticking a tape near a fellow's crotch?"

"How about sales, then?" She wasn't looking at the salesman with his nice suit and slicked-back hair, but she could feel him glaring at her through his owlish eyeglasses.

Mr. Fountain shook his head. "Afraid not."

She gave them a little "toodle-oo" wave of the fingers, just to show that she was undaunted, plucked a business card from the counter, and left. . . .

From there, it had taken her two hours to walk home in her waitress shoes.

A moment after she kicked them off, Mrs. Murray was shoving an envelope over the chain lock. "This came for you. A man in a rumpled suit. Said his name was Buddy."

If she'd had anything in her stomach, Vivian might have vomited.

Buddy Clapper had been sniffing around ever since he first noticed her nibbling a grilled cheese in the Steam Engine Diner. He bought her a piece of pie that night, then started courting her. But it wasn't love he wanted, as this note proved: "Three guys from Chicago. Convention canceled thanks to Japs. Big spenders looking for fun. Meet at Steam Engine, 9PM. Wear pumps. Make $100. Buddy C."

KEVIN CUSACK FINISHED READING *Everybody Comes to Rick's* around six. He'd been so lost in it that he barely noticed the comings and goings in the rest of the department.

When Rick told Victor Laszlo to take the girl and go, Kevin was right there with him, happy and sad at this fine act of self-sacrifice, a fine sentiment on the first day of war. As soon as he closed the script, he was wondering . . . who could they cast? His first thought for Rick was James Cagney. And the girl? Mary Astor? She was a hot property after *The Maltese Falcon*.

Kevin wanted to talk to someone about it. So he headed down to the office that Sally Drake shared with another girl from the East, Cheryl Lapiner.

Sally wasn't there, but Cheryl was at her desk, in the circle of light drawn by a hundred-watt gooseneck lamp. Without looking up, she said, "They're gone. The whole gang. Jerry Sloane was supposed to tell you. But I guess he wants Sally all to himself."

"Where'd they go?"

"Musso and Frank's. They said they needed some cheering up, and the crowd might be thin tonight. A bunch of script readers might get a booth in the back room."

Kevin perched on the edge of her desk and said, "Let's crash their party. It'll be fun."

"You mean you want me on your arm to make Sally jealous?"

He put on a German accent and said, "You do not like fun, *Fraulein?* You do not like to make other pretty girls jealous?"

Miss Lapiner gave him a blank stare. She'd passed thirty-five, secure in the knowledge that her big break wasn't coming. True, the head of the story department was a woman named Irene Lee, but in the backstabbing world behind the camera, big breaks for the ladies were rare.

Kevin grabbed the desk lamp and aimed it at Miss Lapiner's face. "Ve haff vays . . . of making you come out for a drink."

"Go find Sally." She flipped the lamp back to her keyboard. "I think she likes you more than she likes that other jamoke."

So Kevin headed for his car. When he pulled off the lot and aimed for Hollywood Boulevard, he watched the rearview mirror to be sure that no one was following him. If you spent your spare time spying on Nazis, headlights in the rearview might mean trouble.

MARTIN BROWNING DECIDED THAT James Costner had sold his last suit. Picking up bits of intelligence from Lockheed executives was less important now than avoiding suspicion. He had to assume that if Kessler or Stengle had been arrested, they'd break under questioning. And the caretaker was sure to be in some federal detention center, feeling the heat. So Martin Browning went cautiously into his Burbank neighborhood.

There were dozens like it around L.A., straight streets, small houses on small lots, all with the same floor plan, each with some special detail. People might trudge off to work among the faceless multitudes, but they came home to their own little islands of identity, as defined by an odd trellis or a fancy bit of brickwork or a pink front door that matched the camellias blooming in the yard.

James Costner defined himself only by the blandness of his existence. He rented his room from a nice German couple—a retired dentist named Edgar Stumpf and his wife, Edna. He walked to work. He carried his shoulder satchel with him. And he left nothing incriminating in the room. He burned any communication, like letters from his father, mailed from Flatbush to Heidelberg, then forwarded to L.A. through the Bund. And he always moved cautiously into his neighborhood, which was darker than usual because some folks were already observing the blackout.

He stopped diagonally across the street, beneath the shadow of a magnolia.

From there, he could see the Stumpf house without being seen. Something seemed off. He scanned the street. In this world of cars, no car ever appeared completely out of place. But that big black Chevrolet . . .

Then a voice hissed from the camellia hedge: "This is serious, Ash."

In the instant before he recognized the voice, Martin Browning had the metal loop of his knife around his middle finger and his fist ready to punch into a throat or an eye. Without turning his head, he said to the camellias, "Stengle?"

"I rode out, rode up to Mulholland, left the horse, hitchhiked."

"And Kessler?"

"He ran up the steps. I heard a tommy gun. I don't know if they got him. What . . . what do I do now, Ash?"

"That Chevy by the streetlamp . . . have you noticed anyone in it?"

"No."

Still, something felt . . . *off* to Martin Browning. He glanced at the green Dodge coupe directly across the street. It contained his other identity: the wardrobe and sample case of one Harold King, salesman of seeds and agricultural products. Martin always parked it a few doors away from the Stumpf house and moved it every few nights.

He needed that car right now because he needed to *become* Harold King.

He also needed Stengle to leave . . . leave the street, leave the cell, leave the Bund altogether. He didn't want to kill an out-of-work laborer, although Stengle was very killable because he was very naïve, which was a kind way of calling him stupid. And Martin Browning could be kind, but kindness in wartime was almost as dangerous as stupidity. He whispered at the hedge, "You will be inducted soon, I think."

"Yes."

"Get to a marine recruiting office first. Tell them you're an expert marksman. Tell them you want to enlist. Tell them you want to kill Japs. Be sure to call them *Japs*."

"I'd rather kill Japs than go around sayin' 'Heil Hitler.'"

"I'm sure the Führer will be very disappointed. Now go."

"But Kessler said he'd kill me if I didn't show up tomorrow morning. He said we have to do everything as usual. Every Tuesday and Thursday, he picks me up on the Hyperion Bridge, and we go looking for work. He lays the brick. I mix the mortar. We're a team."

"If he needs you to mix mortar, you have nothing to worry about."

"He's a Bund storm trooper, Ash. He carries brass knuckles. He scares me."

"So just do what I'm telling you," said Martin. "Go."

Stengle reached through the hedge to offer his hand. That crossed the line from naïve to completely stupid.

"Go," said Martin. "Go now."

The hand disappeared into the hedge. Stengle disappeared into the shadows.

And Martin decided: he was driving out. If the Chevy tried to follow him, it would have to make a U-turn. But Martin knew the neighborhood. He knew the streets. He knew the alleys connecting all the garages and trash barrels behind all the bungalows. He could shake the Gestapo if he had to. Shaking the FBI would be easy.

He pulled on a pair of calfskin gloves. He took out the Dodge key. He studied the Chevy. He saw nothing in the shadows . . . no movement, no flaring cigarette. Nothing.

In an instant, he was across the street and behind the wheel. He'd disconnected the dome light, in case he had to get into the car at night without attracting attention. And he'd practiced putting the key in the ignition with his eyes closed. He practiced anything that took fine motor skills. They called it muscle memory. The key went right in. The engine thrummed. He put the car in gear.

As he rolled past the darkened Chevy, he saw . . . no one.

False alarm. His instincts had been picking up interference, probably from stupid Stengle. He stepped on the gas and was gone.

KEVIN CUSACK HAD NEVER seen Musso & Frank's so quiet. It was crowded, as usual. Most of the tables in the front room were taken, as usual. Behind the counter, the grill was sizzling with steaks and chops, as usual. People had to eat. They also had to drink. And in Hollywood, drinking was a bigger deal than eating. But the din of conversation in here was usually louder than the kitchen at an Irish wake. Tonight, it was all but silent, as if the corpse was in the room and the neighbor ladies were murmuring the Rosary.

Kevin noticed a few familiar faces.

Humphrey Bogart, a Warner contract player who'd finally hit it big as Sam Spade, was sitting alone in a booth, nursing a highball and staring at an empty glass on the other side of the table. Probably his wife's. They'd probably been fighting. She'd probably stalked out. They weren't called the "Battling Bogarts" for nothing.

And a thought struck Kevin: Bogart, sitting there . . . looking like a guy whose guts had been kicked out . . . Rick Blaine, maybe?

But . . . where were Kevin's story department pals? Not in their usual spots at the grill. Could they really be in the back room, also known as the Writers' Room because so many writers had gotten stewed in there over the years?

A waiter named Larry sidled up in his red jacket. He'd made a nice living as an actor in the silents with his wrinkled mug and a lower lip that looked like it was picking a fight with the rest of his face. But the talkies had put him out of work, because his voice squealed like a trolley going by on Hollywood Boulevard. "Your gang's in the back with that Huston guy."

"*They're* in the Writers' Room with John Huston and Bogart's out here?"

"Nobody's in a mood to pull rank tonight. Not with a—what do you call it?"

"State of emergency?"

"Yeah, and nobody wants to sit with Bogie's wife when she's drinkin'. And I heard Huston say he liked the report that Sally Drake done for him."

Huston probably liked her ass, too, thought Kevin. Most guys did.

He walked toward the back and peered into the Writers' Room. He could see the long, cadaverous face of John Huston, regaling the story department kids in the first booth. Huston noticed Kevin. And Sally Drake followed Huston's gaze. And Jerry Sloane saw Sally turn, so he turned, too, and scowled at the competition.

Neither Kevin nor Jerry had much of a chance if Huston wanted Sally. The hot new director always got the girl . . . not the writer and never, *ever* the reader. Still, Kevin squared his shoulders to enter the fray.

That's when the men's room door swung open. A guy in a blue three-piece suit came out and headed for the grill counter. No one paid him any attention. But Kevin knew that this guy never showed up anywhere without a reason. So Kevin caught Sally's eye and jerked his head at Huston, as if to say, *Good luck;* then he went to the counter and asked the guy if the stool next to him was taken.

"Be my guest."

Kevin sat, opened a menu, and whispered, "Shouldn't you be out arresting Japs?"

"Japs *and* Germans." FBI special agent Frank Carter ordered two highballs.

Kevin said, "I picked up a tail on Cahuenga. Was it you?"

"Better me than some Nazi, but I had you at the studio gates. A guy who's called 'LAJCC Confidential Agent Twenty-Nine' should be more . . . *confidential.*"

"So what's up, other than a war?"

Carter looked around to be sure no one was paying attention, then pulled a brass shell casing from his pocket and placed it on the counter. "Do you know what that is?"

"A cartridge?"

"Thirty-ought-six. Standard issue for a Springfield '03." Carter now put another cartridge on the bar. "Do you see a difference?"

Kevin said, "It's shorter."

"It's 7.63-by-25-millimeter. Probably a pistol."

"So?"

Carter swept the two cartridges off the bar and put them back in his pocket. "I'm curious about the pistol cartridge."

Just then, the ladies' room door banged open, and a woman shouted, "You son of a bitch!"

A scene. Someone was making a scene. Everybody looked up.

Bogart's wife, Mayo, came stomping back to their table. Bogie barely reacted.

"I told you to order me another Scotch," she shouted. "Why does my goddamn glass have nothing in it but ice?" She snatched the glass and wound up to throw it at him.

Bogart jumped up and grabbed her arm. Ice cubes flew. He growled something at her. Then he dragged her toward the door, shoving a bill into Larry's
hands as he went. Mayo son-of-a-bitched him again, and they were gone.

Frank Carter said to Cusack, "Nice town."

"Nicer than Boston . . . in December anyway."

"There's more to life than good weather."

"That's what my father used to say."

"So why aren't you back in Boston, studying law like a good Irish boy?"

The highballs appeared. Two sips, and Kevin said, "Grandpa Cy owns a
theater on Blue Hill Avenue. Second-run Warner pictures, mostly. I loved that
old movie house since I was a kid. When I graduated from Boston College, I
told my father I liked Grandpa Cy's business better than lawyering."

Carter sipped his drink. "Grandpa Si?"

"My mother's half German Catholic, half German Jew. That's why her
parents ended up in America. Catholics and Jews don't usually fall in love in
Germany."

"Your friends in the Bund better not find out."

"Simon Steinberg changed his name to Cyrus Steiner. Small change, big
difference to the Jew haters." Kevin sipped and kept talking. "When he heard
what I wanted to do, he was the proudest Jew in Boston. Took me to the Warner distribution office in Bay Village. Got me a job as an office boy—"

"And here you are"—Carter looked at Bogart's table, where Larry-the-
waiter was cleaning up—"hobnobbing with all the Hollywood big shots for—
what is it?—a buck twelve an hour."

That hurt. Kevin knew he should have been doing a lot better by now. And
he would have been if he'd gone to law school. But he didn't need to remind
himself. He said, "So . . . back to the cartridges."

"I want you to get down to Deutsches Haus and see what the talk is."

Deutsches Haus on Figueroa and Fifteenth, clubhouse for the German
American Bund of Southern California and mecca for Nazi sympathizers from
all over the West.

"Talk?" said Kevin. "About what?"

"About a raid in Rustic Canyon this morning. About those cartridges.
About a guy practicing with a pistol that fires a 7.63-by-25-millimeter round."

"A lot of these amateur Nazis practice with sidearms. At the Bund, Hermann
Schwinn always says that when *der Tag* arrives, they'll do their killing up close."

"So find out what Schwinn is saying about *der Tag* tonight."

"Now? You want me to go down there now?"

Carter glanced at his watch. "Get there by eight, you'll have an hour."

"What's the big deal?"

"We're raiding them at nine. J. Edgar Hoover's orders. We're arresting anyone who's a threat to the internal security of the United States. Schwinn's at the top of the list."

Kevin looked toward the Writers' Room.

Carter laughed. "Forget it. You already had your chance with that snooty D.C. dame."

"I was hoping—"

"She's sitting next to the guy who made *The Maltese Falcon*. He's probably got his hand halfway up her skirt right now."

"She wears slacks," said Kevin.

"Slacks? That means maybe she likes girls instead of guys."

"Maybe she just likes slacks."

"But if she likes girls, that's information the director would like."

"Huston?"

"Hoover. He's the only director you need to worry about now. And he still hates Commies more than he hates Nazis. He'd love to find out that the daughter of a Commie professor from George Washington U. is what you call a . . . lesbian."

Kevin just looked at Carter. Sometimes he worried about what these guys could do to you if they didn't like you. At least they were finally going after the Nazis.

For his part, Frank Carter didn't care about lesbian Communists or Hollywood tough guys who couldn't handle their own wives in public. He had real work to do. Back at the office, the teletypes were firing like machine guns, and all across L.A., Nazi troublemakers were going underground. He sensed that Kevin Cusack might be able to find out things at Deutsches Haus that FBI agents never could.

But now Sally Drake, the Communist's daughter, came loping toward them through the cigarette smoke. "Hey, Kevin, who's your friend?"

Carter offered his hand. "Bob Smith. An old pal from Boston."

"You say 'Bahstahn' like you grew up in Noo Yawk." She took his hand.

Carter gave a phony laugh and said to Kevin, "She's good with accents."

"Why, bless your little heart." Sally did her best Scarlett O'Hara.

Kevin liked that she could mix it up with the guys and never seemed intimidated.

Carter said, "I sell concessions to movie theaters back East. I met Kev when he was hangin' around his family's theater on Blue Hill Avenue, rootin' for Jimmy Cagney. Said Cagney reminded him of his grandfather."

"The Irish grandfather or the Jewish one?" She tapped Kevin's forehead. "I see Cagney in there, an Irishman who'd stand up to Jack Warner himself. But I also see some smart Jewish boy, too."

Kevin didn't like this talk. If word got around that a guy with an Irish surname and German grandparents was actually one-quarter Jewish, it could go badly for him down at Deutsches Haus. So he changed the subject. He said to Sally, "It looks like you've got an Irishman on the hook right now."

"Huston? An all-Irish drinker with hands like an Italian."

"Don't tell Jerry Sloane."

"Don't worry about Jerry." She headed for the ladies'. "And don't go anywhere."

Kevin turned back to Carter and whispered, "For Chrissakes, keep my Jewish grandfather out of it. The Bund has big ears."

"Big mouths, too. So let's find out what they're talking about tonight."

Kevin drained his highball and looked toward the ladies' room door. "She's leaving on Friday, Frank. Going back East. And she and I used to be—"

"*Used to be.* Now Jerry Sloane's in the lead, with Huston moving up fast on the outside. You'll be lucky to finish in the money."

"Competition everywhere," said Kevin.

"So be a winner. Help the FBI catch Nazis." Frank Carter patted Kevin on the shoulder, like a pal. "Get down to Deutsches Haus and prick up your ears."

"Prick up." Kevin finished his drink. "Bad choice of words."

IN THE RAIL YARDS, the trains were moving. Vivian Hopewell sat on the edge of her saggy bed and listened to them rumble. There'd be more trains tomorrow . . . and every day and every night for as long as this war went on. Pretty soon, it would get so noisy in the front room of that old dump, a girl wouldn't get a wink of beauty sleep.

So she reread the letter from Buddy Clapper. She knew what would happen if she went to the Steam Engine Diner. She was no fool . . . no virgin, either. She'd paid for the train ride to California with the only currency she had. She'd been to parties in Hollywood apartments where bourbon got spilled and skirts got lifted. And she knew about the casting couch, the last resort.

What she hated was this, the *last* last resort. And she hated Buddy Clapper, that smug bastard. Why was it, if a guy bought you a bowl of chili, he thought he owned you? But Lord, what she wouldn't give for a bowl, or a plate of meat loaf, or pie, just pie.

She heard one boxcar hit another. Maybe it would all be as impersonal as that. One body thumping into another, connecting, coupling, moving on. . . . So she put on the pumps again.

MARTIN BROWNING SLIPPED THE Dodge into a garage in a Glendale apartment complex: two big stucco buildings, four units in each, a driveway between them, leading back to a six-car garage and a little bungalow where the owner, Mrs. Sanchez, lived.

He'd put away the horn-rims and combed his hair with a part on the right, like Cary Grant. He was wearing a leather jacket and a brown fedora. Not even someone who looked him in the eye would see James Costner . . . or Leslie Howard. They wouldn't see much Cary Grant, either, despite the wardrobe from *Only Angels Have Wings.* But his transformation was almost complete. He'd even changed his personality. Harold King was open and friendly, a typical American backslapper, not a supercilious haberdasher with a nasty opinion about every man's suit.

Martin preferred playing Costner. Harold King exhausted him, and he was tired enough already. If he could just get into the apartment without having to perform . . . but from the patio in front of the bungalow he heard, *"Buenas noches, señor."*

"Buenas noches, Mrs. Sanchez." The salesman Harold King would always take time to chat with the landlady. So Martin stopped now.

Mrs. Sanchez said, "I was not expecting you until the weekend."

"No buyers this week. It'll pick up once the shock of yesterday wears off."

She held up a pitcher. "Sangria?"

Martin Browning would have loved a drink, even a glass of that cloying Spanish wine punch, but first he needed food. He needed a nap, too. "Not tonight."

"Tonight is a bad night," she said. "Tonight I am wondering what my husband would think. I think he would tell our sons to enlist." Every evening on her patio, she poured sangria and talked of the man who'd built this little complex before a car accident killed him. But there were no sons, no Sanchez boys. They were only a widow's dream.

Martin understood. Dreams drove everyone . . . at least until daylight came. Dreams had driven his parents from Koblenz to Flatbush. Dreams had driven him back to Heidelberg. Dreams drove the German people, who'd begun by building a new nation from the ashes of 1918 and would finish by building a new world.

So he swept off his hat, bowed, and said, *"Señora,* your husband looks down each night and thinks only good thoughts for you and the tenants you treat like family."

"Gracias, señor. Not only are you handsome, but charming in your words."

Martin clamped the fedora back onto his head. "Your sangria . . . I think it enhances your vision, Mrs. Sanchez."

She laughed. "It is always here, the sangria. So am I."

As he went up the stairs, he allowed himself a salacious thought. A certain exotic beauty still shone in the face of the Spanish widow. And every man had his urges.

The apartment was called a "railroad flat," five rooms lined up like train cars. The front room faced the Verdugo Hills. The back looked up at the ridge where Forest Lawn invited the living and the dead for a pleasant stroll or an eternal sleep.

And sleep was what Martin yearned for. He knew that if he lay down, he'd sleep for hours and awaken ravenous. But he was more than tired.

To go through the world like a knife, unsheathed but hidden, to use his knife as he had that day, that was work to exhaust body and spirit both, a performance punctuated by moments of extreme fear and professional brutality that might extricate him from trouble but did nothing to cleanse his soul or soothe his nerves.

If he'd been on the Russian front, he'd have shouldered a rifle and served in the epic cold. But here, in sleepy Glendale . . . a little nap would be no dereliction of duty. Then he'd go down to the Steam Engine Diner for a nice plate of meat loaf.

VERMONT AVENUE DROPPED OUT of the Hollywood Hills and ran thirty miles, straight as a Roman road, all the way to San Pedro. On the radio, they were saying that the port was under curfew and blackout. But most of L.A. was still a vast sea of lights, a plankton-stirred surface that seemed to undulate and glow and rise and fall with every roll and swell of the earth. And as far as Kevin Cusack could see, the traffic lights were working.

That meant he'd get down to Deutsches Haus in about twenty minutes, though he had to pull over twice for military vehicles speeding toward Exposition Park. The National Guard had established a base there so that if the Japs attacked at Long Beach or landed on the broad, smooth sands of Santa Monica, the Guard would be ready.

As he drove, Kevin watched for tails, and when he parked on Figueroa, he made sure that no one was spying from the shadows, because Frank Carter was right. This was dangerous business, especially for amateurs.

Kevin had gotten into it in '37, when he wandered into the storefront of the Hollywood Anti-Nazi League. He liked their cause and their roster of celebrity supporters, including the famous director John Ford. He thought that if he met Ford, he could play on their mutual background as second-generation Irish and New Englanders, too, and that might lead to a job. He never got Ford's attention. He did, however, draw the eye of a Jewish war vet named Leon Lewis.

Lewis ran the Los Angeles Jewish Community Committee, which had been infiltrating pro-Nazi groups since 1933. It was dangerous business. The local Nazis and their fascist friends were violent, thuggish, and committed. But with the FBI chasing Commies and the LAPD filled with fascist sympathizers and anti-Semites, too, somebody had to watch the Heil Hitler boys.

Lewis liked Kevin's background—Irish, German, a little Jewish. And when Kevin revealed that he'd had a grandfather in the IRA who'd worked with German agents in the Great War, and that one of those agents was Emile Gunst, now the self-proclaimed life of the party at Deutsches Haus, Lewis made his pitch:

Had Kevin read the anti-Semitic leaflets that the Bund spread around? Did he know the meaning of "*der Tag*"? Did he know that Bundsmen had talked about releasing cyanide gas in the Shrine Auditorium on the night of the '38 Anti-Nazi League rally? Did he ever worry that if the Nazis were successful in America, his Jewish grandfather wouldn't be able to *go* to a movie, let alone own a theater? Would he commit to stopping the rise of Nazism in his own country? Would he endure the danger?

A young man frustrated by the high walls of Hollywood liked having a higher purpose. Kevin liked Lewis, too. So he became an undercover agent for the LAJCC and infiltrated the German American Bund.

Then one night, he came home to find Agent Frank Carter sitting in his apartment, in the dark, puffing a cigarette.

Carter had come with a warning: *Be careful.* He said the FBI had been watching a girl named Sally Drake because of her father's Communist leanings. He'd been discussing her with his LAPD liaison, Detective Bobby O'Hara, and Kevin's name had come up.

"O'Hara's watching you," Carter had told Kevin. "He's got it in for the LAJCC. And he's figured out that you're their agent, a backslapper at Deutsches Haus every night, a slave to the Warner Brothers Jews during the day. He says he'd love to make an example of you."

"Pure vengeance," Kevin had answered. "I was the guy who found out O'Hara was on the take, looking the other way when these half-assed Nazis vandalized synagogues and spread anti-Semitic propaganda. I sent the info up the chain, it reached the police commissioner, and O'Hara got busted from division commander down to street dick. I'm always careful around Detective O'Hara."

After that, Kevin and Carter had started communicating directly. But until tonight, Carter had never tracked Kevin into a public place. Tonight, it was that serious.

ORDINARILY, DEUTSCHES HAUS GLOWED inside and out—lights playing on the stucco façade, lights in all the floor-to-ceiling windows, lanterns illuminating the portico—all to announce that an outpost of the Reich was a place of incandescence, even in glitzy Los Angeles. But tonight, it looked like every place else in town—subdued, shocked, frightened into semidarkness.

Kevin tried the doors that were usually opened wide and welcoming to all but Jews and coloreds. *Locked.* He rang the buzzer. A curtain on the door snapped back, the sergeant at arms peered out, and the door swung open, admitting Kevin into quiet gloom.

On one side of the foyer, the Aryan Book Store sold European histories, Bavarian cookbooks, and Nazi propaganda. On the other side, the Gaststube fed Angelenos hungry for schnitzel or bratwurst. And straight ahead, in the auditorium, they celebrated the new Germany with songs and "*Sieg heil*"s beneath a portrait of the pasty-faced Führer. Tonight, the bookstore was closed, the Gaststube quiet, the auditorium dark.

Hermann Schwinn came out of his office on the second floor. He usually strutted around in a half-assed military uniform with epaulettes, jodhpurs, and shiny boots. But lately, he'd been favoring a "civilian" look—everything neat and trim, from bottlebrush Hitler mustache to rimless Himmler glasses to dark double-breasted jacket. He looked down from the balcony and said, "Ah, Cusack. A friendly face. *Guten Abend.*"

"Good evening, Herr Schwinn." Kevin gestured to the door. "Locked?"

"It is a nervous city tonight. And we are expecting visitors."

"Visitors?"

"The FBI."

Had they been tipped off about the raid? About him? Kevin felt his mouth go dry, but he tried to speak calmly. "You can't keep out the FBI."

"Oh, *nein, nein.* We can't. We won't. We have nothing to hide. But there may be others, more violent, less disciplined. So tonight, we keep the doors locked."

Kevin grinned. "I'm here for the beer."

"And the beer is here for you." Schwinn gestured toward the Gaststube. Then, without offering his usual "*Heil Hitler,*" he turned back to his office.

In the Gaststube, barkeep Dieter Brandt was drawing a stein of Beck's. "Herr Cusack. Not many Germans here tonight. Glad the Boston Irish are not intimidated."

"The Boston Irish are never intimidated." Kevin took the beer and toasted the barkeep.

This room—with its checkered tablecloths, posters of Bavarian mountain scenes, and huge, pin-covered map of the Wehrmacht's advance into Russia—could be the rowdiest German outpost west of New York. But Kevin sensed fear in the empty silence.

An elderly couple eyed him, then turned back to their bratwurst. Fritz Kessler, waiter and bouncer, leaned against a sideboard and looked sullen. But right in the middle of the room sat Emile Gunst, enjoying a beer and a cigarette as if he hadn't a care in the world.

Kevin went over and gave him a bow. "*Guten Abend, mein Herr.*"

"Ah, Cusack. Sit. Sit. Drink. Order some *Weisswurst.*"

Kevin pulled out a chair. "A bad day."

"A bad day, or the beginning of the good days?"

Kevin sipped his beer. "How long before America and Germany are at war?"

It was true that Gunst had been an agent for the Kaiser in the Great War, run guns to Ireland before the Easter Rebellion, and befriended Irish firebrand Jimmy Cusack back in '16. But since arriving in Lotusland, as some called Southern California, he'd become a lotus-eater . . . and an eater of almost everything else, a fat, happy, sauerbraten-and-dumplings sort of fellow who claimed he visited the Bund because he liked the food, not the politics, and made a good living importing Hummel figurines from the Fatherland.

He always rolled his eyes when one of the Nazi loudmouths was blabbing, and he rolled them now at Kevin. "Roosevelt's been at war with Germany for two years . . . Lend-Lease . . . American destroyers protecting British convoys . . . meetings with Churchill . . ."

"But no declaration?"

"He wants Hitler to do it. That will make it easier for him."

"Easier?" Kevin kept priming Gunst. If he'd come to hear the talk, this was the man to talk to, because Gunst loved to talk.

"The cagey old cripple knows his country is full of people like us."

"Germans and their friends, you mean?" asked Kevin.

"Twenty-five million of German ancestry. Two hundred and fifty thousand German immigrants since the war, and—"

"Guten Abend." The waiter, Fritz Kessler, stood over them.

Kevin always found him brusque and grouchy, as if he'd studied German waiters in their natural element. Tonight, he seemed more irritable than usual, perhaps because of the bandage on his temple.

"What do you want?" Kessler demanded.

What Kevin wanted was to be long gone before the FBI arrived. But he was starving, and it was only eight twenty, and he might never get to taste the *Weisswurst* and red cabbage in the Gaststube again, so he ordered it.

Kessler turned on his heels and stalked away.

Gunst watched him go. "Not much strut to him tonight."

"Looks like someone took a hammer to him."

"Some Germans inspire hammers. For others, a hammer is what you need to get their attention." Emile drained his glass and called to the barkeep. *"Noch ein Bier, bitte."*

Kevin said, "You aren't one of these Germans, though?"

"I am an American." Gunst slapped his belly. "For me, life here has been good."

Kevin led the conversation toward the FBI raids, while Gunst kept lighting cigarettes, swallowing gulps of beer, and serving up opinions. On the day after Germany's Pacific ally bombed Pearl Harbor, he said, the FBI might arrest everyone in Deutsches Haus.

Did he know something? Kevin glanced at his watch. Eight thirty.

Gunst asked, "Do you have a date with a pretty actress tonight?"

"Not tonight."

"There. You just did it again."

"Did what?"

"Looked at your watch. I tell you, Kevin, you are acting very tense."

"Everyone is tense. Everyone is worried."

Emile Gunst laughed. "Everyone, *ja,* even a man who imports overpriced figurines from the Fatherland."

Kevin decided to come right to it. "Have you ever heard of the Murphy Ranch? In Rustic Canyon?"

"Where the Silver Shirts drill?"

Kessler returned, dropped the plate of *Weisswurst* in front of Kevin, scowled, and said, "The FBI raided the Murphy Ranch this morning. You want mustard?"

"Bring me the Bauer's. And . . . what do you know about the Murphy Ranch?"

Kessler grabbed the mustard from the sideboard and plunked it down. "Why do you ask, Herr Cusack?"

Kevin had already planned a good lie. "I bought a pistol. The Bund has a target range in the Hollywood Hills. But I've heard there's one out in that canyon, and—"

Kessler seemed to stiffen. "I would not know."

Gunst gestured to his temple. "What happened, Fritz? Someone shoot at *you?*"

But before anyone could say more, barkeep Brandt said, "*Mein Gott.* They are here." He was peering out the window behind the bar.

"Who?" asked Gunst.

"The FBI. They are coming up the walk."

"How many?"

"*Zwei.* Two. They are taking out identifications."

Gunst laughed and his big belly shook. "Draw them each a beer."

Kevin decided to take his cue from Gunst and act innocent. So he cut into his *Weisswurst* and popped it into his mouth.

Gunst said, "Delicious, no?"

Muffled voices came from the foyer. Dieter Brandt went to the end of the bar, pretended to polish it, and peered out. Under his breath he offered a commentary. "They are questioning Herr Schwinn. He is giving them now the keys, the whole ring of keys."

Emile Gunst looked at Kevin. "The keys."

Kevin asked, "Does he have anything to hide?"

"If he does, he must think it is well hidden," said Gunst.

In walked Agents Frank Carter and Mike McDonald.

Kevin looked at his watch. Ten to nine. They were early. He felt Gunst's eyes boring into him. He knew that suspicions were rising in that jolly German belly.

Herr Schwinn came to the door of the Gaststube and said, "*Damen und Herren,* the FBI would like to check identities. Please have your papers ready."

Under his breath, Gunst said, "Papers. They want papers. Like the Gestapo."

Kevin sensed movement behind him and saw the kitchen door swinging.

Gunst whispered, "Kessler makes himself scarce. Perhaps you should, too."

"And you?"

"I am too old and fat to run." Emile Gunst took a tin from his pocket, slid it open, and popped a tiny tablet into his mouth. "Nitro. I always take it if something upsets me. Even an innocent man may be upset. And I am innocent."

"So am I."

"Are you really?" Emile Gunst looked into his eyes.

Then Agent Carter was standing over them, checking IDs, a driver's license, a Social Security card. He said there'd be questions for Gunst and the barkeep, but the elderly couple and Mr. Cusack were not "on any lists." So they were free to go.

KEVIN HOTFOOTED IT BACK to his car. He had nothing. Nothing about the Murphy Ranch. Nothing about a random pistol cartridge. Nothing but the suspicions of Emile Gunst and the man who now appeared from behind a parked panel truck.

Fritz Kessler, all shadow and bulk, blocked Kevin's way. "Did they let you go?"

"They said I was harmless. What about you?"

"I went out the men's room window. There's an agent watching the back door."

"They must not trust the kitchen staff." Kevin pushed past.

"But they think *you* are harmless?" Kessler's footfalls followed him. "Are you really, Herr Cusack? Are you really harmless? I have heard things."

Kevin got to his car and unlocked the driver's side. "You need to get off the street. Where do you live?"

That caught Kessler up short. "Echo Park. Why?"

"Do you have a car?" asked Kevin.

"My wife uses it on Monday nights."

"Save the life story. Either get in or walk or take a bus. But get out of here."

Kessler went around to the other side of Kevin's car and tried the door.

Kevin knew that this big German could be dangerous. He'd seen Kessler throw drunks out of Deutsches Haus. He'd seen him pummel a few with brass knuckles. Letting him into the car was like letting a strange dog into the house. He might be friendly, or he might bite your arm off. But a ride home might allay Kessler's suspicions. So Kevin reached over and unlocked the door. He hoped it wasn't a mistake.

AFTER A NAP, MARTIN Browning drove down Los Feliz to the Steam Engine Diner on San Fernando Road. As James Costner, he might be a snob. But Harold King liked diners. He liked sitting with the workers and the night people and the eaters of down-to-earth American food. He liked meat loaf.

A neon sign flashed above the big, plate-glass window: a blue steam engine spinning fire-red wheels and puffing white light. He opened the door and felt right at home in this American environment of stainless steel, padded stools, and laminate counters. Booths lined the right side of the room. The counter jutted out in two semicircles.

Martin always headed for the back counter, so he could see the whole place. As he dropped onto a stool, an old waitress with her name—NANCY B.—embroidered on her uniform brought a glass of water. "Hiya, hon. Long time no see. What can I get ya?"

Martin grinned his Harold King grin and raised a finger. "One word."

"Meat loaf?" she said. "Ain't 'meat loaf' two words?"

"And gravy makes three." He laughed. "Coffee, too."

"Coffee's *four*. Comin' right at ya."

Martin sipped the water and scanned the room.

An old man was reading the *Racing Form* by the front window. Two railroad workers in dirty coveralls were shoveling food between comments about "goddamn sneaky Japs." And . . . *the girl*.

She was sitting in a booth just to his left, staring into her coffee cup.

He could only see her from the side. But he knew her. He knew the yellow dress. James Costner had seen it just a few hours before in Mr. Fountain's. If things had been different, he might have offered her a few dollars or a bit of encouragement. Instead he'd given her the dirty look of a salesman worried about commissions. Then he'd gotten back to pumping the Lockheed executive for information. Now he wanted to go over and talk with her. *Just talk*. To allay his own loneliness. He knew she'd never recognize him in his new identity. But his job was to sit and wait. So he pulled the newspaper from his jacket and waited . . . for meat loaf.

Before it arrived, a man did. He sauntered in as if he owned the place, though the cheap suit and sweat-stained fedora suggested he didn't own much of anything, and he didn't even take the hat off when he slid into the booth opposite the girl. Bad manners to go with a bad suit. He said, "Whyn't you get somethin' to eat?"

The girl seemed to cower and muttered an answer.

Martin raised the paper and put his eyes on a headline, RUSSIAN COUNTER-ATTACK STALLS NAZIS, but he kept his ears aimed at that booth.

Mr. Tough Guy snapped his finger. "Hey, Nancy!"

"Yeah, yeah. Keep your shirt on." Nancy was pouring coffee for Mr. Racing Form.

The grill man said, "Nancy! Meat loaf's up."

The two railroad workers dropped a few coins on the table and left.

And Martin triangulated. He did it whenever he sensed trouble. Find three points. Hold them in your vision. Plan to react in any direction in an instant. The left corner was that booth: a fake tough guy and a girl who radiated defiance through her fear. Near the door: Nancy B. and Mr. Racing Form. And to the right, a burly grill man in a white apron watching the room while he worked his spatula.

Martin guessed that the grill man was taking a piece of whatever pimping action Mr. Tough Guy was getting, an established business, and none of Martin's.

Then two high-school kids came in, a girl and the boy trying to impress her. They took a booth and dropped a few coins into the tableside jukebox. A drumbeat began. Gene Krupa leading into Benny Goodman's "Sing, Sing, Sing."

The music made it harder for Martin to pick up the conversation, but along with a sniper's vision, he had the hearing of a safecracker.

The girl said, "I . . . I don't think this is for me."

The guy sat back. "What?"

Martin glanced over the paper, and the guy glared: *What are you lookin' at?* A bully, too, thought Martin, another Hollywood small-timer with big-time attitude. Martin dropped his eyes back to the newsprint.

The guy turned back to the girl. "You can't get out of this now."

She looked into her cup and mumbled something else.

The guy leaned across the table, like a pal. "C'mon, baby. It's a fortune. A hundred bucks for three bums from Chicago, all horny as hell. Good actin' experience."

She raised her head. "Acting?"

"Just act like you're enjoyin' it. You won't even get your sheets dirty."

"My *sheets*? We can't go to my place. Mrs. Murray won't—"

"Ah, don't worry. We're not goin' there. We're goin' to Griffith Park, up by the golf course. In my new Packard. Got a nice roomy back seat."

"Back seat? I'm not some cheap—"

"What's the big deal? Bing-bang-boom. Three guys, one at a time."

"But the *back* seat?"

"So take 'em out on the first tee. I got a blanket."

Nancy B. dropped a plate of meat loaf in front of Martin. Then she made for the booth. "Whaddya want, Buddy?"

But Buddy Tough Guy was standing, as if the deal was done. He waved Nancy off. He gave Martin another dirty look. And he said to the girl, "I'll be outside. Finish your coffee." Then he pulled out a flask and dumped a shot into her cup. "A little sweetener. Oh, and you *are* cheap, baby. Get used to it." Then he stalked out.

Nancy B. said to the girl, "What'll you have, honey? It's on me."

"I'm not cheap, am I, Nancy?"

"Hell, no. And you don't have to go with that Buddy Clapper bum, either."

The grill man said her name—"Nancy"—low and threatening.

Yes, thought Martin. He had a piece of the action.

Meanwhile, the kids talked away, oblivious to the goings-on. The boy was drumming his thumbs on the tabletop, keeping time with Krupa.

The girl in the yellow dress said, "Do I look German to you, Nancy?"

"German? Like a Nazi?"

"Like Marlene Dietrich. There's this one agent—he didn't sign me—but he said he thought I looked like Dietrich."

"Ah, you're prettier than her."

"Well . . . maybe with the war, I can play a German. You know, a good gal in Nazi-land, or a Nazi dame who won't take any guff from the Nazi guys."

"Sure, kid, sure," said Nancy. "Why not? Take nothin' from no one."

"Yeah. Why not? I think I'll start actin' like that right now." The girl got up, drained the coffee cup, hooked her purse over her arm, and walked the length of the diner, as fine and steady as Dietrich on the day she left Germany.

Nancy B. watched her go, then looked at Martin. "How's the meat loaf?"

"Needs salt."

Nancy grabbed the shakers and plunked them down.

Suddenly, Mr. Racing Form was shouting, "Hey! Hey! Cut that out!"

Through the window, Martin saw a swirl of yellow skirt, a car door swinging open, people grappling, all lit by flashing neon.

As the *Racing Form* flew, the old man ran out the door. A moment later, he slammed against the plate-glass window.

Nancy B. rushed out.

The grill man muttered, "For Chrissakes," and whacked the spatula on the grill.

The kids gave a look, then went back to chitchat.

Martin sprinkled salt on his meat loaf and managed to finish half of it by the time Nancy B. had helped the old man back to his stool. "Looks like you got yourself a shiner, there, Jake. I'll get you some ice."

The grill man said, "You're too old to be fightin' like that, Jake."

"But that gal," said Jake, "as soon as she got outside, she said, 'Forget it, Buddy, I'm not goin'.' So Buddy Clapper, the bastard, he grabbed her and shoved her in his car."

The grill man said, "Ah, she'll be fine. Tomorrow, she'll come in here and order roast turkey and Boston cream pie and pay with green cash money she's earned just like an old-fashioned girl."

Nancy told the grill man to shut the hell up.

Martin kept his head down until his meat loaf was gone. Then he asked for the bill.

Nancy came over, took out her pad, did the addition. "Twenty-five cents for the meat loaf. Five cents for the coffee. And five bucks for the egg."

"Egg? What egg?" asked Martin.

"The egg you're sittin' on. You're so afraid to get up and help that gal when they drag her off, I'm thinking you're just a big chicken."

Martin gave Nancy a look that warned her she was coming much closer to danger than she knew. Then he dropped a dollar bill on the table and left. But instead of heading east for home, he turned right onto Los Feliz Boulevard. Destination, Griffith Park.

KEVIN CUSACK PULLED UP in front of an apartment house on Echo Park Avenue. More Spanish, more stucco, more tile trim, a nice view across the street to the man-made lake. Kevin and Fritz Kessler had chatted the whole five miles from Deutsches Haus, but they'd said little, as if neither trusted the other.

The Murphy Ranch, the FBI, the war, these had all floated unspoken in the air between them because Kevin had tried a different approach, asking Kessler first about his family, his hopes, his work.

Fritz and his wife had come to America when the Communists were rising in Berlin and everything was "going to shit." They'd come to Los Angeles for the weather and the work. Kessler was a bricklayer by trade. Work was hard to find, but the weather was wonderful. And the Bund made him feel part of something.

All good answers, thought Kevin, offered more gracefully than he'd expected. But now onto the nub of the matter: "So . . . what do you know about this Murphy Ranch?"

Kessler seemed to inflate with suspicion. "If I ever go out there, I will call you. Do you have a number? An address?"

Kevin knew a clumsy grab for information when he heard it. He didn't like to lie, because lies led to more lies, and crisscrossing lies created an inescapable maze. So he gave up as little as possible. He said, "I know where to find you. If I get a gun, I'll call."

Kessler said, "I have a gun, Herr Cusack. I will use it on *der Tag*."

"*Der Tag*. Right. That's why I want my gun."

"We should all have guns to shoot Jews on *der Tag*. I hope you are ready to shoot Hollywood Jews like Jack Warner and Hal Wallis. Or do you flatter them, too, the way you flatter Emile Gunst and Herr Schwinn when you come to the Bund?"

This was going nowhere. So Kevin jerked his thumb at the door. *Get out.*

Kessler appeared to reach for the handle, but instead came up with a fist that shot toward Kevin's face. Brass knuckles flashed to a stop a few inches away from his cheek, a move so shocking that Kevin threw open his door and rolled out.

A Ford coupe squealed and swerved. A horn blared.

Kevin jumped up and shouted back into his car. "Beat it, you son of a bitch."

Kessler got out on the other side and held up his brass-knuckled fist. "I carry these for men who betray us, for Jew lovers who pretend to be friends of the new Germany. Be glad that I pull my first punch."

Over the roof of the car, Kevin said, "The next time you come at me with those things, I'll have that gun."

"Very wise, Herr Cusack. Very wise." Kessler went up the walk, calling over his shoulder, "We are watching you. *Auf Wiedersehen*."

Kevin jumped into his car and sped away. He didn't notice that the driver in the Ford coupe had pulled over and written down his plate number. On a night when everyone was edgy, good citizens kept their eyes—and their pencils—sharp.

VIVIAN HOPEWELL HUNCHED IN the back seat of Buddy Clapper's Packard. She was still screaming into the gag, furious at Buddy and at herself for getting into this.

"Stop it, for Chrissakes," said Buddy. "I'll give you an extra fifty. Just stop your fuckin' screamin'."

"You want me to whack her again, boss?"

"No, you stupid bastard. We want her lookin' pretty. No shiners."

"She got one of those already."

Buddy was driving, and he'd brought along a bulky thug named Poke, who smelled of beer and onions. Turns out that Buddy was the charm of the operation. Poke was the muscle. From what Vivian could tell, neither of them was the brains.

Buddy looked into the back seat and said, "How about it? Another fifty?"

Vivian nodded. She decided to play it calm until she could run. She didn't want the money. No amount of money was worth this. What she wanted was to go home, home to Maryland, home to life as just plain Kathy Schortmann.

They'd turned off Los Feliz and were now deep in Griffith Park, a world of mountainside, meadow, and canyon six times bigger than Central Park . . . and sixty times wilder, right in the middle of L.A. In daylight, she could've picked out a dozen spots where they'd shot movies. But at night, it was just black on blacker.

Buddy had even turned off his headlights. Maybe he knew there were military vehicles speeding through the park to get up to the observatory. Word was that they'd already sited antiaircraft guns up there. But most of the military action was along Vermont and Western. Down here on the east side, it was deserted.

By the time they got to the golf course, Poke had taken out the gag and untied her hands. She pretended she was calming down. Maybe she could find help in the building at the end of the parking lot. It looked like the clubhouse. But was anyone even there?

The Packard rolled across the lot. Trees lined the curb. The first fairway reached out into the night. Two men were standing by a darkened DeSoto sedan. One wore a double-breasted suit, the other a jacket. A flask flashed. A cigarette flared. A match flickered inside the car, where the third guy was lighting up.

Buddy parked beside the DeSoto. Then he said to Vivian, "Relax, kid. This'll be the easiest dough you ever made."

Poke put a hand on her knee. "And maybe after, we can get a free sample."

She slapped the hand away and said to Buddy, "You better tell this gorilla to keep his paws off me, or I'll scram the second this door opens."

Poke leaned a little closer. "Where you gonna go, baby? You can't run down the fairway in high heels. You'll sink."

Buddy turned off the engine and told Poke to get out and go around to the passenger side and keep watch. Then Buddy got out, too.

Vivian noticed that the dome light didn't come on. These bastards knew all the tricks. She tried the back door on the passenger side. Locked. They'd even removed the little lock knob, leaving just the screw post. Then Poke leaned against that door for good measure. She was trapped.

She heard Buddy say, "So, fellas, did I deliver the goods or what?"

"Does she look like Dietrich?"

"See for yourself." Buddy opened the back door.

The guy in the double-breasted stuck his fat face in. His breath reeked of whiskey. He grinned. "I always wanted to fuck Dietrich."

Then another face appeared behind him, longer, thinner, a cigarette dangling. He had a flashlight. He flicked it on and shone it in her face.

For a moment, she couldn't see anything.

He said, "She ain't as bony as Dietrich. Nicer tits, too. But—"

That was all he said.

The flashlight flew, sending a crazy shadow spinning.

The fat man looked around and said, "What the fuck?" and something that looked like a leather blackjack smashed down onto his bald white head. He bounced off the open door and fell into the car, right on top of Vivian.

Outside, a dark shadow was moving, like a spirit.

Buddy yelled, "*You!* Why, you fuckin' do-gooder." And he pulled something from under his arm. It flashed in the dim light. A gun.

The blackjack struck again. The gun flew. Buddy's arm broke. Vivian heard it snap. Then the blackjack uppercut into Buddy's jaw and dropped him. The shadow whirled and met Poke with another blow. Vivian could almost hear the skull crack.

Was she next? Were they being robbed? Would this guy rape her? Vivian tried to push the fat man off, but he was dead weight. So she twisted around and tried to pull up the screw post and broke two fingernails.

Then she heard a car door slamming and tires squealing. The DeSoto was roaring off in reverse with a terrified conventioneer behind the wheel.

A new shadow appeared over her: a fedora, a leather jacket, a black knit tie. He pulled the fat man's body off of Vivian. Then he extended his hand and said, "A lady should not be treated this way."

She looked at the hand. She looked for the blackjack, but it had disappeared. She looked into his face but couldn't make out the features.

He said, "We should go."

She thought, *yes.* She should go. Going with him might be dangerous, but how much worse than going with Buddy and Poke? She smelled leather and Old Spice. She liked it. So she took his hand and let him draw her toward him.

Kevin Cusack parked on Ivar, half a block above Franklin. He was still shaking from the run-in with Kessler. He wasn't made for this stuff. He'd never come so close to getting his head bashed in by one of those Nazis before. So he'd driven home with an eye on the rearview mirror, and now he did a quick scan of the shadows around his apartment house. All clear. So he got out of his car and headed for the phone booth on the corner.

He hated that phone booth. Drunks used it to call cabs, and sometimes they used it to piss while they waited. But the light went on when he closed the folding door, which made it better than most phone booths, and tonight, extra light gave him a sense of security, even though it made him a target for anyone watching from the shadows.

He dialed the FBI office. Frank Carter picked up on the first ring.

Kevin told him what had happened with Kessler. Then he gave Carter an earful for putting him in danger and blowing the operation by coming in too early.

Carter said they'd seen guys sneaking out the back of Deutsches Haus, so they had to move.

"From now on, you can move without me." Kevin slammed the receiver. Then he opened the folding door. As the overhead light went out, a fist burst from out of the night, right into his face.

Kevin flew back against the glass. He couldn't tell who'd hit him, but he knew it wasn't brass knuckles.

Then he heard the words "She's mine. Stay away from her."

Jerry Sloane, that son of a bitch . . . coming out of nowhere with a sucker punch.

Kevin was jammed into the booth, so he couldn't do much to fight back, and he was too stunned anyway. So he shut the folding door and put his foot against the hinge. The light came on again.

Jerry Sloane's face pressed against the glass, contorted with anger and whiskey. "Fuck you, Cusack. And fuck that Huston, too. She's mine." Then he went staggering off.

Kevin looked down at the blood covering his shirt and tie and decided that getting even with a sucker-punching drunk could wait. He had to take off his sport coat before the blood stained the tweed. Besides, revenge was a dish best served by getting lipstick on your collar, not blood.

MARTIN BROWNING PULLED DOWN the driveway and slipped into his garage. All the apartments were dark. People went to bed early in Glendale. But as he headed for his apartment, he heard a voice:

"Good evening, señor."

He looked toward the little bungalow and the shadow of Mrs. Sanchez on her patio. He touched the brim of his hat. "Good evening."

She said, "I have made a second pitcher of sangria. The first night of a war is not a night to drink alone, I do not think."

He was tempted. But a drink might lead to more. And he had done one foolish thing already that night. He shouldn't compound it by doing another. Every foolish thing he did, whatever the reason, could endanger his mission. So he said good night.

As he drifted to sleep, he considered the job he had been chosen for. And he considered his place in this enormous, ambitious, undisciplined, and profligate country. He'd spent his adolescence here, but he felt no loyalty to America. His loyalty was to the country of his birth. And his responsibility was to history, for it was now within his power to change history: one man with a pistol, firing two shots on Christmas Eve at the Reich's greatest enemy. That would be the real day of days, the real *der Tag*.

And Franklin Roosevelt would die.

TUESDAY,
DECEMBER 9

As DAWN BACKLIT THE mountains, Vivian Hopewell awoke and wondered: *Was this all a dream?* From the lowest point in her life to *this* . . . in just twelve hours?

She lay on clean sheets, in a bed occupied by herself . . . and only herself. That alone was an achievement, because she hadn't screwed anybody to get there. She'd come close, but her mysterious savior had proven to be a gentleman.

She rolled over and ran her hand across the monogram on the pillow: *R*. The Roosevelt Hotel, on Hollywood Boulevard, where Clark Gable and Carole Lombard had rented the penthouse until they moved to Encino.

She sat up and looked around. And yes. It was all real. An open door led to a private bathroom. Tile gleamed. Sunlight slanted. And through the front windows she saw . . . a pagoda? She hopped out of bed and looked across Hollywood Boulevard at Grauman's Chinese Theatre, shimmering as magically at dawn as it did during a nighttime premiere, with fans screaming and searchlights sweeping the sky. *Two-Faced Woman*, starring Greta Garbo and Melvyn Douglas, was the feature.

How many times had Vivian dreamed of her own name on that marquee? Vivian Hopewell starring in . . . *Rescued from Griffith Park?*

It was as if the night before had been a movie, not a dream.

After the fight scene:

EXT GRIFFITH PARK NIGHT: Camera FOLLOWS Vivian and Stranger to his car. She begs him not to hurt her. He promises he won't. She begs him not to take her back to fleabag boardinghouse, as bad guys are sure to follow. He promises they won't.
EXT GRIFFITH PARK LONG SHOT: Dodge coupe speeds out of park. At Los Feliz Boulevard, it turns toward Hollywood, not Glendale.
INT DODGE MEDIUM SHOT: Vivian asks where he's taking her. He says, "Someplace where no one will bother you." She asks, "Who are you, mister?" He answers, "A friend."
INT DODGE CLOSE on Vivian as she thinks that over. A friend? Really?

But that's what he'd proven to be, delivering her to the Roosevelt, paying for four nights, and watching her sign in with "Kathy Schortmann." At the elevator, he'd bid her good night, and she'd asked his name.

"Call me Harry. And if I call, I will ask for Kathy . . . Kathy Schortmann."

"That's my Maryland name, my real name. I might go back to it if I can buy a bus ticket home. But I don't even have the money to buy a hamburger."

He'd said, "Check your pocket."

As the elevator doors closed, she'd pulled out fifty bucks in small bills.

A friend, indeed.

MARTIN BROWNING SLEPT AWAY his exhaustion and didn't wake until ten. Then he walked around the corner to the pharmacy in Adams Square. While the cash register rang and the radio murmured, he sat at the soda fountain and read the late morning edition of the *L.A. Daily News*.

The front page proclaimed FDR's declaration on Japan, but no news of Germany. The centerfold offered photos of the president, the emperor, and a file photo of American battleships in happier days, steaming through a sun-drenched sea.

The next page reported on a news conference at the Los Angeles FBI head-quarters: "Chief Agent Richard Hood announced that his 25 field agents had arrested 325 Japanese, 52 Germans, and 9 Italians. Most of them are still in the County Jail, but three busloads, some sixty in all, have been transferred to the Federal Detention Center on Terminal Island in San Pedro. More arrests are scheduled."

A photo accompanied the story: four men boarding a bus, led by a badge-wearing FBI agent in fedora and dark suit. None of the prisoners looked as arrogant as they surely had the day before. One of them, in rimless Himmler glasses and bottlebrush Hitler mustache, was Hermann Schwinn.

Martin Browning wasn't surprised. He knew the FBI had been watching Schwinn. He expected that they'd been tapping the phones at Deutsches Haus, too. And they were sure to have lists of all the Germans in California. Had they been watching the Burbank haberdasher, or the waiter at Deutsches Haus, or the out-of-work laborer?

With any luck, he'd never see Kessler or Stengle again. And no one would see James Costner. He'd already called Mr. Fountain to quit that morning.

Martin turned now to what he called the murder page: reports on un-timely deaths, the bloodier the better. Over a million people lived in L.A. County, so plenty of room for plenty of people to commit plenty of murders, which meant plenty of fodder for papers that thrived on movie stars and mayhem.

Among stories of wife beatings in Pasadena, stabbings in Venice, and bar-room brawls in Boyle Heights, Martin saw no mention of a body in the trunk of a Lincoln-Zephyr parked at Bob's Big Boy in Burbank, nor any reports of dead men in Griffith Park. They'd find Koppel soon enough. Killing him had been a necessity, but attacking men in a parking lot? To protect a strange girl? Because of his own sense of honor?

Of course, pimps and their hapless marks didn't file police reports. They slinked off to suffer in silence. And it had been good practice for what might lie ahead. Not everyone would be as trusting as Arthur Koppel.

And he'd earned the loyalty of a young woman whose stage name suited her Hollywood dreams but whose Maryland roots spoke of her heart. A sweet Kathy, a nice girl from German stock, someone who might prove useful, es-pecially since she'd shown not a glimmer of recognition when she met Harold King a few hours after passing through the orbit of James Costner.

He sipped his coffee and came to bad news: CORPSE IN L.A. RIVER.

"The body of a man in his twenties was found early this morning under the Hyperion Bridge. He appears to have been beaten, then tossed off the span. Found next to him was a scally cap with a label from Mr. Fountain's Men's Shop. The body has no other identifying articles. Police are calling it a robbery."

That was the bridge where Kessler met Stengle every Tuesday and Thursday. And Martin had given Stengle a hat from Mr. Fountain's as a gift. Had Kess-ler killed Stengle after all? Was he also planning to kill James Costner, in the belief that if you eliminate a cell, you eliminate your own guilty involvement?

Martin Browning decided he'd have to deal with Kessler.

As for Schwinn, would he "sing" like a movie gangster? Would a commit-ted Nazi break under questioning? Browning was glad that Schwinn knew so little. Only one German in Los Angeles knew much. His name was Emile Gunst. Time to visit him.

FRANK CARTER HAD BEEN going for forty-eight hours on black coffee and Black Jack gum. His eyes were starting to vibrate in his head, he was so exhausted. But the noise in the office kept him awake. The clattering teletypes made the place sound like a textile mill. The air had the oily stink of hot ma-chinery. At every desk overworked men were reading orders, writing reports, planning tactics. And off in a side room, four bewildered Japanese and two stone-faced Germans awaited their fates, handcuffed to one another.

Chief Agent Dick Hood had slept a few hours at his desk. Now that he'd shaved and slicked his hair, he almost looked rested. He was in his late forties, steady and solid, like a good insurance agent who saw that every client's house and car were covered. He stopped by Carter's desk. "Go home and get some sleep. That's an order."

"Too much work." Carter gestured to the steamer trunk beside him. "Too much evidence."

The trunk contained piles of cash, Nazi propaganda, and info on Bund members from all over Gau West, the Bund term for the western district of the United States. Carter and McDonald had found the trunk when they tossed Deutsches Haus.

"Hard to hide a steamer trunk in a crawl space," said Carter.

"One of the problems with thinking you're the master race," said Hood, "you're always underestimating everybody else."

"There's a clue in here somewhere."

"C'mon, Frank. I'm giving you six hours off."

"No time off"—Carter held up the shell casing—"until I find this guy."

"Give that to ballistics. Like Agent Twenty-Nine said, all these Nazis carry sidearms. All of them are hepped up for shooting Jews on *der Tag*."

"I wasted Twenty-Nine's time, hitting Deutsches Haus too early," answered Carter. "I should've let him enjoy his girlfriend."

"Sally Drake? The Commie's daughter from D.C.?"

Carter brought his finger to his lips. "You're not supposed to know anything about Twenty-Nine . . . except that he's friends with Emile Gunst."

"You should never have let Gunst go last night."

"A jolly fat man," answered Carter. "Imports German porcelain and likes German beer. Pops nitroglycerine like candy. Harmless."

"If he's German and he's in my district, he's not harmless. Bring him in. Let's have another talk with him." Then Hood shouted to the rest of the room, "All right, listen up! More names from D.C. Two dozen Japs, half a dozen Germans, a few Italians. All Japs go to the new detention camps at Griffith Park. The Krauts and Eyeties come back here."

Just then there was a commotion at the door.

Hood noticed and said, "Another thing. That's LAPD detective Bobby O'Hara who just came in. He's now your contact in case you need paddy wagons or backup."

O'Hara gave a salute to the room. Another plainclothesman in a wrinkled suit, skin blotched from spending too much time in the California sun and the Hollywood gin mills, sharp features poking through a fleshy face, the look of a guy who'd throw down evidence if he thought a perp was guilty or pick up cash if somebody offered a bribe.

Carter was glad that he didn't have to spend much time around O'Hara. And he might warn Agent 29 about him again, too.

KEVIN CUSACK HADN'T COME to this town to work for the FBI or the LAJCC. And if the FBI asked him to do dangerous work, then got in his way while he did it, what the hell good was he? So he was back in the phone booth on the corner of Franklin and Ivar, with a nasty bruise under his eye and a nostril plugged with dried blood.

He lived up the street in the Alto Nido, a building favored by writers who liked Spanish architecture and low rents. He should have been living in some big house in the Hollywood Hills. He should have been driving a new car, too. He should have had an office at the studio. Hell, he should have had a whole bungalow, after all the time and energy he'd spent in this crummy town. But he didn't even have his own telephone.

That was what he'd been thinking as he lay awake half the night, listening to the young couple going at it upstairs. He hadn't even had a kiss since Sally Drake dumped him for Jerry Sloane. And when the lovers stopped thumping above his bed, he'd heard his father's voice, running through his mind like a bad childhood memory, reciting the note that came with the annual Christmas card: "I hate to tell you this, Kev, but Mom had some surgery just after Thanksgiving. It's a cancer of the breast. There's a lot we don't know, but she'd love to see you."

How much worse for the folks back home if Kevin had gotten himself beaten to death by a brass-knuckled Nazi in his own car?

So around dawn, he'd decided. He'd had enough. He was going home. . . .

Now the morning sun heated the little phone booth and brought out the worst of the stink. But Kevin was inside just long enough to drop a nickel, dial a number, and say, "Twenty-Nine in ten." This meant that Agent 29 would be reporting in ten minutes.

Then he drove down to Hollywood Boulevard and parked. He walked by a building diagonally across the street from Grauman's Chinese. A moment afterward, a stooped, graying man in a brown suit came out, made eye contact, and headed for Coffee Dan's, on the corner of Highland.

Leon Lewis didn't like to meet agents face-to-face, but the simple code—phone call, agent number, minutes to arrival—would bring him out. It meant something big was up. Lewis would then take a booth facing Hollywood Boulevard. If he opened his paper, it meant that he'd noticed some fascist trouble-maker lurking on the sidewalk. If he raised his hand and called for coffee, the coast was clear.

Lewis sat and held up two fingers to the waitress. So Kevin slid into the booth and thanked Lewis for seeing him.

"Once war with the Nazis is in the open," said Lewis, "we can dispense with all this cloak-and-dagger business. Now, what can I do for you?"

"Last night, Agent Carter asked me to go to Deutsches Haus."

Lewis gestured to his cheek. "Is that how you got the black eye?"

"No. That's a lover's quarrel."

"Your girlfriend did that to you?"

"The other guy. But back to Carter—"

Lewis nodded. He never pushed for personal details. He said, "Very irregular, your friendship with Carter. If you get in too deep with these G-men, I can't protect you when they use you. Let me deal with them. You deal with the Nazis."

"Carter needed quick info from Deutsches Haus. But he raided the place before I could get anywhere with Gunst or that grouchy waiter, Fritz Kessler. I'd collect whatever you have on Kessler."

"So come upstairs, go through files."

"Mr. Lewis, I have a job, remember? It's also my cover. Hollywood reader by day, German sympathizer beering it up at Deutsches Haus by night."

"I'm thinking they may not pour much more Löwenbräu down at the Gaststube."

"And I'm thinking you may not need much more help from me."

Lewis put his hand on Kevin's forearm. He was generally stiff and formal, so the gesture was shocking in its intimacy. "We can always use committed young men."

"One more studio report, then I'm off. Friday night on the Super Chief."

"But this girl—"

Kevin had come to think of Leon Lewis as a kindly uncle, so he told him the truth. "She's going back on the Super Chief, too."

"With you?"

"She doesn't know that part yet."

"If a man can't rekindle an old flame on the Super Chief, maybe there wasn't much spark to begin with." Lewis offered his hand. "Good luck, son. We'll miss you."

"These Nazis are getting too dangerous for me," said Kevin.

"These Nazis have always been dangerous . . . for all of us," answered Lewis.

"I haven't told Agent Carter that I'm leaving yet—"

"You work for me, Kevin, not the feds. I'll tell him. And . . . Merry Christmas."

Then Kevin Cusack headed for Warner Bros., happy to be done with Hollywood Nazis, except for Major Strasser and the gang in Casablanca.

VIVIAN HOPEWELL TOOK A long soak in the bath. When the water started to cool, she reached out with her foot and turned the faucet to add more hot, a rare luxury for a girl who'd been living for three years in a one-tub cold-water rooming house. Maybe better days really did lie ahead, despite the war.

She put her head back, blew a strand of hair from her eye, and let the warmth soak into every crevice. She felt a deep, sensuous comfort radiating right into her. She ran her hands along her thighs and wondered what it would be like to fall in love.

Back home, her old boyfriend Johnny Beevers had offered sloppy kisses, fumbling fingers, clumsy embraces. Hollywood had offered hard appraisals and lumpy casting couches. Not a lot to choose from, but in that steaming water, it was still easy to dream.

So she decided to take one more shot with the only guy in town who'd ever given her a glimmer of hope. Nat Rossiter ran a six-man agency on the Sunset Strip, and he once told her she had talent. Of course, if she called his office, she'd get the old baloney. "In a meeting." Better to show up and make the pitch. No begging. No kneeling. Just say it straight: "I'm here. I look great. I look German. Get me a job."

But what would she wear? The sweaty yellow dress from yesterday? The answer came soon after she'd wrapped herself luxuriantly in a terry cloth hotel bathrobe. A call from the front desk: delivery on the way up. Then the bellhop was rolling a cart into her room with four large boxes from the Broadway. Christmas, two weeks early.

She felt a rush of air as she lifted the top from the first box and peeled back the tissue paper, revealing blue polka-dot fabric, a dress with a white-belted waist and white collar, a matching pair of white and blue shoes. Beneath was a topcoat perfectly matched to the dress. In other boxes, more dresses, blouses, a lime-green gabardine slacks suit.

Someone had a good eye for colors, *her* colors.

She checked one of the tags: size 6. Good eye for that, too.

The note: "Dear Miss Schortmann, I took the liberty of picking out a few things. I personally selected the outer items. I would take you to dinner this evening at 7 PM. Harold."

Buddy Clapper had expected her to play the prostitute for a slice of pie. Nat Rossiter had promised a screen test for a blow job. What could she expect from this Harold guy, who'd been more generous to her than anyone she'd met in L.A.? She decided to put on a new dress and give Rossiter one more chance, then let Harold take her to dinner and see what developed.

Martin Browning hurried along Broadway, carrying a shopping bag that was named for the department store that was named for the street. He'd bought Miss Schortmann a new wardrobe to be delivered to the Roosevelt Hotel, and he'd gotten himself a navy-blue cashmere overcoat heavy enough for the cold of Washington, D.C., roomy enough to hide a fully assembled Mauser C96 with the shoulder stock.

He planned to refashion the overcoat to carry the gun under the armhole.

Then he'd practice the moves he'd make on Christmas Eve—the opening, the split-second aim, the quick closing after the shots. He always practiced. He always prepared.

But he had two more errands in downtown Los Angeles.

First, he went by the Central Market, crossed Fourth Street, and slowed at the storefront of Gunst's Bavarian Imports. Emile Gunst was dusting figurines in the window. Martin rattled his fingers along the glass, the signal for Gunst to be on the lookout.

Then he kept going another five blocks to Union Station, a marvel of California Spanish stucco and style. In the great hall, travelers could wait in chairs worthy of a Hollywood screening room. Aztec-patterned floor tiles echoed the city's Mexican heritage. Art Deco chandeliers defined modernity. And the massive ticket counter, crafted from hard American black walnut, symbolized what Americans liked to imagine as the hardheaded practicality of the national character. An architectural melting pot, thought Martin, more real than the mythical American melting pot it celebrated.

He'd decided to leave on Friday night's Super Chief, because war between the U.S. and Germany was inevitable. So he'd best get himself into position.

No single compartments available. Too many people heading home in December '41. But he could have a drawing room if he purchased two tickets. So Martin doled out a small fortune in crisp new Nazi bills: $220 per person for himself and Kathy Schortmann, plus another $79 for the room. He might have saved her as an act of honor, but knowledge was meant to be used . . . people, too. And he'd decided to use her, along with one of his other aliases: Harold Kellogg and wife would be traveling together to Chicago.

He'd also decided to board in the desert town of Barstow. Fewer eyes watching in Barstow. So he told the agent to make that notation on the ticket.

Martin had considered spending $300 to take one of the American Airlines DC-3s that flew daily across the country. But on an eighteen-hour flight with three stops, there was no escape, nowhere to hide, and most of the planes were booked weeks in advance. Much safer on a train, just plain Harold and his plain, middle-class American wife.

Twenty minutes later, he was back at Gunst's window.

Emile Gunst, playing the jolly shopkeeper, smiled and nodded through the glass.

Martin pointed to a figurine, two children peering into a bassinette, a perfect bit of phony *Kinder-Kirche-Küche* German nostalgia. Gunst gestured—*that one?* Martin shook his head and pointed to another, a boy and girl, arms raised as if they were waving . . . or giving the Hitler salute. Gunst picked it up and nodded. *All clear.* Martin stepped in.

Gunst stayed in character. "*Guten Morgen, mein Herr.*"

"Good morning." Martin looked around—corners, back room, spots on the ceiling where there might be a microphone planted.

"May I help you?" asked Gunst.

"I'm going east for Christmas. I'd like to bring a Nativity set as a gift." He pointed to a set of nine Hummel figurines in the case, cherubic hand-painted faces and pudgy little bodies, all dressed for a child's Christmas pageant. "How much?"

"Boxed, it will be one hundred and twelve dollars."

Martin carefully counted out the bills and placed them on the countertop.

Before picking them up, Gunst studied the bills. "Four twenties, two tens, one five, seven ones." His eyes widened behind his glasses. "So you really *are* the one? You really are more than a spy pumping Lockheed executives while they buy neckties."

"I'm both."

"I thought so. Once you joined a cell with Kessler and Stengle, I thought so."

"Kessler killed Stengle this morning."

"Kessler is a blunderer."

"Blundering could put the FBI on my tail."

Emile patted Martin's hand. "Don't worry. The FBI are blunderers, too."

Martin pulled his hand away, as if he didn't invite such gestures. "The FBI have friends like Leon Lewis and his spies."

"Jews and Jew lovers. No need to worry about them, either." Gunst picked up the bills. "Crisp. Gestapo?"

"You know as well as I do. The money arrives on our freighters. Schwinn brings it to the Bund and distributes it. I collect it at a post office box."

"You won't be getting any more money from Schwinn."

"I know. I saw the papers. I'm surprised the G-men didn't act sooner."

"I was sitting with a Bundsman named Kevin Cusack when Schwinn gave over the keys, as if to show he had nothing to hide. I hope he did not have a file on you."

"He was my bank. That's all." Martin glanced at his watch. "Now that he's out of business, my bank is in a Hummel box. My ammunition, too. And other papers."

"I have been holding it for this very moment, as ordered by Section Six."

Martin Browning made a snort. "Cheap theatrics."

"Perhaps, but . . . we all have our orders." Gunst went into the back and brought out a mahogany box, staying in character as the jolly shopkeeper. "A beautiful case with gold embossed lettering. You see on the top, the name 'Schwester Maria Innocentia.' She was the nun who created the marvelous little figurines we now know as Hummels."

"Sentimental shit," said Martin. "Open the box."

Gunst muttered, *"Ja, ja, Scheisse,"* with a nervous chuckle that said he understood the danger encased in the leather jacket and brown fedora. He raised the lid, revealing a velvet tray and, in nine neat compartments, nine figurines—the Hummel Baby Jesus, the Hummel Angel of the Lord, the Hummel Christmas Donkey, and the rest. He said, "Lovely, no?"

Martin made an annoyed gesture. *Lift the tray.*

Gunst lifted, revealing maps, a codebook, a notebook, ID photos perfect for creating false credentials, and five Mauser C96 stripper clips, each containing ten 7.63 mm rounds.

"And the cash?" asked Martin. "There should be a thousand dollars."

"Rolled up in Baby Jesus. We should have put it into Joseph because he was a Jew, so carrying cash in his porcelain ass would—"

"Close the box." Martin wanted none of the usual Jew jokes. "Wrap it. Use red paper and a green ribbon. No tape. Tape damages the paper."

"Yes, yes. Red and green. Very Christmas-like." Emile Gunst unrolled red paper from a spool at the end of the counter and went to work with scissors and ribbon. "Why do you need five more magazines? You'll have time for one shot only."

"Two. Two shots. One to range him. One to kill him."

"But—"

"Roosevelt cannot let go of his podium or he will fall. If he hears the first shot, his hands will lock. By then, the second shot will be on its way."

"Such a shot with a rifle would be difficult, but a pistol?"

"I'll be on the South Lawn. The newspapers will describe the security measures before the event. I'll use the information to plan my attack."

"So, you hope for two Christmas miracles? First, that the newspapers will give you directions. Second, that the Secret Service does not change the plan."

"Lighting the National Christmas Tree is a tradition. And Roosevelt promised that he would do it this year on the South Lawn. So he'll do it, even with the war . . . especially with the war. And I'll be there." Martin gestured to the box. "I know my Illinois contact. Is the name of my East Coast team in the notebook?"

"Husband and wife, named Stauer. German-born American citizens, as loyal to the Fatherland as you are. They live in Brooklyn."

"What about Barstow? I was told we have contacts in Barstow."

"The Gobels. Unsavory people, but what can you do? The passwords for getting their help are recorded in the notebook in the box. Mention the word 'varmints' and—" Emile Gunst's eyes opened wide, as the bell above the shop jingled.

Two tall men stepped in. Law enforcement. Martin knew just by a look.

Gunst dropped back into character, pasted a grin onto his face, and handed the gift-wrapped box to Martin Browning. "*Danke, mein Herr.* A pleasure to do business with you. Come again. And have a Merry Christmas."

With the package under his arm, Martin turned as the G-men showed their badges.

Gunst gave out with a big fake laugh. "Ah, the gentlemen from last night. Agents Carter and McDonald. How can I help you?"

Martin stepped around McDonald and directly into the path of Carter, who looked at him with the eyes of a guy who hadn't slept in days. But red rims and half-mast lids didn't hide professional suspicion. Carter was appraising him, he knew. Best to beat a fast retreat. So he said, "Pardon me, sir."

Agent Carter said, "I'll get the door."

Martin smiled meekly as another "Merry Christmas" followed him out. He resisted the impulse to look back or speed up. But he had to know what was happening to Gunst. So he crossed Broadway and ducked into the arched entrance of the Bradbury Building. From there, he could see Gunst's shop without being seen, or so he thought.

The shades came down in the front window. Were they going to beat him? When the Gestapo beat someone, they pulled the shades. But then the door opened. Agent Carter came out first, followed by Gunst and the other agent. They were arresting him. Much easier to beat someone at headquarters.

Martin Browning hadn't finished with Gunst. He hadn't even told him what he'd learned about the fuel tanks on the P-38. And if the FBI was arresting Gunst, the most famous *Fresser* in the Bund, they were sure to arrest the waiters, too. That meant Kessler.

But Agent Carter presented the immediate problem, because he was peering across the intersection, between the trolleys and over the tops of the cars rattling by.

Martin knew that if he stepped out now, Carter would see him, then follow him, then question him. Better to slip into the Bradbury Building and disappear.

In most of L.A., façades surpassed interiors. Not at the Bradbury. The exterior was five dull stories of brick and terra-cotta, but the entry led into an atrium of outrageous fancy, of black iron stairs, ramped and rising, intersecting and descending, all at graceful intervals and angles, connecting a tracery of wrought-iron railings and balconies, with two elevator towers rising in utilitarian beauty to the glass roof above.

Two elevator operators stood guard. One said to Martin, "What floor, sir?"

Martin said he'd walk. Then he hurried toward the rear staircase. A door led out at the back. That would be the logical path, but Martin believed that doing the logical thing was often the least logical decision. So he wouldn't go out. He'd go up. He knew the building, and he was hoping that at least one office would be open to him.

A good L.A. haberdasher served customers from Burbank to Beverly Hills. As James Costner, Martin had often visited the office of an attorney on the fourth floor. He delivered ties, shirts, and altered suits. Maybe he could duck in there and hide out. He went up one floor, then turned toward the front of the building, holding close to the wall so that the G-man wouldn't see him.

He heard an elevator operator ask Carter, "What floor, sir?"

Martin Browning kept going, two stairs at a time up to the third level, then the fourth. He knocked on the door of the attorney. No answer. He tried the door. Locked. He headed for the men's room.

On the street floor, Frank Carter was looking up at the swirl of staircases and railings and the huge bright skylight glaring down, and it all made him dizzy. He brought his thumb and index finger to the bridge of his nose and squeezed. It was a way he had of fending off exhaustion, if only for a few seconds. Then he opened another stick of Black Jack, shoved the gum into his mouth, dropped the wrapper on the floor, and scanned all the balconies and railings above him.

"Hey, mister," said one of the elevator operators.

Carter looked at him. "Did a guy just come through here in a—"

"The wrappers, mister. Pick up your damn wrappers."

Carter realized that, yeah, he must really be tired to be dropping gum wrappers on clean floors. He could be tough, but he tried not to be an asshole about it. He bent to pick the wrapper up and almost tipped over, he was so sleepy. Then he said, "A guy in a leather jacket and brown snap-brim . . . did he come in here?"

"Who's askin'?" The elevator operator was still annoyed about the wrappers. So Carter mustered his best FBI glare and flipped his badge.

The operator turned nice in a hurry. "A guy like that come in a minute ago."

"Which way did he go?"

The operator pointed toward the back staircase.

"Did he go out the rear exit?"

"I couldn't say."

Carter tried to listen for footfalls, but the atrium was like an echo chamber. Footfalls on every floor, voices, slamming doors, electric motors.

Carter thought that maybe the guy had gone out the back. Or was he the kind who did things against the grain, against logic, a guy who could think so quickly that he always thought he was outthinking you?

Carter didn't let anyone outthink him. So he'd go up the front stairs.

The elevator operator called out, "Hey, mister, I said the *back*."

Carter ignored him. At the first landing, a woman came tottering by on high heels. Carter asked her where the men's room was.

"There's one on every floor, bub. And find a better mash line."

At the landing between the second floor and the third, Carter passed a Western Union messenger with a satchel over his shoulder. No. Not the guy.

At the third level, he went to the railing and looked down. The perfect place for a murder, he thought. Toss a man off, let him hit the floor. And . . .

Carter decided the guy had probably gone to the top, ducked into a men's room, and . . . no, that would be too logical. If he went against the grain, he was probably someplace on the third or fourth level. So Carter went along the balcony, past secretaries and messengers and men in suits moving from office to office, and when he got to the rear staircase, he looked back into the vast birdcage.

And he saw a guy carrying a Broadway shopping bag down the front staircase. The guy's hair was combed back. He wore horn-rimmed glasses and a heavy blue overcoat. On a seventy-degree day? That was strange. So was the sales tag sticking up at the collar. Frank Carter started running.

But Martin Browning was already at street level, already going through the door. And he didn't look back. He quickstepped around the corner onto Fourth, then ran. By the time he got to his car, he was sweating in the heavy wool, but he didn't stop to take it off. He jumped in and sped away.

KEVIN CUSACK ROLLED TWO pieces of paper and a carbon into his typewriter. In the upper right corner, he typed, "Read by: Kevin Cusack, 12/9/41, Everybody Comes to Rick's by Murray Burnett & Joan Alison."

A report began with a few lines of opinion, so producers would know if the synopsis was worth reading. That would be followed with four to six pages of plot, just the story in the present tense. *It's real. It's happening right now in front of you.* That's how all good stories were supposed to work.

He'd only banged out a few words when Sally Drake came by his desk.

He looked up. He resisted jumping up. The tan slacks, the chocolate-brown blouse, the shoulder-length hair, even the horn-rimmed glasses . . . he liked everything about her. Sexy, confident, and smart, too. But he played it cool. He even made a show of looking at his watch. "Jack Warner doesn't like people coming in late."

"Jack Warner will have nothing to say about it after Friday."

He turned his eyes back to the typewriter. "Hollywood will miss you."

"I won't miss Hollywood. Like Dorothy Parker says, 'There's no there there.'"

"I think it was Gertrude Stein. She said it about Oakland. And don't you mean there's no here here? Not for most of us, anyway. Although there's plenty of there for the screenwriter who hits it big with *The Maltese Falcon*—"

"Are you jealous, Kevin? Of John Huston?"

Kevin returned to his typing. "More jealous of Jerry Sloane."

"He came to work today with a bandage on his hand." She gestured to his black eye. "Did he hurt it on your face?"

"He jumped me in a phone booth."

"And you let him get away with it?" She taunted just a little bit.

"My grandfather taught me how to box back in Boston." Kevin kept typing. "I was CYO youth champion of 1922. But I'm a lover, not a fighter."

"They're giving him an assignment, you know."

Kevin stopped typing. "Oh?"

"They liked his report on the biography of Jim Corbett, the Irish boxer."

"Somebody should tell him that writing about boxers doesn't make you one."

"Boxer or sucker puncher?" she asked.

He didn't answer. It was enough that she knew what a sucker punch was.

She said, "It's called *Gentleman Jim*. It's for Errol Flynn."

"And I'm still writing reports." That was all the annoyance Kevin allowed himself. When another writer made it, you were supposed to be glad for them. But it was hard when the guy who'd won the girl also won the job.

Sally came around the desk and looked over his shoulder, then read out loud, "'Excellent melodrama. Colorful, timely background, tense mood . . .'"

"It'll make a helluva movie. Bogart or Cagney, maybe, with Mary Astor."

She said, "I hear it's a love triangle. So . . . Bogart *and* Cagney."

"Put the two of them in a movie, one has to kill the other. Not this time."

She leaned against his desk. She didn't wear cologne, just some kind of French body powder. He'd loved it when he first embraced her. He loved it now.

She said, "I needed a Boston Irishman to protect me from a randy Irish goat last night. Where the hell did you go?"

"I'm a mysterious man." He typed a bit, playing his casual self.

"Mysterious," she said, "or just illusory, like everything else in this town?"

He knew how she played men. So he typed a bit more. *Click-clack-clatter-clatter.*

She said, "Your friend tried to pick me up."

"He has good taste."

"Asking all kinds of questions, like a cop or an FBI agent or something," said Sally. "You know, the G-men are always bothering me, because of my father."

Kevin wanted to change the subject. "I hear you're leaving on the Super Chief. Only the best for Sally Drake."

"My father has lots of credit with Santa Fe. So I get a drawing room."

"Nice father."

"The G-men think he's a Commie because he writes books about them. But when it comes to creature comforts, Daddy's a forty-five-caliber capitalist."

"A drawing room sleeps two." Kevin kept his eyes on the work. *Clack-click-clatter-clatter.* Then he made what sounded like a joke: "Need a roommate?"

"Roommate?" She laughed, but it was plain that he'd caught her by surprise.

He leaned back in his chair. "If I'm illusory, you won't even see me. I'll sleep in the upper berth. It's like a bunk bed. I'll change in the bathroom. And you hate cigarette smoke, so I'll take my butt breaks in the observation car."

"Dream on, boy." She turned to leave, then said, "Are you serious?"

"My mother's sick, and I'm finally sick of this town, and I'm already sick of this war. I have a high serial number, but who knows when single guys in their thirties will get called up? It's time for Christmas at home, maybe the last for a long time."

She picked up the script and flipped through it. "This *Everybody Comes to Rick's,* it sounds like a big potboiler."

"It's about the way war changes people. It's about doing the right thing when it goes against what you want to do. It's sophisticated hokum, but it's pretty good."

She flipped pages, stopped, read a passage, then said, "Bunk beds, eh?"

"Like brother and sister."

That made her laugh. She had a great laugh. He knew that if he could make her laugh on the train, the brother-and-sister stuff would be hard to keep up.

She put the script back on his desk. "We'll talk later."

Dick Hood told Carter, "You're imagining things. You need sleep."

"I didn't imagine that guy watching from the Bradbury Building."

The FBI conference room, separated from the office by a glass wall, now held three sullen Germans and Emile Gunst, who looked like he didn't give a damn about anything. In fact, he was doing what Carter wanted to do: he was taking a nap.

Carter told Hood, "I think that guy went to see Gunst for more than figurines."

"So get a warrant and go through Bavarian Imports."

Carter popped another stick of gum, stood, stretched, pinched the bridge of his nose. This trick was working in ever-smaller increments.

Hood said, "You're so tired your teeth are getting black."

"That's the gum."

"Go home. You're no good to the agency if you're sleepwalking."

"Talk to Gunst first." Carter told McDonald to put Gunst in the interrogation room. "Let's see what we can sweat out of that fat bastard."

Then, for the hundredth time in two days, Carter headed to the coffee urn. He took a clean cup, filled, sipped, and realized that the inside of his stomach felt like fine-grit sandpaper.

And McDonald shouted, "Hey, boss! Boss!"

"What?"

"Gunst won't be doing any more sweating."

Carter and Hood went running, but there was no need. Emile Gunst was dead, head flopped, skin cold and clammy.

Hood looked at the German handcuffed to Gunst. "What happened?"

The German, a skinny lawyer who'd been complaining since his arrest, said, "He closed his eyes and put his head on his chest. I thought he was asleep."

Carter opened Gunst's mouth. No evidence of a broken capsule, no smell of almonds, so no cyanide. Just the stink of half-digested sausage and beer. He reached into Gunst's pocket and pulled out a little box containing a dozen small white tablets.

Carter said to the German, "Did he take any of these?"

"One," answered the German. "He said it would make him feel better."

Carter looked at Hood. "Maybe it did."

FROM OUTSIDE, THE ROSSITER Agency looked like an old colonial mansion on the Sunset Strip. But inside was a hive of offices, reception areas, and meeting rooms, all decorated with glorious posters from the movies that clients had appeared in. *Beau Geste, Bringing Up Baby, Jezebel,* and a lot more.

The receptionist gave Vivian Hopewell the usual runaround. "Mr. Rossiter's at a meeting. If you'd like to leave your headshot—"

Vivian was having none of it. She said, "Tell him I have a one-time-only proposition. If he wants it, he gets the best Marlene Dietrich look-alike in town. If he doesn't, he can go and screw himself, because I sure won't—"

"Why, Vivian . . . hello." Rossiter came in behind her.

She turned, embarrassed. Much easier to stand up to the secretary than the boss.

"I'm just back from Paramount." Rossiter grinned. "Had a breakfast meeting with DeMille. In fact, I was talking about you."

She felt her resolve melt. "DeMille?"

Rossiter told the receptionist to hold all calls. Then he made a little gesture to Vivian. *This way* . . . up the circular staircase to his second-floor office. He held the door for her, then ever-so-quietly closed it and turned the latch.

Just like last time, she thought. *DeMille, my ass.*

He told her to have a seat. He dropped behind his desk and popped a Sen-Sen. Then he leaned forward, put his elbows on his blotter, and tented his fingers as if he were studying her through the lens of his own camera. He was a small man . . . and a little one, too. All comb-over and mustache and dirty thoughts radiating off his round face.

Behind him was one of the best views in town. The Sunset Strip ran along a ridge that overlooked the whole L.A. basin. When she'd been on her knees under that desk six weeks earlier, she'd distracted herself from a distasteful task by admiring the view.

Rossiter asked if he could get her anything.

"A job. You promised me a job six weeks ago. I paid in advance. Remember?"

"Well, there's nothing just now, kiddo. But I've been thinking about you"—he leaned back in his chair and spun toward the window—"and I think I can help you"—he spun back and said—"if you'll help me through a tough time. You see, my wife—"

"Third wife," she said.

"—has left me, and I'm, well—"

"Your fly is down. Pull it up before your soul pops out."

His mood changed in an instant. His voice got hard and harsh. "Hey, listen, baby, you're nothin' but jawbone and bleached-blond rag mop. That's what they all say when I show them your headshot. Broads like you are a dime a dozen."

She stood. She was done. "Worth more than you, you horny little runt." She turned toward the door.

"Hey, Viv," he said.

The sudden, surprising gentleness of his voice made her stop. "Yeah?"

"Tell the guy who smacked you . . . he didn't hit you hard enough."

She brought a hand to her cheek. She'd layered on the face powder to cover up the bruise she'd gotten in Buddy Clapper's back seat.

"And you give a lousy blow job," he added.

"There's no such thing." She slammed the door so hard that the poster from *Gunga Din* fell off the wall.

WHEN SHE STRODE ACROSS the lobby of the Roosevelt Hotel a few hours later, she'd made her decision: unless she fell in love with this Harold guy, she was going home.

He was sitting on the edge of the tiled fountain, the centerpiece of the faux-Spanish lobby. He hopped up at the sight of her.

Such a gentleman, she thought, not like Rossiter or Clapper. So she added a little lope to her gait, a little performance to her walk, just to please him.

He offered his arm and whispered, "You look ravishing."

Outside, he tipped the doorman, who opened her door with a flourish that made her feel like a star. Then they headed east on Hollywood, full of chatter about all the pictures playing at all the famous movie palaces—the Egyptian, the Pantages, and so on—until they came to Western Avenue, where he turned up the hill toward Griffith Park.

Her thoughts began to spin darkly, dramatically, maybe melodramatically. . . . Was this some kind of setup? Had he given her a night of freedom so he could use her now the way Buddy Clapper wanted to? Was she just a pawn in a turf war between pimps?

She said, "Unh, where are we going?"

"Walt Disney's favorite restaurant. The Tam O'Shanter."

And she almost laughed . . . at herself. "Melodramatic" was the word. She said, "In Glendale? On Los Feliz? The one that looks like a British manor house?"

"They say that's why Disney likes it."

Soon, they were seated in a dining room dressed like a set from *Mary of Scotland*, with banners hanging from the ceiling, swords and bucklers on the walls, and an atmosphere that promised skirling bagpipes and kilted rebellion if the steak was overcooked.

Harold pointed out Disney's table by the fireplace, but the father of Mickey Mouse wasn't there that night.

"I expect he's too busy," said Harold. "Movies will help to win this war."

"Disney movies?" She laughed. "Like Donald Duck and Goofy?"

"All kinds of movies," he said. "The visual image is powerful. The Nazis understand. Have you ever seen *Triumph of the Will*?"

She shook her head.

"Disney's *Fantasia*, then?"

She'd seen it. She didn't much like it, except for the part with Mickey Mouse.

Harold said, "I bet you'll never hear Beethoven's Pastoral again without thinking of flying horses, will you?"

"Well, unh . . . no . . . or yes. Or—" She didn't know much about that long-hair stuff. But she remembered the horses with the wings. Kind of stupid.

"Once you've seen *Triumph of the Will*, you can never think of Germans as anything but a race of supermen marching toward the future like a well-oiled machine—"

"—and worshiping Adenoid Hynkel." She *had* seen *The Great Dictator*.

Harold cocked his head, like a dog trying to make sense of a sound. Inside that head, Martin Browning was thinking that perhaps she was too unpredictable for what he was planning to ask her. Then he laughed. "Ah, yes. Charlie Chaplin . . . funny fellow."

"I think he's right about Hynkel . . . I mean Hitler."

"Let's not talk about Hitler," he said. "We're here to enjoy."

And that was what they did, through three courses. They chose the Welsh rarebit appetizer. Then it was on to prime rib and Yorkshire pudding, followed by the famous strawberry trifle, all accompanied by wines that Harold selected and by conversation that ranged from their childhoods to their work to their dreams.

Childhood: He was the son and grandson of tailors from Flatbush, Brooklyn. He didn't mention Koblenz. She was the daughter of a Maryland waterman.

Jobs: He was a salesman of agricultural implements, seeds, and accessories. She had . . . well . . . she had her waitress flats in case acting didn't pan out.

And dreams: His was huge and idealistic—to bring peace to all nations and usher in an era of cooperation through agriculture. Hers was just as huge and, she admitted, just as unattainable—to make people laugh, make them cry, and make them see themselves in the characters she played on the screen.

She also admitted that she wanted to go home. On these darkest nights of the year, in these darkest days of history, she needed to touch something real again.

And Martin Browning knew that he'd chosen well after all.

He ordered two Laphroaigs, a great Scotch to finish a great Scottish meal. Once Vivian had sipped and her eyes were a little glassy and her laugh a little loud, he said to her, "Let me take you home."

She stopped laughing. "To Mrs. Murray's?"

"Home to Maryland, maybe," he said. "But as far as Chicago, certainly."

"Chicago?"

"By train." He had a lie all ready. "My company likes married men. They are very traditional. I told them I was married, and since the boss is meeting the train in Chicago, it would be good for me to have a wife."

She laughed. "You want me to be your beard?"

"Beard?" Here was an idiom he didn't know.

"A disguise. A woman on a homo's arm is a beard, so nobody thinks the guy likes to diddle other guys. A single guy escorting a married woman who's sleeping with the guy's married pal is a beard. It's a Hollywood thing. Get it?"

He got it. A failed actress traveling with a German assassin as his faithful wife, making him seem like just another harmless businessman, would also be a *beard*.

"Will you do it?" he asked.

"Is that *all* I'll have to do?"

"In public, we'll be man and wife. In private, I'll respect your wishes."

"When?"

"Friday."

She swirled the Scotch and tried to make sense of this. "But my things?"

"We're just around the corner from your rooming house." He didn't tell her that he'd brought her here, instead of to some Hollywood hot spot, so that he could move quickly. Once her room was cleaned out, it would be harder for her to back out. He said, "I'll give you cash to pay off Mrs. Murray. I'll wait while you collect your things. I'll watch in case Buddy Clapper is in the neighborhood."

She finished her Scotch. "All right. Just call me Mrs. . . . Say, what's your last name, anyway?"

"Kellogg," he lied.

AN HOUR LATER, VIVIAN Hopewell was back in the Roosevelt, wondering what she'd gotten herself into. At least she had her two suitcases.

They contained three years of life in Los Angeles . . . the clothes she'd brought, the clothes she'd bought, the headshots, and the script for a part she didn't get in a Three Stooges short called *You Nazty Spy!* She would have played a woman looking into one of those silly plastic eight balls to tell the fortunes of the Stooges. She wished that she had an eight ball now to tell her own.

EVERY NIGHT AT TEN o'clock, Fritz Kessler walked his twin dachshunds around Echo Lake. He could do the circuit in fifteen minutes or thirty, depending on how often the dogs stopped to sniff and sprinkle, or how often he met a familiar face and stopped to chat. He could be surprisingly talkative with a man he liked or a woman he'd like to go to bed with.

This evening, the path was all but deserted, until he came to a man—nothing more than a shadow—sitting on a bench beneath a sycamore.

The man said, "*Guten Abend, mein Herr.*"

Kessler came closer. The dogs tugged on the leads. He said, "Costner?"

"We must talk."

"You look . . . different."

"We change, Fritz, as circumstances change."

"Are you alone?"

Martin Browning had escorted Vivian across the Roosevelt lobby and tipped the elevator operator to see her to her room. He'd resisted the impulse to do it himself. Though he sometimes failed, he always tried to resist impulses that might lead him astray. Then he'd driven down to Echo Park.

His instinct now was to let Kessler live. The wider the swath of murder he left, the easier to track him. But Kessler alive was a greater danger than Kessler dead.

"I'm alone." Martin gestured to the little dogs. "Call off your Rottweilers."

Kessler came over, led by the dachshunds, and sat on the bench in the darkness. "What do you want?"

"To meet Miss Hildy and Mr. Hansy." Martin patted the dogs.

Kessler said, "They are my pride and joy. They and my wife, who watches from our apartment each night when we walk."

Martin looked over his shoulder at the building across the street. He saw no one in any of the windows. Then he looked at Kessler's right hand. It was entwined with the two leads. It would be difficult for him to get the brass knuckles in the right pocket.

Kessler went on, "You know, she's very worried, my wife. Worried that Stengle might give us up. Perhaps we should neutralize him."

So now Kessler was lying to him. All the more reason to kill him. Martin said, "Neutralize? Why?"

"To protect the cell. To protect your mission."

"What mission?"

Fritz Kessler looked out at the water. "You show yourself, Herr Costner, by showing nothing. I think you are dangerous. So did Herr Schwinn. That is why he asked me to watch you. I told him how deadly you were with the Mauser. We both wondered what use you plan to make of it . . . and why you always pick up your cartridges."

The dogs tugged at the lead. One of them began to whine.

Martin said, "You were at the Bund when Schwinn was arrested last night?"

"I work every Monday night."

"Who else was there?"

"The old Kraus couple. They cannot live without schnitzel. And Emile Gunst, who will fill his face with wurst every night until he dies. And a Hollywood boy named Kevin Cusack. He is a friend of Gunst. You may have seen him at Deutsches Haus."

"I don't go to Deutsches Haus."

"Another reason they wondered about you." Kessler smiled. "I wondered why a Hollywood boy would go to the Bund last night, of all nights. He asked Gunst about the Murphy Ranch. He asked me, too. He said he had heard of target shooting there."

Martin got up, went close to the lake, watched the lights of the city reflecting off the surface. "What did you tell him?"

"Nothing."

"Good." Martin had heard the name of this Cusack from Gunst, too. So he knew that in this small detail, Kessler was telling the truth.

"Gunst likes him," added Kessler. "I don't."

To put Kessler at ease, Martin asked a bit more about this outlier. "Why do you not like him?"

"A man who asks too many questions may not be who he says he is. He may be a friend of the Jews . . . or the FBI. We know there are informers in the Bund."

Martin would remember the name. *Kevin Cusack.* But that was not why he was here. He took out his calfskin gloves and pulled them on.

Kessler said, "See? I told you I can be trusted."

"I trust you, Fritz. You are a loyal son of the Fatherland." This was the kind of compliment that Martin seldom offered. But he knew how to inflate an ego, if only to put a man at ease. He sat beside Kessler again and said, "So you can tell me, Fritz, is that why you killed Stengle and lied about it? Because you are a loyal son of the Fatherland?"

"I did not kill Stengle."

"Someone did. And that someone might be inclined to kill me."

"So, what will you do?"

"Kill him first." In an instant, Martin's knife was driving upward, into the throat, through the tongue and the back of the mouth, deep into Fritz Kessler's brain. It happened so quickly, not even the dogs reacted.

Kessler's eyes opened wide. He shuddered. Then he was motionless.

Martin withdrew the knife, wiped the blade on Kessler's trousers, then took Kessler's wallet and watch to make it look like a robbery.

By the time the dogs sensed that something was wrong, Martin Browning was in his car. By the time they started to yap, he was halfway to Glendale.

WEDNESDAY, DECEMBER 10

SALLY DRAKE CAME BY Kevin Cusack's desk around ten. She said, "Still working on that thing about Casablanca?"

"I'm going to tell Hal Wallis to buy it."

"Then what?"

He leaned his arms on the typewriter. "Like I told you yesterday, I'm leaving. If they promote Jerry Sloane ahead of me, they'll promote my wastebasket first."

She slipped her glasses down and looked over them like a schoolmistress. "Jerry Sloane writes better than a wastebasket."

"Everything I write ends up in one. A biopic about Andrew Jackson, a Western for Errol Flynn, romantic comedies—"

"You crack better jokes than you write."

"That's not a compliment."

"Tell me . . . did you really mean that 'brother-and-sister' business?"

He held very still at the typewriter. No fast moves. She was asking the right question without any prompting. "Sure."

"So . . . no funny stuff in the compartment?"

"You just told me I crack funny jokes. Can I crack jokes?"

"You know what I mean."

"No, I don't. Maybe I should ask Jerry Sloane." He couldn't resist a low blow.

But she cleared the air. "Leave Jerry out of this. You could be a good beard. You could play my big brother, keep the mashers at bay . . . and the FBI, too."

He wanted to cheer. But he was still playing it cool. So he ignored the FBI remark and went back to typing.

Then she said, "So . . . if I keep my glasses on, will I be safe?"

"Glasses?" He kept typing.

"Like Dorothy Parker also said, and I *know* she said this: 'Men seldom make passes at girls who wear glasses.' Be at Union Station, Friday night at seven o'clock. The train leaves at eight."

Kevin watched her walk away and thought of something that Dorothy Parker never said but should have: "Men *always* make passes at girls with nice asses."

MARTIN BROWNING READ HIS paper at the Adams Square Pharmacy. He expected that no identification had been made of Stengle. It would take weeks for loved ones to notice that a young construction worker with dreams of California and a love of German good fellowship was no longer sending letters back to his parents in Bangor, Maine.

As for Kessler, the LAPD had called it a murder/robbery. Someone in the FBI might cross-reference the name, notice that Kessler was a waiter at Deutsches Haus, and start asking questions, but by then, Martin Browning would be long gone.

Then he saw another familiar name. "Emile Gunst, Dead in Custody." He was not surprised. He sipped his coffee and wondered: Did they beat him to death? Did he talk first? Or did he have a cyanide capsule in the tin of nitro pills? He didn't seem the type for suicide. Maybe he really had died of a heart attack.

In any event, the feds were getting closer . . . much closer. It was good that he had decided to go.

He hurried back to his apartment and got to work with needle, thread, and shears. His father had taught him to pin a waist, hem a cuff, and lengthen a sleeve, skills that helped him when he applied for a job at Mr. Fountain's Men's Shop. Now they helped him fashion a hiding place in the lining of the navy-blue overcoat. He'd made a cut through the right inside pocket. A leather strap from an old belt would hold the gun. He hadn't perfected it yet. But he would. Success lay in preparation.

As the sun reached the south side of the building, he moved to the window in the back bedroom to work in the warmth and light, and from time to time, have a look at Mrs. Sanchez, who came out onto her little patio each morning in a halter top, slathered herself in baby oil, and stretched out on her chaise longue.

He knew she liked the attention. When their eyes met, she smiled.

VIVIAN HOPEWELL SAT IN her room and gazed out at Grauman's. The Japanese fleet might be just over the horizon, but people were still stopping in the forecourt to see movie-star footprints. Even on the day after Pearl Harbor, they'd had Abbott and Costello out there, putting handprints in wet cement, signing autographs, cracking wise. In Hollywood, the show had to go on, no matter what.

Well, let it go on without her. Deciding was like having an aching tooth pulled. Whatever the pain of separation, she knew it would all feel better in a day or so.

When Harry called, she said she'd slept on it and was still in. She'd play his wife as long as he wanted. Then she asked him if they could have dinner that night.

"I have much to do," he said. "I will call if dinner is a possibility."

He was a strange one, she thought, unpredictable, mysterious, dangerous. The way he swept through that parking lot? Normal men didn't do things like that. And she didn't even know where he lived. An apartment house? A mansion in the Hollywood Hills? A fruit crate down by the L.A. River? The truth was that he was the kind of man that mothers always warned their daughters against.

Agents Carter and McDonald went up the stairs to the LAJCC office on Hollywood Boulevard. They didn't worry about Nazi spies watching the front door. If enemy intelligence agents didn't know the local G-men, they didn't pose much of a threat anyway. And Frank Carter wanted to talk to Leon Lewis.

The LAJCC's News Research Service was cramped with filing cabinets, noisy typewriters, and mimeograph machines spinning out the news. Sometimes national papers reprinted their stories about Nazis and other fascists without editing. Sometimes only snippets made it into the papers. But one way or another, the LAJCC had been warning the country about the threat to American Jews and everyone else.

Carter sat in Lewis's little office and got right to the point. "What do you know about the late Emile Gunst?"

"German agent in the last war. Imported German ceramics." Lewis went into the outer room, returned with a folder, opened it, and read, "'Emile Gunst: Bund member, Gau West.'" He looked up. "These Nazis treat us as if we were another province of the Fatherland, with Gauleiters and everything." Then he read on: "'Immigrated to U.S., 1923, after Beer Hall Putsch. Said he feared Nazis and hated Communists, hated them so much they gave him a heart attack.'"

"You could say he left Germany for his health."

"I know a lot of Jews who'd like to do the same thing," said Lewis. "'Wife Helga died 1938. No children. Joined Bund for social atmosphere, oompah bands, bratwurst. Known to eat nitro pills like breath mints. Hospitalized for chest pain three times.'"

"Anybody talk to his doctor?"

"We're not that thorough. Especially if our agent says that Gunst is on our side."

"Agent Twenty-Nine?" said Carter. "Cusack?"

Lewis said nothing, because he never spoke the names of his agents to outsiders.

Carter said, "I think Cusack was wrong about Gunst. He *wasn't* on our side."

"The paper says he died in custody."

"Heart attack or cyanide. They're doing the autopsy downtown."

Lewis nodded. "Twenty-Nine said he'd never seen a man eat so much sausage at a single sitting . . . or complain so much about indigestion."

"A good agent, Twenty-Nine."

Lewis said, "He's leaving."

That disappointed Carter, but he wasn't surprised. "When?"

"Friday night's Super Chief. He suggested we look into someone named Kessler. A waiter at the Bund."

"We know Kessler. Small-time."

"Did you know that he was murdered in Echo Park last night?" Lewis handed Carter a clipping from the *Herald*. "LAPD said it appeared to be a robbery."

"I did *not* know," said Frank Carter. "And appearances can be deceiving."

MARTIN BROWNING SLID THE Mauser C96 from its wooden holster and fitted the metal grooves on the broom handle grip into the grooves on the holster, turning the pistol into a carbine. This would give him much more stability when he took the shot. The Mauser was a fine weapon, accurate and powerful, with an effective range of one hundred meters. If he could get onto the White House lawn on Christmas Eve, he could make the shot from anywhere in the crowd.

He put the gun into the harness he'd fashioned inside the overcoat. Then he stood at the mirror in the front room and practiced: unbutton with the left hand, reach through the lining with the right, keep the gun concealed as long as possible. He even considered sewing in a false lining, so that if he was approached by the Secret Service, he could merely fling the coat open. *See? No gun.* Would they fall for that?

Consumed by this work, he didn't hear the *tick-tock* of heels on the driveway beneath his window. But he heard them on the stairs. And he heard the knock. He pulled off the coat and threw it over a chair. Then he opened the door to Mrs. Sanchez.

She still wore the halter top but had put on a wraparound skirt and mules that showed off her red pedicure. Her brown skin glistened with baby oil. Her eyes glistened, too. She said, "I think you have been working hard this morning. So I have brought you lunch . . . and sangria." She held the tray out. Chicken sandwiches, a pitcher of red wine afloat with oranges and ice, two glasses . . .

Letting her in was a bad idea, but before he could come up with an excuse, she brushed past, went into the dining room, plunked the tray down, then bent over to pour sangria and offer him a nice long look at her ass.

He realized he should have moved the overcoat. He shouldn't have left Gunst's Christmas "gift" on the table, either, or the Santa Fe brochure and tickets. But it was too late.

She turned and said, "Wrapped gifts . . . a winter coat . . . train tickets. You are going somewhere cold for Christmas?"

"I'll be back on New Year's Eve," he said. "Which reminds me, the rent for January." He went for the overcoat, as if to get money from one of the pockets.

But she stepped in front of him and offered a glass. "Sangria first." She also offered a salacious grin. She reminded him of that singer with the voice of an angel and the smile of a lively devil. *Lena Horne*. She had the same kind of light in her eye, too.

What a sin it would be to put it out. But if she went near the overcoat . . .

He took the sangria, clinked her glass, and sipped. They were standing close in the midday quiet, in an airy apartment, in a sleepy corner of Los Angeles. And it crossed his mind that controlling himself in a train compartment for forty-two hours might be easier if he surrendered now to the same desires that brought this widow to the door.

So he removed the glass from her hand, reached around her, and placed both glasses on the table. This brought him close enough to kiss her. And it was a sweet, sangria-tinged sensation.

Then he was carrying her down the hallway, past the kitchen, past the room with the desk on which he'd left gun oils and cleaning brushes, back to the sun-filled bedroom.

He dropped her onto the bed and dropped to his knees beside it. He ran his hands along her brown legs and up under the skirting of the bathing suit. She sighed as if to say that whatever he was doing, he should do more. So he leaned forward and kissed her smooth brown thighs. She gasped, so he kissed higher. And again she showed him that she liked what he was doing, that it was all she could hope for on a Wednesday afternoon.

The halter top came off, then the wraparound skirt and the swimsuit bottom. . . .

When they were done, she pulled up the sheet and lit a cigarette. After a few puffs, she asked him if he would like the lunch she'd brought.

Yes, he would, but he didn't want her wandering around. So he went naked down the hallway, stopped in the middle room to hide the gun cleaners, then went to the dining room to put the Santa Fe info in the topcoat and hang the topcoat in the closet.

They ate in the sunlight on the bed.

Then she swung a leg over him and . . . an hour later, after she'd rolled onto her stomach to entice him a third time, he gave her ass a smack and promised he'd be back on New Year's Eve. It was a lie, of course. And this whole thing might have been a mistake, but it was better than killing her.

KEVIN CUSACK FINISHED HIS last synopsis around two o'clock. He put a few personal items into a shoebox: a fountain pen; a box of Eberhard Faber No.

2 pencils; a bottle of ink; a notebook. Then he took the synopsis and headed down the hallway.

In the front office, Cheryl Lapiner was hunched over her typewriter, as usual.

He dropped his report on her desk. "They have to make this. It'll be sensational."

She read the cover sheet: "*Everybody Comes to Rick's.* Terrible title."

"I suggested calling it *Casablanca.* It captures the romance and danger."

"Romance and danger," she said. "I could use a little of that."

"Well, next time I invite you to Musso and Frank's—"

"But you're leaving."

He took her hand and said, "Good luck in Hollywood. I've had enough."

She said, "I know you're angry about Jerry Sloane getting a job first, but—"

"Nobody ever said this town was fair."

"That's for sure. Take it from one of the girls."

As he left the writers' building, he told himself to look ahead, toward the larger cause facing the country, even if it meant looking homeward. And he walked right into the big guys, Hal Wallis and Jack L. Warner himself.

They were coming back from the set of *Yankee Doodle Dandy,* the George M. Cohan biopic shooting on Stage 4. Wallis was saying that Cagney could win the Academy Award. Warner was worrying about the box office.

Seeing them, Kevin recalled his excitement that first day on the lot. He remembered passing Queen Bette Davis herself. She was wearing kerchief and flats, and he was awestruck, but she barely glanced at him. So Kevin had decided on his second day to act as if he'd always been there. When he saw Errol Flynn strolling along in Robin Hood's green tights, with a trench coat thrown over his shoulders and an unlit cigarette in his mouth, Kevin offered him a light. Very cool.

He assumed that Jack Warner, in his five-hundred-dollar suit and fast-clicking hundred-dollar shoes, didn't have any idea who he was.

But Warner stopped, pivoted, looked at his watch, and said, "I pay you people to work. What are you doing walking around in the middle of the afternoon?"

"Leaving," answered Kevin.

Hal Wallis looked at the shoebox under Kevin's arm. "Leaving?"

"I've handed in my resignation. No more reports on other people's screenplays. No more dancing to other people's tunes. Time to write my own story."

"You want to write?" asked Wallis.

Kevin jerked a thumb at the writers' building. "Everyone in there wants to write."

"Writers"—Warner started walking again—"schmucks with Underwoods."

Wallis lingered a moment, and Kevin thought, *If he offers me a job writing anything, even Rin Tin Tin, I'll take it.* But all Wallis offered was a perfunctory "Good luck." Not even a handshake. People said he was a cold fish, even if he liked you. Then he followed Warner.

Kevin shouted after them, "The schmucks who wrote *Everybody Comes to Rick's* did a helluva job. It'll make a helluva movie."

Warner gave him a look, as if to ask, *Who is this little pisher giving* me *advice?*

Kevin kept talking. "Find a few schmucks to write the screenplay, except for that no-talent Jerry Sloane. You'll make a lot of money." And he went on his way, feeling bigger with every step.

AROUND FOUR O'CLOCK, MARTIN Browning undid the wrapping on the Hummel box. He removed the tray of figurines and took out the notebook containing the names, addresses, and passwords of the contacts who would spirit him across the country and aid him when he killed Franklin Roosevelt.

Working from a template of code words in the notebook, he wrote two messages:

The first: "Delivery of seed samples Sunday SC. President's door." Translation: He would be arriving in Chicago on Sunday aboard the SC, or Super Chief. And he would meet his contact at the Polk Street door.

The second: "Christmas in Connecticut. Arrive 19th at 4 two suitcases zero packages." This was the location, time, and date of his arrival in Washington. Translation: He would meet his D.C. support team at Dupont Circle, Connecticut Avenue and Nineteenth Street, 4:00 P.M. on two and zero, or December 20.

The Adams Square Pharmacy handled Western Union messages, but Martin didn't want the locals chattering about seed samples or Christmas in Connecticut. Best if everyone in Glendale forgot about him.

So he drove down to the main office on Brand Boulevard, a busy place that December evening. Telegraphs tapping out dots and dashes . . . clerks counting words . . . operators sending, receiving, stuffing yellow telegrams into envelopes . . . customers shoulder-to-shoulder, wiring money or Christmas plans . . . the holiday rush, magnified by the crisis of war.

For a few cents, Martin's first telegram would be delivered to a warehouse in Crete, Illinois, that served as the distribution point for Diebold Seed Company. The second would go to a Western Union office on Atlantic Avenue in Brooklyn, then to an apartment in the Heights. Martin had not checked the "Signature Required" box on either. The fewer personal interactions, the better.

The people who received the telegrams would know what to do. If not, Martin would work as he preferred to—alone.

It was nearly dark when he got back to the apartment.

Mrs. Sanchez was sitting in front of her bungalow with the Jeffries sisters, who'd lived in the complex since it opened in 1927.

During their teen years, Marylea and Kimberlea had been actresses, known as "the poor man's Gish sisters," always cast as damsels in distress, bottle-blond Rapunzels at sixteen frames per second. But their movie fame had fled. They were now what Americans called old maids, living with their fading memories and three rambunctious pugs in the second-floor apartment across the driveway from Martin's.

"Sangria, *señor*?" said Mrs. Sanchez.

The landlady and her lover had agreed to keep their afternoon tryst a secret, to act in public with the same formality as always. So for a few moments, there was superficial conversation about the war and the challenges that lay ahead.

Then Mrs. Sanchez said, "Of course, we must all enjoy Christmas."

"Yes," said Kimberlea, the no-nonsense sister. "You're very kind to bake us Christmas cookies, despite the national crisis."

"We do so *love* the cookies," said Marylea with an affected Southern accent, and she tossed her curls at Martin. "Don't you just *love* cookies, Mr. King?"

"Almost as much as sangria," he lied.

"You will find a box of cookies in your unit," said Mrs. Sanchez. "A surprise."

"Surprise?" Martin tried not to let the light drain out of his eyes. Harold King had lively eyes, smiling eyes.

"I do it for all the neighbors," she said. "Surprise cookies before Christmas. And since you're going away—"

Just then one of the pugs began to bark in the Jeffries apartment. So the sisters finished their drinks and announced that it was time to take the dogs for their evening stroll.

Martin watched them go up the back stairs. Then he said to Mrs. Sanchez, "Did you let yourself into my apartment?"

"I have keys. But you can trust me. Our secret's safe. Yours, too."

"Mine?"

"That you are a collector of German figurines."

Martin had not rewrapped the box, a sloppy mistake. He said, "You *saw* the figurines?"

"I love Hummels . . . such smiley little things."

"What else did you see?"

"I saw your train schedule when I brought lunch. You circled the Super Chief on Friday. So where are you really going?" She grinned salaciously. "You can tell your *mamasita*."

He smiled and calculated. "Wherever I'm going, you make it hard to leave."

"Oh, *señor*," she whispered, "you make me feel very good."

And he decided quickly, perhaps too quickly.

He knew that the Jeffries sisters would be walking their dogs soon. If he acted now, they'd make a perfect alibi. So he dumped the last of the sangria into his glass, gulped it down, and said, "We need more to drink. And more fun. More fun tonight."

"Oh, *señor* . . ."

He got up and opened the screen door of her bungalow with the toe of his shoe. "Shall I make more sangria? Or cook? I would love to cook for you."

"You would cook for me? No man has cooked for me in many years."

He held the door open with his foot and let her slip past. He didn't want to touch anything. The fewer fingerprints he left, the better.

She didn't see him pull on his calfskin gloves.

Three minutes later, he came out of the bungalow and called back to her, "Good night, and thank you, Mrs. Sanchez."

The Jeffries sisters were just coming down with their pugs on leashes.

He went over and patted the dogs. "Oh, I love these snuffly, snuggly little guys. You have to bring them upstairs to visit sometime."

The sisters seemed to like the attention as much as the dogs did. Kimberlea smiled. Marylea giggled and batted her eyes.

He said he was bound for Hollywood to meet a friend. Then he watched the sisters walk toward the street. They'd remember that a few minutes after they left the Sanchez patio, he left, too. He'd time his return for ten thirty, when Kimberlea walked the dogs again, so she would be sure to see him again.

THURSDAY,
DECEMBER 11

IN NEW YORK, THE day offered cold gray with a grouchy flurry of snow. But it was warm in the apartment overlooking the Brooklyn promenade. Helen Stauer sat in a straight-backed chair, with a pair of binoculars at her eyes, a cup of coffee steaming on the windowsill, a Philco console tuned to WQXR and Mozart's *Requiem*, a perfect accompaniment to the lugubrious weather.

She was watching an American destroyer steam south past the Manhattan skyline. That meant a convoy was gathering at the Narrows. A convoy meant good hunting for the U-boats that the Führer had unleashed on Monday. And according to the news reports, he had just unleashed the full fury of the Reich with a declaration of war on the United States.

She would relay the particulars of that destroyer—USS *Babbit*, four-stacker, Wickes class, DD-128—to a wireless operator on the Eastern Shore of Maryland, who would relay the information to Berlin. She would also include information gathered by her husband, an accountant who audited the books of weapons, munitions, and chemical plants across the tristate area.

She sat in her slip and white shoes. Her white uniform lay on the ironing board. She was known as the best-pressed nurse on the swing shift at the Brooklyn Navy Yard infirmary, the best-lipsticked, too—dark red to complement alabaster skin and black hair. She was also known as the most punctual, although she didn't say why. If she arrived early, she could stroll and snoop and learn the latest: What ships had arrived for refitting? What was the progress on the new battleship, USS *Iowa*? What new levels of security were they adding? She observed, absorbed, and transmitted it all.

The Stauers had few friends and were seldom seen out and about, except to worship at Blessed Virgin Mary on Sundays or dine at Peter Luger's on Wednesday nights. They appeared to be a common and rather sad American phenomenon, the childless middle-aged couple living out their lives in a small apartment, working hard with heads down because they'd been through the Depression and knew that jobs were still scarce.

The husband, Wilhelm, was quiet, paunchy, balding. But he carried a Walther P38, with which he'd killed three men who'd gotten too curious about his affairs.

Helen didn't need a pistol. She could find a man's carotid just by looking at him and inject him in an instant with a killing dose of sodium thiopental. Among her other skills with small, sharp instruments: extracting bullets, suturing wounds, using mat knives and fine-tipped pens to fit official documents and IDs to her purpose.

When a knock startled her, she thought first of her syringe. But it wasn't charged. So she turned down the radio and went to the door. Through the peephole, she saw an old lady waving a yellow envelope.

As soon as the door cracked, Mrs. Schwartz started talking, "Good morning, Mrs. Stauer. I . . . I went to bed early last night, and when I got up, this was under my door, delivered to me by accident, I think."

Helen took the envelope, turned it over, and said, "It's been opened. My name is on it but it's been opened. Why has it been opened?"

The old lady's smile faded. "I'm sorry . . . when someone sends a telegram, I get so excited, I . . . I opened it before looking."

"And you *read* it?"

Mrs. Schwartz gestured for her to open it. "You've . . . you've been invited to Christmas in Connecticut. That will be lovely."

"Lovely, yes." Helen Stauer wondered if she should kill Mrs. Schwartz for reading her mail. She decided against it and closed the door in the old lady's face.

Then she read the telegram and almost cried with joy. Their man was in motion. The plan was unfolding. *Der Tag*, for the Stauers, was coming at last. She felt the excitement that men must feel when they go to war, a strange, almost sexual exhilaration at the possibilities of danger, death, and fulfillment.

Helen Stauer and her husband had already requested the days off before Christmas, promising to work on the day itself. They'd leave for Washington on the twentieth, meet their man at Dupont Circle, bring him to a safe house, study, prepare, plan, and execute. Before Roosevelt's crippled body was cold on Christmas Eve, they'd be on a train back to the anonymity of their Brooklyn lives.

MARTIN BROWNING TIMED HIS departure to the Jeffries sisters' dog-walking schedule. He was leaving a day early because of the dead body in the owner's bungalow.

Kimberlea saw him first. "Have you heard? Hitler's declared war on us."

"Yes," added Marylea. "How perfectly awful. Oh, what are we to do?" She often talked as if she were delivering dialogue for title cards dropped into silent-movie scenes.

"Perfectly awful, yes." Martin had been energized by the news from Berlin. If he killed lawyers or landladies now, he'd be waging war, not committing murder. And when he killed Franklin Roosevelt, it would be an act of pure patriotism, a gift to humanity.

Imagine Americans without FDR inspiring them as he had in '33, when the only thing they had to fear was fear itself. Such a people without such a leader would be far less formidable. How much easier would it have been to defeat Britain, had Neville Chamberlain been prime minister, rather than growling old Churchill, besotted as he was with tumblers of Scotch, dreams of empire, and the rhetoric of war? Maybe some good German marksman could get him, too.

It would be a mercy to kill them, a mercy to end this war quickly. Fewer deaths recorded . . . fewer resources wasted . . . fewer world-historical treasures destroyed . . . fewer Bolsheviks befouling Europe . . . an equitable balance restored between Germany and the rest of the world. And out of equity would rise the competition of ideas, which would demonstrate the innate superiority of German *Kultur*. A country stabbed in the back by its own leftists in 1918, then abused by the Allies at Versailles, would assume once again its honorable place as a leader of nations.

That had been Martin Browning's goal since his days at Heidelberg, since his first memories as his father's son. And the Nazis offered the quickest path back to honor. He'd followed it from the university straight into Section 6, Reich Security Office, bringing with him his knowledge of America, his brains, and his skill with weapons made by Herr Mauser. Now he would follow that path all the way to Washington.

"We hear you're going on a trip," said Kimberlea.

What did they know? He covered his concern with a little laugh. "I'm heading east for Christmas."

"Have a perfectly wonderful journey," said Marylea.

"Thank you, ladies." He walked back to the garage, with the sisters and their dogs following, keeping up the conversation.

He opened the trunk and put his bag into it. "I'll drive up through the Central Valley and visit some of my customers. Then keep going."

"But . . . Mrs. Sanchez said you were going on the train."

"Train?" He let out with a bigger laugh, which was better than killing them. "No train for me. Too many accounts to visit."

"I've heard there will be gas rationing," said Kimberlea.

"Not until the first of the year," he said. "By then, I'll be back."

One of the dogs began to make little growling sounds and tug toward the Sanchez bungalow. Did he smell something?

Martin closed his trunk, wished the sisters Merry Christmas, and left.

Later they would speak well of Harold King. They'd say he was always nice to them, that he didn't *seem* like a murderer. They'd say he'd headed east by car, not by train. That would deflect suspicion for a little longer.

Martin would have preferred to play James Costner, supercilious haberdasher, introvert, loner. But every decision he'd made since he climbed into the Jewish lawyer's car had driven him inexorably to the next, and every decision to simplify his situation had complicated his life. So it was time to get out of town. That's what he was thinking as Los Feliz Boulevard lifted him from Glendale up into the Hollywood Hills.

"Los Feliz" meant "the happy," and all those people up in all those fine houses surely were, all those movie executives and businessmen and lawyers kissing their wives and mistresses and going off to work. The war would never reach their Pacific Nirvana, only the profit. They'd make money filming war movies. They'd make more money manufacturing war matériel. And they'd make fortunes brokering the land on which the war factories were built and the war workers were housed. They'd never know the devastation that Europe faced. They'd never see Hitler parade down Hollywood Boulevard in an open Mercedes. But their hearts would break on Christmas Eve. Martin Browning would make sure of it, broadcast live on the CBS Radio Network.

As his journey began, that knowledge made him feel like the most *feliz* of *los feliz*. . . .

FRANK CARTER REMINDED HIMSELF that the heavyset woman with the German accent had endured a horrible shock. Two nights before, she'd heard the dachshunds yapping. She'd peered out and seen them running in circles under a streetlamp. She'd hurried out to find her husband dead on a bench.

Now both dogs curled protectively at her feet. She sat in her housecoat, tissues clutched in her hand and stuffed in her pockets. On a chair lay a white shirt with epaulettes, navy-blue jodhpurs, jackboots, and a heavy belt: her husband's Bund uniform.

The LAPD said that Fritz Kessler's death was a run-of-the-mill robbery, but when it came to waiters from Deutsches Haus, nothing was run-of-the-mill.

It had taken Carter half a day to persuade Chief Agent Hood to give him some time, but here he was. He asked her, "Did your husband talk about Deutsches Haus?"

"He loved the Haus. He loved the Bund. They gave him work when he could find none. 'Germans taking care of Germans,' he called it."

"Did your husband ever talk about the people he waited on there?"

She appeared offended at that. She stiffened. A tissue fell from her lap, and one of the depressed little dogs gave it a sniff. She said, "My husband did not gossip."

"The things men tell their wives are not gossip." Carter phrased it to appeal to her.

She dabbed at her nose, and said, "Well . . . there was one man."

"Oh?" Carter thought for a moment this might be a lead.

"On Monday nights, I use the car. I drive to sodality at St. Vibiana's. I am Catholic. Are you Catholic, Herr Carter?"

"No, but Agent McDonald is."

"My mother goes to sodality, too," said McDonald.

"So a man from the Bund drove him home," she said, "a man named Cusack who asked unfriendly questions about the Murphy Ranch."

"The Murphy Ranch?" Carter glanced at McDonald. "What did your husband do out there?"

"*Ach*, he did not say." Mrs. Kessler waved her hand, and the tissue in her fingers sent a flurry of paper bits floating into the air. Then she blubbered, as if this was all becoming too much for her.

So Carter asked, "Can you tell us about his routines, Mrs. Kessler? Sometimes, if we know about a victim's routines, we can learn something—"

"Deutsches Haus was a second job. He went out early on Tuesdays and Thursdays to look for work. Masons start work early. He worked very hard and—"

"Where did he go on those mornings? To a union hall?"

"I told you, he did not tell me everything. He worried that I might gossip."

"What kind of gossip?"

"*Cheap* gossip." Her voice began to rise and her face to redden, as if she'd had enough of this. "Gossip about the Bund and the good men who go there and work there to warn the world about the Jews. Do you know the Jews were sending spies into the Bund, spies looking for gossip? That is what he was afraid of. He thought this Cusack might be such a spy, and . . . Do you work for the Jews, Herr Carter?"

"I work for the United States government, ma'am. And we'd like to know, did your husband have any weapons?"

She said that he did not.

McDonald said, "May we look in his car? There might be clues in his car."

She gave them the keys and pointed to the car parked across the street.

They left believing that if her husband was guilty of anything, she didn't know about it. But in his trunk, they found a Springfield '03 wrapped in an oiled canvas.

"I guess he liked to shoot," said Carter.

"Maybe he was shooting at the Murphy Ranch on Monday morning."

"Somebody was." And Frank Carter knew they'd gotten closer . . . to something. "Let's have a look at what's left of Herr Kessler."

KEVIN CUSACK DEVOTED HIS last full day in Los Angeles to details: First he made a deal with a downstairs neighbor, a car salesman who ran a lot on Western Avenue. If Kevin didn't return by January 15, the dealership could sell the car for a 50 percent commission. Then he paid his bills by check and dropped them in a mailbox. At Thrifty Drug, he bought a packet of Trojans.

He hoped he'd need them on the train. At the Bank of America on Hollywood, he took all but five bucks from his account—two hundred ninety-six dollars, the sum total of his earnings in the movie business—but he kept the account open in case Boston was just too damned cold and he decided to come back. At the Chinese laundry, he picked up his shirts, four starched for dress, two casual.

Back in his room, he packed the shirts, a suit, two sport coats, two turtlenecks, three pullovers, six ties. He'd grown adept at mixing and matching. As his father always said, the better dressed the man, the more respect he'd command. Supposedly true in Boston or L.A. But his whole Hollywood life could be stuffed into the same two suitcases he'd brought four years before. Dressing the part hadn't done him a damn bit of good.

HAROLD WAS WAITING IN the lobby when Vivian came down with her bags.

"Say, what's the big rush?" she demanded.

"I need to go to Barstow."

"Barstow? That's a hundred and twenty miles. It could take three hours."

"Four with traffic." He led her out, followed by the bellman with her luggage. "That's why we're going today."

"What the hell's in Barstow?"

"An unhappy account. And don't swear. My wife doesn't swear." He piled her into the car, tipped the bellman, and pulled onto Hollywood Boulevard. "We'll get a nice dinner in the Beacon Tavern tonight. Tomorrow we'll eat in Casa del Desierto."

She knew a little Spanish. "House of the Desert? What kind of house?"

"Don't worry. It's not some isolated bordello. It's the train station. It even has a Harvey House restaurant."

She didn't like to think she was so easy to read, but she liked a man who understood her. She said, "I wanted to be a Harvey Girl once. I thought it'd be better than slinging hash in Annapolis."

"No slinging hash on this trip." He dropped the ticket envelope on her lap. "The Super Chief, leaving L.A. eight P.M. Friday, stopping at Barstow eleven P.M. A drawing room."

"Wow. This must have cost you a bundle," she said.

"My company is paying. So we'll go in style."

"Now I know why you want to keep working for them." She pushed in the lighter on the dash and put a cigarette into her mouth.

He snatched it and threw it out the window. "My wife doesn't smoke, either."

"You smoke."

"I'm a man. Smoking is manly. But my wife—"

"Everybody's wife smokes. Every actress in Hollywood smokes. If you want me to play your wife, I need a smoke once in a while."

Martin Browning realized a husband had to give a little. So he gave. "Just don't smoke in public. You're a lady."

For her, smoking was a luxury, and she took her luxuries where she found them. So she lit another cigarette and looked again at the tickets. The name on the envelope: "Mr. and Mrs. H. Kellogg." She asked him, "Say, what kind of name is Kellogg, anyway? Are we the cornflakes couple or something?"

"Very funny. That name arrived with the Puritans." He didn't tell her he'd changed his identity from Harold No. 1 to Harold No. 2. He carried Social Security cards and driver's licenses for both. If the authorities started looking for an unmarried man named Harry King, they wouldn't be looking at a Mr. and Mrs. H. Kellogg.

"Do we have a backstory?" she asked.

"A what?"

"A backstory, a biography, so I know what kind of person I'm playing."

"Ah, yes. Backstory." He reached across her lap to the glove box.

His arm brushed her legs. She moved, as if startled by the touch. She didn't want him to know that she liked it. Not yet anyway.

He opened the glove box, and a road map dropped out. She picked it up: "Los Angeles and the USA." She started to unfold it, but he snatched it away. It should have gone into the trash before he left. But he tried never to leave anything incriminating behind. He shoved it into his breast pocket. He'd get rid of it when he could.

Then he pulled out a pad and pencil. "Take these. Let's create Vivian Kellogg. Do you mind calling yourself 'Vivian' a while longer? I like the name."

"You're the boss." She wrote the name in the notebook and imagined a character.

They tossed ideas back and forth as he found his way over Franklin to Riverside Drive, and onto the new Arroyo Seco Parkway, where he pushed the Dodge up to fifty miles an hour.

The speed filled Vivian with a growing sense of adventure. She might be leaving L.A. behind, but something good was going to happen out there. She just knew it. So she stretched her legs, rolled down the window, and felt the breeze. "I love going fast."

"Someday, the whole country will have roads like this. They already have them in—" He almost said, "Germany," thinking of the autobahns. Instead, he gestured to the notebook. "Back to Vivian. Where do you suppose I met her?"

"I told you I'm from Maryland, from Annapolis, Maryland."

"Then Maryland is our home, and our destination."

"Eastport . . . the working-class end of town." She wondered if he'd still be with her by then. She didn't know that after he killed Franklin Roosevelt, he'd need a safe house from which to make his escape across the Chesapeake. Annapolis would be perfect.

AROUND MIDDAY, A TELEGRAM arrived at the Diebold Seed Company in Crete, Illinois.

Max Diebold was in his office on the upper level of the barn. He came downstairs to greet the deliveryman because he never allowed anyone in the loft. He'd hidden the shortwave up there, behind a wall of hay bales. He tipped the man ten cents and read the telegram.

His son, Eric, came in from the greenhouse. "What's going on?"

Max waved the telegram. "We go to Chicago on Sunday. Dearborn Station."

"To meet the train?"

"What else would we meet at a train station?" The father looked at the dusty black car in the back of the barn. "We should also check the oil and tires and gas up the Ford."

"I'll wash and wax it, too. I bet he'll love a shiny car."

"No. *Nein, Dummkopf,*" said the father. "A waxed car in December? It should be salt-caked, not shiny. We're not trying to attract attention."

For a moment, father and son stared at one another. They were like mirror images, thirty years apart—small, bespectacled, ferret-faced men. But where the father appeared hard and focused, the son twitched with a kind of unnatural excitement at the possibility of a little trip and, perhaps, a little danger.

The father's gaze carried force. The son's conveyed weakness. And soon enough, the son averted his eyes and retreated back into the yard between the barn and the greenhouse. The father went up to the shortwave radio to compose a report for Section 6.

THE L.A. COUNTY CORONER was a cheery guy named Billy Belly Benson. It was easy to see why, thought Carter. If Billy Belly put on a red suit and a fake beard, he could play the lead in the Hollywood Boulevard Santa Claus Lane Parade . . . just so long as they aired him out first to get rid of the formaldehyde stink.

"You sure you don't want to see Gunst?" asked Billy. "I can show you his heart. Arteries plugged like toothpaste in a tube."

Frank Carter said, "We're here to see Kessler."

"Kessler? The other Kraut? He's still on ice." Billy Belly led the G-men to the storage room and pulled Kessler out of a refrigerated locker. "There he is. Cut and dried."

"Cut and dried?" asked McDonald.

"Somebody drove a knife into his throat, just above the Adam's apple, up through the back of his mouth, right into the medulla oblongata. Heart stops beating right away. Not a lot of blood. A dry, clean kill."

"Cut . . . and dried," said Carter. "I get it."

McDonald asked, "Robbery?"

"I tell you *how* he died. Not *why*."

Carter looked at Kessler's face, a human husk, bloated, discolored, all life and emotion gone. "What's that on the temple?"

"Hard to say." Billy turned the head. His belly pressed into the sheet covering the body. "Looks like somebody took a shot at him and grazed him."

"Could've been from Doane's tommy gun," said McDonald.

"But the throat cut killed him," said Billy Belly. "And the damnedest thing—"

"More damned than this?" Carter gestured to the corpse.

"A philosopher we got." Billy chuckled. "Like I said, I tell the *how*, not the *why*, and for certain not the *wherefore*."

"The wherefore?" said McDonald.

"You know, 'Wherefore art we going?' Not a question we ask a lot around here." Billy led them to another locker and pulled out another stiff, an old man with a tan so good, it hadn't faded even in death. "They found this one in the trunk of his own Lincoln-Zephyr, parked beside Bob's Big Boy in Burbank."

Carter almost gagged. "That's no Big Boy burger I smell."

"It was the smell led 'em to the car. Course, we all stink after three days, alive or dead." Billy chuckled again. This work required either the dourest of personalities or the sunniest of outlooks. "Somebody emptied his pockets. So we ran his plate. A widowed lawyer named Koppel. Lived in Pacific Palisades."

"That's where the Murphy Ranch is," said McDonald.

"But get a load of this." Billy put his fingers under the chin of the corpse and lifted. "Same kind of cut as Kessler. Right above the Adam's apple."

"Are you saying the same guy killed him?" asked Carter.

"I'm saying you don't see a cut like that too often. As professional as a surgeon." Carter brought his handkerchief to his nose.

"Yeah, yeah. It stinks," said Billy. "But I got one more thing."

"Make it fast," said Carter.

Billy led them down another corridor to another bank of refrigerated lockers and rolled out another corpse: a young man, eyes swollen, forehead stove in. Carter said, "Who's this?"

"I don't know, but"—Billy pulled a pair of brass knuckles from his pocket and slid them onto his fist—"you know what these are, right?"

"Every street thug in L.A. carries them," said Carter. "So?"

Billy brought his fist to the jaw of this corpse, so that the knuckles made a perfect match with the ugly bruise that serrated the side of the face. "The cops found a knuckle-duster like this in Kessler's pocket. And this guy here was hammered real good, then tossed off the Hyperion Bridge. Landed on his head, broke his neck—"

"So you're saying Kessler killed him?"

"Nah. I leave the speculatin' to you fellas. But there's an awful lot of coincidence around this morgue today. Two guys dead by the same kind of knife cut. And this? You figure it out. It's above my pay grade."

"We're trying." Carter shoved his hands into his pockets and felt the cartridge. "We'll need photos of all these guys."

By four o'clock, Vivian and her "husband" had passed through Pasadena and Covina and Rancho Cucamonga. They'd climbed Route 66 through the Cajon Pass, with snowcapped Mount Baldy so close they could almost touch it. Then they'd dropped down into the high desert. After about fifteen miles of grit blowing against the windshield, they arrived at a dusty parking lot with a sign hanging outside a ramshackle building: GOBEL'S GUNS AND HARDWARE.

Vivian looked at the tar-paper roof, the little lean-to on the side, the barn in the back, and she said, "You drove all the way out here to see the guy who owns this dump?"

"Mr. Gobel is a good customer."

She grabbed her door handle.

He told her to stay put, like a parent speaking to a child.

"But I need a bathroom. We've been driving a long time."

"Give me five minutes. Then we'll go straight to the hotel."

"Harry, I need to pee so bad, I can taste it."

"That's very crude." He reached around her, locked the door, and gave her a look. It wasn't angry or threatening. It was blank. Just blank. "My wife is not crude."

And it scared the hell out of her.

He must have sensed it, because he said, "Stay here, please. I'll be back in a jiff."

With the wind blowing sand and sagebrush across the flat desert, she squeezed her legs together and watched him go into the store. Who was he, really? And what was she doing with him? And why couldn't she go in there and pee?

GOBEL'S SMELLED OF CIGARETTES, gun oil, and smoke from a little woodstove. Two aisles led to a counter at the back, divided by display shelves with all kinds of screws and brads and hinges. Along the wall on the right were seed bins and nail kegs . . . on the left, tools hung for display—wrenches, pliers, saws, claw hammers, tack hammers, and ball-peens, too. Behind the counter long guns hung on racks. Beneath the glass countertop handguns were displayed. A sign taped on the glass read: "California One-Day Waiting Period. No gun 'til tomorrow. Their Law, not Ours." In a side office, country music was playing.

Martin rang the bell on the counter and studied the posters on the walls:

One showed Lady Liberty with an artillery shell cutting off her arm. Her torch was falling toward the slogan "War's First Casualty," which was emblazoned across an orange background. Beneath it, the words "America First Committee." Nearby hung a soldier's portrait, a young man in the uniform of an American doughboy, a Purple Heart pinned to the frame. In a smaller frame on the front of the register was the red-white-and-blue shield, framed by the words "America First."

Martin knew he'd come to the right place. But he didn't know what his contact looked like. German sympathizers took many forms. He'd just use the word "varmint" and see what happened.

A skinny woman shuffled out of the office. She wore an old dress and moth-eaten sweater. A cigarette dangled from her lips, and her skin had the crushed-newspaper tinge of an all-day butt fiend. She squinted over the smoke from her latest light and said, "I'm Ma Gobel. What can I do you for?"

"I need something to kill varmints."

She puffed and squinted a little harder. "What kind of varmints, exactly?"

"Three rats and a mess of squirrels."

She let out a long sigh, as if she'd expected those words but hoped never to hear them. Then she called into the office, "Boys, we got a visitor."

First came a hulk of a man in overalls and flannel shirt with the sleeves rolled up. He folded his arms and said, "Visitor? From where?"

Martin noticed the tattoo on his left arm. A circle and three Ks. Beneath it the words "Klan Forever." An America Firster *and* a Klansman. The only thing better would have been a swastika.

Ma Gobel said, "This feller says he wants to kill *varmints.*"

Martin smiled. He wasn't sure if he should play a role or play himself. He stayed in character as the friendly seed salesman. "Three rats and a mess of squirrels."

The hulk knew what this meant. He said, "What's your name?"

"My name's not important. But . . . can a good America Firster help me?"

Ma Gobel leaned over her son's shoulder and said, "America First dissolved itself today. It's on the radio. Right after Hitler declared war on us—"

"So we'll have to be careful." Another voice entered the conversation, another son, from the looks of him, not quite as bulky, not dressed for hard work.

"America Firsters are good goddamn Americans," said Ma. "But if Germany—"

The second son ignored his mother and said, "I'm Richard. This is my brother, Heinz. You're a friend of Emile Gunst?"

Martin shifted his eyes to their mother.

"Ma knows everything," said Richard. "So speak your piece."

"Gunst is dead," said Martin.

"I told you boys this was gettin' dangerous. Even before the Japs bombed Hawaii, I told you." Ma shuffled into the office.

"Dead? How?" asked Heinz.

"Heart attack most likely." Martin saw no need to mention FBI custody, given how jittery the mother seemed.

"Gunst knew us," Richard said. "He knew America First. He knew the best path for this country was to stay out of war."

Ma shuffled back with a pint bottle in her hand. "Then that Jew lover Roosevelt went and goaded the Japs. So now my boys'll get drafted and killed, just like their pa in '17." She dumped a shot of whiskey into her mug, then toasted her husband's picture.

Richard said to Martin, "Some of us still think the best path would be to send envoys to Hitler, offer to join him, and beat back the Bolshevik Jews."

"Yes, sir," said Ma. "Commies and kikes. They're the *real* enemy. My boys ain't dyin' for Commies and kikes." She offered Martin the pint.

He shook his head. No need to drink to that.

Heinz asked him, "Are you a Bund member?"

Martin said, "I am a friend of Gunst. That's all you need to know."

"We hear the Bund's been raided, shut down." Heinz shook his head. "Too bad."

"Yeah," said Ma. "A good place to get dinner without havin' to sit with a lot of Jews. Can't go anyplace in L.A. without havin' to sit with a lot of Jews."

"They killed Christ, you know," said Richard in total deadpan, so that Martin couldn't tell if he was serious or not. "Now, what do you need from us? Money? Guns? We have two Thompson submachine guns, packed in Cosmoline since 1934."

"Yeah," said Ma. "Goddamn feds and their goddamn National Firearms Act. Federal government shouldn't be able to tell you what kind of gun you can own."

Martin said, "I just need a place to hide my car."

"For how long?"

"Forever," said Martin. "I'll even sign it over to you. Better to stash it in a garage in Barstow than drive it into a ditch in Glendale and attract attention."

"Well, I'll be goddamned." Ma squinted out the window, then reached under the counter and pulled out a shotgun. "Look at that."

Through the side window, they saw a young woman heading for the outhouse at the back of the property. It was Vivian.

Ma said, "I'll give that gal an assful of buckshot for trespassin'."

But Martin shouted that she was his wife.

"Your wife?" said Richard.

Martin grinned. "It was a long ride from L.A. We drank too much Coke."

"Your wife?" Ma grinned, too, revealing that she was a little behind on her dental work. "So tell her to come in and use the real plumbin'."

Heinz flexed the KKK tattoo. "Gunst never said nothin' about any husband-and-wife teams."

"Gunst never told everything to anyone." Martin seethed quietly at Vivian. "Now, I'll leave my car here around five tomorrow. Then you'll give me a ride to the train station. Then you'll never see me again."

"That's it?" said Richard. "That's all you need?"

"One more thing, maybe." Martin looked into the case. "A box of 7.63-by-25-millimeter bottleneck rounds, if you have them."

Heinz produced a box of cartridges. "Rare ammo. Mauser C96?"

Martin saw no need to answer. "Do you have a target range?"

"Drive out Old Highway 58. Just past Jamaica Street, take the dirt road back into the hills. The right fork leads to a shooting range. We own it."

"Thank you," said Martin. "Oh, and it feels like that woodstove is working."

"Of course it's workin'," said Ma. "Gets goddamn cold in the desert in December. That's why I need my sweater and my whiskey, too."

Martin pulled the road map from his pocket. "Throw this in for me, would you?"

"Sure." Heinz opened the stove, snatched the map, and fed it to the flames. "Gone."

"Thank you," said Martin. "How much for the bullets?"

"No charge," said Richard. "Especially if you're plannin' to kill varmints."

Martin didn't tell them that he was planning to kill the biggest varmint of them all.

VIVIAN SAID, "WHAT TOOK you? I was ready to burst."

"Sometimes I need to charm a customer before I can get his signature."

"We drove all the way out here for a *signature*?"

"Mrs. Kellogg, you are asking too many questions. Your backstory says you are a loyal wife, does it not?"

She thought he was kidding, so she looked at her notebook. "Yes. It says here that I am loyal and obedient . . . honey . . . dear."

"So, if I tell you to stay in the car, *stay* in the car. Wet your pants if you have to, but stay in the car."

She turned to the window and resolved not to antagonize him further.

"Now, do you see that?" He pointed to a skeletal hundred-foot tower rising above the low buildings about a mile away. He could change his mood in an instant, as if reading hers. "It's the Richfield Beacon. It's part of the Highway of Lights. Keep your eye on it."

"Highway of Lights?"

"A series of Richfield Oil road stops running from San Diego to Canada. Service for your car, taverns and hotels for your rest, and beacons for airplanes following the roads across California. Like an American dream."

"Better than staying in that shack behind the feed store, I suppose."

"When there's no blackout, the word 'Richfield' lights up in giant neon letters," he said. "Then the beacon sweeps the sky, so that travelers can see it from the road, and planes can find the Barstow airport in the dark."

He gave another look at the little smokestack rising from the Gobel's roof, to make sure that the woodstove was puffing away. Then he followed Route 66 as it turned to parallel the tangle of rail lines, sidings, and switches around this junction town in the desert. Freight was rolling, engines were steaming, and the mighty machinery of American commerce was beginning to turn again in a nation throwing off its shock.

Soon they were pulling up a long drive to the hotel behind the Richfield station. And Vivian was thrilled. This was no roaches-and-mold roadside wreck. It looked like a rambling Spanish hacienda, with balconies and tile roofs and a cactus garden out front.

Inside, it was just as beautiful, and when he asked for two rooms—four dollars each—she knew that she was traveling first class with a man of his word. But she was also slightly disappointed. He was mysterious and a little dangerous. But she had to admit that she liked it. She liked being close to him. She liked looking at him. She liked the way the air vibrated around him. She wondered what he'd feel like next to her in bed.

He handed her the keys and said, "Adjoining rooms. We'll be in close enough proximity over the next few days, so tonight you'll have peace and quiet."

At that, Vivian noticed a newspaper lower in a chair by the fireplace. The guy behind it gave them a look, as if a couple heading off to separate rooms in see-no-evil Barstow was the strangest thing in the world. The roadhouse was halfway between L.A. and a town called Las Vegas, where gambling was legal, marriage quick, and divorce even quicker. Most people stopping here for the night had sin on their minds.

She noticed him again when she and Harold ate in the tavern. He was at the bar, nursing a drink, watching the room as though waiting for a woman.

He was wearing a sport coat of brown and tan houndstooth, along with brown and white wing-tip shoes. So "inconspicuous" was not his fashion. He looked like he belonged in the tout line at Santa Anita. But she thought no more about him . . .

. . . because it was Mexican night, with tostadas and enchiladas, and music from a trio of troubadours in sombreros. Soon, a few couples were dancing to a slow Mexican ballad. She dropped a hint that Harold seemed to ignore. Then she said she loved to dance. But he told her he wasn't a good dancer, and the war news was such that nobody should feel much like dancing. She supposed he was right.

FRIDAY,
DECEMBER 12

Stanley Smith, Pullman porter, stayed in South Central between runs on the Super Chief. He usually spent Wednesday nights a little drunk and lost money in a card game at the Dunbar Hotel. On Thursdays he called up a pretty coffee-colored gal named Janey, bought her dinner, then took her to the Club Alabam to hear some jazz. Then they went up to her rooming house on East Adams and warmed the sheets.

But on Friday, he was right back at Union Station, ready for his next run aboard Taos. Super Chief cars were named for Southwest Indian tribes and their tromping grounds. They were decorated in Southwest colors, too, with lots of turquoise and tan and tones that most people had seen but couldn't quite describe, like ocher and umber. The blankets, the upholstery, even the dishes were patterned like Indian art. And sometimes, they had real Navajos wandering the cars, telling tales and answering questions and calming all the white folks who'd seen too many Hollywood Westerns.

Maybe someday they'd hire costumed slaves for the trains down South. But Stanley wasn't betting on it. He just kept his head down and worked hard because he was proud to work aboard "the Grand Hotel on wheels."

The bosses didn't credit prep time as part of a man's two hundred and forty hours of monthly service, but Stanley devoted himself to preparation, so he'd developed set routines. First he delivered linens and towels—four towels for bedrooms and compartments, six for drawing rooms and suites. Then he did the bedding. Then he fixed small problems he'd noticed on the run from Chicago, like a broken curtain rod or a ratchet that didn't crank when he lowered a berth. Then he read the manifest to learn the names of "his" passengers.

The first name: "Sinclair Cook." He was a regular who bragged on every trip that he was a Hollywood big shot, though Stanley knew otherwise. He also traveled with a different woman on every trip, always called "Mrs. Cook," though Stanley knew otherwise about that, too. And he smeared enough Brylcreem on his hair that Stanley hated changing his pillowcases after every trip. At least he tipped well. But he had the habit of calling for the "nigger porter" whenever he wanted something, which meant he waited.

None of the other names appeared familiar, though one caught his eye: "Miss Sally Drake, plus one, Drawing Room D." That "plus one" made him curious, but he wasn't paid for curiosity. He was paid for service. He hoped that Miss Drake and her mystery guest were good tippers.

Then he noticed a couple named "Kellogg." A notation on the manifest said, "Might board in Barstow." They were scheduled for a drawing room on Navajo. But it was beginning to look like the porter who worked Navajo wasn't coming in. So Stanley might be covering two cars at the rear of the train. Make a big deal of late boarders, see that they had a little snack and a drink . . . double the work, but double the tips.

OVER BREAKFAST IN THE Beacon Tavern, her "husband" invited Vivian to go for a drive. She didn't think there'd be much to see in Barstow, but it beat sitting in her room all day.

Martin Browning had noticed her eyeing his satchel. If he understood anything about intimacy, he knew that you couldn't keep *everything* secret. Tell the truth about the small things so that you could lie about the big things. So he'd decided to show her the gun and concoct a lie for carrying it.

They crossed the First Avenue railroad bridge with the freight yards below. Then they sped through a windblown little neighborhood and out into the desert. Just past Jamaica Street, he took a nameless dirt road and followed it into the hills. The sun was bright, the air so clear they could count every clump of sagebrush.

Vivian said, "Where are we going?"

"A target range. I have a pistol. I like to shoot."

"My father used to shoot," she said.

The car bounced over ruts and potholes, heading deeper into this yellow-brown nowhere until they came to the turnout. Not a building in sight. Not a person anywhere. Down below, a dry wash cut like a scar across the earth. A workbench—two-by-fours and plywood—sat in the scar. Shell casings littered the ground. The sun reflected off white-painted posts at fifty-yard intervals.

He said, "Target shooting keeps my eye sharp."

"Do you think you'll be drafted?" she asked.

"I'm in agriculture. I'm feeding America. That gives me an occupational deferment." He plunked the satchel on the workbench and pulled out the Hummel box. He told her to take the four- and five-inch figurines and put them on top of all the posts.

Her eyes widened. "Even the Baby Jesus?"

"And his parents. The donkey, too."

She looked out, shielded her eyes from the sun, and said, "Glad I wore my flats."

As he watched her move from post to post, her yellow dress fluttering in the breeze, he thought how easy it would be to practice on her. Leave her for the buzzards. Save her from whatever lay ahead. Save himself from the moment when she made a mistake and slipped out of character and left him with a hard decision: Kill her or let her live to cause a new crisis?

But as quickly as it came, the impulse fled. He had a plan for using her. And she was letting herself be used.

When she returned, he was attaching the wooden holster to the pistol grip. He put a stripper clip in the top of the gun and pushed ten rounds into the magazine. Then he held it out for her to touch. "My most prized possession."

She ran her hand over the polished wood and oiled metal. "My father says you can always take the measure of a man by the way he takes care of his tools and his guns."

"I think I'd like your father." And in that moment, beneath that warm desert sun, in that isolated dry gulch, Martin Browning felt a true intimacy with Kathy Schortmann. He said, "Whenever I shoot this gun, I think of my own father. He took it off a dead German in Belleau Wood in 1918." But even in intimacy, he lied.

She said, "Let's see how good you are. But remember, those little figurines are goddamn expensive."

"And you remember that my wife doesn't swear, even when her husband destroys sentimental shit." Then he raised the pistol and squeezed off two shots that made the porcelain explode on the post a hundred yards away. Then he did the same for the target a hundred and fifty yards out. Then, he gauged the wind, steadied the weapon, and fired at a post fifty yards beyond that.

"My God," she said. "I can't even *see* those things."

They walked out and found that yes, he'd hit every one.

At the third post, she said, "Uphill? Two hundred yards? With a pistol? Where did you learn—" She stopped in midsentence because something caught her eye.

He followed her gaze, and far behind them, he saw a puff of dust. A blue sedan was emerging from a low ridge and heading back toward town.

Had someone been watching them? The windshield flashed and the sheet metal glinted. He thought about giving chase, but what would he do if he caught up? He'd brought Vivian out here to manipulate her, not to frighten her. So he stayed put. He was shooting well. He was lying well. And the girl appeared to be trusting him even more.

KEVIN CUSACK HAD ONE last stop: Musso & Frank's. For his farewell lunch in Hollywood, he'd eat in style, even if he ate alone.

He got there around one, gave Larry-the-waiter a wave, and took a seat at the grill. He always sat at the grill when he was alone. He could always find someone to talk to. And he didn't need to look at the menu, because he knew what he was having: fish.

He might be planning to slip into Sally Drake's berth on the train, but he was still a good Catholic boy. So he ate fish on Fridays. And in honor of his coast-to-coast trip, he'd order from both the East Coast and the West: Cape Cod oysters at seventy-five cents a half dozen, California sand dabs in sauce meunière at eighty cents, and for starters, a martini.

He sipped the drink and spun round on the stool to survey the room. Musso's was brighter during the day, with skylights letting in the sun. But the burnished mahogany partitions and red leather booths still made the place feel cool and enveloping.

Anybody famous? No Bogie, but a familiar voice rumbling from a nearby booth. The cowboy actor John Wayne was talking to a blonde. Kevin couldn't see her face, but when she spoke, he heard a German accent. Marlene Dietrich? People said that Wayne and Dietrich had been on-again-off-again lovers. A pretty strange pairing. But Wayne was separated from his wife, so . . . on-again? After all, they were both working on the umpteenth remake of *The Spoilers* over at Universal. . . .

Wayne had gotten a break in '29 with *The Big Trail*. It flopped, but he hung around for ten years, pounding out one crummy grade B programmer after another, waiting for a second break that finally came when John Ford cast him in *Stagecoach*. From what Kevin could see, Wayne didn't have a lot of talent, but he showed up every day and hit all his marks, and now he was a star.

Kevin *did* have a lot of talent—or so he thought—but he never got that first break, and he didn't have a decade to wait for another one. So he was leaving.

But first, oysters on a bed of shaved ice. He slurped one down and had a second halfway to his lips when Larry-the-waiter whispered in his ear, "Say, how come you ain't sittin' in the Chaplin Booth with Raoul Walsh?"

Kevin looked toward the booth tucked into the front corner, the best spot in the joint, secluded enough for privacy, public enough so that the occupants could see and be seen. Charlie Chaplin had always sat there for lunch back in the silent days.

Now, the eye-patched director who'd given Wayne that first break was holding court there. He was also sitting in the Hollywood catbird seat, after directing the big Warners release for December, Errol Flynn as Custer in *They Died with Their Boots On*, and skedded to direct Flynn in *Gentleman Jim*. He was having lunch with his writers on the new project, Horace McCoy and Jerry Sloane. And story department secretary Cheryl Lapiner was taking notes.

What a jolly group, thought Kevin.

Larry said, "Before Walsh got here, Sloane was braggin' to the girl about how good he is with his fists and that's why he's such a good choice for writin' a boxin' picture. He said he had to punch you out the other night just to show you who's boss."

"Fuck him." Kevin drained his martini and swallowed his anger with it.

Larry gestured to Kevin's cheek. "That how you got the mouse?"

"He sucker punched me."

"The bastard. You want I should go over and spill some coffee on him?"

"Nah." Kevin slurped down another oyster and asked Larry to bring him another martini. Then he seethed a little bit more. But what the hell? He wasn't interested in Cheryl Lapiner. And he was done with Hollywood.

Larry delivered the drink. "A double, on me. Farewell to a good tipper."

Kevin finished the oysters and the martini and tried to ignore all the chatter coming from the Chaplin Booth, where they were talking a little plot, a little character, and a lot of boxing.

Then, just as that double martini kicked in, temptation struck.

Jerry Sloane got up and headed for the back.

Kevin told the grill man, "Hold the sand dabs," and he followed Jerry.

In the men's room, no one was at the urinals. Two of the stall doors were closed. Two guys doing their business.

Kevin used the urinal, then went to the sink to wash his hands. The mirror gave him a view of the stall doors, and one of them was opening. Kevin saw Jerry's reflection and decided he'd give Jerry more time than Jerry had given him in the phone booth.

He said into the mirror, "I hear you're bragging about sucker punches. Trying to impress Cheryl?"

Jerry saw Kevin's reflection and stopped.

Kevin turned. "Did you brag to Sally, too?"

"I told her to get lost. She's nothing to me."

"Did she tell you I'm going back East with her?"

"She told me you're a loser running home with your tail between your legs."

"She told me you're a sniveling shit with a little dick."

Jerry grinned. "You got the girl, Kev, but I got the job. Now get lost, or I'll give you another shiner." He raised his fist like a tough guy scaring a punk.

Kevin's answer was a single short right. *Ping.* Right off the jaw.

Jerry Sloane flew back, slammed against the stall door, and landed unconscious on the toilet.

Kevin hadn't hit anyone in a long time. He hadn't forgotten how to do it, but he'd forgotten how much a good punch could hurt. He shook his hand to shake away the pain. Then he heard an admiring whistle from the other stall.

John Wayne was peering over the top of the partition. He stepped out and said, "That punch . . . it didn't travel more than eight inches."

"Because it's real," said Kevin, "not a movie roundhouse."

Wayne jerked his thumb at Jerry. "Who tells Walsh that his new writer is—"

"—indisposed? Let him find out on his own, same way he'll find out his new writer can't write."

"Fair enough." Wayne went back to his German girlfriend.

Kevin went back to his sand dabs, ate, and left at just about the time that Raoul Walsh sent Horace McCoy to find Jerry Sloane.

What a way to burn a bridge.

MARTIN AND VIVIAN CHECKED out of the Beacon Tavern at 4:00 P.M. They'd both napped, and Vivian had taken a long bath. Martin had advised that unless she liked showering in cramped train stalls, she should take full advantage of her room's amenities.

Then they drove to the station, Casa del Desierto, all whitewashed and Moorish, looking as unreal on a Barstow siding as a movie set from *Beau Geste*. A porter unloaded the luggage, and Martin told Vivian he'd be back in twenty minutes. He said he had to leave the car with the Gobels.

She protested but he raised a finger and said, "Logistics." Then he gestured. *Out of the car.* She did as she was told. He was her boss. No arguments. She watched him drive off. Then she turned to the porter and said, "What's 'logistics'?"

"Hard to say, ma'am. Some kind of vegetable, maybe?"

The waiting room was a typical small stop on a big railroad: benches, ticket booth, clock, and the Harvey House restaurant. The Chief, the Super Chief, the City of Los Angeles, and a lot of other trains, local and long-distance, all stopped here. Some even waited while passengers got off to stretch and eat.

After about ten minutes, a local came through on the way to Las Vegas. A dozen people got on. Another fifteen minutes, and Vivian went to the ladies' room. When she came out, the station was filling again with another trainload of travelers. But no Harold.

Where the hell was he?

She sat again, then got up and looked outside, then went over to the restaurant entrance and peered in, thinking she might have missed him in the ladies'. No Harold at any of the tables or along the counter. She went back to the waiting area and sat again.

What if he'd left her? Could he have driven her all the way out here just to leave her? Well, she had her luggage and the tickets. So . . . to hell with him.

Then a man walked over. He had a thin mustache, two-tone shoes, a tweed sport coat. He'd been reading the newspaper on one of the other benches. She hadn't paid him any mind, but she recognized him now. He was the guy who'd been eyeballing them in the hotel the night before. Same shoes, different sport coat.

He said, "Excuse me, ma'am. But you seem in some distress."

She gave him her best cold-fish straight-ahead stare. "I'm fine, thanks."

He had a kind of proprietary air about him, like he owned the station because he hung around the waiting room. He said, "If you need help . . ." and gave her his card: SAMUEL HOLLY, THE HIGH DESERT HOUNDSTOOTH, PRIVATE INVESTIGATOR.

She thanked him, then got up and went outside to get away from him.

She sat for another five minutes on the platform, then ten, then fifteen. The wind puffed the dust into little williwaws of sand on the other side of the road. The sun dipped toward the horizon. And she wondered: *What kind of a bastard did this to a woman?*

Then an old pickup came rattling across the overpass, down the access road, and pulled up. On the door, the words "Gobel's Guns and Hardware."

Harold Kellogg got out, shook hands with the driver, and hooked the leather satchel over his shoulder. The truck puttered away, trailing dust. And there he stood, in the last square of desert sunlight. Beneath the brim of the fedora, his eyes were all in shadow. But he was looking at her, she knew. Looking into her, too. He took a drag of a cigarette, dropped it, squashed it with his foot.

He might be unpredictable, but Lord, he was handsome. If she could have ordered a husband from central casting, he'd have been it. As he came toward her, she stood. He was extending his arm, inviting her.

But she wasn't letting him off that easy. "Twenty minutes, you said."

"Sorry."

"Get one thing straight, Harry Kellogg. If you want me to play your wife, you need to play the husband. And my husband wouldn't run off in the middle of the goddamn desert without telling me how long he'd be gone."

"Any man who called himself your husband would be—"

What? she thought. What was he about to say?

"—a very lucky man." He took her arm, since she wouldn't take his. "And your husband smells grilled meat . . . the famous Harvey sirloin."

"Don't leave me alone like that again."

"The Gobels were late. So I'm late. But I will not leave you alone again between here and Chicago. I promise."

KEVIN CUSACK GOT A cab to Union Station around six thirty. Never hurt to be early. The departure board showed that the Super Chief was on schedule for eight o'clock. But he couldn't check his bags because he didn't have a ticket yet. So he sat in an armchair in the Great Hall, positioned himself with a view of the Alameda entrance, and waited.

About seven fifteen, he saw a familiar face. But it wasn't Sally. He pulled his hat down and slumped into his chair and hoped that Frank Carter wouldn't notice him. But Carter scanned the crowd and the cavernous space and came straight for Kevin, who shook his head. *Don't sit next to me. Please. Find somebody else to bother.*

Carter dropped a folder in Kevin's lap, walked around to the next row of chairs, and took a seat just over Kevin's left shoulder, facing in the other direction.

Kevin whispered, "So you came down here to wish me bon voyage?"

"Lewis said you're on the Super Chief tonight. Open that."

Kevin flipped the cover: autopsy photos as glossy as movie-star headshots. "Jesus . . . that's Kessler."

"Did you kill him?"

Kevin turned to Carter. "What are you? Drunk?"

Carter ignored that. "According to our friends in the LAPD, some do-gooder saw you arguing with him on Monday night, right near the murder scene. They got your plate. They reported it. The cops also have you for assault in Musso and Frank's this afternoon. Detective Bobby O'Hara is looking all over town for you."

"He has forty-five minutes to find me. Then he can come to Boston."

Carter lit a cigarette. "It does look suspicious, you skipping town just now."

Kevin turned to Carter. "I almost got my head beaten in for you, Frank. That Kessler mug carried some nasty knuckles. If you're playing me—"

Carter said, "Look at the other picture."

Kevin glanced down. "Never saw him before."

"Never saw him at the Bund?"

Kevin looked at the name. "A Jew named Koppel? You're kidding, right?"

"Somebody cut him the same way they cut Kessler. Anybody ever talk to you about Bund boys who were good with a knife?"

"Gunst said a few things but . . . no names." Then Kevin saw Sally come through the Alameda entrance, followed by a porter wheeling her suitcases. He said to Carter, "If Professor Drake's daughter sees me with you again—"

Carter pulled his hat low, stood, and in one smooth motion took the folder and started walking. "Get on the train with your girlfriend. I'll cover with the LAPD."

"Nice knowin' you." Kevin got up and hurried toward Sally.

They met in the middle of the station.

Her first words were "So, did Rick have a happy ending?"

"Rick?" Then he remembered. "Oh, Rick from Casablanca? He was never as happy as I am right now."

"Such a romantic. But let's scram. The FBI is everywhere."

"FBI?" Kevin looked around for Carter, who had disappeared.

"If they think your father's a Commie, they watch you all the time. It's half the reason I'm leaving L.A. I'm tired of being watched. Tired of being followed."

"Well, now they have Nazis and Japs to follow."

Two uniformed cops were coming by in their dark shirts and matching ties. They couldn't be looking for him, though, not unless Leon Lewis or Frank Carter had tipped them off. Lewis would never rat him out. He wasn't so sure about Carter.

The PA crackled, "Now boarding, Santa Fe Super Chief for Chicago. Track nine."

THERE WAS NOTHING LIKE the Super Chief, nothing like it in the world. Every traveler got a thrill as they came up onto the platform and saw the drumhead shield at the stern of the observation car, or felt the rumble of the big diesel engines up forward, or rode along with the crowd surging toward the train.

But as Kevin and Sally moved ahead, she was still looking around, apparently more spooked by the FBI than she'd let on.

Kevin said, "Relax. We're on our way."

She said, "Remember, you're my brother."

They went past the nameplate on the observation car: NAVAJO.

She looked at her ticket. "We're in the one called Taos."

At every car stood smiling Negroes in blue coats and black sable hats with shiny silver plates that read PULLMAN PORTER. High class all the way. One of them was calling out, "Good evening, folks! This is Taos. This way to board Taos and Navajo, too."

The guy walking ahead of Kevin was leaving a little fog of Brylcreem in the air. He had a young woman clutching his elbow, and he'd been bragging to her about all the big shots that rode the Super Chief and how he was a big shot at Warner Bros. Kevin had never seen the guy in a production office or on a soundstage or in the commissary. But as he approached Taos, the Negro at the door treated him like the biggest shot in town. "Why, Mr. Sinclair Cook. Welcome back. And is this Mrs. Cook?"

"As always, George," said Mr. Cook.

"My, my, sir, but you sure are a lucky man." The porter grinned.

Kevin knew there wasn't a chance in hell that she was the guy's wife.

But the porter didn't seem to care. Checking passenger lists was his job. Checking morals was not. He said to the woman, "My name's Stanley, ma'am, Stanley Smith. Anything you want, just tell me. Ain't that right, Mr. Cook?"

"Best porter aboard," said Cook, and he gave the girl a boost onto the train.

Now the porter turned to Kevin and Sally. "Good evening, folks, and welcome to Taos, the finest car in the consist, which is the finest on the Santa Fe line." He looked at their ticket and said, "Drawing Room D." He helped Sally onto the folding wooden step. "I'll be along presently to see how you folks are doin'."

Kevin thanked him. "You said your name was Stanley?"

"Yes, sir. Stanley Smith." The porter grinned. He had a great smile, thought Kevin, and big hands from hard work on that train.

"So why did that man call you 'George'?"

"Well, sir, sometimes passengers forget a porter's name. So they say 'George.' Easy to remember." Stanley didn't add that most porters considered it an insult. A slave took his master's name. As George Pullman was the first master of this company, calling his porters "George" was only a little better than calling them "slave" . . . or "nigger."

"I'll remember your real name," said Kevin.

Then he and Sally boarded. He told himself to enjoy the luxury, because Sally wasn't sending out any signals beyond "strictly business." He was her brother, and there wouldn't be much fun in that.

Once in Drawing Room D, she yanked down the shades and flopped onto the sofa, as if she was relieved to be out of the crush and crowd.

Kevin looked around at the chairs in Navajo red and black with shiny chrome trim, a sofa bursting in orange and yellow, like a desert sunrise. "It's easy to see why they call this the Grand Hotel on wheels, even with the shades down."

"I'll pull them up once we get rolling," she said. "But I like my privacy."

He said, "Now, about the upper bunk—"

She jerked her thumb to the ceiling berth, presently closed and locked. "Don't get any ideas, *Brother*. This drawing room was the only space available. If it was smaller, you'd still be in L.A., working for the FBI."

"The FBI?" he said innocently.

Sally usually played it like a smartass dame who could mix it up with you and still you'd want to make love to her. But tonight, she seemed snappish and annoyed. "That guy at Musso's the other night? The one you were talking to when I came into the station just now? He and his FBI stooges have been watching me for months. If one of them comes looking for me, and I'm with you, maybe they'll back off."

So, he thought, she'd known all along. He said, "You're giving me too much credit."

"Like I say, you make a good beard." She kicked off her shoes.

That, he thought, was a start.

Then they heard *knock, knock,* and the porter's voice: "All aboard, all visitors off, please." *Knock, knock.* "All aboard, all visitors off, please."

AT TEN FORTY-FIVE, THE Super Chief rumbled toward Casa del Desierto in Barstow, California.

When they heard the horn wailing, Mr. Kellogg took his "wife's" arm and together they stepped out onto the platform, out into the late-night desert chill. The ground began to shake. A bright beam shot along the track. The engine came out of the darkness, flashing the famed Warbonnet colors—red and yellow and silver—with the words "Santa Fe" just beneath the headlamp.

Vivian Hopewell wanted to feel the excitement, but she could barely keep her eyes open. They'd split a bottle of wine over dinner, and she'd seldom had such a full stomach since she got to Hollywood, and it all made her just . . . too . . . damn . . . sleepy.

IN THE OBSERVATION CAR, Sally tossed back her third rum and Coke, stood, and said, "While the train is stopped, I'm going back to our room. I'll need half an hour. So have another drink."

"Half an hour for what?" asked Kevin.

"Ten minutes to get undressed, ten to read, ten to fall asleep. When you climb into your berth, watch where you step."

MARTIN BROWNING WAS GLAD that Vivian was so sleepy. He'd planned it that way. He'd plied her with so much alcohol, he didn't even need to add a Veronal tablet to her wineglass. Now, she was nearly legless. But he'd run out of conversation. Solitary men sometimes did.

At the entrance to Taos, the porter was putting down a wooden step. He said, "Evening, folks. You must be the Kelloggs. Welcome aboard. I'm Stanley."

"Good evening, Stanley," said Martin Browning. "My wife is very tired, so—"

"I'll make down the bed right away, sir." Stanley took their three bags and directed them down the passage on the port side of the car.

"Please make both," said Martin.

"Yes, sir." Stanley could see that the pretty blond lady, who looked like that actress in *Destry Rides Again,* was way beyond tired. So he said, "You know, your missus so sleepy, there's a drawing room right here on Taos, bed's already made down. You can take it, and the lady don't need to wait."

"Taos?"

"Your room's on Navajo. That's the observation car. You got folks comin' and goin' and chitchattin' away till midnight, and some of us porters grabs forty winks back there, too, after everybody go to sleep. Taos is much quieter, sir."

"That sounds better. Thank you."

The train lurched. Vivian stumbled against Harold, who caught her and stumbled into a young lady coming from the observation car.

Stanley said to her, "Evenin', Miss Drake. Your beds are ready."

The train kicked into motion. Miss Drake staggered, mumbled something to Stanley, and disappeared into her room.

Martin followed Stanley, with a firm hand on Vivian so she wouldn't fall over.

Then a shout came from the front of the car: "George! Where's George?"

Sinclair Cook was stepping out of his room with a big grin on his face. Stanley knew why. Cook was a noisy one, and he'd made plenty after Pasadena. He got noisy, and then, while his girl got some sleep, he got a drink. Now he was barreling into this Barstow-boarding couple, stumbling, apologizing, then glancing again at Vivian.

Martin Browning, who never missed the smallest gesture or slightest change in the climate of the moment, saw eyes narrow, as if this guy with the clipped mustache and the shiny hair had seen Vivian before.

Then Cook said to Stanley, "A highball, George. Bring it to the observation car."

"Yes, sir, Mr. Cook. Right away, sir."

Cook poked a finger in Stanley's face. "Canadian Club, two cubes. Can't sleep without it, especially after a busy night, if you know what I mean," and he kept going.

Crude man, thought Martin Browning.

Stanley explained to the Kelloggs that this room was usually prepared for regular passengers who'd canceled at the last minute. So . . . lucky for the sleepy Kelloggs. He showed them the room features—temperature control, radio, separate bathroom—and excused himself.

Martin put Vivian's bag on the lower berth. "Can you change into your nightgown yourself?"

She smiled. She felt dreamy and sexy and a little foolish. She looked at the bed. "Nice . . . and room for two."

Martin saw the sloppily seductive look of a woman who'd had too much to drink. He was glad he'd spent himself with Mrs. Sanchez. Even a man in his thirties needed a few days to recover after a lunchtime triple. The Spanish widow had paid a high price so that Martin Browning might be cold-blooded now. He said, "Good night, dear."

Vivian sat on the bed, flopped back, and passed out. He lifted her feet and slipped off her shoes. Safe to leave her. Safe to leave his satchel. Time to reconnoiter the train.

He went forward to the next car—Oraibi. Like Taos, it had six bedrooms, two drawing rooms, two compartments. He kept going into the dining car, Cochiti, where two Negro cooks were working in the stainless-steel galley kitchen. Next in the nine-car consist was Acoma, the club car and dormitory. He passed the sleeping compartments of the train workers, pushed through a swinging door, and stepped into a bright, colorful space with the bar at the front, tables and seats along the sides.

He ordered Laphroaig neat. Then he headed back through a hundred yards of streamlined aluminum and steel all the way to Navajo, the observation car: twenty chairs, side tables, and short-waisted drapes swinging with the sway of the train. But only two men there at this late hour: the crude Mr. Cook, in the first seat on the right, and halfway down on the left, a young man sipping from a tumbler while reading a magazine.

Martin took the seat diagonally across from the young man.

Cook looked at Martin's glass. "Hey, how'd you get that before I did?"

Martin said, "I got it myself."

Cook snorted. "Mister, you got to make these niggers work. Start doin' their jobs for them, and before you know it, they'll have *you* gettin' drinks for *them*."

Martin said, "I'll remember that." He noticed the young man shift his eyes toward the loudmouth, then glance at Martin, as if to say, *You talk to him. I have no patience.*

Martin put a cigarette into his mouth and pulled out his lighter. He snapped it a few times, then said to the young man, "Bad for your health anyway."

So the young man flipped his lighter across the aisle.

Martin caught it, lit the cigarette, admired the gold case and the inscription: "For Kevin, to light your way when good wishes won't. Grandpa C." Martin asked, "What does the 'C' stand for?"

"Cusack. Kevin Cusack. Nice to meet you." Kevin raised his glass.

Martin raised his in response but . . . where had he heard that name before?

The door swung open, and Stanley Smith came in with Cook's Canadian Club.

"It's about goddamn time, there, George," said Sinclair Cook.

"You know I always take care of you, sir," said the porter.

Martin watched this interchange, then turned back to the young man. "I'm Kellogg, Harold Kellogg. A pleasure to meet you, too, Mr. Kevin Cusack." Sometimes saying a name out loud helped him to remember. And he did. He'd heard the name from Emile Gunst . . . and from Kessler just before he killed him. *What* was Kevin Cusack doing here?

And the Super Chief thundered east.

PART TWO

ACROSS AMERICA

SATURDAY, DECEMBER 13

IT WAS STILL DARK when the train rolled into Seligman, Arizona, at 6:20 A.M.

Martin Browning had barely slept. The specter of Kevin Cusack had kept him awake all night. Who was the guy working for? The FBI? The LAJCC? Martin had replayed the conversation in the observation car again and again. But he couldn't recall a glimmer of surprise or the slightest flicker of recognition on the face of Cusack, who was either clueless or the coolest customer aboard.

Martin decided to watch him. Play him. Figure out if he was dangerous or just a walking coincidence. After all, there were only so many ways to go from the West Coast to the East. Two weekly runs of the Super Chief, a few other trains, a few planes, and a lot of people wanting to get home for their first—and perhaps last—wartime Christmas.

Martin dropped from his berth and glanced at Vivian. She hadn't moved from the position he'd put her in the night before. The wisdom of bringing her along was already obvious. If Cusack really was an agent, a "wife" could only deflect suspicion.

Then he went in search of coffee.

THREE SCOTCHES AND THE steady rocking of the train had kept Kevin Cusack sleeping like a stone. It was the stop that woke him. He peered out at the station and thought about going outside for a smoke. But this was a no-passenger stop. Service only.

So he jumped down and glanced at Sally. She slept on her stomach, and from the sound of it, she was sleeping up a storm, which was a nice way of saying that she snored, which was good, because it distracted him from the curves beneath her blanket.

A gentle knock brought the Negro porter.

Kevin opened the door. "You're up early, Stanley."

"We work round the clock, sir. Grab a few winks where we can. I got three hours so I feel right chipper."

"I bet you sleep for two days when you get home."

"Oh, no, sir. Too busy doin' odd jobs for my mama, takin' her to the Eastern Market on Saturdays, takin' her to the Methodist church on Sundays—"

"Where's home?"

"I like to say the railroad's my home, sir, but Kingman Park in Washington, D.C., is where I grew up. Now . . . the lady ordered coffee."

Sally popped up as if she'd heard a fire alarm. "Coffee?"

Stanley took the silvered pot from his cart. "How does the lady like it?"

"Black, no sugar," she said.

"Yes, ma'am," said Stanley. "And you, sir?"

"Cream."

Stanley filled two cups and handed them to Kevin. "Breakfast starts at seven, folks. Sit on the right side, so you can watch the sun come up. And order the Santa Fe French toast. Can't ride the Super Chief without havin' that famous French toast."

"Coffee, first." Sally reached from under the blanket for hers.

After the porter left, Kevin said, "Black, no sugar? That'll put hair on your chest."

"Leave my chest out of it."

"But you said I could crack jokes."

"Finish your coffee, then go and have a smoke so I can get dressed."

First, he slipped into the bathroom: sink, toilet, mirror, barely room to turn around. He set his cup down and studied his reflection. The bruise under his eye was fading. The bruised knuckles still hurt. But he—not Jerry Sloane—was riding with the girl. Now to impress her. He had a day and a half to do it. So he lathered up and shaved.

VIVIAN HOPEWELL OPENED THE door of Drawing Room F. The Negro porter was holding a cup of coffee sent by her "husband."

At the same time, someone was pushing by. She heard him say, "Two coffees, George. One in the drawing room for my wife, one in the observation car for me. And put a little somethin' extra in mine."

"Yes, sir," answered Stanley. "Comin' right up, sir."

Vivian saw the man go past, then pop back and look in over Stanley's shoulder, like a comic doing a double take in a cheap two-reeler.

The sight of that mustache and slicked hair almost made her throw up.

The first Hollywood bastard who'd ever lied to her was looking right at her, that Brylcreemed bullshit artist, Sinclair Cook. She turned to the window and hoped that he hadn't recognized her, that he was just grabbing an extra gander at a girl in a nightgown, like any low-class lecher. From what she remembered, Sinclair Cook would leer at a nun.

She took the coffee, closed her door, and remembered things she'd tried to forget, like meeting him back in '37, when she was eighteen, waiting tables in the G&J Grill in Annapolis. One day when business was slow, Cook came in.

He noticed that she was reading *Photoplay*. He said that he worked "in film," so he went out to Hollywood a lot.

She said that going to Hollywood was her dream.

He gave her the once-over and said, "With swell gams like that, you're a cinch to be a star."

Afterward, he came through town every month and always brought fan magazines and Hollywood gossip and bragged that he was a big shot out there, because without him, they wouldn't have film to put those movies on. And one day, he popped his question: Did she want to go? It wouldn't cost her anything, and he'd teach her plenty along the way. "Whaddya say, doll? It'll be a lot more fun than servin' pie à la mode in Maryland."

And she went. Her mother was furious. Her father was confused. But she had to take her shot, and how else was a poor girl going to get to Hollywood?

They rode the Union Pacific's City of Los Angeles from Chicago. And as the train crossed the Mississippi, she learned the truth: "in film" meant he was a film salesman, but he sold Kodak to the home photo trade. He didn't know anyone in Hollywood except a still photographer at MGM. What he liked to do was run card games on the train and have sex to celebrate if he won . . . or to raise his spirits if he lost.

After doing things in Sinclair Cook's compartment that she hoped never to do again, she was almost relieved when he left her in front of the L.A. station with her suitcase at her feet and fifteen bucks in her purse.

But she wouldn't let him spoil her ride this time. She'd eat in the dining car and drink in the club car and enjoy it all. She colored her hair now and dressed a lot better, thanks to Harold, so Cook might not even recognize her. And if he did, she'd introduce him to her "husband" and his leather blackjack.

THE DINING CAR, COCHITI, had thirty-six seats, tables for four on the right, tables for two on the left, white linens, custom china with Navajo patterns, plum-colored carpet, and veneered red paneling that the maître d' called "bubinga wood, very rare, very carefully coordinated with the color palette of the car."

Martin Browning requested a table for four so that his neighbors from Taos might be seated with them. A dollar gratuity sealed the deal. He was using Gestapo money, so he'd spread it around like Rockefeller.

Soon Vivian came in, looking crisp and refreshed in her new suit. It was light green, as if chosen to complement the Navajo colors around her. She wore sunglasses to ward off the glare and cover the shadow of the black eye from Monday night. A skim of face powder and red lipstick completed the picture.

Her "husband" smiled and said, "You're looking lovely, Mrs. Kellogg."

She gestured to the other side of the car. "Why not sit at a two-top?"

"A what?"

"Restaurant lingo. A table for two."

"It looks better if we appear sociable, don't you think?"

"Whatever you say, dear." That was how she was supposed to play it. No sarcasm. No smart answers. Just . . . smile sweetly, Vivian.

Then Kevin Cusack appeared, and the maître d' directed him to the Kellogg table, where Martin Browning went to work. He stood and offered his hand. "Mr. Cusack, I asked them to seat you with us, you and your wife—"

"Sister," said Kevin. "She's coming along."

"Sister?" Vivian raised a brow. "Sister" was almost as good as "faithful wife."

The waiter, another Negro—they were all Negroes here, too—took their orders.

Then Kevin said, "We're heading back East for Christmas."

"So you're from Los Angeles?" asked Vivian. "Where do you work?"

"Warner Brothers."

Martin felt Vivian almost bubble over. He gave her a look: *Calm down.*

She got the message and settled her voice. "Warner Brothers? Really?"

"Really." Kevin would never see these people again, so what did it matter if he pumped himself up?

And here came his "sister," looking gorgeous. Tousled or touched up, Sally Drake always looked gorgeous. Once she combed that no-nonsense hair and put on that red lipstick, she could turn overalls into high fashion. But "Sally Drake" and "chipper morning chitchat" didn't meet in the same sentence. She lurched in, mumbled a greeting, then plunked herself down on the other side of the car.

Vivian whispered, "Should you go over and sit with her?"

"She just needs coffee," said Kevin. "But . . . tell me about you two. Where are you headed?"

"Home," said the husband. "My wife wanted to see what a salesman of agricultural products does on long trips. Isn't that right, dear?"

"Oh, yes," said Vivian. "We *were* going to Hawaii for a vacation. But not—"

Martin liked that detail. He added, "No second honeymoon after Pearl Harbor."

Vivian said, "So tell me, Mr. Cusack, what do you do at Warner Brothers?"

"I'm in the story department."

Her eyes brightened. "You write stories?"

"I *read* them. Then I write *about* them."

Now, Vivian was positively riveted. "What have you worked on?"

Kevin saw the look that Sally shot across the aisle. But he was enjoying himself. The farther from Hollywood he went, the more impressed people were that he'd even been there. He said, "I just finished work on something set in Casablanca. I can't give it away. But it's a natural for Humphrey Bogart."

"I loved Bogart in *High Sierra*." She looked at her husband. "Didn't you, dear?"

"I like *The Maltese Falcon*." And he liked the way that Vivian was doing his work for him. Every question revealed a little more.

She said, "This Casablanca story, do you think it would have a role for—"

"Not the Marlene Dietrich business, please." Harold Kellogg told Kevin, "My wife thinks she looks like Marlene Dietrich."

Vivian knew she'd gone off script. She adjusted. "What my husband's saying is that you can take the housewife out of Hollywood, but you can't take Hollywood out of the housewife. Of course, I *do* have German blood."

And Cusack gave up a bit more information. "A lot of us have German blood."

Then Mr. Brylcreem bustled in with his young "wife" and gave them all a big "G'morning, folks." He sat at one of the tables for two, raised his hand, snapped his finger in the air. "Hot coffee, boy."

A Negro waiter was beside him in an instant.

Kevin shook his head and whispered, "My father always said you can tell a lot about a man by the way he treats the help."

Vivian said, "I think I'd like your father."

"Is he German?" asked her husband.

"He is, as they say, as Irish as Paddy's pig," answered Kevin.

And they all laughed, though Martin wondered about that German heritage.

Breakfast arrived, and the French toast was as advertised—thick bread soaked in egg and cream, browned, then baked, then sprinkled with powdered sugar. . . .

"Like biting into a cloud," said Vivian. "A sweet, fluffy cloud."

Kevin said, "You have a way with words. Maybe you should be a writer."

"Oh, no," she said. "I'd rather act."

"Now, dear," said her husband, "don't be bothering the man with your fantasies."

So Vivian looked out at the sun lighting the desert and changed the subject. "Isn't it amazing . . . we can be going so fast and still sitting here, enjoying this lovely meal—"

"And not thinking at all of war," said Kevin.

"But it's a world at war," said Mr. Kellogg. "And we all have a part to play, whether our name is Roosevelt or"—he looked at his wife—"Vivian Kellogg."

Kevin said, "You sound like a character in that Casablanca script."

"Is he the hero?" asked Vivian.

Kevin said, "At the beginning he sticks his neck out for nobody."

"And he's the *hero*?" said Harold.

Kevin lit a cigarette. "He changes."

On the other side of the car, Sally finished her coffee and muffin, then got up and stopped at their table. "I promise to be more fun at cocktail hour."

"We all will," said Martin Browning, honing the Kellogg charm.

Then Sinclair Cook, the grinning Mr. Brylcreem, came over. "Say, you gents look like you might enjoy a little poker. I'll be running a game in the club car later."

Behind her sunglasses, Vivian concentrated on her coffee and prayed that he didn't recognize her.

"Ten o'clock tonight," he went on. "Buy-in is fifty bucks. Table stakes. Friendly game. Strictly according to Hoyle. Let me know after dinner if you're interested."

Kevin and Harold Kellogg looked at each other, united in dislike of this guy.

Vivian gave Sinclair Cook a glance, and he did another double take.

FRANK CARTER AWOKE IN the Ansonia, a residential hotel near Wilshire and Alvarado. It wasn't much, but good enough for government pay. He staggered to the window, looked out at Westlake Park, saw sunshine, and cursed.

If the sun was already warming the bums in the park, it meant he'd overslept. He was also sick of sunshine. Another day of sun in an endless stream of sunny days made you forget just how special the sunshine really was. In a way, it was a lot like freedom.

You never appreciated something until it was gone. But too much of a good thing could make you complacent. You never appreciated the guardrails that kept people on the path until somebody bent them into roadblocks, like the Nazis had in Europe. That's why Carter had joined the FBI . . . to hold up the guardrails.

Then the bathroom door opened, and Stella Madden came out. Frank stopped thinking about guardrails and started thinking about . . . garters.

The silk stockings he'd rolled down the night before were again held up by garters that looked so . . . enticing. . . . against her white skin. Also back in place was the Beretta she carried in a holster strapped to her thigh. She fished in her purse and pulled out her lipstick. She said she wore bright red to distract from her broken nose. He told her he liked her nose just fine. He didn't tell her that he also liked the seams that ran down the backs of her stockings. He knew that she already knew . . .

. . . because as she turned to pick up her skirt, she said, "Down, boy. Once I put my lipstick on, I'm done."

"You know . . . this is very unprofessional."

She pulled on the skirt. "In our line of work, sometimes it's all we get."

Stella was one of the few licensed female private detectives in L.A. She had an office on Wilshire, near Westlake Park, and this was not her first visit to Frank's room.

He'd bumped into her the night before in Union Station.

Her opening line: "What is it this week, Frank? Commies or Krauts?"

"Both . . . and Japs, too."

She'd said she was shadowing a guy at the ticket window. "His wife thinks he's cheating on her. He's so fat he couldn't find his dick with a flashlight, never mind find another woman to pull it for him—"

"Nice talk for a lady."

"But I think he made me, so I'm laying back. Amble on over there, willya, and see if you can pick up on where he's going."

"I do you a favor, you do me one." Carter had pointed out Sally Drake, who'd just click-clacked by on her high heels. "There goes the Commie of the night."

"Deal."

So Stella had followed Kevin Cusack and Sally Drake onto the Super Chief. Frank had traced the cheating husband to the coffee stand. Then they'd had dinner and gone back to his room, because even the good guys couldn't always be good.

Now, Carter pulled the cartridge from his pocket. "What do you make of that? The ballistics boys say it's from a Mauser C96."

She knew guns and ammo better than most men. She said, "A bottleneck round, 7.63-by-25-millimeter . . . a Mauser C96."

"Good gun?"

"At fourteen hundred feet per second, highest muzzle velocity of any pistol other than your .357 Magnum. Superior penetration. Long barrel for long range. The manual says a hundred meters, but a good shooter can do a lot better with the shoulder stock. Of course, that makes the gun illegal, but–"

"Our guy won't be worried about that." Frank Carter threw his arm around her and gave her a kiss on the cheek. "Thanks."

"For what?"

"A lead. Whoever he is, this guy can probably shoot the eye out of a squirrel with a C96 at maximum range. Time to grill the local Nazis about Bund marksmen."

MARTIN BROWNING WATCHED THE desert roll by, flat and wide and preternaturally empty. How insignificant it made them all seem, all those people on that train, with all their troubles and emotions and ambitions, all speeding across the sand of some ancient seabed, on an orb spinning at a thousand miles an hour, circling the sun at sixty-six thousand more. Yet what an impact one man could make with a single bold act.

Then he heard the toilet flush, and it brought him back to the moment.

There was an unholy intimacy in a train compartment. And he didn't like it, but he liked learning to read Vivian's expressions and inflections. He'd also relaxed about Kevin Cusack, who was most likely what he appeared to be, just another traveler. But what about the guy with the Brylcreemed hair and the Clark Gable mustache?

The porter's knock interrupted his ruminations. "Everything up to snuff, sir?"

"Up to snuff?" Martin was thrown by one of those figures of speech that had never quite penetrated his formal and orderly understanding of English.

"Up to the specifications of yourself and the missus, sir."

When passengers left for breakfast, porters got to work. A good porter could make up every sleeper assigned to him, straighten everything, stow bed-clothes and mattresses, all in an hour.

"We're quite pleased. And Stanley"—Martin pulled out a roll of cash—"can you tell me about the man last night, the one who ordered the highball, the one named Cook?"

Stanley put up his hands, as if to ward off the money. "Now, sir, a good porter never talks with one passenger about another."

Martin peeled off a bill. "Have he and his wife ridden the train before?"

Vivian stepped from the bathroom wearing fresh lipstick and more powder over her bruise.

Martin told her, "We're discussing that man who invited me to play cards. The one with the slicked hair and the mustache." He watched for a reaction, and yes . . .

Her eyes shifted. Her laugh came out more nervous than amused. "You mean the one trying to look like Rhett Butler with a beer belly?"

Martin said to Stanley, "I bet Sinclair Cook never tipped you a fiver."

Contrary to the expectations of Martin Browning, who'd had little direct contact with Negroes but had seen too many Hollywood movies, Stanley's eyes didn't widen into bright white saucers at the sight of cash. They narrowed instead.

"Nobody tips me a five 'cause he likes how I make up a room." Stanley was careful to add a "sir" at the end.

Martin put another bill into the Negro's hand. "I tip lots of fives for infor-mation."

"Well, sir, you never heard it from me. But if you plannin' to play cards with Mr. Cook tonight, take a nap this afternoon. Once that game gets goin', they play till breakfast. If Cook is winnin', he'll play right the way through to Chicago, and sometime around three in the mornin', when everybody's gettin' sleepy, he'll start dealin' from the bottom."

"Thanks, Stanley," said Martin. "I'll pace myself."

As soon as the Negro stepped out, Vivian went to the control panel for air-conditioning, lighting, and radio and asked, "What kind of music would you like?"

Martin said, "Do you know how important it is to know your enemy?"

"My enemy?"

"A man who stalks a railcar, smelling of cheap aftershave and hair cream, leering at other men's wives, even with a wife of his own on his arm? Such a man is a bluffer."

"She's not his wife." Vivian turned up the music. Glen Miller, "Sunrise Serenade."

"How would you know?"

And she decided on the truth. "Because I was his wife . . . once."

"Married from Chicago to Los Angeles?"

"I performed wifely duties to earn my fare."

"And then you regained your innocence?"

"I never regained my innocence. But I never lost my self-respect."

And he thought better of sarcasm. He said, "You're not expected to perform wifely duties for me, except in public."

"I'd have ridden a covered wagon to get to California. That's how big my dreams were. But California can kill your dreams."

"So can men like that. Sometimes I think they're the ones who deserve the killing."

She didn't hear the chill in his voice, only the confidence of a man who'd protect her from predators. She liked it. She stepped closer. The wheels rattled as the train curved toward the north and the warm rays of the morning sun slanted in.

She whispered, "That's why I trust you. Cook was a pig."

"Most men are. But he will not come rooting in our clean cabin."

Glen Miller hit a high note as the gentle turn of the train caused her to lean into her "husband." And she stayed close, so that their bodies were touching.

He whispered, "The room is too small to dance."

"But to kiss?" She pressed her lips to his.

And he kissed her back. He couldn't help it. He was not that cold.

KEVIN CUSACK COULD HAVE gazed out the window all day. It was like a Technicolor movie going by. Instead, he asked Sally, "What are we doing till lunch?"

"I'm doing it." She held up her copy of *Life* magazine, the December 1 issue, with the B-17 on the cover. "And you wanted time to write, so write."

"Writing wouldn't be a bad idea," he said, "if I had any ideas."

"So . . . write about your friends in the FBI."

Before that sarcasm blossomed into outright hostility, there was a knock: Stanley Smith, checking to see if everything was "up to snuff."

"Snuffed up nicely," said Kevin. "You work fast."

Sally said, "Tell me, Stanley, about that couple my brother had breakfast with—"

"Oh, I don't work Cochiti, ma'am. Dinin' car is Harvey Company territory."

"But the Kelloggs—are they regulars?"

"Now, ma'am, we don't talk about other passengers." Stanley waited to see if a hand dipped into a pocket, but some people never tipped until the end. So he offered a little gossip now for a bigger tip later. "They're ridin' my car for the first time, ma'am."

After Stanley left, Kevin said, "Why did you ask that?"

"Something about that Harold Kellogg. I can't place him, but—"

"He's not FBI, if that's what you're worried about." Kevin grabbed his briefcase. "I'll be in the observation car. I need a smoke. Helps me to think. Maybe I'll think up the Great American Screenplay."

FORTY-FIVE MINUTES SOUTH OF downtown L.A., Terminal Island gave home to three thousand Japanese and their American-born descendants, all living close-knit around the tuna fleet and the cannery, a whole community of experienced fishermen, hard workers, good citizens, and since December 7, all suspects. So nobody was getting on or off the island ferry unless they had a good ID, like Frank Carter's FBI badge.

Seaside Avenue, the main drag, ran past Japanese homes and docks, down to the new federal detention center at the southern tip of the island. The steel bars and poured concrete were all painted a pretty yellow, and a red tile roof made the whole joint look like one of those Spanish missions. In Hollywood, even the slammer had a false front.

Among the Germans at Terminal: Hans Schmidt, caretaker of the Murphy Ranch, and Hermann Schwinn, self-proclaimed *Führer* of the Bund.

Frank Carter called first for Schmidt, who'd pleaded ignorance on Monday morning and by Saturday acted as if he'd been struck dumb. No, he had no list of the marksmen who used the target range. No, he didn't know the dead men in the autopsy photos. No, he'd have no more to say. He'd respect the chain of command and let Herr Schwinn speak for them all.

So Carter sent Schmidt back to his cell and called for the big fish.

While he waited, he reread the file on Schwinn: former bank clerk who migrated to America in 1923; ran a travel agency for tourists to Germany; became leader of the Bund in 1934; suspected to have planned the theft of weapons from armories on the West Coast; plotted the kidnapping and hanging of

Jewish movie executives; bribed L.A. police officers; and planned a gas attack in the Shrine Auditorium during the '38 Anti-Nazi League rally. Most of the plots had fizzled, thanks to incompetence and info from spies in the LAJCC.

But if these Nazis were flops as terrorists and saboteurs, they were hotshots at publicity, and in Hollywood, that was the name of the game. Every few months, Schwinn had sent Bundsters to the roof of some building on Hollywood Boulevard to toss leaflets. They called it snowstorming. But their stunts weren't about selling movies. They sold hate: "Jews! Jews! Jews everywhere! Out with the Jews! Let white people run this country as they did before the Jewish invasion."

Schwinn had lost his citizenship on a technicality, but he was married to an American, so he'd avoided jail or deportation . . . until now. He sauntered into the interrogation room looking relaxed and arrogant in a denim shirt and blue dungarees.

Carter gestured for him to sit, then threw a folder on the table. "You know what's in there? Names, money, maps . . ."

Schwinn looked at the folder. "Did you get them from the Jew Lewis?"

"I got them from you, when you gave us the keys at Deutsches Haus."

Schwinn folded his arms, as if to say that he—and not they—were in charge here.

"You really think you're smarter than you are, don't you?" said Carter.

"Smarter than *we* are," added Agent McDonald, who took his lead from his boss.

Carter pulled out an envelope containing a wad of cash, big bills, all crisp and new. "We also found this."

"I hope you signed for it." Schwinn spoke perfect English, right down to the sarcasm.

"It's not counterfeit. That would be too easy. But you're getting this dough from somebody who thinks big envelopes of cash are a good investment."

"In what?" asked Schwinn.

"In doing the stuff that put you in prison denims."

Schwinn said, "Denims or Bund uniform, it's all the same if you serve an idea."

"What do you serve?" asked Carter.

"I serve the ideals of German culture," answered Schwinn with a kind of bland detachment. "I am no anti-Semite, and I have no connection to any Nazi officials."

"Stop the bullshit!" Carter slammed his hand on the table.

McDonald jumped back, as if shocked by such a show of anger from Carter. Good cop and bad cop was the play.

Schwinn smoothed his little Hitler mustache and straightened his rimless

Himmler glasses and shot a glance at McDonald, as if to ask, *What's wrong with your boss?*

Carter leaned over Schwinn's shoulder, opened the folder to an autopsy photo. "Who's that?"

Schwinn looked. "Emile Gunst."

"He took cyanide to keep from talking."

That was a lie, but maybe the picture would get Schwinn talking. It didn't.

So Carter flipped to another photo. "This man was found in the trunk of his car in the parking lot of the Bob's Big Boy in Burbank."

Schwinn looked at the name. "'Arthur Koppel.' A Jew. In the Bund? Do you *try* to be funny, Agent Carter, or does it come like nature?"

Carter flipped to the next picture. This time, he heard a sharp intake of breath.

Whether Schwinn knew of Kessler's death, he was shocked by the sight of him, cold, naked, cut and dried, in glossy black-and-white.

Carter let Schwinn swallow his shock, then said, "We think the same guy who killed the lawyer killed Kessler. Same weapon. Same cut. Quick and clean. Kessler worked for you, didn't he?"

"What would Kessler have in common with a Jew lawyer?"

"He was also one of the Bund bouncers. Did he carry brass knuckles?"

Schwinn said, "A good weapon stops trouble before it happens."

"Speaking of weapons"—Carter flipped to the photo of a Springfield rifle—"we found this in Kessler's trunk. His prints were all over it. The only other prints belonged to this man"—Carter turned to another photo—"found under the Hyperion Bridge."

Schwinn drew another breath, brought a hand to his mustache, then to his glasses.

McDonald gave Carter a nod. They both knew a giveaway when they saw one.

Carter said to Schwinn, "Who is he?"

Schwinn shook his head. "I know Kessler, but this one—"

"Don't bullshit us." Frank Carter homed in. "The coroner's report says he died from the fall, but first, somebody beat the shit out of him . . . with brass knuckles." Carter flipped to a picture of the bloody bruise in the victim's rib cage.

Schwinn turned toward the barred window, as if none of this were his concern.

Carter put a rifle cartridge on the table. "I picked up a dozen of these on the target range at the Murphy Ranch. We think these two stiffs were there Monday. Shooting."

Schwinn straightened his glasses again.

Carter produced the other cartridge. "We also think there was another shooter, practicing with a pistol. Maybe a Mauser C96. Who are the pistol champs in your Bund?"

"You have my papers," said Schwinn. "Go through them."

Carter kept pushing. "Whoever the third man was, he killed Kessler, didn't he? And he was a trained professional, too, not like the slobs in the Bund."

"I know of no third shooter."

"But somebody killed Kessler after Kessler killed this young guy—"

"His name is Stengle. Thomas Stengle." Schwinn said the name as if he'd decided to give up *something*. Was he cracking . . . or playing them? "A tradesman, like Kessler."

Carter looked at McDonald. "Now, we're getting somewhere."

"They practiced at the Murphy Ranch on Monday mornings," said Schwinn. "Just the two of them."

"One with a Springfield and one with a Mauser?" asked Carter.

Schwinn nodded. "Stengle spoke often of how much he loved his Mauser. Find his apartment, you might find his gun."

"What's his address?"

"I can't do all your work for you. Find it yourself."

"We will," said Carter. "But help me to understand something, Hermann: Two men practice shooting in a secluded location. One of them kills the other. Then he's killed by a guy who also kills a Jewish lawyer. What's going on?"

"Coincidence?" Schwinn rolled his eyes. "Or logic."

"Logic?"

"Kessler could be annoying. Jews are annoying. Therefore killing Kessler is like killing a Jew."

"Is it coincidence," asked Carter, "when the dead Jew lives in Pacific Palisades, right up the street from the Murphy Ranch?"

Schwinn offered nothing but another round of telling fidgets.

Carter leaned close. "There was a third man on that range, wasn't there?"

Schwinn raised his chin. "Kessler and Stengle practiced together. They were getting ready for *der Tag*. That is what I know."

"What we know is that you're a good liar. You might even be good enough to get by when they haul you in front of the Alien Enemy Hearing Board. But if something bad happens, something that includes a Mauser C96—"

"I have told you what I know."

"—I'll haunt you for the rest of your life, which may be very short if you end up in general population." Carter swept everything up and called for the guard.

KEVIN CUSACK WAS SITTING in the observation car. He lit a cigarette and looked around. At the writing desk, a mother and her little girl worked on a coloring book. On the other side, two older women who looked like sisters talked and laughed as if they hadn't seen each other in a long time. In a seat by herself, the young "wife" of Mr. Brylcreem thumbed a magazine and looked worn out. *By what?* he wondered.

And that was how a writer was supposed to work. Observe the surroundings, consider the people inhabiting them, collect details, take notes, invent situations. Maybe that's why they called this the observation car.

Now, Harold Kellogg pushed through the door, saw Kevin, came toward him.

Kevin liked this guy, who seemed more relaxed than most salesmen, as if he was so confident of his product—or himself—that he knew both would sell themselves. In a world of glad-handers, a guy like this stood out.

He dropped into the chair next to Kevin and asked, "How's your sister?"

"She's reading. It puts her in a better mood."

"My wife's reading *Gone with the Wind*. I had to leave when she started blubbering over the death of little Bonnie." In truth, Martin Browning had removed himself after kissing Vivian . . . *because* he'd kissed her. She was a tool, he told himself, not a plaything. He put a cigarette between his lips, and Kevin flicked his lighter. After a drag, Martin asked, "So how is it that your name is Cusack, and your sister—"

Kevin leaned closer. "Can you keep a secret, Harry?"

Harry: So they were now on a nickname basis, thought Martin. Americans quickly overcame any pretension to formality. It was a quality that he disliked. But he was glad his deception was working. He said, "I am excellent with secrets." He did not say he would *keep* them, because secrets, like everything else, were meant to be used.

Kevin Cusack said, "She's not my sister."

Martin wondered if that revelation was a ploy to gain his trust or actually revealed how little Kevin Cusack knew about the man he was talking to.

"Not every couple aboard is married," said Kevin. "Not like you and your wife."

If Cusack was looking for information, thought Martin, he wouldn't get any. He said, "The talent agencies are full of girls who got to Hollywood with the help of a gentleman who was neither her husband nor her brother—"

"Nor a gentleman," said Kevin.

"And when those girls give up, they go home the same way they got out here. Like her." Martin gestured toward Mr. Brylcreem's "wife." She'd pulled the curtains behind her and appeared now to be asleep behind her sunglasses.

Kevin said, "I've traveled out and back twice. Seen a lot of guys like Sinclair Cook. Cheats on his wife, probably cheats at cards, too."

Martin Browning was still on his guard, but the concerns of Kevin Cusack seemed to have nothing to do with Nazi hunting. He asked, "Will you play in his game tonight?"

"I hope to be otherwise engaged."

Martin Browning laughed. When a man told you something so private, best to laugh like a brother and file the information. Then he picked up the *L.A. Times.* Kevin Cusack looked again at his work. And there they sat, sipping coffee, smoking, reading and writing, while the train roared across the desert.

After another ten minutes, Martin looked over Kevin's shoulder and said, "What are you writing? Something ripped from the headlines, maybe?"

"Plenty of headlines to rip from."

"Imagine the story you could tell about this place"—Martin held up the newspaper—"this Deutsches Haus." The headline read, DOWNTOWN BUND HALL SHUTTERED; FBI RAID LEADS TO ARRESTS.

Kevin glanced at the paper and said, "The Bund Hall? On Fifteenth at Figueroa."

Martin noticed a tightening of the voice, a shifting of the eyes. "You know of it?"

"Everybody knows where the L.A. Nazis hang out."

Martin noticed "Mrs. Cook" look up and pay attention from behind her sunglasses. Talk of Nazis could get anyone's attention these days.

"But what do I know of Nazis?" said Kevin. "It's just something I heard."

Martin smiled an innocent smile, straight out of the Harold Kellogg smile book.

Kevin said nothing more. None of it mattered anymore. He'd left the Bund behind. He'd left the LAJCC behind. He'd left Hollywood behind. He was done sticking his neck out.

IN THE OFFICE, FRANK Carter requested another day to look for the third shooter.

Chief Agent Hood's response: "Schwinn said there were only two."

"You don't believe him, do you?"

Hood waved a sheet of paper. "I have a list of *real* people to arrest. And I'm operating in the most spread-out city in America, but *you* want to find a phantom."

"I'm looking for a German national who may—"

"Who may not exist," said Hood over the noise of teletype machines and ringing telephones.

"We found Stengle's address. Let me go toss the place."

"Give it to the LAPD." Hood walked away.

Carter followed him into his office. "But *we* know what we're looking for, Dick."

"Do we?" Hood plunked down behind the desk.

"A Mauser C96. If I find it, we keep looking. If I don't, I'm done."

Hood threw up his hands. "All right. You can go. But not McDonald. I need him."

That hurt. Carter liked someone watching his back. He liked another set of eyes. So he went to his desk and dialed a number.

A man answered: "Madden Detective Agency."

"Is this Bartholomew?"

The voice grew softer. The suspicion oozed. "Yes."

"It's your FBI friend, Frank Carter."

"Friend?"

"We don't care what color your underwear is, Barty, baby, as long as it's not Commie red." Carter heard a hand go over the receiver, then a muffled conversation.

Stella came on the line. "Are you harassing my secretary, Frank?"

"As long as his boyfriends are over eighteen, he's got nothing to fear from me. Are you busy? I could use some help this afternoon."

"You putting me on the payroll?"

"I'll take you to dinner."

"I'm in the mood for chili."

"El Cholo?"

"I didn't peg you for a cheapskate, Frank. Chasen's or no deal."

"El Cholo makes better chili, but if you want Chasen's, I'll float a loan."

He picked her up on the corner of Wilshire and Alvarado, and they headed north. The Thomas map directed them across the L.A. River to a squat two-story building where the Hyperion Bridge merged with Glendale Boulevard.

McGee's Machine Shop was on the first floor.

McGee wore a greasy leather apron and a dirty T-shirt, just a working stiff making a few extra bucks renting rooms at the edge of a nice neighborhood called Atwater Village, probably in violation of every zoning law in the book. And he wasn't too friendly, even after Carter flipped the FBI badge.

So Carter showed him the autopsy photo. "Is that Tom Stengle?"

"Jesus," said McGee. "Somebody beat him up real good."

"Let's see his room."

McGee led them up a rickety outside staircase to a little balcony. Stengle's room wasn't much: a table by a window, a fifth of Four Roses on the table, a dresser with clothes hanging out of open drawers, an unmade bed, a view across the bridge toward the hills on the other side of the concrete flood-controlled riverbed.

Stella took a sniff from the bottle and made a face. "Whiskey cheaper than water."

Carter asked McGee, "What about visitors?"

"None that I saw. Always met his morning ride on the other side of the bridge. Said the guy didn't like making the U-turn at the light."

Carter took out the autopsy photo of Kessler. "Could it have been this guy?"

McGee said, "Like I told you, he never pulled up here. And from the looks of that, he won't be pullin' up anywhere."

Carter figured that Stengle wanted to protect the identity of his associates. Always a suspicious sign. "How was he with the rent?"

"This ain't exactly high cotton, mister. I get paid once a week or you're out on your ass. What I want to know is . . . who pays now?"

Carter swiped an envelope from the dresser. "Write and ask them. Mom and Dad. Return address, 'Bangor, Maine.' Go write it now."

Then they searched the room. They found Nazi propaganda in the bottom of the dresser, including a bunch of anti-Semitic leaflets. They found a Springfield rifle under the bed, in a long box labeled CURTAIN RODS.

"But where's the Mauser?" asked Stella.

"If we don't find one, maybe he never had one."

"Which means we're done?"

"Which means there was a third shooter, and he's still on the loose."

Then Stella looked at the label in one of Stengle's shirts. "Mr. Fountain's Men's Shop. This guy didn't live in the high cotton, but he bought nice cotton shirts."

Carter opened Stengle's folder, and yes, the hat found next to Stengle's body came from Mr. Fountain's. He said to Stella, "Want to go to Burbank? I think I need a necktie."

"You could use a new suit, too."

ON THE SUPER CHIEF, lunch was served as the train crossed New Mexico.

Harold told Vivian to go on without him but to keep to herself. He needed a nap because he hadn't slept well. He didn't add that when the moment demanded, he could go forty-eight hours without sleep. In truth, he was just tired of company, hers or anybody else's.

So she made her way alone to the dining car, saw the man from Warner Bros. sitting by himself, and immediately forgot Harold's instructions. She asked if she could join him. She said she'd love to hear a few more Hollywood stories. She didn't add that as the train sped toward winter, she was already missing the warm dreamland she'd left behind.

Kevin explained that his sister wasn't hungry. He didn't add that he was frustrated because he couldn't make any headway with her. And they'd reach

Chicago in just twenty-five hours. By then, he'd either be back in love or hopping the lonely train to Boston.

Vivian took off her sunglasses to study the menu. "Omelette of Virginia ham . . . cold ox tongue . . . broiled Lake Superior whitefish . . . What?"

Kevin was looking at her cheek. He hadn't noticed the bruise in the morning. Now he wondered: *Did her husband whack her around?*

She touched it, then pointed to his. "You got one, too."

"You got a story for yours?" he asked.

"You first."

"I walked into a phone booth door in the dark. You?"

"Blame mine on the dark, too." She put on her sunglasses again.

He knew she didn't want to talk about it. So he changed the subject. "You know, I saw Marlene Dietrich yesterday in a Hollywood restaurant. She was with John Wayne. I think they were having a postcoital lunch."

"Postcoital? You mean, right after they . . . did it? How could you tell?"

Kevin shook his head. That wasn't the point of the story. "I couldn't. But, you really do resemble her . . . only prettier, softer."

"Thanks."

"I speak the truth." Kevin looked at the menu, but he could feel her looking at him, feel her mind working.

Then she said, "Do you really think I could be a movie star?"

"I bet your husband thinks you're a star now. And what they think about you at home is what matters."

She looked out at the desert speeding by. "Yeah. Home. No place like it."

He heard a wistful note, as if some dream hadn't come true. Was it her marriage? Hopes for a career? Kids? Or maybe he was hearing it because he was feeling the same way himself. He said, "We all want to go home for Christmas. Where's home, again?"

"Annapolis, Maryland."

"The navy town."

"We call it 'Crabtown.' My dad's a waterman. He had big dreams. But he ended up culling jimmies and sooks and raking oysters like a lot of locals."

Then they ordered. Lake Superior whitefish for him, an omelette for her.

And he told Hollywood stories all through lunch. When he described Errol Flynn bumming a light in his Robin Hood tights, she laughed out loud. He liked her laugh. He liked her. He hoped her husband didn't hit her too often . . . or too hard.

Then he said something that made her feel good all afternoon: "You know, you may look like Marlene Dietrich, but you remind me more of Jean Arthur."

"Really? I love Jean Arthur."

"An all-American girl with a heart of gold and good backbone, too."

"Coming from an actual script reader, that's a real compliment."

"Don't lose that backbone, kid."

A SIGN HUNG ON the door of Mr. Fountain's Men's Shop: CLOSED FOR LUNCH. Frank Carter knocked anyway. Mr. Fountain appeared and pointed to the sign. Carter flashed his badge, and the door swung open.

Mr. Fountain seemed to be a product of his own expertise: perfectly tailored navy-blue suit, gray vest, polka-dot blue bow tie, forced smile. "What can I do for the FBI?"

It didn't take Carter long to figure out that Mr. Fountain didn't remember a customer named Stengle. Yes, he sold scally caps, although he preferred to sell "a nice Borsalino." But a sale was a sale. And—

Frank Carter pulled out the Stengle autopsy photo.

"Oh, my." Mr. Fountain recoiled. "You just spoiled my lunch."

"You don't know him?" said Stella.

Mr. Fountain shook his head and waved a hand in front of his face as if to fan himself and keep from fainting.

Carter gave Stella a jerk of his head. *Let's go.*

And Mr. Fountain apologized for being curt. He said he'd been worked to a frazzle since his best salesman quit.

Carter pivoted back. "Your best salesman?"

"He called on Tuesday, said he wouldn't be coming back, right out of the blue."

"Bad luck," said Stella. "All alone at the height of the Christmas season."

"Christmas and war," said Mr. Fountain. "James was a whiz with all those Lockheed executives who come in looking for a few clean shirts before they go to Washington. He'd ask them about the P-38s and their fuel tanks and their guns, and all the while, he'd be talking them into buying a new sport coat or cuff links or—"

"P-38s?" said Carter. "Lockheed guys? What was James's last name?"

"Costner."

Frank Carter looked at Stella. "I think I saw that name in one of Schwinn's Bund ledgers."

"He rents a room from the Stumpf family," offered Mr. Fountain.

"Germans?" Carter was becoming more interested.

"Burbankers, as loyal as FDR. They came right after the last war. A retired dentist and his wife."

A few minutes later, Frank Carter drove down a street right out of the twenties bungalow boom. The houses were pretty. The magnolias gave good shade. The camellias in the front yards were bursting with red and white.

Edna Stumpf answered the door. She looked to be in her seventies, small and stooped, gray-haired and gray-sweatered. When she smiled, it was plain that her husband had practiced on her, because her teeth were too big for her face.

Carter said, "FBI, ma'am. We'd like to ask you a few questions."

Someone was moving from another room, coming toward them, a dark shadow, moving fast. Frank noticed Stella slide her hand into the pocket of her skirt. The pocket was slit so that she could get to her pistol without showing her legs. Another reason Frank Carter was glad to have her along.

But Edgar Stumpf was smiling, too.

Carter pegged them for two gentle souls, nothing more.

"Vat iss this, Edna? Visitors?" Edgar Stumpf's man-made teeth were better fitted.

Carter showed his badge. "Afternoon, sir. We're looking for James Costner."

"Not since Monday do we see him," said Edna through the screen door.

"Why? Is he in trouble?" asked Edgar. "He is not a boy to get into trouble."

Carter said, "We just need to talk to him."

Then Stella said, "Is that sauerbraten I smell?"

"*Ja, ja,*" said Edna. "Sauerbraten I cook on the second Saturday of the month."

"Could a nice Irish girl get the recipe?" asked Stella.

In a moment, they were in the front room with the overstuffed chairs and the antimacassars and the Philco playing a Brahms symphony.

While Mrs. Stumpf wrote out the recipe, Frank Carter asked about Costner. "What kind of person is he?"

"Very polite. Very quiet," said Mr. Stumpf. "Pays rent in advance. Travels on weekends. Gives gifts . . . nice clothes from Mr. Fountain's. And last Christmas—" He pointed to a mahogany box on the coffee table. Embossed on the top of the box, in gold, the words "Schwester Maria Innocentia."

"*Ja, ja,*" said Mrs. Stumpf, waving a little recipe card in the air to dry the ink. "We planned to bring out the box on Christmas Eve. But with all the bad news, we think today that some happy Hummel Jesus-children will brighten the night."

Mr. Stumpf opened a mahogany box, revealing a blue velvet tray, nine neat compartments, nine figurines.

And Frank Carter said, "I've seen him."

Stella was reaching for the recipe card. Her hand stopped in midair. "Where?"

"In Gunst's shop. I looked him right in his eye."

Edna and Edgar turned to each other, plainly confused.

Stella asked them, "Can you describe James Costner?"

Edna said, "Have you seen the wind movie? With the handsome Herr Gable."

Stella said, "He looks like Clark Gable?"

"No. No. Like the other man he looks."

"In *Gone With the Wind*? Leslie Howard?"

"*Ja, ja*. I even heard a friend one morning, calling to him from his car, calling him 'Ash.' I asked him why. He said they thought he looked like Ashley Wilkes."

Carter didn't remember that the customer in Gunst's shop looked like Leslie Howard, but the guy he saw from a distance, the guy in the blue overcoat with the price tag sticking up and the owlish glasses? Maybe.

Edgar Stumpf said, "I think he looked like Leslie Howard when he wore the round glasses, what you call the horn-rim—"

"*Ja, ja*," said Edna, clapping her hands as if this were a game, "the round glasses like he wore in the pig movie."

"Pig movie?" said Stella. "Porky Pig?"

"No, no," said Edgar Stumpf. "*Pygmalion*."

AFTER A DAY OF "alone" time, Sally Drake's mood improved. She said they should go to dinner as if it were a nightclub, which meant she'd need the whole drawing room to dress. So she banished Kevin to the bathroom and spread her clothes—pleated skirt, matching jacket with a nipped waist, white blouse—on the sofa.

Kevin was knotting his tie when the train lurched and the door slid open enough to give him a breathtaking reflection in the mirror: Sally bending over in black panties.

Without turning, she said, "Close the door, Kevin, or you can get off in Raton."

"Raton is a service stop. Nobody on or off." He relatched the door. "Ditto La Junta, Colorado, and Dodge City, and Newton, Kansas. The soonest you could throw me off is tomorrow morning in Kansas City."

"Just keep the door shut until I say you can come out."

When she gave the okay, he emerged with his tie knotted but his cuffs undone. He handed her a small box, then extended his right arm. "Would you do the honors?"

"The cuff links?" She smiled. They'd been her birthday present to him. Each was a double strand of gold knotted like the symbol for infinity—a figure eight on its side—with a red garnet where the strands crossed. She helped him with the right cuff, then said, "Do the left yourself. I'm still mad at you for leading the feds to me in Union Station."

"That G-man wasn't even looking for you."

"But he found me. He knows I'm on this train. That means some agent will probably be waiting in Chicago to follow me to Washington."

"Let me make it up to you." He leaned forward to kiss her.

She put a hand to his chest to hold him off. "Brother and sister, remember? So put on your jacket, because your sister wants a Manhattan."

They passed from Taos to Oraibi and into Cochiti. At the Dutch door to the kitchen, Kevin stopped to marvel at the ballet of two Negro chefs dancing from stove to oven to icebox, all in the narrow stainless-steel galley, all oblivious to the rocking of the train, all the while working wonders for the thirty-six diners in the front of the car.

Sally said, "Come on, before I die of thirst," and they went along the passage to the dining room. At night, with the lights low and the darkness speeding by, it could compete with the most romantic spot in L.A.

The tuxedoed maître d' said, "I'll take the liberty of seating the Kelloggs with you when they arrive, since you enjoyed their company this morning."

Kevin slipped him a dollar bill and ordered two Manhattans.

"You're generous," whispered Sally as they sat.

"Easy to be generous when you're traveling for free."

The waiter, in white jacket and apron, delivered the drinks: Jack Daniel's, sweet vermouth, maraschino cherries so sugary they made your teeth ache.

Sally said she liked Manhattans because her father did. "He always jokes that the red cherry reminds him of the Russian flag."

Kevin laughed. He could feel her relaxing. His hopes were rising.

She said, "So you spent all day in the observation car."

"I spent it wondering . . . Why should I keep trying?"

"Because you have talent."

"But no luck."

"Talent's more important." She raised her glass, and they toasted. "To talent."

Then there was silence between them. But on a train, the rhythm of the wheels made even the silence feel like part of a larger plan. It was a comfortable silence. And comfort, he hoped, might be a prelude to other pleasures.

She ordered two more Manhattans and, for the table, the Romanoff malossol caviar at $1.25. Her treat, to make up for being "such a bitch" at breakfast.

"You just take longer to warm up. That's all," he told her.

"When women are honest, they're called bitches. When they take charge, they're called bossy." She plucked the cherry from her drink and popped it into her mouth.

Kevin folded his menu. "So take charge of ordering. I like to be bossed."

She laughed, which Kevin took as another good sign.

And the Kelloggs made their appearance. They'd been in the club car. And they'd been drinking. But Kevin didn't sense any tension between them. If a guy smacked his wife around—or vice versa—a few drinks would usually bring out the worst in them, like the Battling Bogarts. But with the Kelloggs it was laughter and high spirits.

Vivian giggled. "I'm glad you ordered appetizers. I need to soak up the martinis."

Then her husband announced that he'd treat them all to champagne in honor of their new friendship. He called for Veuve Clicquot, which cost $9.95, a small fortune but a good pairing with caviar. It also went a long way toward loosening everyone up. He didn't add that the Gestapo was paying.

Soon, they were all toasting "confusion to our enemies," and ordering dinner. Vivian chose the swordfish steak in a sauce meunière. Harold was having the roast larded tenderloin in Madeira sauce. And Sally picked the most expensive meal on the menu at $2.50: sirloin steak for two, medium rare. To wash it down, Martin chose a Pontet-Canet Pauillac '34 and put it on his bill.

The nation out there in the dark might still be rousing itself from shock. But here on Cochiti, luxury and laughter prevailed, if only for a little while longer. And Martin Browning wanted to keep it that way.

He'd passed most of the afternoon staring at the landscape and visualizing the events that lay ahead on the South Lawn of the White House. Thanks to Scarlett and Rhett, Vivian had proven to be the best kind of traveling companion, the quiet kind. Sitting with her that afternoon had reminded him of something his mother said when he asked why she and his father could sit so long and say so little. She'd told him that being comfortable with someone and not saying a word was the perfect description of love.

Martin wasn't looking for love, but he considered wordlessness a true gift. Harold Kellogg, on the other hand, was chatty and charming to the point of ingratiation. When the meals arrived and the waiter sliced the big sirloin tableside for Kevin and Sally, he even applauded. Then he cut into his own tenderloin, glistening with Madeira sauce and melted lard.

And Sally Drake said, "Well, *there's* a coincidence."

Martin stopped cutting. He didn't believe in coincidence. And certainly not over steak. He looked up.

Sally said, "Your cuff links."

"My wife gave them to me," he answered. "Isn't that right, dear?"

"For your birthday." Even when half lit, Vivian could ad-lib.

Sally said, "I bought a pair in Burbank, at Mr. Fountain's, and—"

Vivian looked up from her swordfish. "Hey, I was in that shop the other day."

That was the worst thing that could come out of her mouth, thought Martin. What would the wife of a traveling salesman from Maryland be doing in a posh Burbank clothes shop? Martin, as Harold, said, "I think you've made a mistake, dear."

"Oh. . . . Oh, yes. You're right, dear."

Martin recovered and said, "Actually, I bought these in Washington."

Kevin raised an arm to show a cuff. "Good taste, Harry, wherever you shop."

Harold Kellogg laughed, but inside his skin, Martin Browning had gone cold and analytical. They'd entered a danger zone.

Sally said, "The salesman told me they were custom-designed for Mr. Fountain."

"Salesmen will tell you anything." Harold Kellogg went back to eating, but Martin Browning tried to remember. Had he sold her those cuff links? He'd been a hard seller, because cuff links had a nice profit margin, and Mr. Fountain liked the extra effort.

Kevin Cusack was more interested in sirloin and sex. Whatever lay ahead, whatever he'd left behind, he was enjoying himself tonight. And enjoyment started with food and drink. He was also enjoying the conversation of Mrs. Kellogg. When she started asking about the Battling Bogarts, he gave her all the gossip he could think of.

And Martin let them chatter on to distract from the cuff links.

But Sally was aiming her horn-rims at him like gun barrels. In male company, most nearsighted women took off their glasses, because glasses on a woman implied brainpower. Sally kept hers on, as if to say that if men didn't like her brains, too damn bad. And if men found her confidence intimidating, to hell with them.

Martin Browning preferred to be in control. He said, "If you and your brother were so successful in Hollywood, Miss Drake, why are you leaving?"

"We weren't *that* successful. And maybe we're just going home for a visit."

"Maybe you're running away . . . you and your *brother* with a different name." Martin knew that would put her back. "Different fathers, too? Or different mothers?"

Kevin took a sip of wine and said to Sally, "He knows."

"That you're my 'beard'?" said Sally.

Vivian Hopewell caught herself before she said, "You, too, hunh?"

Kevin said, "That's me. Cusack the beard."

Sally looked at his cuff links. "I gave those to someone I . . . I really liked."

"A nice gift," said Vivian. She knew it wasn't her best line, but as a reward, her "husband" poured her more champagne.

And did he also drop a tablet into his wife's glass? Kevin couldn't be sure . . .

. . . because the guy was very smooth, and he was looking right at Kevin.

"So why are *you* going home, Mr. Cusack? To marry this lovely lady, perhaps?" He grinned. Control the situation. Never give an advantage. He set down the bottle, tugged at his sleeves so the cuff links showed nicely, and went back to his steak.

Kevin sipped his wine and calculated. He had about eighteen hours left. He'd avoid this guy for the rest of the trip. The shiner under his wife's eye . . . the Mickey he'd just slipped her . . . none of it was Kevin's problem. He had other things on his mind.

Then Vivian changed the subject and sealed the fate of at least one person at the table. She said, "Amazing how fast the time goes when you're reading a good book."

"What are you reading?" asked Sally.

"*Gone with the Wind*. I loved the movie. So I had to read the book."

"The book is always better," said Sally.

"I still see Vivien Leigh and Clark Gable when I read about Scarlett and Rhett."

"And Olivia de Havilland as Melanie," said Sally. "But Ashley? Do you ever dream of Leslie Howard?"

"Scarlett wouldn't fall for him," said Vivian. "I never see him when I'm reading."

"You know"—Sally gazed across the table—"I think I see him now."

Martin had just put a piece of steak into his mouth. He stopped chewing.

"Has anyone ever told you that you look like Leslie Howard?" asked Sally.

Kevin laughed. "People tell me I look like Tyrone Power and—"

"You look more like him than I look like Leslie Howard." Martin tried laughing it off. He didn't give one of his better laughs.

"I don't see Ashley Wilkes." Sally took off her glasses and held them up, as if framing his face. "I see Leslie Howard as Henry Higgins in *Pygmalion*."

Martin looked at the glasses, then picked up his wine and took a drink.

"And I've seen him before," said Sally. "But where?"

"You see too much." Martin knew exactly where she'd seen him.

She said, "Are you sure you never sold cuff links in Burbank?" She was taunting him, emboldened perhaps by drink, and she seemed to be enjoying it.

"Very sure." He laughed, but he could feel Vivian looking at him, too. Was she dimly recollecting the encounter at Mr. Fountain's on Monday afternoon? He couldn't have that, either.

Sally said, "Come on. Humor me. Put 'em on."

But there was no humor in this. Nobody was laughing.

Then Mr. Brylcreem broke the tension, blustering in and parading over to their table. "So, are you gents in or out? I got five in the game. I need at least one more."

Kevin shook his head.

Martin Browning said, "I'll play." Then he began to triangulate, to calculate, to consider: If he decided to do what now appeared necessary, how could he use Kevin's absence from the card table, and his own presence, to his advantage?

"WELL, THAT WAS INTERESTING." Sally dropped onto the sofa in Drawing Room D. "It's none of that guy's goddamn business why we're going east."

"He thought you were playing him," said Kevin, "so he played *you*."

"Something tells me he doesn't play nice," she said. "And I swear, I've seen him before. Did you ever go into Mr. Fountain's?"

"Forget Mr. Fountain. Forget Mr. Kellogg." Kevin flipped off the light, so that the moonlit landscape came to life outside. Then he turned up the music. "Stardust." Perfect. He dropped onto the sofa and put his arm around her.

"What are you doing, Kevin?"

"Forgetting that guy."

The only sounds were the clack of the wheels and the clarinet of Artie Shaw.

Sally's glasses reflected the moonlight, but she didn't take them off, which meant she wasn't looking for a kiss.

Maybe he was moving too quickly. But once he'd begun, he couldn't retreat. He put a hand on her thigh and whispered, "I like it when you wear a skirt."

"Most men do. That's why I usually wear slacks."

He brought his face along her cheek and whispered, "My FBI friend thinks you wear slacks because you don't like men."

"What did you tell him when he said that?"

"I told him he was misinformed." And he brought his lips to hers.

She pulled away. As he moved in again, she said, "He wasn't."

He stopped in midmotion. "Wasn't what?"

And the confession tumbled out of her, as if she'd held it in for too long, but the booze had loosened her tongue. "I'm sorry, Kevin. I've . . . I've tried. But I can't stand it anymore. I went to Hollywood to meet handsome men. All I saw were starlets and costume-department butches in tailored slacks."

"What? What are you saying?" He felt himself deflating, in more ways than one. "We dated for months."

"I enjoyed it. I really did. I hated myself when we split. I was never interested in Jerry Sloane. I really like you. I was hoping this train ride would rekindle something."

He leaned back. He didn't like all the past tense . . . or all the new information.

She said, "I even let that John Huston feel me up. I thought some male celebrity might . . . might give me the desire I wanted to have."

"But—"

"I think I know who I am. That's what I learned in California. And right now, we all have to face truths about ourselves and the world we live in."

"Truth? If you like girls and not guys, this world may not be very kind to you."

"Just the slobber from the FBI will give me rabies. Nobody knows, but I have a friend, a special friend. She lives on the canal in Georgetown. Mary Benning is her name. She's a teacher. She's the real reason I'm going back."

"You're going back for a woman? Jesus." Kevin didn't want to hear more. "I need a smoke." He got up and opened the sliding door to the passage.

She called his name.

And he said, perhaps too angrily, "What?"

"I'm sorry."

"I'm sorry, too. Sorry I ever got on this goddamn train." He slammed the slider behind him. He didn't know if he was angry at himself or at her or at fate in general.

And he turned directly into Mr. Brylcreem, who was coming along the passage. He gave Kevin a leer. "Throwin' in your cards with that dame so soon?"

Kevin pushed past Cook and headed for the observation car.

Cook called after him, "Like I always say, pal, gotta have jacks or better to open, even if all you're openin' is your fly."

MARTIN BROWNING LEFT VIVIAN asleep in the cabin, dosed with martinis, champagne, and Veronal to knock her out cold for the night. Now the real game began: poker in Acoma, murder in Taos.

He had to do it. The longer Sally Drake thought about those cuff links, the more likely she'd remember the man who sold them. And if she announced it at breakfast, where might it all lead?

First, he went forward to the club car and the sound of rattling poker chips.

Sinclair Cook was running the game and handling the money. Based on the deference the waiters gave him, he must have been a big tipper. He said, "Welcome to the party. Too bad your friend would rather drink in the observation car."

"I can't speak for him." Martin pulled five twenties from his pocket and put them down in front of Sinclair Cook. "But I'm in for a hundred."

Cook looked at the cash and began to count out a hundred dollars in chips. "Boys, I think we got a card shark . . . or a mark."

The other players: two young guys with big hands and suntans who claimed they played in the Chicago White Sox minor-league system, a fidgety lawyer who'd been in California taking depositions on a case to be tried in Chicago, and a businessman from Los Angeles.

Martin Browning took a seat to the right of the lawyer.

Sinclair Cook cut open a new pack of cards, shuffled, and announced, "Seven-card stud, jacks or better to open."

KEVIN SAT AT THE back of the observation car, nursed a Scotch, and wondered: How could he have been so wrong? How could he have missed her signals? When Sally dumped him for Jerry Sloane, was she just trying on another pair of shoes that would never fit, no matter how hard she pushed her feet into them?

He knew about girls who liked girls. He was from the town that gave the all-female partnership its name. The "Boston marriage," they called it. But . . .

He decided not to give a damn, at least for a while. He'd just sit there and smoke and drink and feel the rhythm of the rails . . . and feel sorry for himself, too.

THE SHUFFLING CARDS PLAYED counterpoint to the spinning thoughts in Martin Browning's head. He knew something had gone wrong between Sally and Kevin. He'd heard the end of an argument when the door to Drawing Room D opened. He'd heard Sally say that she was sorry. He'd heard Kevin say that he was sorry, too, sorry to be on the train . . . with her? He'd heard the slam of the door and the voice of Sinclair Cook.

After six hands, he'd won five. The others were getting resentful, because he knew how to play the cards and play them, too. But he was playing a larger game.

"Check to you," said Cook.

Martin tapped the table. Another check. He was standing pat. But he couldn't stand pat on the mission. He had to protect it at all costs, from any threat. So the next time the play came to him, he threw in his cards. He said he'd give them a chance to win some money from each other while he went to find his replacement.

Sinclair Cook said, "Something else on your mind? I guarantee a fine night ahead." Then he winked. "Take it from me."

Martin wanted to kill Cook, too, just for being crude. Maybe later.

He moved quickly through Cochiti, Oraibi, into Taos—foolish names honoring Indian tribes these Americans had done so much to dispossess. They'd treated the Indians worse than the Nazis had treated the Jews, he thought, with much less reason.

In Taos, he noticed the porter stepping out of Drawing Room D. He heard Sally's voice: "Thank you, Stanley." As he went past, he glanced in and saw that the bed had been "made down." And Sally was alone. Excellent.

But he went on to the observation car, just to be sure.

He found Kevin Cusack slumped in a chair, a cigarette in his lips, a tray of butts in front of him, his tie undone, and a cloud of smoke around his head. As Martin approached, Kevin looked up and said, "Cleaned out so soon?"

"Resting. Let them clean each other out. Then I'll go back for more plunder."

"I'll play when a spot opens."

"Then stay right here. If you go to bed, you'll miss your chance."

"Okay." Kevin folded his arms and legs. "I'll just take a little nap."

This couldn't be working out more perfectly, thought Martin. The observation car was empty, except for Cusack. If he stayed here awhile longer, the deed would be done.

Martin looked at his watch. "I'll keep playing as long as my hand's hot. If nothing opens up before the next stop, get off in Kansas City and stretch your legs. Fill your lungs with fresh air, then come in with a clear head and take my seat."

"How long's the layover in Kansas City?" asked Kevin.

"Half an hour, I think." Martin lied about that. But if it worked, all the suspicion would be on Kevin Cusack. "I'd better get back. Do you want another drink?"

Kevin drained his glass, held it up, rattled the ice. *Yes.* He should have been more suspicious, but two Manhattans, champagne, Pauillac, and three Scotches had left him more than woolly. He was downright drunk.

And Martin Browning knew it. He hurried forward again. Passing between Navajo and Taos. He felt the rush of air as the doors opened and closed. He stopped in the vestibule of Taos and pulled on his calfskin gloves.

IN THE OBSERVATION CAR, Kevin finished a cigarette and pulled out his pack of Chesterfields. *Empty.* He had another pack in the room. Maybe he'd go get it. He didn't want to confront Sally just yet. But he really needed another smoke.

IN TAOS, MARTIN BROWNING tapped on the door of Drawing Room D. A muffled voice asked who was there.

"Kevin." Martin Browning was skilled enough at disguise that he could adjust his voice, and if need be, mimic a Boston accent. Since he'd heard their argument, he said, "I'm sorry . . . about everything. And I forgot my key."

IN THE OBSERVATION CAR, Kevin staggered as the train leaned into a curve. He was drunk enough that the motion caused him to fall into another chair. And miracle of miracles, he saw a cigarette on the floor. Someone had dropped it, as if they knew he'd need it. He reached across the aisle to pick it up and almost landed on his face.

Lord, he was drunk. But he had his smoke. He didn't need to go back to his room.

In Taos, Sally Drake opened the door. "I'm sorry, Kev—"

And that was all she said.

The hand closed around her throat so quickly that not a breath could escape.

She screamed and all she could force out was a hiss, like a cat. When Martin Browning heard that sound, he knew he had her. The clean kill would come quickly. So he pushed her into the room and kicked the door shut.

Her hiss became a strange squeak. She was pouring every bit of voice and air into her scream. He could feel her trying. He could feel her punching and kicking. But he was focused. He was doing a job that he hated doing but would do well.

There were things he wanted to say to her . . . that she was right about Mr. Fountain's Men's Shop, that she was right about him, that she was very perceptive, so perceptive that he had to kill her. But he didn't say anything. Talking would only intensify the horror for her. Talking would only make it worse for both of them. So he focused on killing her until she was dead.

Then he put her limp corpse into the made-down bed and covered her with the Navajo blanket.

Ten minutes after leaving, Harold Kellogg was back at the game.

Sinclair Cook said, "Where's the other guy?"

"Not interested just now. Can I get my chair back?"

The lawyer said, "My luck's changed. So take the seat to my left."

Martin might have treated that as an insult. The lawyer was suggesting that Martin might be cheating. But he just laughed, because that's what Harold Kellogg would do.

He took a new chair and waved to the waiter. "Brandy. And there's a gentleman in the observation car who could use a Scotch. Make it a double . . . on me." And he added a bit of his own crudity. "He looks as if he's worn out."

"Worn out from what?" Mr. Brylcreem grinned like the lecher he was.

Martin winked at him. "I think you know."

Mr. Brylcreem chuckled, as if to say, *We* both *know, and we're both well versed . . . with the same woman.*

Martin considered how easy it would be to throw him from the train the next time Sinclair Cook headed for the men's room. But he wasn't worth it. Martin tried to kill only when necessary, not when it would bring him mere personal satisfaction.

And the Super Chief sped deeper into the night.

SUNDAY,
DECEMBER 14

WHEN THE MOTION AND sound stopped, Kevin Cusack opened his eyes. He hadn't been sleeping. He'd been passed out. He knew because his skull was throbbing, and he was still sitting in the observation car. Drunks passed out in chairs. Sober men slept in beds . . . or berths.

A porter stuck his head into the car and said, "Hey, man, get up. Kansas City. We all got passengers to tend to, 'cept for you, so go get the newspapers."

Stanley Smith popped out of a chair near the front of the car, rubbed the sleep from his eyes, saw Kevin and said, "Good mornin', sir," then hurried off to work.

Kevin glanced at his watch: 5:20 A.M. They must have burned grass all the way across the prairie to get there so early. They weren't scheduled to leave until 6:25. So maybe he'd take that walk. The cold might constrict the blood vessels in his head, which would soothe the pain. Then he'd play cards, if the game was still going.

He stopped first in the drawing room because he needed a couple of aspirin. But Sally looked so nicely tucked away, sleeping so soundly, he decided not to wake her by fumbling around. He pulled down the big shades and hung the DO NOT DISTURB sign on the door handle.

Then he stepped out onto the platform and saw his breath for the first time in years. But the cold stopped the throbbing behind his eyes. And the aroma wafting out of the station promised that somewhere inside, someone was cooking bacon and eggs, the best Cusack remedy for a big head. He could eat and be back aboard in plenty of time. So he followed his nose.

When it came to train stations, L.A. had nothing on Kansas City. And Kevin wasn't surprised to see so many people about so early on a Sunday. It was wartime. There'd be no more sleeping-in. Newsboys were hawking papers. Travelers were hustling. The PA was calling out an arrival from Omaha and a departure for Chicago. But Kevin ignored it all, because Kansas City was headquarters of the Harvey Company, and he was homing in on their flagship restaurant. He grabbed a seat at the counter, gave his order to the waitress in the bibbed apron, and watched her fill his cup.

Hot coffee burned off some of the alcohol fog, and he realized that he'd been a jerk to Sally the night before. He decided that for the rest of the trip, he'd be as decent to her as he could be. He didn't understand everything in life, but it would be a lot easier for him than for her, no matter what.

When breakfast arrived, the Harvey Girl refreshed his coffee and asked him where he was headed.

"Chicago," he said. "On the Super Chief."

"The Super Chief?"

"Yeah. I just got off for a bit."

"This *morning's* Super Chief?" She looked past Kevin to the clock in the main hall.

Kevin turned and saw the time. "Hey, that clock is fast. It's off by an hour." And even as he said it, the last wisps of booze-brain vaporized.

He jumped up, threw a dollar on the counter, and ran across the concourse . . . dodging travelers . . . leaping over suitcases . . . pushing past porters . . . racing out onto the platform. And . . . never in his life had he felt so deflated . . . or so goddamn stupid.

The wind whipped down the empty track. A newspaper hopped from tie to tie and puffed up into the air. A porter came over and asked, "Can I help you, sir?"

Kevin Cusack just shook his head. Welcome to the Central time zone.

FRANK CARTER AWOKE IN the Ansonia next to Stella Madden. He was getting to like her company. She was as hard-nosed as a man. She was easy to talk to. She had a beautiful round bottom. And she could do it all night.

Too bad he didn't have the day off. But Sunday was now a workday for the FBI, because they were undermanned and overburdened and way too busy grabbing Nazis and Japs, grabbing and grilling and arresting like hell. Pretty soon, he thought, they'd run out of space for the Nazis at Terminal Island. And the Griffith Park camp was already full of Japs. But Hoover was on Hood from Washington. So Hood was on Carter and every other agent in L.A. No days off until the internal security of the United States was assured.

Carter went to the window and looked across at the old Olympic Hotel on Alvarado. A few months earlier, he'd led a raid on the apartment of the Japanese naval attaché in the Olympic. And they'd learned plenty. They'd even found a list of three thousand Japanese Americans who were *not* likely to turn against the U.S. Too bad they couldn't find a list of good Germans, too. Eliminating threats saved a lot of legwork.

The Japanese might be the immediate problem. But Carter worried more about the Germans. They looked like ordinary white Americans. A lot of them were. They could mix in anywhere, just like the guy who'd shot that 7.63 mm round. Where was he? Who was he? What was he up to? And did he really look like the most nondescript star in movies?

Stella rolled over and said, "Good morning."

"When I say the name 'Leslie Howard,' what do you see?"

"Oh, for Chrissakes." She popped out of bed. "I see coffee. Just coffee."

AT TWELVE THIRTY CENTRAL time, the Super Chief was speeding through the Chicago suburbs. And Pullman porter Stanley Smith was delivering what he called his "get-goin' knocks."

A DO NOT DISTURB sign remained on the door of Taos Drawing Room D. Stanley hadn't seen the "brother" since early morning in the observation car. He figured they weren't really brother and sister after all. Most likely they were spending a final morning in a single berth before reaching Chicago. But that was none of his business. Getting them off the train was. He put his ear to the door and heard nothing. So he gave one more knock. "Thirty-minute warnin', folks." Then he moved on.

At Drawing Room F, Mr. Kellogg answered on the first knock.

"Mornin', sir," said Stanley. "Thirty minutes to Chicago. All doors open. You can pick up checked bags in the station."

"We only have three, Stanley." Mr. Kellogg gestured to them, all packed and ready. "One for me, two for the missus. And Stanley, we're in a rush. Can you have these bags at the front?" Then he began peeling twenties. One. Two. Three. Four.

How long could Stanley wait him out? *Five.* He could wait five twenties, a hundred-dollar tip. Who tipped a hundred dollars?

This guy did. He put the money into Stanley's hand and gestured to the suitcases.

Stanley nodded. "I'll put these right at the front, sir. You'll be first off. And there'll be a boy waitin' to carry your bags up to the street."

FRANK CARTER AND STELLA Madden were sitting in the Original Pantry on Figueroa. The sign outside: BREAKFAST 24 HOURS.

While they waited for waffles, Stella sank into the *L.A. Times.*

Frank said, "Looking for clients?"

"Or gossip."

"So what's the gossip this morning?"

"Sleepy old Glendale is getting to be a very dangerous place. First they find Stengle's body under a bridge leading into town. Now, there's a corpse in an apartment bungalow near Forest Lawn."

"Convenient anyway. What was it? Robbery? Jealous lover?"

"If it's robbery, there's nothing in it for me, but if it's jealousy or some other messy emotion, somebody might need a private detective." She handed him the paper.

He didn't see anything special, but one detail jumped out: "Police have questioned all the tenants, except for a traveling salesman who left before the body was discovered." Carter lowered the paper and said, "How about a ride to Glendale before I go to work?"

"Is this about Mauser man?"

"Could be."

"I thought our guy was a haberdasher, not a traveling salesman."

"Could be both."

"A two-headed snake?"

"Could have three heads . . . or even four."

Breakfast arrived: flaky waffles, sausages, whipped butter.

"So let's eat"—Frank grabbed the syrup—"then go snake hunting."

"I hate like hell to miss Mass."

"You got a lot of sins to confess."

"The more, the better."

IN DRAWING ROOM F, Vivian was dressed and ready and befuddled. She also had a headache. She blamed it on all she'd drunk, not on the pill he'd slipped her the night before. And the rhythm of the rails, so steady and calming for so long, was beginning to slow, as if to announce that this fantasy trip was ending. She knew there'd be no better time to ask: "Harold, what . . . what happens after we meet your boss?"

"What do you mean?"

"Are you leaving me here . . . in Chicago, I mean?"

For a moment, he just stared. He had a powerful stare, and she couldn't read it. He was dangerous, yes, but so magnetic, especially when he flashed the smile he finally gave her. She didn't want it to be over, and the smile said it wouldn't be.

He sat next to her. "I want you to play my wife all the way to Washington. I'm going there for meetings, and Annapolis isn't much farther, so—"

It was almost like a marriage proposal. Her headache evaporated in an instant, and she threw her arms around his neck. "Oh, gee, I thought you'd dump me, like that Brylcreemed bastard did. I thought—"

"You should know better."

She only heard the words, not the flatness in the voice. And she kissed him with all she had, kissed him her lust, kissed him her passion, even kissed him her love.

He'd planned it this way. He'd left her hanging until the perfect moment. Then he gave her hope. It was how a captor controlled a hostage or a strong male controlled a weak woman. Rescued from the abyss of desertion, she'd continue to trust him, no matter how terrible the news she might hear before they got off the train . . . or after.

Another knock broke their embrace.

Martin answered with a big Harold Kellogg grin. But Stanley Smith's expression said that the body had been found. "What is it?"

"Sorry, sir," said Stanley, "but, have you seen Mr. Cusack?"

"I saw him step off in Kansas City. Why?"

Stanley turned to leave. "Can't say. But—"

"Oh, Stanley . . . What we talked about? The baggage?" Martin shoved three more twenties into Stanley's pocket. "We need to get off quickly."

"Thank you, sir." *Thunk* . . . the door closed behind Stanley.

Vivian said, "He seems bothered by something."

"Whatever it is, it's not our problem. We must meet my business connection at the taxi stand. If we miss him, the whole trip's a waste. So follow my lead and do what I say."

She agreed, but . . . then what? Would they hurry for the Lake Shore Limited? Would they fly? An airplane trip would be thrilling. But she was ready for anything.

Now they heard voices in the passage, feet shuffling, doors banging.

Martin opened the door and peered out.

Stanley was saying, "She looks dead, sir."

The white conductor, who usually paraded through the train like a plantation boss in his blue uniform and gold watch fob, stepped—no, stumbled—out of the drawing room and turned an even paler shade of white. He took off his glasses, cleaned them, put them back on, looked again into the drawing room. "We'll need the police to meet us."

Martin Browning pulled his head in and closed the slider.

Vivian was wide-eyed. "Did they just say 'dead'? My God."

"I heard them arguing last night." Martin flipped off the radio.

She said, "Will we have to stay and answer questions?"

"It's not our concern, and I told you, we can't be stuck here." He looked around the room. "I need a pen and some paper."

IN GLENDALE, A UNIFORMED officer guarded the crime scene. And yes, he said, the medical examiner had removed the body. If the FBI had questions, they'd get answers from the detectives executing a warrant on the apartment of one Harold King.

So Frank and Stella went upstairs. Frank tapped the open door, showed his badge, and stepped into the front room with Stella close behind.

The lead detective—skinny guy, shiny blue suit, cigarette ash on his tie—didn't look too happy. "G-man? On a local case?"

Carter ignored the comment and asked him how the deceased met her end.

"Strangled. Quick and professional."

"A hired killer . . . for a landlady ?" asked Carter.

"I don't know about that," said the cop, "but the guy knew what he was doing. A hand at the throat, a hand on the back of the head, push the hands together, and *adios,* Señora Sanchez."

"What enemies would a Spanish landlady have?" asked Stella.

The detective gave Stella a puzzled look. A dame working with the FBI? Then he said, "Who knows? Who knows if she's even Spanish?"

"Yeah." The guy dusting for prints looked up. "Could be Mexican. You know the difference between Spanish and Mexican, don't you?"

Stella said, "I'll bite."

"If your name ends with 'z' and you make more than ten bucks a week, you're Spanish. If you make less, you're Mexican."

Stella turned to Carter. "Now you know why I went into private practice."

Carter asked the cops, "Do you mind if we have a look around?"

The detective glanced at his partner. "Does the warrant allow that?"

"Of course it does." Carter was already heading down the hall. "We're the goddamn FBI."

"Hey—" The detective went scrambling after him.

In the first room on the right, a desk. Nothing on it but a lamp. Beside it was a wastebasket with crumpled newspapers. Carter picked up one of the papers and noticed that it was covered in oil. He took a sniff, turned to the detective. "Gun oil, maybe?"

Then they moved on to the back bedroom. The low December sun flooded in. Carter asked the detective if the sheets had been inspected.

"Semen stains. Sex but . . . no evidence of rape on the body," said the detective.

Carter looked down the hall. "Where's Stella?"

"She saw those old child-star dames from across the way. Went out to talk to them."

Carter soon caught up to Stella and the Jeffries sisters in the driveway.

Marylea was basking in the chance to portray melodramatic silent-movie horror at all that had happened in their little world. She was even wearing false eyelashes, waiting for her close-up. "Mr. King, a killer? I can't believe it."

Stella turned to the other sister. "What do you think?"

"We think he's a very nice man." Kimberlea seemed cooler, less excitable.

Marylea shook her bottle-blond tresses. "He's what girls nowadays call a dreamboat."

Carter looked at Kimberlea. "Dreamboat?"

"Like a movie star. He didn't *look* like Cary Grant, but he dressed like him."

"Nice suits, you mean?" said Stella. "Like Cary in *His Girl Friday?*"

"More like *Only Angels Have Wings.* Cary in leather jacket and fedora."

Carter and Stella glanced at each other. Were they getting closer?

"Oh, I loved his outfit," said Marylea. "So dashing."

Stella asked the sisters, "Any idea where he's dashing to?"

"He told us he was going east . . . driving," said Kimberlea. "To see his family."

"Yes," added Marylea, "but Carmelita—poor Mrs. Sanchez—she told us she'd seen train schedules and tickets out on his table."

"Santa Fe schedules," said Kimberlea. "But he left in his car."

"What kind of car?" asked Carter.

"A Dodge coupe, ugly pea-soup color," said Kimberlea.

"I remember the plates," said Marylea. "76 B 2344."

"How can you be so sure?" asked Carter.

"Even in the old days, we memorized our lines," said Marylea.

"Helped us convey the emotions." Kimberlea rolled her eyes.

Marylea said, "I keep my memory sharp so I'll be ready for my next role. I can certainly remember a license plate I saw hundreds of times."

Carter took out his notebook and wrote down their info.

The dogs were tugging at the leashes and snuffling around everyone's feet.

Marylea told them not to be bad little boys or Mommy would spank them.

They kept snuffling, as if they didn't give a damn what Mommy thought.

Stella told the sisters, "You two were great in *Distressed Damsels*."

Marylea batted her eyelashes so hard that one of them fell off, and one of the dogs pounced on it like it was a bug. Marylea cried, "Oh, no! Oh, you bad boy." Then she crouched and started fishing in the dog's mouth.

Kimberlea said, "She hasn't worn those things in years. Now she thinks we'll have a comeback because of all this. So she's blinking like a stoplight."

Marylea stood and wiped the dog spit from the eyelash. "If we have a comeback, it'll be thanks to my talent. I'm the star. You're just a featured player." Then she gave a toss of her locks and led the dogs toward her front door.

Kimberlea said, "I can't leave her alone for too long. Is there anything else?"

Carter glanced at Stella, hoping she'd come up with a good question, and she did: "If Harold King didn't look like Cary Grant, who *did* he look like?"

"I always thought he looked more like Leslie Howard."

Frank Carter and Stella Madden watched Kimberlea go into her building. Then they turned to each other and said, at the same time, "It's him."

As the Super Chief rolled into Chicago, Vivian watched Harold watching the platform. She didn't know that picking out plainclothesmen was one of his skills. He was looking for the long overcoat, the bored look that could bore right through you, the cigarette or the stick of gum to heighten the affect. . . .

He said they had to get off the train and out of the station without any police interaction, or they'd be stuck for hours.

Stanley knocked and told them their bags were at the front, but the conductor was asking passengers to stay on board because there might be questions from the police.

Harold said, "I told you what I know, Stanley. And I've written a description." He'd put it into a Santa Fe envelope and left a nonexistent New York address on the back flap.

It read: "At nine thirty last night, I heard an angry argument in Drawing Room D. Mr. Cusack told Miss Drake he wished he hadn't come on the train with her. I believe Sinclair Cook heard this conversation, too, and should be questioned. Based on my earlier conversation with him in the observation car, also witnessed by Mr. Cook's wife, Mr. Cusack spoke warmly of the pro-Nazi Bund in Los Angeles. He may now be connecting with Nazi agents in the Midwest. I believe he is armed and dangerous."

Martin gave Stanley the envelope and pulled another twenty from his pocket.

Stanley looked him square in the eye. "Sorry, sir. Orders. You can't buy me off with another twenty, no matter how brand-new crisp it is."

Vivian didn't have a script, but she improvised. She put her hand on the porter's arm and said, "Stanley, I'm . . . I'm with child, as they say."

Stanley's eyes dropped involuntarily to her belly.

"Three months, so I'm not showing. But I'm headed east to give Mom the news."

"That's fine, ma'am, but—"

When she wasn't reading *Gone with the Wind,* Vivian had been studying train schedules in case her "husband" left her in the lurch. "We need to get over to La Salle Street Station to catch the Lake Shore Limited at three o'clock, otherwise, we won't make New York tomorrow."

"But, ma'am—"

"My mother is *dying,* Stanley. I . . . I only hope I'm not too late to . . . to—" She dabbed a tissue at her nose. "You see, we just *can't* miss that train."

And Stanley relented. "Well . . . I guess. You left your address and all on this envelope, so the police will know where to find you, so . . . well . . . I guess."

After the porter left, Harold said to Vivian, "A dying mother . . . absolute genius."

No man had ever made her feel better.

SOON ENOUGH, THEY WERE off the train, hurrying through Dearborn Station, and stepping out into the cold.

Vivian followed Harold past people queuing up for cabs on Polk Street, toward a man wearing a black overcoat and hat. If she hadn't already been freezing, the sight of Max Diebold would have made her go ice cold.

He looked at her with eyes small and judgmental behind rimless glasses. "I did not expect a wife."

This puzzled Vivian. Wasn't "seeing the wife" the whole point? She shot her "husband" a look.

He took her arm and said, "Mr. Diebold, I told you I was married."

Diebold raised a gloved hand and a black Oldsmobile 98 club sedan pulled round the corner.

Vivian didn't know what was going on, but she was going along. She had no choice. And as long as she held Harold's arm, she had no fear.

The driver popped out and popped the trunk. He looked like a younger version of Diebold, rimless glasses, three-piece tweed suit, skinny torso. He opened the back door for Vivian. "Welcome to Chicago, ma'am. I'm Eric Diebold."

She looked at Harold, as if to ask if it was all right to get in.

He nodded, then turned to the father, who was glaring at her as if he hated the sight of her. Meanwhile the son was sneaking peeks at her, as if she was the best thing he'd ever seen.

At least the car was warm. She pulled down the armrest and sank into plush gray upholstery. Wherever they were going, they'd get there in style.

But Harold and Diebold were still out on the sidewalk having a sharp conversation. Vivian thought she heard Diebold ask, "How much does she know?"

Harold answered in low tones, hard to hear in the echoing noise. It sounded as if he were the boss and Diebold the underling. But when he got into the back seat, he was all smiles and servility. He said to Vivian, "Now, dear, for a nice drive. Isn't that right, Mr. Diebold?"

"My son is an excellent driver," said Max Diebold in a voice as cold as the wind whipping down Polk Street.

The son looked into the rearview mirror. "Excellent, especially for pretty ladies."

"Thank you." Vivian tried to keep the trepidation out of her voice. She'd learned her lesson about getting into fancy cars with strange men.

KEVIN CUSACK WAS EATING. More food might help him to forget how stupid he was.

After eggs at the Harvey House restaurant, he'd found a coffee stand, where he scarfed down three doughnuts. Now he'd landed at a lunch counter. It was open to the concourse, so he could watch the world go by. And a radio was playing, so he could hear the news. And sirloin steak topped the menu at thirty-five cents. In Kansas City, you had steak, but he'd just dropped ten bucks on a Union Pacific ticket to Chicago, so he'd eat the cheap stuff instead of the famous Harvey sirloin. People said that in Kansas City, even the lunch-counter steak was choice.

But no amount of food could stop the sign flashing in his head: STUPID. STUPID. STUPID. How could he have been so stupid? That son of a bitch Harry Kellogg had played him, had told him to wait up for the card game, had suggested that he get off in Kansas City and stretch his legs. But why?

He didn't know. He could barely think. The PA was echoing . . . the NBC Radio Network announcer was delivering the national news . . . and the Salvation Army bells were ringing. It might be a week after the greatest disaster in American history, but Christmas was still on its way.

The steak took Kevin's mind off Kellogg. Charred on the outside, rare on the inside, just the way he liked it.

"And now, the local news," said the radio voice.

As Kevin popped the rarest slice into his mouth, he barely heard what he was hearing until he heard his own name: "Kansas City police have issued an all-points bulletin for a man identified as Kevin Cusack of Los Angeles."

Kevin stopped chewing. Then he stopped breathing.

"The suspect is wanted for questioning in the death of Sally Drake, described as his sister but believed to be his traveling paramour."

Kevin would have thrown up, but the steak caught in his throat.

"Her body was found in her berth when the Super Chief reached Chicago. Police believe the suspect got off in Kansas City. He's about six feet tall, black hair, blue eyes, wearing a tweed jacket, white shirt, and red necktie. If sighted, inform authorities. He is a known member of the pro-Nazi German American Bund and is wanted for questioning in Los Angeles for murder and assault. He is believed to be armed and dangerous."

Pro-Nazi? Armed and dangerous? Police?

And here they came—two cops—walking right up to the counter, looking right at him. Kevin just sat there, trying not to choke on the steak.

The waitress said, "Afternoon, fellers." Then she plunked two coffees down in front of them.

"In other news, the Kansas City Board of Trade will . . ."

Kevin needed a gulp of coffee to sluice the steak down, but his appetite was gone. He dropped forty-five cents next to his plate and got up without another glance at anyone. Before he realized where he was going, he was on the sidewalk in front of the station. The wind slapped him in the face and reminded him that this was no dream.

The curb captain said, "Do you need a taxi, sir?"

Kevin shook his head. He didn't need a taxi. He needed a drink. He needed a cigarette. But first, he needed a friend.

So he went back into the station and found a line of phone booths. He dropped into one and slammed the door. In the close quiet, he snapped off his red tie and put up the collar on his sport coat. He was already acting like a fugitive.

Then he dropped a nickel into the phone and gave the operator the FBI number in Los Angeles. Collect, person-to-person, but he decided to use a false name that Carter would recognize: Sam Spade.

No answer. Not surprising on a Sunday morning.

So he dialed the operator again and gave the LAJCC number. He knew that Leon Lewis spent part of Sunday in the office. He might be there now.

A familiar voice accepted the charges. "Kevin? What's this about an all-points bulletin?"

"You know already?" said Kevin.

"That Detective O'Hara was here. He said you're wanted for murder."

"I'm no murderer."

"I believe you, but if I were your counsel, I'd tell you to turn yourself in."

"You *are* my counsel." Kevin peered onto the concourse. "And there's cops everywhere."

"So pick one out and turn yourself in," said Lewis.

"But the radio's calling me a Nazi. These local cops might shoot me on sight."

"My advice would be the same."

"I've read enough scripts to know how easy it is to frame a man."

"We'll vouch for you, despite the evidence."

"Evidence?"

"Someone named Kellogg. He said you discussed Nazi ideology, and he heard an argument in your drawing room last night. O'Hara said the guy made a signed statement. He's calling it an affidavit, which, of course, it isn't, but—"

"That Kellogg guy is railroading me, Mr. Lewis. He must have done it."

"What do you want me to do, then? How can I help?"

"I . . . I don't know." Kevin's mind was lurching from one terrible possibility to another. And while he heard Lewis's voice telling him to keep calm, he also heard, *Accused of murder, Nazi sympathizer, armed and dangerous.* . . . These were not terms to encourage calm. These were terms to make a man's throat constrict. These were terms to make a man in a tight phone booth sweat like a stevedore. Kevin said he needed air.

"Call back in half an hour," said Lewis. "Maybe you'll see things more clearly."

THE LAST GUY CARTER wanted to see when he got to work was Detective Bobby O'Hara. The last guy he wanted to smell, too, all stale cigars and yesterday's boxer shorts and a few beer farts, too. The last thing he wanted to hear was O'Hara gloating as he told the story.

"We got him this time," said O'Hara. "We got Cusack."

"But murder?" Carter tried not to show his shock. "Kevin Cusack?"

"Don't bullshit me. We know you call him Agent Twenty-Nine."

"Right. Agent Twenty-Nine, LAJCC. So go talk to Leon Lewis."

"We did. Typical lawyer, typical Jew. Gave me the runaround. Says he hasn't heard anything. Says Cusack's going back to Boston."

"So call Boston."

"I would, but Cusack's in the Midwest, leavin' bodies everywhere." O'Hara sat on the edge of Carter's desk, uninvited. "You got this morning's victim, the Commie's daughter. You got Kessler, last seen in a car with Cusack on Monday night. And there's that screenwriter who filed a complaint after Cusack beat the shit out of him in Musso and Frank's . . . with John Wayne as a witness. Cusack's a very volatile guy, Frank."

"You want him because he helped put you back on the street."

"I want him because he's a fuckin' Nazi," said O'Hara.

"He never took payoffs from the Bund, Bobby. You did."

"He's a Nazi. He even likes to talk with a funny German accent. That's what the secretary at Warner Brothers says. And she was there when he smacked her boyfriend around at Musso's. I'm tellin' you, Frank, the guy's bad news . . . and gettin' worse."

Carter just laughed. "He works for the Jews, and the Jews work for us."

O'Hara waved that off. "The Jews are a pain in the ass, too, thinkin' they can do our work, makin' us look bad, rattin' us out. Who told them to be spies, anyway?"

"I sometimes wonder, Bobby, who do you hate more? Jews or Nazis?"

O'Hara grinned. "I don't hate anyone. But accordin' to my guy in K.C.—"

"You have a *guy* in K.C.?"

"I have guys everywhere. And they'd all love to collar some Hollywood smartass on a killin' spree. You feds may go struttin' around, stickin' your noses wherever you want, but we got jurisdictions, Frank, and Cusack has fled mine."

Carter asked, "How did the girl die?"

"Strangled. Like a pro."

That got Carter's attention. Another strangling. Like the Sanchez woman?

O'Hara said, "C'mon, Frank. Help me out here. I make some calls, you make some calls, we run this guy down and both look good."

Dick Hood stalked up to Carter's desk and dropped a folder. "Today's Krauts." Hood turned to O'Hara. "And you, get your fat ass off that desk. It's federal property."

O'Hara stood and saluted. "Yes, sir."

"What the hell are you doing in here, anyway, annoying my agents?" asked Hood. "The LAPD is supposed to be helping us, not getting in the way."

"The uniforms are downstairs. The paddy wagons are ready." O'Hara headed for the door. "But I have murderers to catch, whether the FBI helps or not."

Hood said to Carter, "Murderers?"

"He's after one of our informers," said Carter.

Hood shook his head. "I never did like that guy."

Carter followed Hood back to his office. "About our missing shooter—"

Hood put up his hands. "I'm not hearing it, Frank. You don't have a suspect. You don't have a crime. You don't have a *potential* crime. All you have is a cartridge."

"I have four murders in L.A., and maybe one more on the Super Chief."

That seemed to surprise Hood. "The Super Chief?"

"That's why O'Hara was here. Somebody killed that Sally Drake. They found her body when the train got to Chicago."

"Sally Drake, the Commie's daughter . . . and one of our informers?"

Frank Carter began to formulate a story that might get him more time to investigate. He hated to hang Kevin Cusack out to dry, but he'd do it if he had to, then reel him in when he could. "Our guy fled the jurisdiction Friday night, when the LAPD wanted to talk to him about killing Kessler. I think Kessler knew the guy with the Mauser C96, so maybe our informer did, too, so—"

"But you say he's in Chicago. Let Chicago handle it." Hood pointed to the door. "Two interviews in Burbank, two in North Hollywood. Get going."

Carter knew that arguing was useless. So he went back to his desk, called Stella, and asked her what she was doing.

"Looking at the movie listings. Have you seen *The Maltese Falcon*?"

"In the flesh. And let me tell you, Sam Spade ain't so tough."

"Want to see it this afternoon?"

"Maybe tonight. But in the meantime—"

"You want me to do more of the work that Dick Hood won't let you do?"

"A lot more." He filled her in on what he knew about the murder on the Super Chief. "The Jeffries sisters said Harold King had Santa Fe train schedules. Go down to Union Station. See if you can get a list of passengers on that train."

"What's in it for me?"

"El Cholo at seven. Then we'll go up to the Wiltern and see if Bogie's any tougher on the screen than he is in real life."

She said, "It's a deal."

He hung up and shouted, "McDonald! Let's roll."

A moment after he left, the phone on his desk rang.

Agent Dickie Doane answered. He refused the charges. But he left a note on Carter's desk: "Collect call from Sam Spade."

KEVIN CUSACK HUNG UP. Then he used the same nickel to call Leon Lewis again.

Lewis had two addresses: a lawyer who'd help Kevin turn himself in and a driver who'd help him get out of town. "I suggest you call the lawyer. But you can trust the other guy, too."

Kevin said, "I'll let you know. I need to think."

"Think hard."

Kevin hung up and sat in silence, thinking as hard as he could. And the heat in the booth started him sweating. In Hollywood, they called it "flop sweat," the salt river that soaked you when you knew you were about to blow it, whatever *it* was. He feared that whatever he did, he'd be blowing it. But he had to do more than hide in a phone booth. So he stepped out, right into the path of two more cops. He turned the other way and saw a scruffy newsboy coming toward him, hawking papers. "Extra! Extra! Dragnet in K.C.! Hollywood Nazi wanted for murder!"

Hollywood Nazi. Good God. He already had a nickname. When the press gave you a nickname, you were all but convicted. He started walking, eyes front, chin up. He didn't even glance at the hot-off-the-presses headline, but it helped him to make up his mind. He wasn't turning himself in.

Of course, a guy walking around Kansas City in December would look damn suspicious without an overcoat. So he headed back to the lunch counter. He remembered a wall of coats hanging on pegs. He saw a tweed that might fit. He strode in like he owned it, grabbed it along with a hat, and never looked back. He just aimed for the exit, jumped into the first cab he saw, and gave the driver an address.

"That's in the stockyard, Mac. You sure you want to go down there?"

"Just drive."

THIRTY-FIVE MILES SOUTH OF Chicago, the Ford sped across the snowy fields of Crete, Illinois. The white landscape had faded to cold blue. The December dark was coming fast.

And Vivian had said almost nothing. She figured if Harold wanted her to speak, he'd start a conversation. But the only chitchat came from the son, who commented now and again about the traffic or the roads or some pretty view of Lake Michigan. She could see his eyes in the rearview mirror, flicking in her direction whenever he thought she might be looking the other way. He gave her the willies. So did his father.

Martin Browning was worried, too. Max Diebold was a veteran of the Great War who'd migrated to America with all his prejudices intact, and he disapproved of Vivian. The dirty looks, the cold comments on the sidewalk, the colder silence in the car . . . those said it all.

Now the car was pulling off the road and bumping up a long, rutted driveway. The house and outbuildings sat on three flat acres rimmed with skeletal trees. Beyond the trees, fallow fields rolled toward faraway clusters of buildings, shadows in the dusk, lights twinkling as feebly as distant stars. Around here, neighbors were measured in miles.

Martin was planning to drive to Washington. It would take three or four days but it would be the safest way to get there. He wanted to leave soon and leave the suspicious Diebolds behind. But a light snow was sputtering down, just enough to make the roads slick. So he decided to wait until morning and start fresh.

Eric opened the car door and said to Vivian, "Welcome to our humble abode."

Vivian stepped out and looked up into the first snowfall she'd seen in four years. It made her shiver. Maybe going home wasn't such a good idea after all.

A '37 MACK E series box truck headed east into the darkness on Route 50. The cab was blue, the container a shade lighter. The gold lettering on the box read, KRAMER & SONS, KOSHER MEATS, KANSAS CITY, MISSOURI, and beneath that was a white Star of David.

Kevin Cusack hulked down in his stolen overcoat, turned up the collar, and listened to Dilly Kramer.

"Listen" was the operative term. Kevin couldn't get a word in. Not that he wanted to. He didn't have much to say. And Dilly was a guy who liked to talk. He seemed to have an opinion for every decoration on his scally cap, which was covered in political campaign buttons, baseball pins, advertising buttons, so many that a strong magnet could pull that hat right off his head. Dilly had been talking for an hour, with seven hours more to talk before they got to St. Louis.

"Yes, sir, any friend of Leon Lewis is a friend of mine," Dilly was saying. "I knew him in the war. I guess you could call it the first war, now that we got another one." Dilly laughed. He had big hands and big features and a big laugh. And that was all Kevin wanted to know about him, especially since Dilly didn't know anything about Kevin except that he came from Hollywood. He didn't even know Kevin's real name. "Tom Follen" was the pseudonym that Leon Lewis had suggested. "Anyway, we kept in touch afterward. I sure envied him when he left for California. I said, 'What? You goin' off to eat oranges and date tomatoes?'"

"Tomatoes?" said Kevin.

"Dolls. Broads. Dames. Chicks. Say, is it true them Hollywood gals'll give you a blow job for an acting job?"

"I wouldn't know."

"What? Good-lookin' guy like you?"

"I was a story analyst. That's lower than a writer."

"Writers are low? Ain't they the ones who dream everything up?"

"There's an old joke in Hollywood: How do you tell if a starlet's too stupid to memorize her lines?"

"How?"

"She sleeps with the writer."

Dilly laughed. He got it.

"So now," said Kevin, "I just want to go home. Home to Boston."

"You want to leave all that good weather for Boston?" Dilly shook his head.

"There's more to life than good weather."

Dilly snorted. "That's what my father said after the war. I wanted to go to California, too, but he said, 'If you go, who'll take over the business? Stay here and help. You can do the drivin' and your brother'—I got a brother who's a rabbi—"

"*Mazel tov,*" said Kevin.

"Hey, you know the lingo?"

"Irish name but a Jewish grandfather."

"Well, *mazel tov* to you, too." Dilly chuckled and got on with his story. "So, my father says, 'You can do the drivin' and your brother can do the butcherin', while I make the best damn dill pickles in Kansas City.' He knew I like dill pickles. That's how I got my nickname. You know, *Dilly.*"

The truck hit a hole and the sides of beef thumped and rumbled on their hangers.

"So here I am, drivin' kosher meat across the Midwest. Best decision I ever made, too. Married. Three kids. Respect in the community—"

Kevin looked ahead at the dark landscape. What better place for a Hollywood Nazi to hide than a kosher meat truck? But why did he feel more like a man hurtling into an abyss than a guy just trying to get home for Christmas?

A GUST OF WIND shook the Diebold farmhouse. Outside, the windmill rattled and the pump brought up water for the night. The snow was beginning to swirl. But the warmth in the kitchen made Vivian think of home. Three pots simmered and steamed and filled the air with the pungent, mouth-tingling aroma of vinegar marinade.

While his father scowled, Eric played the host, pouring glasses of Riesling all around and promising more comfort as soon as the stove warmed the front parlor.

Vivian noticed that the table in the dining room had been set for three. She said, "If you weren't expecting me—"

"We'll feed you," said Max Diebold.

Eric smoothed things with a grin. "We have plenty, Papa. Plenty for a pretty lady. As Mama used to say, always plenty in the Diebold house."

"Don't speak of your mother in the presence of strangers." Diebold turned and went out the back door.

So, thought Vivian, perhaps it was grief that made Mr. Diebold so grouchy.

Eric said, "Sorry about my father, but he has many emotions. And—why don't you go into the parlor. It should be warm there now."

Vivian said, "I'd rather stay in here and help out."

Eric grinned again. "You would? Oh, Mother always loved having pretty ladies in the kitchen. She said it made the work go more quickly."

Vivian said, "I'm thinking there's potatoes in one of those pots. And you know . . . I'm an excellent masher."

Eric gave a snicker. "They say I'm something of a masher myself."

Martin Browning didn't know much about the son, except that there was something "off" about him, too eager, too quick with the grin and the sniggering wisecrack, too obvious with the sneaky sidelong looks. His whole persona was undignified, not German at all. But the environment that he and his father had built was as German as could be. Everything spotless in the kitchen, the firewood neatly stacked by the stove, the dishes shining behind glass pantry doors.

Martin could have puzzled all night over the son, but he was more concerned about the father. From the way that Max was acting, he wondered if the Diebolds had been turned. Anything was possible, and part of his job was preparing for any possibility. So he stood by the window to watch what was happening outside. When a lantern flickered to life in the barn, he decided to investigate. He told Vivian he needed some air.

"It's freezing out," Vivian said, and then she added "dear" for good measure.

Martin turned up his collar. "I'll be just a minute."

Eric called after him, "Better not leave me alone with such a pretty lady."

Martin didn't take that seriously, and Vivian took her cue from her "husband."

Eric picked up a knife and sliced into a loaf of bread.

Vivian went closer to the stove and said, "So which of these pots has the potatoes?" She lifted one of the lids.

And a German authoritarian snapped to life in Eric Diebold. "Do not *touch*!"

Vivian stepped back, shocked at the sudden anger and the big knife Eric held at his hip, pointing at her, as though he considered using it.

Then he smiled. "I mean . . . if you take the lid off, you let out the steam."

"I'm so sorry," said Vivian.

"Don't be sorry. Just . . . just be pretty." Eric went back to slicing.

IN THE BARN, MARTIN Browning stepped quietly onto the rickety stairs and went up quietly, too, toward the faint light. In the far corner of the loft, in a

little makeshift compartment created by hay bales and rough boards, the slender shadow of Max Diebold was working a key connected to a shortwave radio.

Martin stepped out of the darkness. "What are you sending?"

"Information to our man in Maryland," said Max calmly. "You escape via
the Eastern Shore. A U-boat will be monitoring American radio broadcasts.
Once they hear that Roosevelt is dead, you have twenty-four hours to get to
the beach."

"And if I'm not there on Christmas night, between five and six, they will
leave."

"They will also leave if they see *two* people in your raft." Max moved a sheet
of paper that he had been working from.

Martin grabbed it and read: MB b-r-i-n-g-s g-i-r-l n-o-t p-a-r-t o-f p-l-
a-n a-d-v-i-s-e n-e-x-t e-i-g-h-t h-o-u-r-s. Beneath the letters, another line of
code. Martin read it aloud, then whispered, "Advise in the next eight hours . . .
of what?"

Max Diebold was clearly not afraid of Martin. He said, in the tired way that
a teacher talks to a dull student, "Advise of what to do with the girl."

VIVIAN HAD RETREATED TO the doorjamb between the kitchen and the
dining room, just to stay out of the way. She was making small talk to take the
edge off the tension. "So . . . on this farm, do you raise animals?"

"Oh, no," said Eric. "We raise flowers and vegetables, just as you've heard.
Diebold's Seeds, a famous brand. I would have thought you'd know about us."

"My husband probably told me, but"—Vivian tried a gesture she'd seen
from Dietrich, a little shrug—"I don't always listen to him."

Eric's eyes brightened. "Oh, you don't? Does that extend to fidelity?"

"What do you mean?"

"A wife was not part of the plan, and then you show up? My father is suspicious."

Vivian laughed nervously. "I'm no one to worry about. I'm an innocent."

"How innocent?" Eric put the knife on the counter, then came toward her.

Vivian folded her arms around her waist and stepped back.

Eric kept coming. "If I kiss you, will you cry out like an innocent? Or will
you allow the kiss, especially if I promise to tell no one that you are a whore
playing a role, an imposter interfering with our operation?"

IN THE BARN, MAX Diebold was saying, "Are you in love, Browning?"

"Don't ask stupid questions."

"You cannot endanger our other agents with a love affair. Leave her here.
Leave her to us. Your car is ready. Multiple plates and registrations, some with
your new name, some with another alias. Michael Milton, we're calling you.

Take the car and go. You're a lone wolf. You always have been. Operate that way."

"I operate as I see fit. I use those I need to use, including you."

Diebold turned away, as if he'd said enough. He began tapping again on the key.

Martin said, "Stop sending, Max."

"If you cannot leave the girl, you cannot—"

"I said stop sending." Martin unplugged the key.

Max Diebold pulled a pistol from under the codebook and pressed it against Martin's forehead. "I will do my duty to the Reich."

Martin Browning knew that Diebold was ruthless in his defense of Germany, and in the half second he had to decide what to do—

A scream cut through the night, a female scream . . . followed by a male cry and the sound of something crashing in the house.

Max Diebold's eyes shifted, but he still held the gun against Martin's forehead. He said, "You should never have left him alone with that girl."

Martin said, "He's *your* son."

They heard the back door slamming open, Eric calling into the wind for his father.

Max Diebold went hurtling down the steps, with Martin close behind.

Eric Diebold was stumbling out of the house, hands on the hilt of a knife buried in his side. He dropped to his knees in the snow. The wind gusted, and he fell on his face.

Max Diebold ran to his son, rolled him over, touched the hilt of the knife.

Eric screamed, "No. Don't pull it out."

Vivian's shadow appeared in the doorway, her hands braced against the doorjambs.

Max glared at Martin. "The knife is in his liver. He needs a doctor or he'll die."

Vivian took two or three steps into the swirling snow. She tried to speak. But she couldn't get her lips to move and fell back into the house.

Martin knelt and looked into Eric's eyes, which were searching above him, blinking and fluttering in the falling snow. The knife must have struck a major vessel, because he moaned every time his heart beat more blood into his belly.

Max said, "She did this. She stabbed my son. She cannot—"

But Martin had already made another decision. Until he'd seen Max at the telegraph key, he'd never expected it to come to this. But he knew what he had to do to protect the mission . . . and Vivian.

Max Diebold surely did not see the blade in Martin Browning's hand. He may have felt it drive into his throat, just above the Adam's apple, through the sinuses, and into the brain. He may have known that it was a killing blow. But then he knew nothing.

Martin let the body drop onto the son, then covered Eric's eyes with his hand, ignored Eric's blood-strangled cry of "Nooooo," and cut off whatever was left of the young man's life.

IN THE KITCHEN, VIVIAN was sitting at the table, staring at the floor, at the spilled potatoes, at the blood mixed with the potato water.

Martin said her name.

She said, "I told him to stop. But he pinched . . . he pinched my nipples. It hurt. But he wouldn't stop. He called me a whore interfering with your operation and—what did he mean by all that?"

"I don't know."

"I jumped back. He grabbed the knife and came at me again. He said he needed to test my . . . my commitment. I thought he was going to hurt me even more, so I threw the boiling potatoes at him. He stumbled back and slipped and somehow fell on the knife. Is he—"

"He'll be fine. His father has taken him to the doctor."

"They drove off? I didn't hear the car—"

"Let's not worry about them. Worry for you." He took a bottle of Veronal from his pocket and dropped two tablets into her wineglass.

"What is that?" she asked.

"It will help you to sleep."

At first she resisted, but he held the glass to her lips. "You need your rest. Please." And she drank. Then Martin got about the business of cleaning up.

MEXICAN FOOD WAS ONE of the things Frank Carter liked most about L.A., and El Cholo was the place to get it. Chili that burned your lips and warmed your belly. Enchiladas, tostadas, and the best green-corn tamales north of Jalisco.

Stella was waiting for him in a booth. "Glad you finally made it. The mariachis keep coming over and playing sad songs, like I've been stood up or something."

Carter picked up the beer on his placemat. "I'd never stand up a girl who's already ordered me a Dos Equis."

"Not if you know what's good for you." She opened her notebook. "I also got you some info. There was no Harold King on the Super Chief. The only Harold, 'Mr. Harold Kellogg,' as in 'Mr. and Mrs.' A note on the manifest said, 'Might board in Barstow.'"

Carter dipped a corn chip in the red salsa. "What about Cusack?"

"The manifest says 'Sally Drake plus one.'"

"Cusack was the 'plus one.'" Carter ate the chip.

"So where is Cusack now?" she asked.

"Somewhere on the snowy prairie." Carter showed her a slip of paper that Agent Dickie Doane had left on his desk. "He tried to call me collect, using the name 'Sam Spade.' I suspect he's scared shitless. They're calling him a Nazi spy in the papers."

"Nazi spy?"

"The police report quotes a statement from this Kellogg guy, tying Kevin to the Bund. But Kellogg and his wife got off the train before they could be questioned. They were rushing for the Lake Shore Limited, or so they said. The porter let them go. When Santa Fe found out that they tipped the porter a hundred and sixty bucks, they let *him* go."

"Maybe someone should meet that Lake Shore Limited in New York tomorrow."

The food arrived. Chile rellenos for her. Tamales for him.

"Enough shop talk." Stella looked at her watch. "We can still make the nine o'clock showing of *The Maltese Falcon*, the stuff that dreams are made of."

"I can think of something else dreams are made of . . . more fun than the movie."

MONDAY, DECEMBER 15

KEVIN CUSACK HAD LEARNED a lot on the ride from Kansas City because Dilly Kramer could fast-talk like a Hollywood hustler or ruminate like a Harvard philosophy major . . . about anything that came into his head. And he never stopped. So Kevin now knew . . .

. . . that there were 352 kosher butchers in New York City and about the same number in the rest of America, which meant that Kramer & Sons took up the slack, delivering to a wide area otherwise underserved.

. . . that there'd never be a baseball season like 1941 again, with one player on a fifty-six-game hitting streak (Joe DiMaggio) and another batting .406 (Ted Williams).

. . . that *Citizen Kane* was an okay movie, but Orson Welles was a show-off.

. . . that Hitler didn't read history, or he'd have known that Napoleon marched into Russia with six hundred thousand men in the summer of 1812 and left with twenty thousand the following winter.

. . . that somewhere on snowy Route 50, it was easy to fall asleep, even if you were a fugitive from justice.

When Kevin awoke, they were backed up to a loading dock in St. Louis. The sky to the east was brightening, and something cold was pressing against his neck. It was a knife. Then he smelled coffee on the hot breath of Dilly Kramer:

"You know what I do for a livin', right?"

"You drive trucks."

"I also sharpen knives for the rabbi." He moved his hand so that Kevin could feel the razor edge. "I can cut your throat or trim your foreskin with two flicks. Now, who are you?"

"I told you, my name is Tom Follen."

"Well, Mr. Tom Follen, the radio says a guy who looks a lot like you is on the lam. His name's Kevin Cusack. They're callin' him the Hollywood Nazi, armed and dangerous."

"Framed and frightened is more like it," said Kevin.

With his left hand, Dilly fished Kevin's pockets. First he pulled out the red tie. "Yeah, they said the guy was wearin' one of these." Then he found Kevin's wallet. Inside was Kevin's California driver's license. "You're him."

"Lewis said I could trust you to get me closer to home."

"They'll arrest you in Boston, too."

"At least they'll be Boston cops. My Irish grandfather buys half of them beers in Doyle's. The other half get free movie tickets from my Jewish grandfather."

"Did you kill that broad on the train?" Dilly pressed the knife a little harder.

"No. But I'd like to kill the guy who did. Or get the FBI after him."

"FBI? Don't bullshit a bullshitter."

Kevin knew how that sounded. He said, "Listen, you can't keep that knife on my neck all day, and I don't want to get you into trouble. Let me get out here and—"

Dilly took the knife away. "Nah. You're a good listener. And Leon Lewis asked me to take care of you. Next stop, Cincinnati. I might even let you drive. But I ain't takin' you to Boston. Lexington, Kentucky's as far as I go."

Kevin said, "I'll take what I can get."

"Now, reach behind my seat. There's some clothes might fit. A denim shirt, jeans. Put 'em on. You ought to look like a workin' man, not some Hollywood pantywaist."

FOUR INCHES OF SNOW covered a multitude of sins. Martin Browning had cleaned the blood from the kitchen. He'd burned all the codebooks. He'd dumped the bodies and the shortwave radio down the well. Eventually they'd be missed . . . by someone. But he'd be long gone. And he was wondering again if he should go alone. Instead of two dead bodies, what if the police found three? A German father and son . . . and a failed Hollywood actress? That would befuddle them for a week.

Maybe Max Diebold had been right. Maybe bringing her along had been a mistake. It had certainly been out of character. Martin put on his gloves, then took the knife he'd pulled from Eric's liver, and considered using it on Vivian.

He stepped into the parlor and looked at her, sleeping on the sofa, close by the woodstove. Her head was turned, offering her white neck. She wouldn't feel a thing. He took a step. But then she stirred, and he stepped back into the kitchen.

She raised her head, rubbed her eyes, looked around.

Again he came toward her . . . this time with a mug of coffee. "Time to leave."

"Where . . . where are the Diebolds?" she asked.

"They didn't come back. They must've admitted Eric to the hospital."

"Will I get into trouble?"

"Eric slipped and fell on the knife. A kitchen accident. That's what they'll tell the doctors." He put a hand under her arm and helped get her to her feet. "Now freshen up. Then let me take you home." Something had kept him from using that knife. He hated to call it love. It was such a dangerous emotion.

GERMAN AGENT HELEN STAUER stood by a pay phone at Atlantic Avenue in Brooklyn. She was waiting for the 10:12 A.M. call. If the phone rang, she would answer it. If not, she would buy a paper and leave.

The snow that had fallen overnight in the Midwest would reach New York by afternoon, but the morning was bright, and the sun reflecting off the buildings gave the illusion of warmth. So she angled her face to catch the heat and waited.

At the appointed time, the phone rang. She picked it up and said, "Is John there?"

The voice on the other end was male. She'd never met him. She didn't know what he looked like or where he lived, although she guessed somewhere on the Eastern Shore of Maryland. And his name was not John.

Without introduction, he said, "There's a woman with him."

"Not part of the plan. Where is he now?"

"He should be driving east. There was a murder on the train. Authorities are looking for someone named Cusack. But it sounds like our man's work."

"He sounds dangerous," she said. "Or sloppy. Or efficient."

"Or all three. And Diebold has gone silent. Our man may have killed him."

Helen Stauer would file that bit of information. "Anything else?"

Click.

FRANK CARTER AWOKE IN Stella Madden's bed. She lived well for a private detective. The St. Germaine on Serrano at Ninth was a lot better than the Ansonia. A nice neighborhood, a doorman, no bums on the sidewalk . . . and right from her bed, he could see the famous white sign that real estate developers had put up in 1923 to promote "Hollywoodland" in letters fifty feet tall. The "H" had fallen over. Someday, the whole thing would disappear.

He smelled coffee . . . and bacon. It reminded him of mornings with Mom in the kitchen and little sis listening to the radio. Dad had disappeared in '33—confidence ruined, manhood in tatters, another Depression father who just up and left. The Carters lost their house and moved to a tiny Queens apartment, all because there were no guardrails on an economy that crashed and took everyone with it. Frank didn't have money for college, so he did two years in the army, then . . .

. . . those memories flashed and disappeared, because Stella was bringing him coffee. And all she was wearing was a silk bathrobe. She sat on the edge of the bed and gave him a mug. "Up and at 'em, tiger. There's phone calls to make and Nazis to catch."

"I made the call. You were sleeping." He sipped the coffee and looked around. "Nice digs you got, especially in the daylight."

"Daddy bought L.A. real estate when it was cheap. So I live well. But I hate being bored. So I detect things. . . . Now, about the Lake Shore Limited. What if the Kelloggs aren't on it?"

"We backtrack to Barstow. Do you know anyone up there?"

"A private dick named Sam Holly. Calls himself the High Desert Hounds-tooth. Spends a lot of time watching the hotels and the train station. Barstow's a good spot for a guy to jump the outbound to nowhere."

"We might have to visit this Sam Holly."

"Not today. I'm testifying in a divorce case. Due in court all day and maybe all week, depending on how pissy the lawyers get. I'll give Sam a call."

Vivian watched the sun creep over the top of the east-running clouds. She was still woolly-headed from Veronal and shock. The coffee hadn't helped, nor the eggs she'd barely touched, nor a good face wash with hot water and a change into slacks and waitress flats. She'd simply gone through the motions. She'd tried not to look at the floor where Eric's blood had been, or at the place in the yard where Eric had fallen, or into the eyes of the man she didn't know, no matter how much she learned about him.

When the black '36 Ford Deluxe rolled out of the barn, she'd simply done as she was told and gotten in. She hadn't noticed the Ohio plates. Even if she had, she wouldn't have asked about them. She wasn't thinking straight enough.

For two hours they'd followed the Lincoln Highway across a prairie un-rolling as gray and flat as the clouds. He'd found a classical station to match her mood. But as the sun appeared, the landscape turned white and the light dazzled her from her torpor.

In the sudden clarity, she turned to him and said, "Who are you?"

He didn't take his eyes from the road. "What are you talking about?"

"Who are you? You seem so calm and steady, but everywhere you go, there's violence. At Griffith Park . . . on the train . . . back at that farmhouse."

"The girl on the train was traveling with a Nazi. That's what the radio says. He was probably violent. Such people are. He probably killed her."

She thought that over, then asked him again. "But who are you?"

He offered her a gentle laugh, like a paternal pat on the head.

She said, "That isn't even your real name, is it? Harold Kellogg?"

He kept smiling. "You must allow me some mystery, Vivian."

"And what did that Eric Diebold mean when he called me an 'imposter interfering with our operation'? What operation?"

Martin spun the radio dial to some swing station. "Chattanooga Choo Choo." The No. 1 hit got lots of play.

She reached over and turned down the radio.

That caused his anger to flare. Was she defying him? He couldn't brook defiance, but he should resist anger, so he turned his eyes to the road ahead and said, "Eric Diebold is a half-wit. I thought that was obvious."

"Then why did you leave me alone with him?"

"I thought he was a harmless half-wit."

"He isn't." She looked out at the frozen flat heartland, the source of America's strength, or so the writers said. It was a world as alien to her as the moon.

And they rode for a time in silence. Then, suddenly, he threw the wheel over and ran the car onto the shoulder, into the edge of a snowbank.

"Hey, what's the big idea?" she demanded.

"Get out. If you're not going to trust me, if you're going to look out the window and sulk when I tell you the truth, get out." He didn't mean it. He said it to control her.

But she shocked him *and* herself. She said, "Okay, Hitler, open the trunk and get my bags."

A few moments later, she was standing by the side of the Lincoln Highway, alone and shivering, watching the black Ford roll away.

No other cars crossed the landscape, not for five minutes, not for ten. The sun glared off the snow. The wind rattled the yellow corn stubble that poked through it. And she began to wonder if she'd made a mistake.

Then a flatbed truck appeared, heading east, drawing closer. She stuck out her thumb, and the truck skidded to a stop. The passenger door swung open.

The driver was wearing a barn coat and a wool cap with the earflaps turned down. He squinted at Vivian, then looked around as if he were expecting Orson Welles to pop out of a snowbank and announce that she was an alien starring in another broadcast of *War of the Worlds*. He said, "You . . . you lost, lady?"

She decided to play the Hollywood smartass. "Do I look lost?"

"I'd say you look about as lost as a two-year-old in a train station." The man put the truck in gear. "But if you want to keep standin' there—"

"No, wait." She picked up her bags and said she'd appreciate a ride. Then she saw a black Ford speeding back.

It cut to a stop right in front of her. Her "husband" popped out and said, "Get in."

She said, "I have a ride."

He came around and grabbed her bags and said, "Vivian, get in the car."

The Indiana man said, "That your husband, lady?"

She nodded.

"Well, don't let him hit you again, not in the face anyway."

Vivian thanked the driver and got into the Ford.

Martin Browning gave the man a big salesman's grin and said, "Women."

"Yep. Can't live with 'em, can't live without 'em."

As soon as Martin was back in the car, Vivian said, "Do you apologize?"

Martin Browning was not the sort for apologies, but Harold Kellogg was, so he pointed the car east, stepped on the gas, and said, "I'm sorry for leaving you. All right?"

So she pushed a little further. "Now, tell me about your operation."

"I told you, there is *no* operation. It was the fantasy of a half-wit."

"So why are you going to Washington?"

"Business. War business. Government business. Our work will help millions."

She said, "Not good enough, Harold."

He looked into the rearview mirror. The pickup was a few hundred yards behind. So he tamped down an impulse to snap the punching knife from his shoe and stab her in the neck. Instead he said, "Does the Department of Agriculture mean anything to you?"

"It's part of the government."

He nodded and said, "All right, then."

And they rode for a few minutes in silence except for Artie Shaw's clarinet on "Begin the Beguine."

He thought it was over; then she said, "All right then, *what*?"

"People like me are flocking to Washington," he said. "Airplane contractors to the Defense Department, bankers to Treasury, farmers to the Agriculture Department . . . we'll all have a part to play. I'll tell you more when I can."

That sounded canned, like something he'd heard someplace, and she'd heard it, too, but she couldn't place it, so she made an act of thinking it over and said, "Promise?"

"Promise."

And she turned up the radio, as if to say, *Promise accepted*. She was going to get home, no matter how. And she didn't want to be left at the side of the road again.

In response, the car sped up so suddenly that it knocked her back against the seat.

She said, "Harry, what are you doing?"

"Leaving your new protector behind. Sometimes a man may decide to play the knight in shining armor." He also didn't want anyone writing down that stolen license plate. He only had one more, from Indiana. He'd know when to use it.

After a few miles, she said, "I'm glad *you* did."

"Did what?"

"Decided to play my knight, even if your armor's a little dinged-up." All might not be forgiven or forgotten, but for a few days more, Vivian could play her role.

The report arrived at 10:39 a.m. Pacific time. "No Kellogg on Lake Shore Limited. None on passenger list or known to conductors. None answering public address."

Frank Carter tore the sheet off the teletype and brought it to Dick Hood's office. "I need to go to Barstow."

Hood glanced at the sheet and said, "I'd laugh but I'm too tired."

"The answer's in Barstow."

"Answer to what? How long it'll take for the wind to blow your hat off?"

"Answer to this." Carter pulled the cartridge from his pocket. "The guy who fired this is out there killing people. If he boarded the train in Barstow, maybe somebody saw him. Maybe he left his car there. Maybe the car can lead us to him."

"Maybe you should do what you're paid for." Hood gestured to folders on his desk. "Krauts. Interview and arrest as necessary. Maybe then we'll talk about Barstow."

Carter didn't even argue. He went back to his desk and called Stella. Instead, he got Bartholomew, her secretary, who didn't like Frank Carter. Bartholomew liked men but not in positions of authority. He liked them in other positions.

Carter enjoyed tweaking him. "Barty, baby, is Stella there?"

"Not today. Not tomorrow, either."

"Just give her a message: They weren't on the train. Time for her to call Barstow. And tell her I'll see her tonight."

"Oh, goody for her."

Smartass, thought Carter, but at least he gave as good as he got. Carter hung up and called to McDonald, "Let's go." But he wasn't out the door when Doane was shouting, "Collect call for Frank Carter. The guy says his name is Sam Spade."

Carter went to his desk, accepted the charges, and said, "Where the hell are you?"

"In a phone booth in a diner in Indiana. And I didn't kill her."

"I know. But somebody fingered you . . . *and* smeared you with the Nazi label."

"His name was Kellogg. Harry Kellogg. Find him."

Carter wrote the name down on his notepad, in all caps, and underlined it three times. "You *talked* with Kellogg?"

"For two goddamn days."

Carter wrote down: "Looked K. in eye." Then he said, "What about the wife. What was her name?"

"Vivian." In the Indiana diner, Kevin was looking through the door of the phone booth. Dilly was sitting at the counter reading the paper. The cook was sizzling up two grilled cheese sandwiches. The place was quiet, but for the Andrews Sisters on the juke.

Carter asked, "Why did he finger *you*?"

"Because *he* did it. He killed her and pinned it on me. The question is why."

"What did this guy look like?"

"Oh, Christ, I don't know . . . Sally thought he looked like Leslie Howard."

Carter wrote, "It's him."

Kevin was suddenly distracted. "Wait a minute."

Two state cops had just pulled into the parking lot on motorcycles. They dismounted and sauntered over to the big blue box truck displaying the Star of David.

At the counter, Dilly was trying to act casual while shooting glances out the window.

In the booth, Kevin put his back against the glass and said to Carter, "If I'm arrested, I'm giving the phone to you."

"Stay calm," said Carter. "Not sure you want to be arrested just yet."

"So get me some FBI cover."

Carter couldn't even get *himself* onto this case. How much harder to get an agent involved from some Midwest field office? But he didn't want Kevin to know that. So he said, "I have friends in high places. They might help you. But—"

"You owe me." Kevin watched the motorcycle cops inspecting the truck. He remembered something his IRA grandfather used to say: "Don't trust a cop, unless he's Irish, and if he's wearin' them puffy jodhpur pants, don't trust him even if he's from County Kildare."

Carter asked, "Did that Kellogg say where he was going?"

"No, but his wife talked about going home to Maryland."

Carter wrote: "Maryland. Not New York."

"The husband was too busy snookering me into talking about the Bund, right in the observation car, right in front of a witness. Now, it's on the radio and all over the papers."

"Yeah, and the LAPD slobbered it down, too."

"O'Hara?"

"He's hot on this one, Kevin. He wants your ass."

The cops came in and looked around. It was easy for them to pick out the

Jew, probably the only stranger in the joint. Kevin saw words exchanged. He couldn't tell if they were friendly or not. Then the cops sat down next to Dilly.

Carter said, "Talk to me, Kevin. What's in Indiana?"

"Route 50. It runs from Sacramento to Washington, D.C., then on to Maryland."

"Look, Kevin, before you do anything too crazy—"

"I gotta go. I'll call you same time tomorrow."

The cook had just put the two grilled cheeses down on the counter. The cops gestured to Kevin's plate, said something to Dilly, like, "Where's your partner?" Dilly was gesturing to the phone booth, waving for Kevin to come and get it.

Kevin hung up, stepped out, nodded to the police, and sat. He'd been starving twenty minutes earlier. But the sight of those jodhpurs and shiny boots killed his appetite.

Dilly said, "Tommy, meet my two pals, Muldoon and Healy. Indiana's finest. And fellas, Tommy's my new help."

One of the cops gave him a perfunctory wave. Kevin, a.k.a. Tommy Follen, waved back, then turned his attention to his sandwich.

Dilly winked. *Stay calm.* "Tommy, why don't you go out and grab those two briskets I got wrapped up in the back of the truck. A nice dinner for two nice officers."

Half an hour later, they were on the road again.

Dilly said, "Kosher brisket. Better than money when you have to grease your way across the great state of Indiana . . . or anyplace else."

AT 10:30 P.M. EASTERN time, Franklin Roosevelt broadcast a message to America. It was the 150th anniversary of the Bill of Rights, and he said that the date should not pass without a few words. It was why they were fighting, after all.

His voice came out of a radio in the St. Germaine in Los Angeles, where Frank Carter and Stella Madden were more interested in the pleasures of the flesh than in presidential speeches. After they finished, but before the president did, Stella called a number in Barstow: the Holly Detective Agency. And for the fifth time that day, there was no answer. Stella couldn't figure it. Even the poorest private dick had an answering service.

Roosevelt's voice also crackled in a motor court in Ohio, where a black '36 Ford Deluxe was parked in front of a little gimcrack cabin. Inside, two people occupied separate beds in a cold room. They'd told the proprietor that they were married. But they'd hung a sheet between the beds. The "husband," quoting Gable in *It Happened One Night*, had called it "the walls of Jericho." Neither of them slept well.

On Route 50, Roosevelt's voice resonated in the Kramer & Sons truck. While Dilly slept, Kevin Cusack drove and listened and watched the headlights bounce a hundred feet ahead. Though he wanted to go home, the lights were leading him on, and the way ahead was coming clear. He was going to Washington and then to Maryland. He owed it to Sally to see her father . . . and her female friend. He owed it to himself to find the Kelloggs and clear his name.

TUESDAY,
DECEMBER 16

TWO VEHICLES PLOWED EAST, one on the Lincoln Highway, the other on Route 50. The drivers didn't know that they were converging on the same place, the South Lawn of the White House, at the same time, on Christmas Eve. The only man who might put it all together was driving around Los Angeles, interviewing German schoolteachers and car mechanics and waiting for a small-time gumshoe in Barstow to answer his phone.

When Kevin called Carter that morning and told him his plan for Washington and Maryland, Carter told him to keep going. He told him he *needed* him to keep going, though he didn't explain why. He told him his friends in high places were all in Washington, and he had a hunch that Kellogg was heading there, too. He didn't add that if the "Hollywood Nazi" remained a murder suspect, the real killer might let his guard down. With a fake Nazi drawing attention, the real Nazi might get careless. And a careless Nazi might reveal himself.

Then Frank Carter might be able to stop him before he used that pistol, however he planned to use it.

And as darkness came early in the darkest month, the '36 Ford Deluxe and the Kramer's Kosher truck traveled deep into the night before their drivers stopped at last to rest.

WEDNESDAY, DECEMBER 17

ALONG A WIDE FRONT from Kentucky northeast into Pennsylvania, cold rain fell and froze everywhere. Roads became dark rivers of invisible ice, and ice played hell with the plans of milkmen, coal men, mailmen, even icemen. It slowed Martin Browning. And it slowed the man who had decided to find him.

Browning went shifting and slipping and skidding for hours before following a sand-and-salt truck right into Pittsburgh, where he booked two rooms in the William Penn Hotel. He told Vivian that if they had to lay over a day, at least they'd do it in style.

THREE HUNDRED AND EIGHTY miles southwest, Dilly pulled up at the Greyhound bus station in Lexington, Kentucky, set the brake, and offered his hand. "Sorry to see you go. All the way to Washington, eh?"

"Yeah, but not in a big blue truck with a Star of David on the side." Kevin shook Dilly's hand. "You've done me a huge favor, Dilly, a mitzvah, as my Jewish grandfather used to say."

Dilly looked up at the neon GREYHOUND on top of the building. "I don't guess there'll be any cops lookin' for you in Lexington, Kentucky, but be careful."

"Thanks." Kevin opened the door.

"Wait a minute." Dilly pulled a roll of cash from his pocket.

"Dilly, I can't—"

Dilly forced the money into Kevin's hand. "Just say I'm doin' it for Leon Lewis. Doin' it for a guy who's chasin' Nazis. Doin' it for the tribe. Now, give me your hat."

Kevin handed Dilly the fedora he'd stolen in Kansas City.

Dilly took off his cap. "Anybody lookin' for a Hollywood Nazi won't be lookin' for a guy wearin' a hat with a Kramer's Kosher pin."

Kevin put the cap on. "How do I look?"

"Like an Irish rabbi who voted for Roosevelt." Dilly tapped the Roosevelt pin on the side of the hat, as if to say goodbye to his favorite talisman.

Kevin said, "I'll mail it back to you."

Kevin watched Dilly drive away. Then he went into the station. No police checking travelers, no suspicious eyes, just a Negro couple waiting for connections and two sailors with seabags waiting for war.

The squinty guy behind the ticket counter wore a Greyhound vest with a name tag: BOBBY PEPPER. He gave Kevin the once-over. "Where to?"

"Washington, D.C."

"Off to see the president, are ya?" Bobby pointed to the Roosevelt button on the cap. "I was a Willkie man myself. But now we're at war, we're all in the same boat, eh?"

"A big damn boat," said Kevin. "So, how long to Washington."

"You got freezin' rain, so buses between here and Charleston ain't even runnin'. But I got one leavin' at two thirty for Bristol. Roads are better down Bristol way. Should get you to Charleston in time for the eight o'clock to Roanoke." Bobby Pepper worked his pencil through Lynchburg to Richmond, then looked up. "Mister, you should make Washington tomorrow night. But with the ice, I'll promise Friday morning."

"How far is it?"

"About five hundred miles."

"And it takes forty-eight hours? That's about ten miles an hour."

Bobby gave an even squintier squint. "You can always walk."

Kevin knew that he should be doing his best not to attract attention, so he made a joke. "Nah. My legs'd get tired. What do I owe you?"

"Eight dollars and ninety-seven cents."

Kevin counted out the money. He could feel Bobby giving him a closer look. He told himself to keep calm. If there was a picture of the Hollywood Nazi behind the counter, the cops would already be on the way.

But Bobby was studying Kevin's new cap. "I'd say you'll be there in plenty of time for the lightin' of the Christmas tree—"

"When's that?"

"Christmas Eve, of course. Right on the White House lawn. Carols . . . speeches . . . sure would like to see it, but I don't guess you fellers are interested."

"Us fellers?"

Bobby tapped the side of his head and pointed to Kevin's cap.

The Star of David on the Kramer's Kosher pin. Kevin's new identity was working. He grinned. "I might just go. Like you say, we're all in the same boat now."

"Well, if you go, don't wear that Jew button."

"I'll wear a holly sprig. And if I see FDR, I'll tell him hello from Bobby Pepper."

AFTER TWO DAYS OF phoning, Stella Madden finally got the High Desert Houndstooth. As soon as she hung up, she called Carter to fill him in:

Sam Holly had given his secretary time off because her brother had been killed on the *Arizona*. But even in wartime, business was business and men were always cheating on their wives or embezzling their bosses or disappearing because they just couldn't take it anymore. So Holly'd been working all week, covering his usual haunts—the train station, the restaurants, the motor-court hotels along Route 66.

One of his jobs—a contract with an L.A. agency—was to watch for a quiet guy and a good-looking blonde. On Thursday night, he was in the lobby of the Beacon, eyeballing the check-ins, when a couple showed up who fit the bill, even though they booked separate rooms. The next morning, he followed them, expecting they'd head for the train. Instead, they drove up into the hills.

"And get this," said Stella. "They went to a target range . . . with a pistol."

Frank Carter wrote "TARGET RANGE" on his notepad.

"*And* they were driving a green Dodge coupe, California plate 76 B 2344."

"So . . . the Burbank haberdasher who became a traveling salesman has a wife."

Stella went on: Holly saw them again that evening, when he was watching the station. The guy dropped the woman off and didn't come back for over an hour. She got pretty steamed waiting, so Holly gave her his card, on the principle that a lonely woman dumped in a train station might make a paying client.

"Did he get her name?" asked Carter.

"The hotel register didn't list her, only the husband, Harold Kellogg."

"Did he describe her?"

"He said she looked a little like Marlene Dietrich."

"Dietrich traveling with Leslie Howard," said Carter. "Good casting."

"Eventually the husband came back in a pickup truck from Gobel's Guns and Hardware. The Gobels are big America Firsters. And big trouble. The town bullies."

Holly said that the girl told Kellogg that if she was going to play the wife, he'd better start acting like a husband. He made nice with her, and they went into the Harvey House restaurant, all lovey-dovey. When they got on the Super Chief, Holly made his report to the L.A. agency. "Turns out they weren't even the couple he was supposed to watch."

"But I'm glad he did," said Carter. "We have to talk to these Gobels. We have to go up to that target range and look for shell casings."

"Holly can do it, but it'll cost."

"Is he reliable? Can he be trusted?"

"I trust him . . . if he's on the wagon."

"And if he's drinking?"

"Well, that's why he works in Barstow, not L.A."

THURSDAY,
DECEMBER 18

THE ICY GLOOM OF Wednesday gave way to cold clarity the next morning. Bright sun gleamed along the Lincoln Highway and the Greyhound bus routes of West Virginia. And for a few hours, the frozen rain on the trees and lamp-posts made the world shine like a sugar-coated confection in a bakery window.

Kevin Cusack didn't much care. Thirty-three degrees was too damn cold for any Californian, even one transplanted from Boston. Besides, he was too exhausted to care. He'd spent the night sleeping upright in the Lynchburg bus station, because he'd missed his connection to Roanoke. And he feared that he'd miss a few more before he got to where he was going.

When his bus was called in Lynchburg, he did one last thing before boarding: he phoned home. His father answered in Dorchester, Massachusetts, and Kevin started talking right away, talking quickly so the call couldn't be traced: "Don't believe a word you've heard, Pa. I'll be home when I'm in the clear." Then he hung up.

EAST OF PITTSBURGH, VIVIAN fiddled with the radio. She liked that he let her control the music. So she spent the morning looking for the best swing tunes. From time to time, she'd pass a classical station and leave it on. She knew he favored the longhairs, and she wanted to keep the peace. It wasn't hard. He was a good companion, quiet and calm behind the wheel, polite and decent to her at every stop along the way.

Riding into the glare of the low winter sun, she could almost forget the ugliness in the Diebold farmhouse or the murder on the train. But just west of Chambersburg, Pennsylvania, she dialed up a news report about the worldwide ugliness: the Japanese were moving in the Pacific, the Germans were digging in on the frozen Russian plain. She said, "It seems so far away, but—"

"But it isn't," he said. "The war is everywhere. Even here."

Then they heard this: "Kevin Cusack, known to authorities as the Hollywood Nazi, wanted for murder on the Super Chief, remains at large."

"So," he said, "they're still after him."

"Do you really think he's a Nazi?" she asked. "Did you call him a Nazi when you scrawled that thing for the Pullman porter?"

"I wrote that he knew a lot about the L.A. Bund. That's all."

"But . . . a Nazi who worked for Warner Brothers?"

"Let the authorities figure it out."

She hadn't asked him again about the "operation." She'd decided to do nothing to provoke him. The threat of violence he presented was never aimed at her. Desertion—being left on the side of the road again—was what she feared most.

And then, as if to change the subject, he asked about her house in Annapolis.

She talked about the kitchen. And the smells. And her mother. There were things about her mother that she'd tried to forget, things that she'd purposely left out, things that caused her trepidation to grow as she drew closer to home. She loved her mother, but she preferred to discuss her father and his boat.

Martin brightened at the mention of boats. He didn't tell her that if he was to escape across the Chesapeake, he'd need one. He asked, "What kind of boat?"

"A nice Chrysler, eight cylinders, sleek lines, prettiest oysterman on the bay. He bought it back in '29."

"Was he a rumrunner? Nobody was buying Chryslers in '29 unless they made good money. And the only way to make good money on the water was rum-running."

"Just drive." Vivian didn't want to talk any more about either parent.

He sensed it and changed the subject. "You know, we're driving into history."

She'd never much cared about history until she saw *Gone With the Wind*. But Martin Browning was a student of the Civil War, and the Lincoln Highway was following the route that the Confederates took to Gettysburg.

He studied the Civil War because it was one of the few wars that ended with an assassination. Plenty of wars had *begun* with them—from Roman times to 1914—and the names of the assassins were well-known. Historical and literary fame followed Brutus, "the noblest Roman of them all." Ignominy stained John Wilkes Booth. But if Booth had killed Lincoln *before* the bloodshed, so that the North let the South leave the Union in peace, what would historians have said? No man had ever committed assassination at the start of a war and thereby made himself an instrument for ending it. That was what Martin Browning hoped to do.

Killing the president who equipped the Russians and fed the British and was now preparing to turn America's industrial might fully to war? This would be an act of patriotism for Germany and an act of charity for humanity. Of course, Martin knew that Americans wouldn't stop fighting, whether Roosevelt was leading them or not. But if you cut the spider from the middle of the web, would the web not weaken and collapse?

He was driving up the long slope toward McPherson's Ridge as these ruminations spun in his head. On either side lay open fields and split-rail fences, and right at the crest, a statue: General John Buford, who decided to make a stand on the high ground and started the pivotal three-day battle. A single man redirecting the flow of history.

Martin Browning admired such men. He believed he was one himself. But he should have been looking at his temperature gauge instead, because directly under the gaze of General Buford, he blew a radiator hose.

Ten minutes later, he was elbow-deep in the engine.

Vivian, standing beside him with her arms folded against the cold, saw flashing blue lights. She said, "Here come the cops."

He said, "I'll do the talking."

"What if he asks for ID? For registration papers?" And for the first time, she noticed the plates on the Ford. "Ohio?"

"Cleveland, Ohio," he said. "Do you have a Social Security card?"

"Well, yeah, but—"

"Leave it to me. And call me Michael. The car is registered to Michael Milton."

The cop was out of the car and coming toward them. He was a young guy, fresh-faced, well armed, wearing a nice brown uniform and brown leather jacket.

Martin had considered ditching the car in Pittsburgh. If the bodies of the Diebolds had been found, the house would have been searched, and paperwork on a '36 Ford Deluxe might have been discovered. Police might have issued an APB. But there were so many black Fords on the roads, Martin had decided to keep driving.

Now he pulled on his calfskin gloves, then slid his hand into his pocket and made sure he could pull the blackjack quickly.

"Afternoon, folks," said the officer. "Radiator?"

"Radiator or water pump," said Martin.

"Could be the thermostat." The officer was friendly, used to dealing with tourists.

Martin kept smiling and glanced at Vivian, as if to say, *You smile, too.*

The officer gestured to the plates. "Ohio, eh? Where you headed?"

"I've always wanted to see Gettysburg," said Martin, "and—"

"—and I've always wanted to see Washington at Christmas," added Vivian, brightening into her "actress" face, smiling like a star. "We're going to see the president light the Christmas tree in Washington."

Martin's head snapped around. Why that? Christmas Eve, the National Christmas Tree, FDR? Well, it was in the papers. And it was a tradition.

The policeman leaned into the engine. "Gotta be a pressure buildup somewhere."

Martin slipped his hand into his pocket. What the officer said next would determine his fate . . . and perhaps Vivian's.

He said, "My brother runs the gas station in town. I'll call him. Get you folks to Washington in time to light that tree."

"We have to keep up our traditions, eh?" said Martin.

"Good for morale," said the officer. Then he asked for Martin's license and registration, took a quick look, handed them back. "Thank you, Mr. Milton."

As the cop walked back to his cruiser, Martin relaxed. He was glad that driver's licenses did not include pictures.

Vivian looked at him. "Michael Milton?"

"Just call me Mike."

FRANK CARTER ARRESTED FOUR Germans that day. Back in the office, another pile of names sat on his desk for Friday. He complained, but Hood just waved a hand. "You can have Saturday to go to Barstow."

"Saturday may be too late."

"J. Edgar gives me orders. I give them to you. I give you Saturday."

So Carter headed over to Stella's office in the 1900 block of Wilshire.

Bartholomew Bennett answered the door. He wore an impeccable double-breasted suit with a carnation in the lapel and a paisley pocket square.

Carter sniffed at the cologne in the air. "Oh, Barty, you smell so good."

Bartholomew pursed his lips. "We're just closing."

"Off to the Run, are you?" Carter was referring to the row of downtown hangouts where Los Angeles homosexuals met to socialize.

"If anyone really needs to know," said Barty, "I'll be at the Biltmore Bar."

"Don't show them your gun," said Carter. "You might frighten them."

"I'll just show them the barrel." Bartholomew patted his pocket square and the Beretta holstered beneath it. "Licensed in California."

"But the Beretta 418 is a lady's gun," said Carter.

From the inner office, Stella shouted, "I gave him that gun."

Barty shouted back, "Is this G-man really your new boyfriend?"

"Good *night*, Barty," said Stella.

"Gah." Barty slammed the door after him.

Stella was behind her desk, waiting for the phone to ring. She said to Carter, "Barty can hit a hummingbird at fifty yards with that gun. I carry the same model myself."

"You prove my point. A lady's gun." Carter dropped into a chair.

"Lay off, or I'll think you're a bully instead of a nice guy with a hard job."

His response was to offer her a cigarette. She poured two glasses of bourbon. And they waited for the call that Sam Holly had promised for five thirty.

It never came.

Around six, Stella called Holly. No answer.

They had another bourbon, waited another half hour. Then Stella said, "I told him I'd pay him him fifty bucks. The Sam Holly I know would take off his two-toned shoes and walk across the desert in his bare feet for fifty bucks. Tomorrow, I'm driving out there."

"I can't go," said Carter.

"I'll take Barty. Like I told you, he's a dead shot."

KEVIN HAD MISSED THE early bus to Washington. That meant he'd have to wait until the wee-hours milk run, which meant a stop in every Podunk town and Civil War skirmish site in the state of Virginia, which meant sleeping half the night in a sitting position on a bouncing bus and not arriving until morning, bleary-eyed and exhausted and probably confused as hell.

Then what? He didn't have much. Carter had told him to stay in the open. And Carter was his only friend, except for Leon Lewis.

Now that he'd been running for four days, it would be a lot harder to talk his way out of a murder charge, unless he could find the real murderer himself, because in a world where everyone was chasing Nazis and Japs, catching a fake Nazi might be better than catching no Nazi at all.

He took a seat in the waiting room next to an old man and his wife. The man glanced, then gave him a second look. Lots of people were giving him second looks lately. But it wasn't that they recognized the Hollywood Nazi beneath the three-day stubble. They were looking at the buttons on his cap, including that Star of David. A lot of these people had never seen a Jew before.

He nodded and smiled and silently thanked Dilly Kramer again.

Somebody'd left a Washington newspaper on the bench. He flipped through it until he came to this: "DC Man Suspended over Hollywood Nazi: Pullman Porter Stanley Smith worked the car where Sally Drake, daughter of a professor at The George Washington University, was killed. In Chicago, he allowed two witnesses to step off the train before police could question them. He was also found to be carrying a hundred and sixty dollars in cash, an enormous sum. 'Somebody overtipped him,' said railroad authorities, 'and he disobeyed orders. Disciplinary action has been taken.' Smith returned to the District yesterday."

Kevin decided that if he couldn't find the Kelloggs, he'd find Stanley Smith.

THE MECHANIC IN GETTYSBURG knew his stuff. So Martin Browning now knew that the Ford Motor Company had enlarged their water pumps in 1938 to improve the cooling systems. You could still get a pump for a '36 Deluxe, but you'd have to go to Harrisburg to get it . . . in the morning. Martin considered throwing some money around. Maybe an extra fifty if the service station could get the pump and put it in right away. But that might attract more attention that it was worth. Besides, he'd already told the cops that he'd come to enjoy the history.

So he and Vivian checked into the Gettysburg Hotel as Mr. and Mrs. Michael Milton. Then he hired a guide, who took them from McPherson's Ridge to Little Round Top to the Angle. Along the way, the guide made speeches about the bravery of men whose spirits would now inspire another generation of Americans, and Martin nodded with patriotic fervor, even though he knew that those men had probably been like soldiers in every war: scared to death one minute, fatalistically throwing their lives away the next.

And all afternoon, Martin worked on answers for Vivian's questions: Who was Michael Milton and why did he keep a car in the Deibold barn? By dinner, he had his lies lined up.

Gettysburg was quiet in the week before Christmas, in the first month of war, so the hotel dining room was only about a third full. Martin and Vivian both had the Thursday night special, pot roast and gravy, along with Yuengling beer, the brew of Pennsylvania.

Martin began by toasting to Vivian's quick thinking. "Lighting the National Christmas Tree . . . a genius touch." He knew she liked a compliment.

"I read about it in the paper," she said. "I'd love to see it."

"You'll be home by then. Home with your mother. Much better."

"Mom . . . I love her but she loves her late-afternoon highballs a little too much. The truth is, closer I get to home, the worse I feel."

He asked her, "Do you wish you stayed in Los Angeles?"

"When I'm there, I dream of home. When I'm almost home, I dream of the big, bright California sun."

"We always want what we don't have. It's the nature of existence."

She laughed. "Since we're talkin' about *existence*, does Michael Milton exist?"

"He's a fictional character. You know about them. You've played your share of them."

"Yeah, but I don't carry their driver's licenses."

He took another sip of beer. "Before the end of Prohibition, Diebold distributed whiskey across the Midwest. His agricultural supply trucks made good cover. But the syndicate liked their drivers to carry false IDs and registrations, just in case. . . ."

"So you were a rumrunner? Like my father?"

He knew that he'd hit the right note, presenting himself as a man who worked hard to make his way and sometimes coasted close to the edge of the law, like her father.

And he saw a bit more deeply into her. A young girl from a home of contradictions. When she was growing up, bootlegging was a good way to make a living, but afternoon drinking was a bad way for a mother to show her daughter her love.

His explanation worked. He put his hand on hers, and she opened her palm.

She leaned across the table and said, "So why are you really going to Washington?"

He pulled his hand back. "I hoped that by now, you'd trust me."

"I trust you," she said. "But you don't trust me. Otherwise you'd tell me something more than you have."

"Please, just trust me."

"You've been good to me. I guess that's enough." She slid her other hand across the table to his. "So, *Michael,* is tonight the night?"

"The night?"

"The night that Joshua fights the battle of Jericho."

"And the walls come tumbling down?"

And they did.

Vivian gave herself to him.

He accepted with pleasure and a sense of something more. He couldn't tell if it was love or guilt. But he promised her that after his work in Washington was done, he'd come back to her. He didn't tell her the truth, that on Christmas Eve, he'd be coming for her father's boat, not for her. He didn't even know if it was the truth anymore.

PART THREE

WASHINGTON, D.C.

FRIDAY,
DECEMBER 19

KEVIN CUSACK STEPPED OFF the bus at Greyhound's sleek new terminal on New York Avenue. He was scruffed and smelly, but he knew that if he walked confidently toward some destination in the middle distance, there wasn't a cop in the country who'd pick him out as the Hollywood Nazi.

And from what he could see, there were cops everywhere, uniforms in the station and out on the sidewalk and probably a few cops hidden under overcoats and fedoras, too. But he blended into the crowd of government workers, then ducked into the first phone booth he saw and called L.A.

Frank Carter accepted the charges and congratulated himself that his man had made it all the way to Washington. "I expected to hear from you yesterday."

"I'm on the run, remember? Sometimes, not even Sam Spade can find a phone."

Carter was still going on the theory that the best way to flush Kellogg was to let him think he was in the clear. So, he'd used his L.A. newspaper contacts to plant stories that the G-men were looking for someone else. He didn't know if it was working, but if he was playing puppet master, at least he had Pinocchio on the line. He said, "You need to help me, Kevin. You need to stay on the run."

"What about your friends in high places?"

"Just keep moving. Keep looking."

Kevin knew that Carter wasn't above setting him up. Leon Lewis had warned him. Friendship only went so far with these government guys. "Why do I have to stay on the run?" he asked.

Carter said, "Well . . . because . . . I need you out there." It was all he had.

"All right," answered Kevin. "Be at your phone this time tomorrow."

"Where are you going?"

After a long pause, Kevin said, "Home for Christmas."

"But you can't."

"Not yet. So for now, I'll try the best hotel in Washington." *Click.*

VIVIAN AWOKE NEXT TO her "husband." She leaned on her elbow and watched him sleep.

He opened one eye and said, "Good morning."

She said, "I can get a train from Washington to Annapolis, you know. So take me to Washington. One more night before we say goodbye."

"I'm not saying goodbye." He almost believed it. "Get the guest room ready."

"Guest room?" She laughed. "In my parents' house? Don't make me laugh."

He put a finger to her lips, then kissed her. A kiss led to more. When they were done, he rolled over and stared at the ceiling.

"What are you thinking?" she asked.

"I'm thinking you're right." He had one night in Washington before the Stauers arrived. He could check into the Willard with Vivian, and they could stroll arm in arm around the White House grounds, just like any tourist couple.

AROUND 11:00 A.M. PACIFIC, Stella Madden drove through the sand-scoured outskirts of Barstow, California. She slowed as she passed the sign squeaking in the wind: GOBEL'S GUNS AND HARDWARE. Three tumbleweeds went rolling by, just like in the movies.

She said, "I don't see a Dodge coupe . . . or a pickup."

"All I see is hell . . . or purgatory," said Bartholomew Bennett.

"Save the melodrama. Read the map."

He directed her a half mile farther, to Rimrock Road, which led past more scrub lots, more sand, more bungalows leaning into the wind.

Stella pointed her Studebaker Champion at three spindly palm trees and pulled into the driveway next to them. A shingle on the front door of the little house read SAMUEL HOLLY, PRIVATE DETECTIVE, THE HIGH DESERT HOUNDS-TOOTH. The carport was empty.

"Forget purgatory." Barty looked around. "Hell. Definitely hell."

Stella knocked on the door, then peered in a window.

A neighbor lady tending her roses called over, "He ain't been home for two days."

Stella offered her card. "Did he say where he was going?"

"Always goin' somewhere." The lady was shaded under a sunhat that she'd put on a few decades too late, considering that her face looked like a worn baseball glove. "Could be anywhere in the high desert. That's why they call him—"

"—the High Desert Houndstooth. Yeah. I know."

Back in the car, Barty said, "God, I hate houndstooth."

"I think somebody else does, too," answered Stella.

"I mean the fabric," said Barty.

"I mean the guy," answered Stella. "The fifty I promised him would buy a lot around here. More houndstooth, another pair of two-tone shoes—"

"A one-way ticket out of town."

"Right." Stella threw the car in gear. "So let's go punch ours." She drove back to Gobel's and pulled up beside the squeaking sign.

Barty said, "How do you want to play this?"

"I go in alone . . . like I'm lost. You get out and stretch your legs, take a walk, check out that barn back there. Look for the green Dodge, plate number 76 B 2344."

"Bartholomew in a barn?" Barty tugged at his bow tie. "The things I do."

"If you see it, come in and say you've figured out how to get there. I'll ask for the Richfield Beacon Tavern. It's the big landmark around here."

"Why not ask for Sam Holly? That might get a rise out of them."

"Just act casual . . . and be smart."

"My dear, a man can't be casual *and* smart." Barty adjusted his pocket square. "He's either one or the other."

Stella stepped into the store. Two aisles divided by shelves . . . a wall of tools hung for display . . . a woodstove puffing away . . . a glass counter . . . an American flag, photos, long guns for sale.

Ma Gobel sat behind the counter, reading a magazine. The radio was tuned to some Western twang-and-wail station. A pint bottle was open on the counter. She said, "Afternoon, pretty lady. What can I do you for?"

"I'm a little lost."

"Ain't we all?" Ma put a cap on the bottle and put the bottle in her pocket.

Stella approached the counter. "Could you direct me to the Beacon Tavern?"

Ma raised the shade on the window behind her and pointed to the Richfield tower. "Just head thataway."

"Ah, yes, I see it now. Thanks."

"Nobody knows Barstow better than ol' Ma."

Stella turned, fumbled with a cigarette to buy time, then decided that getting a rise out of this old lady might be a good idea after all. So she asked, "Could you tell me where to find the office of Samuel Holly?"

"Sam Holly?" Ma's eyes narrowed down. "Just who exactly is askin'?"

Yes, thought Stella. They knew him. He'd been here. And not to buy a hammer.

The bell jangled, and Barty stuck his head in. "Oh, Stella darling—"

Ma gave Barty a scowl.

Barty came down the aisle on the right. "I figured out where we're going, dear." He jerked his head toward the side window. *Take a look at that.*

Stella saw the green Dodge coupe swing by the building, leaving a trail of dust. She tracked it right into the barn.

Ma Gobel followed Stella's gaze and said, "Lost, are you? Lookin' for Sam Holly, are you? Lookin' for my green Dodge coupe, too?"

Stella said, "Thank you, ma'am. We'll be going now."

Outside, Gobel's pickup truck was stopping, a door was slamming, a big guy in overalls was getting out.

Barty said, "Yes, honey. It's time for us to go."

"Yes, *honey*," said Ma, aping Barty. "What do you two think? I'm some kind of goddamn old drunk you can come in here and pump for information?"

Stella backed down the aisle.

"You *better* get goin', goddamn you," said Ma.

"Thank you, ma'am," said Stella, as if talking to an angry watchdog.

And her tone set off the old hag, whose hands dropped behind the counter and came up with a shotgun. "Thank you, my ass."

At the sight of the ugly double barrels, Barty cried, "Watch out!"

Stella hit the floor.

Barty came from the other side, clearing his Beretta at the same time.

Ma swung the gun toward him, and a double-barreled blast shook the shingles of Gobel's Guns and Hardware. A spray of buckshot smeared the room from one wall to the other. It tore Barty's chest open and knocked him back against a barrel of nails. It struck the tools hanging above Stella's head and sent pellets pinging everywhere.

A few even hit the big guy in overalls, who was bursting through the front door. He staggered, then lurched toward Stella.

She began to crawl backward. But she could hear Ma behind her, reloading and mumbling, "You lyin' bitch, you think you can come in here and spy on us? What are you? Some kind of Jew?" The spent shells hit the floor. "Lyin' and lookin' and askin' if we know the biggest snoop in Barstow. And gawkin' at our new car like we stole it or somethin' . . ." One shell clicked into the gun, then the other.

The big guy shouted, "What the hell is this, Ma?"

"This bitch is lookin' for Sam Holly, like we killed him."

The son grabbed a ball-peen hammer from the wall display.

The mother snapped the shotgun shut.

Stella wondered which would get her—buckshot or ball-peen? She rolled into a sitting position, looked up the aisle and down. To her right: son brandishing hammer. To her left: mother aiming shotgun.

The son said, "Don't shoot, Ma. You already hit me once."

Ma hesitated.

That gave Stella time to dig into her pocket and snap the pistol off her thigh.

The son raised his hammer.

He didn't see the gun, but Stella had an angle on him. So she shot him through the fabric of her skirt. Then she waited for Ma to blast her.

But a pistol shot cracked from the other aisle. A small-caliber hole appeared in the middle of Ma's forehead and she dropped like a sack of feed.

The son, staggered from the first shot, said "What the—" and looked toward the other aisle, toward Barty, who was bleeding into the floorboards but just alive enough to hit his target. This gave Stella the chance to pull her pistol clear, point, and fire again, right into the son's belly. He took the shot like a slap in the face, stumbled a bit, scowled, then lurched toward her.

She crab-walked backward, pushing frantically with her feet and hands, back and back, away from the hammer, back toward the glass counter. When she bumped against it and could go no farther, she raised the pistol and fired again and hit the big guy in the belly again, but he kept coming.

So she fired again, and the fourth shot stopped him. He raised the hammer but wobbled where he stood, as if the hammer suddenly was so heavy it was pulling him over backward. She put another shot into him, and he finally fell.

Then it was silent in Gobel's Guns and Hardware.

From the corner of her eye, Stella saw Barty, propped against the nail barrel, his hand holding his pistol, his head flopped to one side. Blood was seeping out of a dozen holes in his chest. The light was going out of his eyes.

Then a pair of two-tone shoes appeared beside her.

Sam Holly? She looked up . . . and saw another stranger. Another son?

This one was holding a tommy gun. He said, "Who the fuck are you?"

And that was all he said.

Barty had one more shot in him. . . . right between the eyes.

KEVIN CUSACK COUNTED HIS money. With the hundred that Dilly had given him, he had over three hundred dollars. So he picked the Mayflower Hotel on Connecticut, near Dupont Circle. Nobody would be expecting the Hollywood Nazi in that high-toned D.C. palace. But first, he went to Garfinckel's and bought some things—underwear, clean shirts, a shoulder bag to hold his new stuff and his dirty stuff, too.

He'd never shown identification in a hotel, but two weeks after Pearl Harbor, the deskmen were likely to be asking. Would they be looking for a guy named Kevin Cusack? He signed the register as Kevin *Carroll*, Boston, Massachusetts, scrawling the last name the way he usually scrawled his own.

The desk clerk looked at the register. "Very good, Mr. Ca . . . Ca . . ."

"Carroll." Like a lot of Boston Irish sons, Kevin had done construction work, so he had a union card. He flashed it to show the scrawled signature and the oversized "C" that he always wrote. Then he made up a story about coming for a special meeting of the International Laborers' and General Construction Workers' Union.

The clerk gave the card a quick look. "Mr. Carroll, yes. Room 812." Then he explained that Mr. Carroll shouldn't be surprised by the wartime measures in the hotel. There were air-raid sirens on every floor, lookouts on the roof, and the barbershop had been turned into a first-aid station, "So I'm afraid you'll have to shave in your room."

Kevin didn't care. He was happy to step into a quiet space that wasn't starting and stopping and jerking with every terrain change and gear shift.

First, he called the front desk and asked how long it would take to get a tweed sport coat and wool trousers sponged and pressed. *Overnight?* That would be fine.

Then he showered. For fifteen minutes, he let the hot water steam him and clean him and renew him.

Then he put on a hotel bathrobe and flopped onto the bed. He realized he was starving. A room-service burger and beer would be just the thing. So he reached for the phone, but after almost a week of sleeping upright in trucks and buses, he was as tired as a man could get. Before his hand reached the phone, it dropped and he fell dead asleep.

IN THE WILLARD, VIVIAN pulled back the sheer and looked out at Pennsylvania Avenue. Martin checked his watch: four twenty. The sun would set in half an hour. When it did, he wanted to be standing where he could study the light and see the terrain.

But Vivian said, "Let's order room service."

"Mrs. Milton, you are growing too fond of your luxuries."

She dropped onto the sofa and kicked off her shoes. It was a big hotel room, maybe the biggest she'd ever been in. "You've spoiled me."

He watched her lay back, tempting him, but he wanted her upright. So he handed her the waitress flats. "I need to stretch my legs after all that driving. A nice walk, then dinner in your favorite Washington restaurant. You name it."

She slipped on the flats and said, "Do you see these shoes? Women who wear shoes like this don't eat in fancy restaurants. So . . . *you* name it."

"I've heard of the Old Ebbitt Grill. We'll go there. But let's go . . . now."

Out of the hotel, they took a right on Pennsylvania, which ran into Fifteenth at the eastern edge of the Executive Area. Directly in front of them was the Treasury Building, columned and corniced like a Greek temple.

He turned her south on Fifteenth. At Treasury Place, a pair of soldiers stood in front of a little house that guarded the entrance to the president's grounds. Probably new since December 7, thought Martin. They kept walking with the evening traffic, down to E Street, which separated the South Lawn from the Ellipse, the fifty-acre open field between the White House and the Washington Monument.

He hoped to get onto the South Lawn on Christmas Eve. But for now, he'd settle for a look through the fence. When he heard the boom of the evening gun from Fort Myer, just across the river, he picked up his pace.

Vivian scrambled to keep up. "Say, what's the big hurry?"

"I've never seen the White House at dusk," he said. "I've heard it . . . it's—"

And there it was, tinted rose in the glow of the setting sun.

"—beautiful. Just beautiful."

The famous view reached across the South Lawn, past the fountain, all the way to the White House Portico. A small group had gathered on the sidewalk with cameras and appropriate awe. Even in wartime, or *especially* in wartime, this vision of American stability and continuity had a powerful resonance.

"So . . . so beautiful," he repeated.

She saw a strange look in his eye, as if he were seeing a majestic mountain. And there was something in his voice, too, an almost erotic excitement. She'd heard it the night before in the big double bed in the Gettysburg Hotel, when she'd rolled a leg over his waist and slid down onto him.

"How far away do you think it is?" she asked.

"Six hundred and seventy-five feet. Two hundred and twenty-five yards. Two hundred and five meters."

"You know exactly?"

"I could tell you in inches, I have dreamed of this sight so often."

Sometimes, she thought, he said strange things. She hooked her arm into his. "Well, we've seen it, and I'm starving. Let's go."

He told her he wanted to wait a while longer to watch the dark come down. So they did, another fifteen minutes, until the dusk was gone and the lights were twinkling in the mansion. Then the lights disappeared. Someone inside was pulling blackout curtains.

And Martin Browning knew he could make the shot.

Franklin Roosevelt was a dead man.

CHIEF AGENT DICK HOOD didn't argue. He even authorized a private flight from Burbank to Barstow. Around 4:00 P.M. Pacific, a local patrol car brought Frank Carter to Gobel's. The wind was still blowing. The dust was still swirling. The sign was still squeaking.

And Stella Madden was sitting in her car, staring into space.

At Carter's approach, she shook her head, as if to say, *Not yet*. No talk yet.

So Carter went inside. The bodies lay where they'd fallen. Highway Patrol detectives were working the scene. A camera flashed above the body of Ma Gobel.

The police chief—fifties, red-faced, shaken—glanced at Carter's FBI badge and shook his head. "I knew the Gobels were America Firsters, but *Nazis*?"

"The Nazi we're after was driving a green Dodge coupe," said Carter.

"It's in the barn. We ran the VIN." The chief looked at his notepad. "Registered to a Harold King of Glendale, California, legally signed over to the Gobels, who legally registered it this afternoon. Brought the car back from the DMV while Miss Madden and her assistant were here. I don't know what started the shootin', but—"

"They were looking for Sam Holly," said Carter.

"The High Desert Houndstooth." The chief motioned to Barty. "That poor bastard might still be alive if he knew we found Holly's car up in the hills . . . burned right down to the rims, with a blackened body behind the wheel, a *shoeless* blackened body."

"Shoeless?" asked Carter.

The chief pointed to the two-toned wingtips on the feet of Richard Gobel.

"What was Holly doing up in the hills?" asked Carter.

"Snooping at the Gobel target range, it looks like."

"Did you pick up any cartridges?"

"Nah. Folks been shootin' up there for so long, there's thousands of cartridges. But we did pick up some funny pottery." The captain took a piece from his pocket and handed it to Carter. "Looks like a Christmas angel with its head shot off."

"A Hummel," said Carter, almost to himself. "It's him."

"He made this shot from two hundred yards. Uphill."

"Jesus," said Carter.

"He got Jesus, too." The chief pulled another shard from his pocket, the face of a smiling baby, *the* smiling baby.

Another cop came from the inner office with a pile of papers. Carter flipped through them. The usual Bund stuff: mimeographed Nazi speeches, flyers, posters. *Hooray for Hitler. America First.* Guys in hoods marching beneath crosses and flags.

Carter asked, "Did you go through that Dodge coupe yet?"

"Nothing special. An owner's manual. A receipt for an oil change. An old road map with the edges singed, like somebody threw it into a fire or somethin', then thought better of it." The chief laid them out on the countertop.

Carter opened the map. One side showed the state of California with an insert of L.A. Pencil routes traced from Glendale to Deutsches Haus, to downtown Burbank, to the Murphy Ranch, and all the way to the Long Beach docks.

On the other side: a map of the entire country, and a pencil line traced along Route 66 through Barstow, Kingman, Amarillo, Winona, Flagstaff, then Gallup, New Mexico, Oklahoma City, and St. Louis, where the line broke off and followed Route 50 right into Washington.

So there it was. The Nazi bastard was going to Washington, and he forgot his map, or he tried to burn it, but somebody rescued it from the fire because maps cost money. Kevin Cusack's instinct had been true. Carter's hunch had been a winner.

Then Carter sensed Stella beside him.

She'd come in quietly and stood staring at Barty. Her eyes were empty, her voice flat. She said, "I want one thing, Frank. If you go after him, I go with you. If that Nazi bastard didn't stop here, Barty would be alive."

Carter showed her the map. "He drew us a picture. Washington, D.C."

"We can fly," she said. "Eighteen hours, three stops, three hundred bucks a person if you can get seats. If your boss won't pay, I will."

SATURDAY, DECEMBER 20

JUST BEFORE 8:00 A.M., the Stauers stepped from a taxicab in front of Penn Station, in New York.

Helen gazed up at the neoclassical majesty of the columned façade, then turned to admire the Empire State Building.

Her husband said, "I know what you're thinking. If we had transatlantic bombers, they could use that tower as their aiming point."

"We will do more damage on Christmas Eve than the whole Luftwaffe."

He leaned in for a kiss.

She put a finger up. "My lipstick."

"But you look ravishing in your Prussian-blue outfit, and—"

She tapped his lips with her fingertip. "After we kill him."

"Anticipation is half the pleasure."

They looked like holiday weekenders heading for the Congressional Limited. But Helen had packed a Mauser Karabiner 98k and a 4× Zeiss telescopic sight, model ZF39. The gun was forty-one inches long and barely fit in her oversized suitcase. In her purse, she carried a weapon that was just as lethal in her hands—a hypodermic syringe. Wilhelm wore his Walther P38 under his arm and a stiletto in a sheath at his wrist.

KEVIN CUSACK OPENED THE inner panel of his door in the Mayflower. His clothes were hanging, cleaned and covered in protective paper. Even in wartime, small services continued, small luxuries comforted, and small conveniences made life a little more civilized. He put on his wool trousers and starched white shirt and felt like himself.

He ordered room-service eggs and bacon with grits. Washington was a Southern city, so you always got grits. Then he went to work on the Washington phone book. The room didn't have a Maryland book, so Stanley Smith was his first target. But in a population of 650,000, there were a lot of Smiths. And what if the phone was in his mother's name? Did they even *have* a phone?

Beyond that, what could Stanley Smith offer that might lead Kevin toward Vivian Kellogg? Would she even want his help? Or did she already know that her husband was a murderer? And what else did she know?

Kevin counted five Stanley Smiths. After breakfast, he called them all. Two "not homes" and three who were definitely not Pullman porters.

Up next? His morning call to Los Angeles. But he wasn't giving away his refuge to phone-tapping feds just yet. He'd find a pay phone. And maybe, somewhere in his memory, he'd find the name of that market where Stanley took his mother on Saturdays.

MARTIN BROWNING AWOKE WHEN Vivian rolled out of bed. He watched her walk to the window and pull back the drape, letting the sunshine frame her blond hair and the curve of her hips. She was a vision, whether clothed and lipsticked at the Old Ebbitt Grill, or naked and innocent in the bright morning light.

The sight of her transported him, as he'd been transported on the day after Pearl Harbor, when Koppel's Lincoln-Zephyr reached the Pacific Coast Highway. And his thoughts were much the same: Who could know a moment like this and not believe that all man's troubles might be soothed, or even solved, by the sight of a beautiful ocean or a naked woman limned in sunshine? Who could hope for more in life, after all the wars were fought and all the battles won, than to awaken to this?

He didn't know if this was love, but it was more than lust, because his thoughts weren't purely sexual. Then she leaned forward, as if to look at something down in the street, and those thoughts spiraled quickly toward lust.

She looked over her shoulder. "You like what you see, don't you?"

The sheet across his midsection was rising.

She gave her bottom a twitch and said, "Do I look like an imposter?"

"An imposter?"

She turned and leaned against the sill. "An imposter interfering with your operation?" She asked it playfully, but she wasn't playing. And she'd broken the mood.

The sheet settled back. He could surrender to his anger or try to recover his lust. He swung his legs out of bed and went toward her, took her by the shoulders and kissed her and pressed against her. And in this, he wasn't lying.

She stood on her toes. He dropped his hands to her bottom and lifted. She gripped his neck. He carried her back to the bed, where he planted his feet and drove himself into her, hiding his anger beneath his lust, burying his anger inside her, but she felt only the lust and answered with her own.

After their breathing had settled, she said, "So the operation will go forward?"

He'd had many women, but never had he allowed himself to feel like this about any of them, nor allowed any of them to talk to him like this. "My operation will bring me back to you on Christmas Eve, Vivian. That's all you need to know."

"So there *is* an operation? And the Diebolds?"

He rolled off her. "I'm a broker for seed producers, including the Diebolds."

She knew nothing about brokering, nothing about the government's interest in seed production, but she knew what she'd felt when she got into that car in Chicago. "Why was Diebold angry to see me?"

"He's always angry. Angry when he nearly lost his business in the Depression. Angry that he had to work for bootleggers to keep it. Angry that he had to drive to Chicago to get us." Martin jumped up and went to the bathroom. "It's wartime, Vivian. People are angry. And you're making me angry. I have business with the secretary of agriculture. That is the 'operation.'"

"On a weekend?" she said.

"In wartime, there is no weekend." He turned on the shower. Then he grabbed a towel and wrapped it around his waist and came back into the bedroom.

She was sitting up with the covers pulled to her neck.

He sat on the edge of the bed. "I've brought you this far, haven't I?"

"It's been a bumpy ride, but yeah."

He gave her leg a squeeze. "So trust me awhile longer."

THE ATT OPERATOR ASKED if Agent Carter would accept charges from Sam Spade. A voice that wasn't Carter's said, "Yes."

"Go ahead, please," said the operator.

"This is Agent McDonald. Mr. Cusack?"

"Yes." Kevin was hunched in a phone booth in Union Station.

"Agent Carter's on his way to Washington. American Airlines. He'll be there at six o'clock tomorrow morning. He's booked into the Willard Hotel." McDonald's voice dropped to a whisper. "He says you're to lie low until he arrives."

Kevin remembered McDonald. He'd been on the raid at Deutsches Haus. But could he be trusted? Could Carter? Could anybody?

He said, "So the feds aren't looking for me? Are the D.C. police?"

"We've planted a few stories to throw them off. We'll try to protect you. I can't make any promises."

Kevin had seen the morning papers. They'd all run articles about the "Hollywood Nazi." None of them were on the front page. But they kept the story alive, quoting Carter: "We think he's heading for Boston. Train stations and bus stations from Providence to Portland are under surveillance." If Carter was orchestrating this, thought Kevin, what was he after?

But that wasn't what he asked. Instead, he said, "The Willard? On a government expense account?"

"Carter has a new girlfriend. She's paying."

"He's bringing his girlfriend?"

"Some guys get all the luck."

As soon as Kevin hung up, he thought of more questions: If Carter was coming with his girlfriend, was it an official FBI visit, or had he been canned? And if Carter was operating on his own hook, what did that mean for Kevin?

He peered through the door at the crowd of travelers. No one needed a telephone just then, so he stayed in the booth with the D.C. phone book and, more important, the books for Baltimore and Anne Arundel counties. He searched the name "Kellogg." But after twenty minutes of calling and coming up empty, he realized he could dig all day and find nothing. Instead, he had to find that Negro porter.

He stepped out of the booth just as a pair of police approached. *Act casual. Lean against the wall. Take the newspaper out of your pocket. Pretend to read. Hope they don't ask you why you're loitering.*

Of all the Union Stations he'd seen, Washington's was the most magnificent, a fitting crossroad of democracy, with an enormous barrel-vaulted ceiling and a mighty undercurrent of echoing sound. But even here, the cops were always on the lookout for shady characters around the phone banks . . . bookies, pimps, truck hijackers, and in this town, Republicans, too . . . or maybe Democrats.

But the cops went by with no more than a glance.

Kevin kept his nose in the paper a few minutes longer, just to be safe. He'd opened to the food advertisements. On one page was a logo: DGS, for District Grocery Stores, with the motto "The Owner Is Your Neighbor," and specials on Corby Cake, "Pure as Mother Made It," 59 cents, or Carnation Evaporated Milk, 10 cents. Then his eye tracked to the words "Shop the Eastern Market."

That was it. *That* was where Stanley Smith had said he shopped on Saturdays with Mom.

Ten minutes later, Kevin walked down Seventh Street to the huge redbrick market building that had served Washingtonians since 1873.

Not even Japan's march across the Pacific could dampen the spirits here on the weekend before Christmas. At one outdoor stall, they were selling wreaths and trees, at others handmade trinkets and toys. Salvation Army bells were ringing, and the shoppers, all coated and muffled in the chilly morning, pushed from one stall to the next.

Kevin "no, thanks"ed his way past hard-selling vendors, went by a bunch of guys warming their hands over a smoky barrel fire, and entered the main hall. The din rose with voices hawking oysters from the Chesapeake and home-cured bacon from Virginia and oranges and tangerines straight off the overnight train from Florida, male voices and female voices, and a choir singing Christmas carols, too.

It would be harder to find Stanley here than in the phone book, he thought, because half the shoppers were Negroes. A D.C. melting pot, it was. Still, Kevin walked the length of the hall, beneath shafts of sunshine slanting through the skylights, bought a cup of coffee, and took a seat at a table in the middle of the floor, from which he could view the whole concourse.

He'd wait an hour, then go for a walk, then come back for another hour. He had all day and didn't have a better idea. So he waited and wondered at how far he—and the country—had traveled from the blissfully ignorant world of Saturday, December 6. Back then, he still had hopes of writing a movie for Errol Flynn, of bedding Sally Drake, of living the high life in the California sun. Now, the nation was at war and he was a fugitive from justice. And that was just how fast life could change.

It was enough to make a guy feel sorry for himself, make him want to roll over and give up, which he was thinking of doing until he noticed an older Negro woman, heavyset, in an ankle-length overcoat, and a man who looked like her son, weighted down with shopping bags. . . .

They worked their way from one stall to the next. And by the time they got close, Kevin was certain. He'd found his Pullman porter. And he liked the solicitous way that Stanley helped his mother and pulled cash from his pocket whenever she asked. A man who treated his mother so well was a man to trust.

Then he heard the mother say, "How about a shrimp and oyster gumbo for supper?"

"That be just fine, Mama."

So Mama went to the seafood stall while her son stood in the middle of the floor and studied the chalkboard above the cheese vendor.

And Kevin said to Stanley's back, "I'd love some of that broiled Lake Superior whitefish they serve on the Super Chief."

Stanley's head whipped around.

Kevin peered from under the scally cap. "I had the whitefish last Saturday."

"You." Stanley lowered his voice. "I don't want nothin' to do with you."

Mrs. Smith came up behind her son. "Stanley, who you talkin' to?"

"Nobody, Mama."

Kevin popped up and removed his cap. "I've had the honor to ride in one of your son's cars. Just complimenting him on the fine job he does, ma'am."

"You're so right, sir," said Mama. "And ain't it nice? They like what he done so much, they give him the whole Christmas season off, right on up to New Year's."

Stanley looked at Kevin and his eyes said, *No, don't tell my mama anything.*

Mrs. Smith said, "Stanley, if we havin' gumbo, we need okra."

"Go buy it, Mama. I'll be right along." Then Stanley turned on Kevin. "There's eyes everywhere. People watchin' to see who I see. You the *last* person I want to see."

"I didn't kill her, Stanley."

"I don't care."

"When you saw me in the observation car on Sunday morning, I'd been there all night, drunk as a skunk. Drunk and stupid."

"Well, I ain't stupid, and that's what they been callin' me in the papers, sayin' how stupid I was to let that Kellogg off the train. I don't like it one bit. That wife said she was pregnant and had to get home to her dyin' mama on the Lake Shore Limited. Played me for a damn sucker."

"I don't think they ever took the Lake Shore, Stanley. I think they're in Maryland. And I need to find them. I think it was Kellogg who killed Sally Drake."

"Ain't no proof of that."

"Not yet, but ask yourself, would a decent man smack his wife hard enough to give her a shiner, especially if she was pregnant?"

"Men hittin' women all the time. Men screwin' women who ain't their wives all the time. Men screwin' women on trains all the time. If I worried about all of them, I couldn't do my job." Stanley looked over at the vegetable stand, where his mother was finishing up. "So get lost, mister."

Kevin wrote his name and hotel phone number on a corner of the newspaper and gave it to Stanley. "Help me find them, so we can both clear our names."

Stanley took the piece of paper. "I could be arrested just for *talkin'* to you."

"I didn't do it."

"Like I told you, I don't care." Stanley pivoted away.

Kevin stood with the crowd bustling around him like a stream swirling over his rock. And he wished again that it was December 6.

IF MARTIN BROWNING COULD have chosen a place *not* to escape to after shooting the president, it would've been Annapolis. Here in the nursery of the U.S. Navy, thirty-five miles east of Washington, the war felt very close. Young men were finishing their studies early. Security around the Academy was tight. Armed guards were everywhere. But for a man who did things against the grain, this might be the best place to hide.

Vivian directed Martin down Duke of Gloucester Street, across the little bridge that spanned Spa Creek and over to Eastport, a workingman's neighborhood of neat bungalows, close-built and modest. In one of them, on the corner of Chesapeake and Second, a cardboard Santa stood on a porch, waving: *Come on in. . . .*

Vivian said, "That's it. Pull over."

The weather had settled to a chilly gray, the kind of day that she always hated. And she hated being back, too. After three thousand miles of giving the performance of her life, her show was over, and she hated the empty feeling in her belly. She said, "I'll take it from here."

He said, "I'd like to meet your parents." He wanted them to know what a nice guy he was, so that when he showed up on Christmas Eve, an hour after Roosevelt was dead, they wouldn't suspect a thing.

They both got out, and Martin pulled her bags from the trunk.

The front door opened. A woman in her sixties stepped onto the porch, lit a cigarette, glanced at them, then looked more closely and said, "Kathy?"

"Hello, Mama."

Mary Schortmann stepped off the porch. She was tall like her daughter but wore a bib apron and another thirty pounds around her midsection. Her hairnet didn't quite hold her bun in place, and the holes on the sides of her shoes didn't hold her bunions. She came over to the fence and studied them, as if convincing herself that she wasn't seeing ghosts. Then she said, "Well, isn't this a nice surprise?"

"Merry Christmas, Mama."

"Oh, your dad'll be so happy." Mary Schortmann pushed open the little gate and after a moment, embraced her daughter.

For Vivian, the smell of her mother came rushing back, not the surface odors of food and Lucky Strikes and maybe a little afternoon nip, but something deeper, a sense more than a smell, of a small life lived in a small house with the shades pulled and the hopes dim, of a past wasted and a future invested in a pretty daughter whose beauty, like all beauty, was sure to flee. It took Vivian a moment to reach through all that and remember that no matter how happy she'd been to leave home, there really was comfort in coming back.

Then Mary Schortmann looked at Martin. "So Kathy, who's your friend?"

"Call me Vivian, Ma. It's my movie name. And this is Harold. He's come to Washington to see the secretary of agriculture."

"Is that a fact? My, my."

Then a leathery little guy in a flannel shirt and stretched blue cardigan poked his head out the door. "Mary, who's that?"

"Your daughter."

Les Schortmann all but leaped across the lawn and threw his arms around her. "I always knew you'd come back, baby."

"For Christmas, Dad. Just for Christmas."

"And a happy Christmas it'll be." Her father beamed at her, then offered his hand to the man behind her. "Who's your good-lookin' friend?"

She introduced him. "He has business in Washington. But he'll be back on Christmas Eve. Can he stay?"

"We'd be flattered," said Les, "flattered right out of our shoes."

Martin gave a big Harold Kellogg smile.

Vivian said, "Maybe you'll take him for a Christmas boat ride, Pa."

"Always gassed up and ready to go," said Les. "I still do a bit of crabbin' on the *Kathy S.*—that's her name—" The father shot a loving look at his daughter.

Martin kissed Vivian on the cheek—a gentleman would not kiss a girl on the lips in front of her parents—and he got back in the car.

They watched him drive off, and Les Schortmann said, "Seems like a fine young man, even if I don't see a wedding ring on your finger."

"Now, Pa—"

"Don't know what Johnny Beevers'll say, but"—the father made a wave with a pipe—"your ma and me, we wasn't married when I went off in '17, and . . . well . . ."

She hooked her arm into his and said, "It's great to be home."

BACK IN WASHINGTON, MARTIN Browning changed hotels and identities. The Hay-Adams was perfectly sited, with a view across Lafayette Square to the White House. The new identity was pulled from his collection of fake IDs. He was now Nigel Hawkins, of Hawkins Imports, London and New York. He put on his blue suit, then the overcoat with the special lining and the gun in place, so he could practice moving with a fully assembled Mauser C96 under his coat. Then he headed out to meet his team.

Nobody was waiting where Nineteenth and Connecticut came together like spokes in a wheel. So he took the crosswalk onto Dupont Circle. A curving bench surrounded the fountain in the center. Shoppers were hurrying with packages and bundles. Others sat in the fading afternoon light. And a street-corner choir sang Christmas carols. Martin recognized "Joy to the World." It sounded ironic and hopeful at the same time.

Then he noticed a woman sitting alone. She wore a Prussian-blue overcoat, matching hat, shoes. He said, in a British accent, "Merry Christmas."

She said, "Merry in Connecticut, too."

He came over and sat down. "Connecticut and Nineteenth."

The proper exchange, in the proper order.

She shifted her eyes toward a man—paunchy, slouched, brown raincoat, brown hat—now rounding the fountain from the other side.

Martin said, "I hope he's with you."

"My husband"—Helen Stauer stood—"scouting for American agents."

The man walked right past them and kept going.

Helen looked at the outline of the wooden shoulder stock beneath Martin's coat. "If one of them sees that, you could be arrested. Why are you carrying it?"

"To see if you'd notice. I think the better of you because you did."

"I have not decided what I will think of you." She didn't smile when she said it.

He sensed that she didn't smile often. But he found something both severe and attractive about Helen Stauer. The blue outfit suggested a sense of style. The black hair and red lipstick against the pale skin suggested she knew how to use her assets. And the way she turned on her heels suggested that she was German to the bottom of her soul.

They made no small talk. That was fine. Martin liked meeting someone who'd only talk when she had something to say, which didn't happen until they'd followed her husband to the old Cairo Hotel, one of the tallest buildings in town.

When they arrived in the suite on the twelfth floor, the husband was pouring Scotches. He wore a brown three-piece suit and a black knit tie. His vest emphasized his paunch. His baldness emphasized the soccer-ball circularity of his head. Had he existed in two dimensions, he would've looked like two circles balanced on two sticks. He surely didn't look dangerous. But the best agents never did.

"Welcome to our safe house," he said. "I am Wilhelm. My friends call me Will."

Helen gestured to a room on the right. "You sleep there. Where are your bags?"

Martin took the Scotch and looked around. If he had to be cooped up with other people, this wouldn't be bad. "Nice apartment."

"The German consul kept a mistress here," said Will. "When she left him—"

"What makes you think the FBI isn't watching right now?" Martin picked up the lamp on the end table and inspected it for a hidden microphone.

"Don't worry," said Will. "We've already checked."

"The Gestapo pays the rent through a dummy Irish corporation," said Helen.

"The Irish are neutral," added Will.

"No one is neutral," answered Martin Browning.

"Your bags?" said Helen again.

Martin ignored her and went to the window. The view pointed south to the White House. A Zeiss 4× scope lay on a table. Martin picked it up.

Will Stauer said, "We can study the target right from here."

Martin balanced the scope in his hand. "This usually comes with a rifle."

"Mauser Karabiner 98k," said Helen. "We brought one."

"Smuggled in through the New York Bund." Will took a small leather toolkit from his pocket. "I'll attach the scope tonight."

"I'm taking the shot," said Martin, "with my C96. It's my job."

"It is our job to consider all possibilities," said Will.

Martin put the scope to his eye and brought the White House much closer. "With this, the K 98k has an effective range of five hundred meters, around a third of a mile. But the White House is a mile from here."

Will said, "We'll be shooting from the south side, from much closer."

"As I just said, I'm taking the shot," said Martin.

"Your bags, Herr Bruning," said Helen, sounding annoyed.

"No bags." Martin drained his Scotch. "This is a spy trap. Twelve floors up. No back way. No good. Not staying."

"Section Six has other safe houses in the city," said Will Stauer, "but—"

"We operate as a small cell," said Helen. "That's the preference of Section Six. Involve as few people as possible. And the plan is for you to stay here, Herr Bruning."

"We're adjusting the plan," he said. "Meet me tomorrow at noon, Constitution Avenue, a nice public place. Sit on a sidewalk bench. Face north with the Washington Monument behind you." Martin put on his fedora and his British accent. "And my name isn't Herr Bruning. It's Nigel Hawkins, British businessman, here to feed at the American trough, old girl."

"Forget the 'old girl' business and tell us about *your* girl," said Helen. "The girl you brought on the train. The girl Max Diebold telegraphed about."

"Nigel Hawkins is a homosexual. He doesn't like girls"—Martin tugged his brim—"except as friends."

"Are *you* a homosexual?" asked Helen.

"I'll be whatever I need to be. And you'll do whatever I ask." Martin saw the look that passed between them. "If you disagree, we can contact the wireless operator on the Eastern Shore and get an answer from Section Six tonight."

Helen stepped closer to him. "A girl only complicates things."

"She's served a purpose," said Martin. "So will you. Good evening."

ON SATURDAY NIGHTS, THE Schortmann menu never changed: knockwursts and sauerkraut, B&M baked beans, brown bread, bottles of Budweiser. But on this Saturday night, Mom set the table in the dining room to celebrate the return of her daughter.

So why did Vivian feel so . . . so out of place?

In her little bedroom, the same shabby curtains hung limp. The same single bed with the maple headboard was pushed into a corner, making room for the same pile of fan magazines on the floor. The matching nightstand and chest of drawers wore the same layer of dust, thickened by a few more years. And the same Hollywood dreams still flickered in the pictures she'd pasted and tacked and taped to the wall. . . .

Covers from *Photoplay*, glossies she'd sent away for . . . Clark Gable without a mustache in *Mutiny on the Bounty*, Clark Gable with a mustache in *San Francisco*, Astaire and Rogers dancing on the cover of *Life* . . . all those dreams that drove her to Hollywood, dreams of drama, of adventure, of life lived only as it could be on the screen, they all seemed to be taunting her. She changed into a pair of old blue jeans and a wool sweater and went back downstairs.

Her mother's eyes brightened at her daughter's comfort clothes. "You look like my Kathy now . . . not like some girl puttin' on Hollywood airs."

Vivian let that pass.

Mama said, "I sure am glad I bought extra knocks and kraut. You just don't know how long we'll be able to get German food now that we're at war again."

"In the last war," added her father, "they took to callin' knocks 'Liberty Sausage.'"

Vivian didn't have much appetite. Mostly she talked, and they hung on every word, but she didn't tell them everything. She mentioned DeMille but not Nat Rossiter. She talked about Harry Kellogg but not Buddy Clapper. She talked about the adventure of riding on the Super Chief but didn't mention murder on the train.

Mom and Dad talked, too, about Cousin So-and-So and Auntie Such-and-Such and Johnny Beevers and all the other people that Vivian would be seeing soon, and about how all of them would want to know what movie stars she'd met and why she'd come home and why this and why that and why the other thing.

Then her father got to talking about crabbing. He cracked his knuckles and massaged his hands. She'd forgotten how outsized his hands were. He'd hauled so much line and worked so many traps, his hands looked like they belonged to a man twice his size. "Sometimes, I think I'm getting too old for this."

"Maybe you should go back to selling," said Ma.

"Nah. Havin' my own boat was always my dream."

"It's good to have dreams," said Vivian.

"Good to wake up, too." Her mother gave her one of those hardheaded digs.

And Vivian wanted to go back to L.A. right then, or at least back to Harold. Instead, she helped her mother with the dishes. Then she went into the living room, where her father was already snoozing in front of the Philco. *The Adventures of Ellery Queen* was playing, with *Abie's Irish Rose* to follow at eight.

On the American Skysleeper, the stewardesses were handing out blankets. After stops in El Paso and Dallas, the DC-3 was in the air again. Next stop: Nashville.

Stella came back from the lavatory and stepped around Carter, into her fold-down berth. "Teeth all brushed, face all washed, time for a good night's sleep."

"I wish we'd taken the train," said Carter.

"Stop complaining. Most of those poor saps down there make about five hundred bucks a year. We're spending more than that for one flight across the country."

"Uncle Sam is paying for me."

"So get some sleep. You want to hit the ground running. Uncle Sam won't be too happy if this is some kind of wild-goose chase."

"Neither will Dick Hood. He said if I don't come back with the biggest collar of this war, I shouldn't come back at all."

SUNDAY,
DECEMBER 21

KEVIN CUSACK CALLED THE Washington Airport at 7:00 A.M. Had the American Skysleeper from Los Angeles landed? *No.* Mechanical troubles, still on the ground in Nashville, not expected until six that evening.

So what to do until then? Mass, maybe? He could say a prayer for his mother, who was sure to be saying one for him. Afterward, maybe he'd visit the Smithsonian or the Washington Monument.

Then the phone rang. It was Stanley: "How come you wrote 'Kevin Carroll' on that note you give me?"

"False name. I'm on the run, remember?"

"How about runnin' up to Baltimore? You pay for the gas?"

"What's in Baltimore?"

"A guy who uses a lot of Brylcreem."

SUNDAY PAPERS AND ROOM service in the Hay-Adams. Nigel Hawkins, as polite and British as could be, told the busboy to put the cart by the window. That way, he could study the White House while he ate. Watching the guards come and go could tell him a lot. But the front page of *The Washington Post* told him more: SECURITY TIGHT AS PRESIDENT LIGHTS NATIONAL TREE ON CHRISTMAS EVE.

First came a paragraph of who, what, where, and when. Then specifics: "Multiple law enforcement agencies are involved in the event. The Washington Metropolitan Police, the Capitol Police, the National Park Police, and the U.S. Military will all be coordinated by the United States Secret Service."

A formidable array, thought Martin. But with so many interlocking, overlapping agencies, there was as much chance of a slipup or blown assignment as of redundancy.

"Two hundred card-holding guests will be admitted to special seating. The rest of the public will find standing room in roped-off areas on the South Lawn. All visitors will be at least two hundred feet from the South Portico.

"White House gates open at 4:00 P.M., in advance of the Marine Band concert at 4:30. Members of the public are to be admitted via the Southeast and Southwest gates. Cardholders are requested to enter by the Northeast Appointment Gate for direct access to their seats."

These cardholders, he wondered, who were they? And could a card be forged? Or could a cardholder be found and separated from his card?

"The gates will be guarded by members of the U.S. Army. Uniformed and plainclothes Secret Service will be deployed across the grounds and throughout the crowd. No packages will be allowed, and the main gates will be equipped with 'electrical searchers' that show an alarm if any quantity of metal passes."

Electrical searchers? Martin had heard of such things. But were they any good? And would the VIP gate have one? The paper suggested not.

He read on: "It is anticipated that some twenty thousand will be admitted. There is concern that such a large crowd presents a target for enemy saboteurs or even for enemy airplanes, although there is no evidence that the Luftwaffe have aircraft capable of mounting an attack on the continental United States."

The Luftwaffe should have been the least of their worries, thought Martin Browning, because in a pushing, swirling, happy mob, he knew he could get through, even with the so-called electrical searchers. But in such a crush, could he raise the pistol and aim? And could he take two shots? One to range him, one to kill him?

He had to consider every possibility, even using that Karabiner 98k from a greater distance.

Vivian Hopewell awoke as Kathy Schortmann. She knew because she was staring at the same ceiling crack that had been widening in Kathy's bedroom since 1934. She put on Kathy's old slippers and scuffed down to the kitchen, where she found her mother at the stove, lifting bacon strips from the black frying pan onto the draining rack.

She reached for one and her mother smacked her hand with the spatula. "We cook the bacon. We go to Mass. When we come home, the bacon's drained and ready to crisp in the pan. No bacon till after Communion."

"Oh, yeah, I forgot. Communion." Maybe she'd be struck by lightning.

Vivian went back upstairs and put on the blue polka-dot dress that Harold had bought for her. She loved how it flattered her. He had such wonderful taste. She missed him. But maybe she could talk to him. So she dug into her purse and pulled out a handful of business cards: *The Rossiter Agency, Representation for the Stars . . . The Roosevelt Hotel, in the Heart of Hollywood . . . Jules White, Columbia Pictures, Producer & Director, The Three Stooges . . . Mr. Fountain's Men's Shop, Burbank . . . The Willard Hotel.*

She called the number of the Willard and asked for Mr. Milton. *Checked out.*

She threw the Willard card in the wastebasket. She swept up the others because they all had some sentimental value, even the card from the men's shop where she'd gone looking for work, the one that sold the cuff links. Maybe if she could find the D.C. shop where Harold got his, she'd go there and buy the matching tie clip for his Christmas gift.

Then her mother's voice cut through the quiet. Time to go to Mass. Time to endure curious gazes and answer nosy questions. Time to dodge Johnny Beevers. Time to *dominos* the *vobiscum*, as her high-school friends used to say.

STANLEY SMITH DROVE OUT Rhode Island to Route 1, a.k.a. Baltimore Avenue. Along the way, he told Kevin about Sinclair Cook, who'd ridden the Super Chief many times with many young women, all of them "wives." Before the card game on Saturday night, Cook had come looking for some inside dope. "He told me he'd used Kellogg's wife once."

"Used?" asked Kevin. "You mean screwed?"

"Hey, man, a gal wants to get to Hollywood, she uses what she got. And she *gets* used, too. That story's as old as dicks 'n' pussies."

And as slimy as Cook's hair, thought Kevin.

Stanley said that Cook wanted to know if the Kelloggs were really married, because nothing made a cardplayer angrier than knowing that another player had screwed his wife. And a pissed-off cardplayer was a good mark.

"I told him I thought they was married," said Stanley. "Couldn't be sure."

Kevin hadn't considered that the girl named Vivian might not be married to Harold Kellogg, or that she might actually be part of his game . . . whatever it was.

An hour later, Stanley parked his '33 Chevy with the rotting rocker panels on Mount Vernon Hill in Baltimore. The street had a little greensward in the middle, with bare trees breaking up the winter sunlight. At the top, a pillared monument to George Washington loomed over the city. Just beyond rose the spire of the Mount Vernon Place Methodist Church.

"Nice neighborhood," said Kevin.

"Used to be nicer. Lots of rich folks livin' in fine rows. Changin' now. Rows gettin' busted up. More reg'lar folk movin' in." Stanley looked at his watch. "Our boy should be in church."

"How do you know?"

"He always leaves junk for me to clean up on the train, newspapers and pint bottles and such, and once, a newsletter for that church up there. Got my attention 'cause my mama's a Methodist who likes to see all the churches hereabouts."

Stanley popped out of his car just as people started to flow out of the church.

Mr. Brylcreem, hatless even on a chilly December morning, was leading his wife and daughters down the hill. The girls looked to be ten and twelve. The older one was moving on crutches and leg braces.

Accosting a man walking home from church with his family? Including a daughter with polio? Even this guy? That was low, thought Kevin. But Stanley didn't hesitate, so Kevin followed him up the hill.

Of course, everyone noticed the Negro. Eyes met. Eyes shifted. Mr. Brylcreem did a double take.

As planned, Kevin said, "Why . . . is that Sinclair Cook?"

Cook shook his shiny head: *Please, not here. Not now.*

"We met on the train," said Kevin. "The Super Chief. Remember?"

Cook pretended to think it over, then gave them both a greeting and told his wife, "Take the girls in the house, honey. I'll be along presently."

With a suspicious eye for these strangers, then for her husband, the careworn Mrs. Cook led their daughters across the street.

And Cook rounded on the men. "What the hell do you want?"

"The address of the Kellogg girl," said Kevin, "the one from the train."

"That isn't even her real name," said Cook.

"So what is it?" asked Kevin.

"How the hell should I know?" Sinclair Cook turned to Stanley. "Why did you bring this guy around here, anyway?"

"I guess 'cause he never called me 'nigger,'" Stanley said. "I told him what you told me on the train, that she used to be one of your gals."

"And you told him where I live? Where I *live*?" Then Cook settled down a bit. "Listen, fellas, my wife's not well. And my Nancy—you saw her—she's got the polio. I had all I could do to keep them from seein' the newspapers—"

"We don't want anything but her name," said Kevin.

Cook looked at Stanley and said, "Is this guy on the level, George?"

"My name is Stanley. You call me Stanley."

"No," said Kevin. "Call him *Mister* Smith."

Cook ran a hand over his Brylcreem and wiped it on his raincoat. He'd clearly lost his strut. "I don't make much selling film. If I wasn't a good cardplayer, my family—"

Kevin said, "What's her *real* name?"

"I don't remember. I met her slingin' hash in Annapolis. I don't even remember the restaurant. We changed her name on the train, changed it to Vivian Hopewell."

"Will anybody in Annapolis know her by that name?"

"How the hell should I know? It's a small town. Go and ask around."

"Sinclair!" called the wife from the front stoop. "Pot roast is ready."

Stanley glanced at Kevin. "Y'all like pot roast?"

"No. Makes me fart."

So Stanley said to Cook, "Remember, if you tell the cops about my friend here, I'll tell your wife about them dirty sheets I change off your berth after every trip."

"In honor of all the Georges," added Kevin.

As they headed back to the car, Stanley said to Kevin, "Makes you fart? Pot roast makes you fart? You a funny guy."

MARTIN BROWNING STOOD ON the knoll by the Washington Monument and looked north across the Ellipse to the White House, then east to the Capitol, west to Lincoln's memorial, south to Jefferson's. And he could not deny the power of it all. Those grand structures proclaimed the grandeur of a government that was as open and expansive as the landscape, as pure and highminded as the white stone that fashioned them. It might all be an illusion, but people needed illusions. They needed symbols. Any German knew that.

He'd been to the Nuremberg rallies. He'd seen enormous red swastika banners stretched as taut as Hitler salutes in the sunshine. He'd seen searchlights sending pillars of light into a black sky. He'd seen thousands of Nazis marching in lockstep by day and night, marching toward the future on a grand German stage. But on this stage, for *their* first communal wartime act, Americans would light a Christmas tree and sing happy songs.

Whose truth would be the more enduring? He didn't know.

But just as he considered himself a student of grand national symbols, Martin also studied the intimate, unspoken language of bodies. So for a time, he observed the Stauers, who sat on a bench on Constitution Avenue, as instructed, and he concluded that this husband-and-wife team was well attuned, like a shortwave sender and receiver.

The wife sat upright, posture erect, feet together, head alert. The husband leaned back, stretched an arm across the top of the bench, crossed his legs, with an ankle on a knee, which suggested he was more supple than most pot-bellied men. She was the blade, he the blunt object. Both would have their uses.

Martin came down the slope and walked past them. The husband glanced up, but didn't react. He was probably looking for a blue overcoat, not a leather jacket, fedora, and shoulder satchel. Then Martin made eye contact and jerked his head. *Follow me.*

They all crossed Constitution, walked under the double row of trees, and came out onto the Ellipse, fifty acres that enticed weekend strollers, scampering children, and energetic young men with loud voices and flying footballs. Once they were ambling along, as innocent as ministers, Helen Stauer said, "Why are you dressed like this?"

"To see how sharp-eyed you are."

"No more tests, please," she said.

As if sensing the tension, Will Stauer changed the subject. "It's a lovely morning for a stroll."

Martin ignored that and led them across the Ellipse, to the crosswalk at E

Street, then right up to the fence on the edge of the South Lawn. After they'd all taken a good look at the White House, he said, "The portico is two hundred and five meters. Roosevelt will be there, lighting the tree for twenty thousand."

Helen said, "Your pistol has a range of a hundred meters."

Martin said, "If I can get through security, I can take the shot from two hundred feet. That's like letting me walk up and put the gun to his head."

"But the newspaper mentioned 'electrical searchers,'" said Helen.

Martin said, "I hope that the wooden holster will insulate the metal."

"Hope is not a strategy."

Martin had no rejoinder. He knew she was right.

For a few minutes, they stood in silence, studying the roll of the ground, the pathways, the tree cover, and all the angles that a shooter might use if he could get onto the White House lawn. Half a dozen other groups came and stood along the fence. Some took pictures. Some chattered away. No one paid the assassins any mind.

Helen pointed to the two thirty-foot spruces about a hundred feet from the fence. "The one on the right is the Christmas tree. The paper says it's to be decorated by the children of Washington the day before the event. Perhaps—"

"Perhaps we could get in then and hide a gun on the grounds," said Will.

Martin said, "Easier to plant a weapon at night—"

"So we should reconnoiter at night," said Helen, "but plan in the cold light of day. That means we consider everything that could go wrong. So we mustn't forget the last time an assassin shot at FDR—"

"The Italian anarchist in '33," said Martin.

"Yes, in Florida. He fired from a crowd, five times with a .32-caliber pistol from fifty yards. But a woman next to him grabbed his arm and the shots went wild. One killed the man shaking Roosevelt's hand, the mayor of Chicago, but none hit Roosevelt."

"My plan," Martin told her, "is to have you on my right, covering my movement."

"Use the girl." Helen leaned closer. "Take the shot, drop the gun beside her, disappear into the crowd. We will be outside, ready to help you escape. That's *my* plan."

Martin let the life drain from his eyes, as if to tell her he didn't like her plan at all.

But Helen Stauer could give a cold look of her own, and she spoke the truest, coldest words he'd heard in two weeks: "You are on a suicide mission, Herr Bruning. We all are. But if we work together, we might survive. Now, there is much to consider, from many perspectives." She turned and headed back across E Street.

Martin Browning watched the slight woman in the Prussian-blue overcoat walk away, high heels clicking. He asked her husband, "Where is she going now?"

Will Stauer pointed to the white obelisk dominating the city. "Up there."

"View a battlefield from the highest point," said Helen over her shoulder.

Martin agreed, but he didn't move until Will said, "It is best to follow. She likes obedience."

KEVIN CUSACK PULLED OUT his wad of bills. "If you drive me out to Annapolis now, Stanley, I'll pay you fifty bucks. I have to find this girl."

"Then what?"

"I don't know, but it's the first step."

"Like I told you, man, Sunday dinner's at one. If I drive you to Annapolis, I'll miss it. And I don't need Mama mad at me, not when she's makin' chicken and dumplings."

So Kevin told Stanley to drop him at Union Station. If he had to, he'd go by train.

"Call tomorrow," said Stanley. "I'll drive tomorrow, if Mama don't need me."

"Thanks."

During the week, the Pennsylvania Railroad ran hourly between D.C. and New York, first stop Odenton Station, where you could catch a trolley to Annapolis. But reduced schedules on weekends. Every three hours. And Kevin had just missed the one o'clock local. He cursed. So . . . now what?

Maybe a walk across Washington. He could imagine himself as James Stewart in *Mr. Smith Goes to Washington,* awed by all the grand symbols of American democracy. And what grander symbol was there than the Capitol dome? So he aimed toward that and remembered Walt Whitman's words: "I like to stand aside and look a long, long while up at the dome. It comforts me somehow."

Maybe the monuments would comfort Kevin, too. He needed some comforting. He needed some inspiration. He'd left L.A. because he was done sticking his neck out. And here he was, sticking his neck out. Why him? Then he wondered . . . there in the grim December of 1941, why *not* him?

He thought about going over to Professor Drake's house in Foggy Bottom. But how would that look to the G-men who were probably watching the Commie's door? And what would he say? "Hello, Professor. I didn't kill your daughter"? No. He'd visit Mary Benning instead. He'd tell her how Sally really felt. He'd tell her that Sally loved her and was coming back because of her. That would comfort her. And maybe it would comfort him, too.

According to his pocket map, it was three miles to Georgetown. A good walk, plenty of time to think and plenty of time to change his mind. He dropped down onto the Mall and headed west, collar turned up and cap pulled low. When two Park Police clip-clopped by on horseback, they barely glanced at him.

He passed the new National Gallery of Art and the huge Museum of Natural History and knew that he could lose himself for days in either, lose himself so completely that not even J. Edgar Hoover could find him. But he was drawn irresistibly to the white stone obelisk in the center of the Mall.

If you'd never been in a city before, you went to the highest spot to make sense of it. In L.A., you drove up to the Griffith Park Observatory. In the city of monuments, you visited the most famous monument of them all, the tallest stone structure in the world.

He bought a ticket and got in line with young families, men in uniform, and a pair of young women talking about their jobs as government secretaries. A ranger shouted instructions and answers to unasked questions: "Form a line to the right. Let downward-bound riders exit the elevator before boarding. Move to the back. You must ride to the top, five hundred and fifty-five feet, but if you wish, you may walk down, all eight hundred and ninety-seven steps." After a ninety-second lift, the doors opened to a burst of light from the little windows at the top.

Another ranger in gray shirt and stiff-brim greeted them. "Please step off, folks. Room at all four sets of windows, or you can start in the exhibit room one flight down. That's where you'll board the elevator when you leave."

Kevin let the families have the windows first. He went down to the exhibit room, which was packed because this was the first day the monument had been open since December 7. He excused his way past people queued up for the "down" elevator. And he bumped a lady in a blue overcoat. Their eyes met briefly, two strangers passing.

Then he squeezed into the corner to look at a display of photos showing the monument's construction. When the elevator doors popped open, he glanced toward the sound. A ranger shouted, "All aboard," and Kevin saw the woman in the blue overcoat again, moving onto the elevator. And . . . right behind her, a brown fedora, a leather jacket, a male face. And . . .

. . . *thunk* . . . the elevator doors closed.

Kevin took a second to consider. A familiar face? Leslie Howard? It couldn't be.

He reached for the elevator button pad, but the ranger said, "Do not touch that, sir. Only federal employees may touch the elevator."

"How long for the next one?"

"Ten minutes."

"How long to walk?"

"Ten or fifteen, depending on how many people are on the stairs."

If he ran, maybe he could make it in five.

So down he went, down two steps at a time, three at a time, down the dim shaft, past dozens of people . . . some going slowly, some quickly, and some stopping on every landing to read every three-by-five-foot stone marker commemorating every state, city, Masonic lodge, and church that contributed to the building of the monument.

He plummeted past all of them. Step to step, step over step, across the landing, around the walkers and gawkers and down, all to get another look at the face beneath the brim of the brown fedora.

And with every step, he saw the actor that Sally had seen when she looked across the table on the train. The Pimpernel in *The Scarlet Pimpernel*. Henry Higgins in *Pygmalion*. The bastard who looked like Ashley Wilkes in *Gone With the Wind*.

Down and down, hurtling down and flying down and doing his best not to cause a cascade of people falling down in front of him. And still, it took ten minutes to the lobby, to the statue of Washington, to the park policeman who barely glanced at him. . . . but no leather jacket and brown fedora.

Outside, Kevin looked east, west, south, and nothing. Had he really seen Harold Kellogg? *Nah. Couldn't be.* So he walked down to Constitution Avenue, perched on one of the benches for a moment, and pulled out the pocket map. Enough with the monument. Time to visit Mary Benning on the Georgetown canal.

He didn't notice the paunchy guy in a brown three-piece suit and dirty raincoat sitting on a nearby bench. He hadn't noticed him up in the monument, either. But that was the point. Nobody noticed guys like that.

MARTIN BROWNING ASKED THE cabbie to drive around the monument again.

"Sure, buddy. It's your dime."

They circled back to the Constitution Avenue crosswalk just as the guy in the button-covered scally cap and raincoat started walking.

Helen Stauer whispered, "Is that him?"

Martin said, "I can't be sure."

"Coincidence, then. But best that he not get another look at you."

"What in hell is he doing in Washington?" Martin was seldom perplexed. But he was thinking he should have stayed and found a way to kill Kevin Cusack.

Helen Stauer said, "Leave it to Will."

VIVIAN WORRIED ALL THROUGH the gospel and sermon. She knew that if she stayed in her seat at Communion, the parish busybodies would see it as an admission that she hadn't been to Mass or confession since she left town. And if she went up to the rail and made a show of kneeling and taking the host, those same old biddies would be yammering that a girl who'd spent three years in the Hollywood fleshpots shouldn't be receiving Communion until she'd spent a whole day in the confessional and said five hundred Our Fathers and a thousand Hail Marys. Damned if you did and damned if you didn't.

Her father stayed at her side when she chose to stay seated. And he hustled her through the crowd of busybodies after Mass. And she loved him for it. But he couldn't get her past Johnny Beevers, who caught up to them outside.

"Kathy! Kathy, I . . . I heard you were back in town."

She gave her old boyfriend a warm smile. She still liked him.

He'd gone to Towson State, come home, and gotten a job as an intern in the Annapolis statehouse. That led to a job as an aide to the governor. From there, he'd grown into his gangling height, grown into his brains, and grown up enough to look like he actually belonged in the three-piece suit he was wearing.

He asked her if she'd have a cup of coffee with him.

"Not today," said Les Schortmann. "We get her for Sunday breakfast."

"That's okay, Mr. Schortmann. How about Tuesday? Or Christmas Eve? I have two VIP passes to South Lawn for the tree lighting. How about coming with me?"

Les whispered, "Should I tell him you got a beau in Washington?"

Vivian gave her father the wave-off. *Get lost, Dad.* Then she thanked Johnny and said she'd always wanted to go to the tree lighting, but she'd have to think about it. "I'll tell you over coffee on Tuesday morning."

"Then it's a date," said Johnny. "Eleven thirty, Tuesday, at G and J's."

"My old stomping grounds," said Vivian. "I'll wear my waitress flats."

Johnny looked at her legs and said, "I always liked the pumps better."

KEVIN CUSACK THOUGHT A neighborhood called Foggy Bottom might be more dramatic. A swamp maybe . . . or some mist rising from a sewer. But Washington was a company town, and the company was the U.S. government, so the buildings along Virginia and Twenty-Third Street were square, flat, and dull, all the way to Washington Circle.

He went through the "campus" of George Washington U. More basic buildings, more city streets, but that was where Sally had lived, so he tried to imagine her, and it was where her father had taught, so he kept an eye out for him, too, and kept plodding up to Pennsylvania. At the overpass above Rock Creek, he stopped in the middle to watch the cars speeding along the new parkway. That was when he noticed a guy in a dirty raincoat leaning against a lamppost on the east end of the overpass, reading a paper.

Kevin started walking again, and the guy started walking, too, toward the west end, where Pennsylvania joined M Street, the main drag that led through old, redbrick Georgetown. Kevin glanced over his shoulder. The guy was now on the other side of the street, looking down at the parkway.

Confront him or keep walking and see if he followed? Kevin picked up the pace. M Street was a steady, seven-block uphill slope past businesses, shops, and restaurants, all the way to the Key Bridge. And Kevin knew that the faster he went, the more he'd wear this guy out, and the longer he went, the more time he'd have to figure him out.

At the corner of M and Thirtieth, he stopped and pretended to read a menu in a restaurant window. Out of the corner of his eye, he looked down the street. But . . . nothing. He scanned both sides of the street. And . . . the guy was gone. A false alarm?

Kevin shrugged it off and kept walking.

He turned down Thomas Jefferson, which was lined with old two-story brick buildings, all nicely kept. The Potomac shimmered at the end of the street. But he was only going half a block to the little bridge that crossed the canal. There he turned for another look. But the guy was nowhere in sight. Gone . . . and forgotten. Just a false alarm.

So he headed down onto the towpath that ran along the stone-lined waterway, the obsolete relic of a system that once carried goods almost two hundred miles from the Appalachians to Washington. He'd found Mary Benning's address and figured out that she lived between Jefferson and Thirty-First, on the north side of the canal, in a little first-floor apartment.

As the shadows deepened on the shortest day of the year, Sunday strollers went home, or sought out places where lights were burning and life was going on. Down here it was quiet. The wet stones of the canal made the whole atmosphere clammy and damp.

At Mary Benning's door, Kevin took a deep breath and knocked. When it cracked, he smiled and said, "Mary?"

"Who's asking?"

"Sally Drake sent me."

Mary was a petite brunette with short hair and a manner better suited to a precinct sergeant than a schoolteacher. She said, "Who are you?"

"Did Sally ever speak about a guy named Kevin Cusack?"

"He killed her," she said, and she tried to close the door.

But Kevin put his foot on the threshold. "He didn't. I didn't. I swear."

"I have a knife."

He put up his hands. "I'm friendly."

She looked up the canal and down, as if expecting someone else to appear from the bushes. "The police have been here, you know."

"Asking about me?"

"Sally's father sent them. I think he knew about us."

"Sally was coming back to be with you. Let me in, and I'll tell you the story."

A moment of decision followed, Kevin uncertain of what to say next, Mary obviously uncertain of whether to let him.

Finally he said, "Please. I'm harmless."

Maybe it was his vulnerability, maybe her curiosity, but she opened the door.

Soon, he was sipping coffee in her little living room: a table, a sofa and chairs, a console with radio and record player, and behind a screen on the back wall, a little kitchen area. A stairway on the side led up to her bedroom and bath.

She said, "Sally told me you were a good guy."

"I am."

"Good enough to keep our secret?" she asked. "Mine and Sally's?"

"So long as you keep mine."

And on that basis, they talked for an hour . . . about Sally, about Hollywood, about why he'd come to Washington. He told her about his love affair with Sally. She told him about hers. He told her how angry he was when Sally left him for Jerry Sloane. She told him how unhappy she was when she and Sally decided they could never be together.

As he left, she said, "Sally was right. You are a good guy. And you were never here. But if you need help, I'm always here."

And for the first time in a while, Kevin felt good about something. He'd made a friend in a city where friends were hard to find. And if he had to lose in love, losing to Mary Benning was better than losing to Jerry Sloane.

WILL STAUER SAT IN the suite at the Cairo. He had a bump on his forehead and a glass of Scotch in his hand.

Helen stood over him, hands on hips. "You *lost* him?"

"I tripped." Will swallowed half the Scotch.

"On what? Your stupidity?"

"On a curbstone. I was on the other side of the street, making myself invisible. I stepped into a storefront when he looked my way. When I stepped out, I tripped. But I think he took Jefferson. I think I could find him again."

Martin stood by the window and listened to husband and wife bicker, but he was more interested in the Karabiner 98k. He hefted it, held it to his shoulder, worked the bolt. At 8.6 pounds, plus two pounds for the ZF39 sight, it was as finely balanced a rifle as he'd ever held. And they were going to put it in the hands of this clumsy oaf?

Will shook his head. "I'm so sorry, dear. So sorry, Herr Bruning."

Helen said, "You are a fool. But . . ." Like a mother who was done chastising her child, she wrapped her arms around Will's head. "It's all right. It's all right, darling."

Martin worked the bolt a few more times. Its metallic click brought the Stauers out of their little embrace and back to reality.

Helen asked him, "What do you suppose our man was doing in Georgetown?"

"We don't even know if it *was* our man," said Martin.

Will looked up. "He was wearing a hat with all kinds of buttons. Roosevelt buttons. St. Louis Cardinals buttons. Even Jew buttons."

"Which team do you think he likes better?" asked Martin. "The St. Louis Cardinals or the Los Angeles Jews?"

"Los Angeles has such a team?" asked Will.

This, thought Martin, was why he worked alone. They missed his sarcasm, so he changed the subject and gestured to turtleneck, trousers, and stocking cap—all black—on the sofa. "My wardrobe for tonight?"

"Tonight, you should be difficult to see," said Helen.

"Tonight, I should be invisible," said Martin. "But tomorrow, we meet in the open, like tourists. Natural History Museum cafeteria."

"Why there?" asked Helen.

"I like the stuffed elephant." He took a screwdriver from Will Stauer's little leather tool kit and undid the split rings that held the scope in place. "I would not have come back to this spy trap . . . but for this."

"Please be careful with it," said Will.

"If I'm scouting a shot, I like to see the shot."

THE DC-3 WAS THE workhorse of the air. But the horse that carried Frank Carter and Stella Madden had pulled up lame in Nashville, this time for another six-hour layover to replace the carburetor on the left engine. Estimated arrival in D.C.: TBD.

Stella said, "I sure could use a bed. A shower, too."

Frank Carter said, "And maybe some barbecue, since we're in Tennessee."

But first, he had to call the Willard Hotel to hold the room. While he went to a phone booth, Stella bought a newspaper and took a seat in the waiting room.

Carter was back in five minutes. "I heard there's good barbecue just up the road."

Stella kept her eyes on the paper and said, "I know why that Nazi bastard's going to Washington."

Carter sat next to her. "Why?"

She pointed to the headline below the fold. SECURITY TIGHT AS PRESIDENT LIGHTS NATIONAL TREE ON CHRISTMAS EVE.

MONDAY, DECEMBER 22

ASSASSINS WORKED BEST IN the dark. So, around 2:00 A.M., Martin Browning dressed in the black turtleneck and trousers. Then he put on the stocking cap and his navy-blue cashmere overcoat. In the hotel lobby, he told the night man that his favorite cure for insomnia was a long walk.

He promised he'd be careful. He didn't add that he carried a leather blackjack in his pocket and a punching knife in his shoe and any street thug who accosted him would catch the worst of it. Instead he joked: "If I'm not back by three, send the cavalry, as you chaps say."

And out he went, across Lafayette Square toward the statue of the French hero at the southeast corner. There he hunkered down and peered across Pennsylvania at the Northeast Appointment Gate, the VIP entry point for Christmas Eve. Two uniformed Secret Service men stood outside the grim little guardhouse, but he didn't notice any kind of extra equipment. The papers were right. No metal detectors for the VIPs.

Then he hurried onto Fifteenth and went down the east side of the street. At Treasury Place, he counted two soldiers in the little guardhouse, beyond which he could see what looked like a huge steel doorframe: the "electrical searcher." If he couldn't figure out how to defeat it, or get one of the VIP cards, he'd have to hop the fence and plant a gun in the middle of the night.

Americans had been notoriously lax about protecting their thirty-two presidents. Three shot dead from close range in eighty-five years, both Roosevelts shot *at*. And yet, until 1938, the fence surrounding the White House grounds had been a mere three feet tall. Then the Secret Service had doubled the height and topped each spoke with a sharpened point. But before December 7, the grounds had been entirely open during the day. Visitors could wander right up to the South Portico and take a picture. Not anymore.

Martin wasn't worried about scaling the fence. But how often did the guards walk the perimeter? Did they have dogs? Was the fence wired? He went down to E Street and crossed to the sidewalk that ran along the north side of the Ellipse. Evergreens and bare-limbed deciduous trees edged the lawn and the elliptical track where Union officers had once exercised their mounts. He found a thick spruce, slid into its shadow, and watched.

He timed uniformed Secret Service patrolling inside the president's fence. He followed the sound of an army vehicle that completed a circumference of the Executive Area, from Seventeenth to Pennsylvania to Fifteenth and back to E Street every eight minutes. Then he saw a pair of Capitol Police walking east on E Street, in and out of the streetlamp shadows.

He crouched and pulled a pint of whiskey from his pocket. If they noticed him, he'd douse himself, take a few swallows, and play the drunk. But they kept walking and talking . . . about the upcoming heavyweight fight between Joe Louis and Buddy Baer.

Once their voices had receded toward Fifteenth, he decided to test the fence. In German concentration camps, they had "talking" fences with thin cables connected to microphones on the spokes. If vibration activated the microphones, a light would flash in a guardhouse and men would come running.

Martin found a couple of rocks and let one go. It hit the fence with a loud *thwang*.

No lights came on. No guards appeared with guns drawn, dogs snarling, or flashlights bobbing. The White House fence wasn't talking . . . yet.

More knowledge stored. More to collect. So he retreated south, keeping in the shadow of the trees, until he reached Constitution Avenue.

The Washington Monument rose, as dark as the night sky above it. The streetlamps, however, cast a strong downward light, and they were spaced more closely on Constitution than on E Street. He'd keep away from them and from the row of American elms along the avenue. He'd work from the inner rim of trees, fifty feet north of the sidewalk, fifty feet closer to the target.

These trees—more elms and a scattering of evergreens—gave decent cover and offered branches low enough for a nimble man to climb. Could he scale one of them unseen, then hold his position with a K 98k, until the moment came to fire?

He picked a tree, second in from the main path, on the left. He stood beside it and put the scope to his eye. He was right on the axis with the White House, and its distant shadow suddenly filled his field of vision, like the detail in a photograph beneath a magnifying glass. When the spotlights were lit on Wednesday night, Roosevelt would appear close enough to touch.

He reckoned he was about five hundred and fifty meters away, at the outer limit of his ability with the K 98k. He'd rather shoot the C96 from the South Lawn, but if he had to, he believed that he could make the shot from here.

Then he heard voices, more talk of boxing . . . the two Capitol Police, still walking the perimeter of the Ellipse. They were passing under a streetlamp on Constitution. He pulled himself against the trunk and waited. If they walked on, fine. If they took the path onto the Ellipse, he was in trouble. They took the path.

He looked up into the branches and sprang, then grabbed, then practically ran up the side of the trunk, his feet scraping against the bark.

One of the police officers said, "Did you hear that?"

Martin grappled higher and got another branch. He wished he had a rope to sling over the branches. A rope would give him leverage. He'd remember to bring one on Christmas Eve.

But now flashlights were approaching, sweeping suspiciously.

Martin heard an engine downshift: a box truck on Constitution, a night delivery speeding across the District. He waited until the truck was close enough to muffle any other sounds. Then he launched himself higher, grabbing a big branch fifteen feet above the ground, lifting and pulling, molding himself against the trunk, until he was no more than the shadow of a branch himself. Then he carefully moved a hand to his turtleneck and pulled it up over his chin and nose, so that if a flashlight pointed in his direction, it wouldn't reflect off his white face.

A beam bounced across the branches around him. Another went over his foot. If they found him now, he couldn't play the drunk. What drunk climbed a tree? He'd have to attack . . . and quickly. Better to hold his breath and hold his place. Hold and hold. Don't even move for the knife.

One of the cops said, "Raccoon or rat?"

"Raccoon," said the other. "Let's go. I need to take a leak."

And they moved on, their voices receding. He watched them go back to Constitution and walk all the way to the corner of Seventeenth, where they disappeared into a little stone building, the old Lockkeeper's House from back in the days when a canal followed the line of Constitution Avenue. Now it was a public restroom.

Martin's hands were shaking and his legs were weak from holding motionless. He relaxed against the trunk. And now, he knew how easily he could get into the tree. Could he do it with a rifle under his coat and the police watching the area in the Christmas Eve dusk? And could he hit his target? He raised the scope to his eye again and filled with confidence. Whether he shot from the South Lawn or from this tree, Franklin Roosevelt was a dead man.

At 9:30 a.m., a taxi delivered Frank Carter and Stella Madden to the Willard Hotel. Carter climbed out and held the door for Stella. Then he stood for a moment and looked up and down Pennsylvania Avenue, taking it all in.

"What?" said Stella.

"Not how I hoped to arrive back in town."

She patted his cheek. "Before you hit the ground running, you need a shave."

"And a good night's sleep."

"Next time, we'll take the Super Chief."

After airplane waiting rooms and a cramped DC-3, the Willard lobby felt like a Hollywood vision of some Roman villa, with marble floors and columns, marble reception desk, and Kevin Cusack sitting in a shaft of sunlight, reading the paper.

Carter saw him straightaway, walked up to him, stood over him.

Without looking up, Kevin said, "What kept you?"

Before Carter could answer, Stella said, "We've been followed."

Carter turned to her. "We're the goddamn FBI. We do the following."

Stella pointed out the front window. "Two guys. I had them in the airport."

They were getting out of a car at the curb. Long overcoats, fedoras, and badges they were flipping for the doorman, as if to say, *Leave the car right where it is.*

Stella said, "Maybe this guy should get lost until we sort this out."

Kevin said, "You must be the girlfriend."

"You must be Sam Spade." Stella pointed to a long, mirrored, palm-lined corridor. "That's called Peacock Alley. There's a door at the end. Go."

"She's right," Carter said. "Let us sort this out. The local dicks don't need to know about my secret weapon just yet."

"What secret weapon?" asked Kevin.

"You," answered Carter. "Beat it. Call in half an hour."

Kevin didn't argue. He glanced at the two cops coming into the lobby, then disappeared down Peacock Alley. He didn't stop to admire the potted palms or the carpets or his own reflection in the mirrors. He didn't think he looked too good, anyway.

Meanwhile, in the lobby, the cops were showing their badges to Carter. The skinny one with the five-o'clock shadow said, "I'm Detective Mills, Washington Metropolitan Police." He gestured to his partner, a slouchy older guy. "This is Detective Conway. You must be Agent Carter. May we ask you a few questions?"

Carter looked at his watch. "I'm due at headquarters."

"A contact of yours fled the L.A. jurisdiction ten days ago. By the name"—Detective Mills flipped up his notebook—"Kevin Cusack. We've been asked by L.A. to check up on him in Washington."

"He's also wanted for murder on the Super Chief," said Conway.

"A dangerous guy, he sounds like," said Stella.

"Yes, ma'am," said Mills. "And you are?"

"She's my assistant." Carter saw eyes roll at that. "What makes you think your suspect is a contact of mine?"

"Detective Bobby O'Hara," said Mills. "He helps us in L.A. We help him in D.C."

"If your suspect crossed state lines," said Carter, "he's *our* problem. You boys can stand down."

"Not if he's running around our city," said Mills. "O'Hara thinks you've been in touch with him. We hope you'll share what you know so somebody can bring him in."

"Somebody will bring him in," said Carter, "wherever he is."

Stella said, "The FBI always gets their man."

"So do the Washington Metros." Mills handed her his card. "Stay in touch. And one more thing, ma'am, if you've brought a firearm to D.C., you need to register it."

"This is all the gun we need." Carter opened his coat. "Smith and Wesson .357 Magnum, Model 13. Carried under authority of the United States Congress."

FROM HIS WINDOW IN the Hay-Adams, Martin Browning looked down at St. John's, the little yellow church just across Sixteenth Street, on the north edge of Lafayette Square. It was known as the Church of the Presidents, since every one of them had worshiped there. If it was FDR's Christmas Day destination, maybe Martin could take the shot right from his sofa.

But he knew that by Christmas morning, both he and Roosevelt were likely to be dead. If he shot from the South Lawn, his own death was a certainty, as promised in today's newspaper, which added a new detail to the tree lighting: "Once admitted to the White House Grounds, no one will be allowed to leave until the event has concluded." Gates locked. Escape impossible.

That tree on Constitution Avenue was looking better and better, because Martin Browning was having second thoughts. He should never have let Vivian into his life. She'd given him a vision of something more, something that was weakening his resolve, something for men and women living in some other moment in time, not December '41. So he decided to talk to her. Talk might dispel second thoughts, especially if she started badgering him.

And she started right away. "I've called every hotel in D.C. asking for Harry Kellogg, asking for Michael Milton, and . . . Say, have you run out on me?"

"I checked out of the Willard to join my working group," he answered.

"Where?"

"Not important." He changed the subject. "How has your time been at home?"

Vivian's anger cooled. "Boring. Radio shows. Sunday Mass. And outside of church my old boyfriend asked me on a Christmas Eve date. It's like I never left."

"I hope you told him you're busy on Christmas Eve."

"I was tempted."

"You were?" Was that jealousy that Martin Browning felt flickering through him?

"Remember how I said I wanted to see the White House tree lighting?"

Martin took a breath and held it. "Yes."

"Johnny—I told you about him—he has VIP tickets. So—"

Martin was now sitting on the edge of his chair. "What did you tell him?"

"That I'd let him know. Now, I'm rushing to catch the ten o'clock train to D.C. because I plan to stand in front of the Agriculture Department until you—"

Jealousy sputtered and was replaced by coldhearted resolve, a much more familiar emotion to Martin Browning. He said, "Catch the train. I'll buy you lunch. Meet me in the cafeteria of the Museum of Natural History. It's right across the Mall from the Department of Agriculture. Twelve thirty." And he hung up.

Then he ordered a big breakfast. People always said that talking about your problems helped you to solve them. No more second thoughts.

HALF AN HOUR AFTER he'd disappeared down Peacock Alley, Kevin Cusack called Frank Carter's room.

Stella answered. "Frank's in the shower, then due at FBI."

Kevin said, "If you two are giving me the runaround—"

"Frank's trying to help you while you help him."

"Frank's trying to help Frank," said Kevin.

"Believe what you want," said Stella. "But the LAPD is after you, and now so are the Washington Metros."

"They have nothing."

"Except a murder in L.A., a murder on the Super Chief, and an assault in the Musso and Frank's men's room. They even have a witness to that one."

"John Wayne? You're joking."

"He said you threw a good punch," answered Stella. "Frank wants you to meet in the Willard lobby at five. He says you have to trust him. So trust him. I do."

"Yeah. Sure." *Click.* Kevin was coming to believe that he should trust no one. Not even the man that he called next to ask for that ride he'd been promised.

"Not today," said Stanley Smith. "I got two flat tires."

"Forget it," said Kevin. "I'll take the train." And he headed again for Union Station.

FRANK CARTER STOOD ON Pennsylvania Avenue and thanked whatever forces had brought him to Washington . . . even if they included a Nazi killer and a Hollywood script reader running for his life. This was where he'd always seen himself, right in the heart of American law enforcement, the headquarters of the U.S. Justice Department.

He showed his badge at the front desk and soon was in the office of his oldest FBI pal, Dan Jones of South Bend, Indiana. Jones had parlayed a sharp mind, sharp elbows, and a sharpshooter's eye into one promotion after another. Now he was agent in charge of the Espionage Unit, the man who wrote all those custodial detention memos that J. Edgar Hoover signed.

Carter looked around and gave a whistle. "Nice digs. Windows and everything."

"We've come a long way since Quantico," said Jones. "I'm glad you got Dick Hood to send you east on this. Maybe we can get you back here permanently."

"You took the words right out of my mouth."

"So you have a Nazi for us? The Hollywood Nazi?"

"He's not the one who fired this." Carter put the 7.63 mm cartridge on Jones's desk. How small it seemed to him, yet how large it might loom in history.

Jones picked it up and sniffed for powder residue, like the old forensics man he was. "This is a hot little round. Really packs a punch. Mauser C96, maybe? A dangerous weapon in the right hands."

"That's what has me so worried." And Carter retold the story from the raid on December 8 to Stella's shootout in Gobel's.

"Stella Madden," said Jones, "I remember her from my L.A. days."

"She's with me."

"*With* you?" Jones raised his eyebrows. "Very irregular, Frank."

"She has a special sense. Intuition, you might call it. And . . . well, she thinks the guy who shot that round plans to shoot the president on Christmas Eve. We need to stop him, Dan, or stop the tree lighting."

Jones thought that over and said, "What we need is to bring Mike Reilly in on this. He runs the White House Secret Service detail."

"Will he buy the intuition of a female private detective?"

"Ask him yourself. I'm sending you over to see him. Meanwhile . . . this guy?" Jones handed Carter a rap sheet for Kevin Cusack, a.k.a. the Hollywood Nazi, a.k.a. LAJCC Agent 29.

Carter said, "I've kept him in the field, like a stalking horse for the real Nazi."

"Just tell me, is he a good guy or a bad guy?"

"I'm meeting him at five o'clock. I'll bring him in. You be the judge."

ODENTON STATION: ONE-STORY, BRICK, utilitarian and simple, like scores of stations along the Pennsylvania line, and the Baltimore and Annapolis Electric Railway was rumbling through downstairs.

As Kevin Cusack headed down, he glanced at the other side of the tracks. And he saw her. Just like that. He'd chased her across half the country, and there she was, waiting for the inbound train. He recognized the bottle-blond hair, the sunglasses that might be covering another bruise, and the green slacks that were part of the suit she'd been wearing that Saturday in the dining car.

He bought a return ticket and hurried back to the southbound platform. Once the Washington-bound train was rolling, he moved onto the car she was riding. She seemed lost in thought, or daydreams. He considered approaching, but observing might be a better idea.

FRANK CARTER HAD NEVER been to the White House before. He did his best to act as if he were *not* impressed when he showed his badge at the Southeast Gate on Treasury Place. A uniformed Secret Service officer waved him toward a big metal arch that was decorated with evergreen garlands and bows, but as soon as he went through it, a bell went off, and three uniforms surrounded him.

One of them asked, "Are you armed, sir?"

"I'm surprised you didn't ask me that already." Carter showed them his Magnum.

"Hey, fellers," shouted the officer, "this Alnor Door is working."

They hadn't been testing Carter. They'd been testing their equipment. They took his gun and told him he could pick it up when he came back. He asked them what an Alnor Door was.

"An electrical searcher," the officer explained. "Standard equipment in prisons. People pass through and if they're carrying metal, it starts buzzing. We just put this one in. Works like a charm."

A good first line of defense, thought Carter.

He passed into the White House by the East entrance and was directed down the central corridor on the ground floor, all the way to the windowless Secret Service office, across the hall from the doctor's office. Now, he thought, he was in the *heart* of the heart . . . of everything.

Dan Jones had given Carter a quick description of Mike Reilly: "Sharp Montana accent, dark Irish scowl, and a fullback's body, which is a job requirement for the guy who might have to carry a crippled president in an emergency."

True to form, Reilly scowled at Frank Carter and told him to sit. "I have ten minutes. Lot going on around here, and now we have a special guest coming. So my work just doubled."

Carter didn't ask who the special guest was. None of his business. Instead, he spun through the story again, concluding, "If someone is planning to take a shot at the president on Christmas Eve, maybe the tree lighting should be canceled."

"Not possible," said Reilly. "The Boss insists. He promised the country he'd invite Americans onto the South Lawn this year. He said he wanted a more 'homey' atmosphere for the tree lighting."

"Homey?" said Carter.

"His word. And he's determined to do it, even though a lot has changed since he made the promise. The war news is all bad, he says, so we need a big public event, something that's a morale booster for the whole country, even if it hurts *my* morale."

"Well, if we can't stop the show," said Carter, "we just have to find the shooter."

Reilly leaned back in his chair. "You say you looked him in the eye?"

"I let him slip through my fingers in L.A. I even held the door for him."

"You held the door for an assassin? Wow." Mike Reilly seemed to Carter like the kind of guy who'd heard it all. But he hadn't heard that one.

"*Would-be* assassin," said Carter.

Reilly said, "So you managed to move heaven and earth to get sent all the way back here to make up for your mistake."

"And do my part to protect the president."

"Thanks, but we've got that covered." Reilly then launched into a description of all they'd done to "harden the target." Before Pearl Harbor there were seventeen cops and six Secret Service agents assigned to the White House. Since December 8, on every shift, he had twenty-two White House policemen, twenty Metropolitan Policemen or twenty uniformed Secret Service guards, and fifteen Secret Service agents, along with machine gun emplacements on the roof and an army reconnaissance car—with a machine gun—circling the Executive Area.

"But you still have to worry about the lone gunman, the guy who can stand two hundred yards away with a pistol and do this." Carter pulled the headless Hummel angel from his pocket and put it on the desk.

"Good shooting." Reilly picked up the figurine and inspected it. "You know, the army's biggest fear is a team of Nazi parachutists dropping onto the White House lawn. Mine is assassination. Some Nazi who can do this, operating alone or with a small team that activated when Hitler declared war . . ." Reilly didn't need to finish.

"Only two guys have looked this Nazi in the eye. Me and Kevin Cusack."

"Isn't Cusack the one they're calling the Hollywood Nazi, the one who killed that girl on the Super Chief?"

"It's my bet that the real Nazi framed him," said Carter.

Reilly reached into a drawer and came up with a thick ring binder. "Since you think you've seen this Nazi, have a look at this. I have to go."

Carter read the cover. "Suspect book for Los Angeles?"

"The White House gets forty thousand letters a month, five thousand of them are threats. We try to check out every threat to determine how dangerous—or crazy—the writer is. The ones we investigate get a page in this book."

"A trained assassin isn't going to write a nasty letter."

"Humor me." Reilly stood and picked up the headless Hummel. "May I keep this?"

"Be my guest. Let it be an inspiration."

"Thanks," said Reilly. "And rest easy, Agent Carter. I have one more surprise for anyone who slips a gun past the Alnor Door. A last line of defense, you might call it."

VIVIAN HOPEWELL GOT TO Union Station at 11:40. She walked over Capitol Hill and down the Mall to the Museum of Natural History. She was early, so she wandered for a time in the exhibit halls. She saw the rhino that Teddy Roosevelt shot, and the noble lion, the elk, the mighty bison. She felt a little sorry for all of them.

She never noticed the man in the button-covered scally cap, even though he seemed to be in every gallery she visited, reading captions about the life cycle of the monarch butterfly or studying exhibits on the ice age.

Around twelve thirty, she strolled back to the main rotunda, where a magnificent, taxidermic African elephant took center stage. It seemed to be running, its trunk raised to the sky . . . or the ceiling. She could almost hear its trumpet echoing off the balconies.

And Harold was waiting for her. She hurried up to him and embraced him. She was overjoyed to see him, and thrilled to be back in the big world of restaurants and museums and roadways to interesting places.

Kevin Cusack almost jumped at the sight of him, but he kept control and hung back behind a pillar. Observe before acting, he told himself. Follow Harold and Vivian downstairs and watch through the door of the cafeteria.

It wasn't fancy: linoleum floor, self-serve counters, noisy scraping chairs, two school groups in the corners, kids loud and boisterous with Christmas coming and classes winding down. Harold and Vivian took trays and went through the line. Baked macaroni, tapioca pudding, and coffee for her. A prepackaged ham sandwich for him. They found a table off to the side. He apologized for the noise, but this was the closest place to the Department of Agriculture.

She dug into her baked macaroni, dripping in melted cheese, guaranteed to put three pounds on her. He unwrapped the sandwich and doused it with mustard.

After a bite, he asked, "So, how is it living in your parents' house again?"

"I can't wait to leave."

"It's only for a little while."

"Do you really mean that?"

He smiled, as if to say yes, he really meant it.

She brought her index finger to her chin.

He got the message and wiped a drip of mustard from below his lip. Then he said, "Tell me about this old boyfriend."

"Even when we were kids, Johnny said he'd work in the statehouse some day. Right out of college, he got a job with our state rep. Then he wrote a report on Maryland roads. The governor liked it so much, he put Johnny on his staff. And now Johnny's got two VIP tickets to the tree lighting."

"So, he found his passion without ever leaving Annapolis. You had to cross the country to find yours. But you gave the performance of your life on that train."

She loved that. It was bromide after her mother's bile.

"Now, I need you to do me a favor. Do you see those people over there?" Martin pointed to a woman in a blue hat and overcoat, sitting with a paunchy man in a brown suit. "They're colleagues at Agriculture. They'd be very impressed if they knew that I was going to be sitting on the White House lawn for the tree lighting."

"But—"

"Do you think you could persuade your old boyfriend to give up the tickets?"

"I . . . I don't know. I'm seeing him tomorrow, at the place where I worked."

"The G&J Grill? The place you told me about?"

On the other side of the room, the Stauers were finishing up, getting up, returning their trays to the dish receptacle. Now they were coming over, all smiles and warmth, all as planned so that they could get a look at the girl. Helen was already extending her hand. "Mr. Kellogg, so nice to see you. Is this your lovely wife?"

Martin introduced them all around.

Helen said, "We were just telling your husband how thrilled we are to have tickets to the tree lighting. He says you might get them, too. Perhaps we could go all together."

"Well, yes," said Vivian. "Maybe." She didn't know it, but they were all playing her. If she could deliver those tickets, all their jobs would be much easier.

"Now, you'll excuse us," said Helen, "but America's work awaits."

"Feeding the world, one meeting at a time." Will Stauer gave a jolly laugh.

Martin got up and said, "Yes. We're all due back at the department."

"Washington is such a booming city now," said Helen.

"So true," said Martin. "Airplane contractors to the Defense Department, bankers to Treasury, farmers to the Agriculture Department . . . we all have a part to play." Then he kissed Vivian on the cheek and whispered, "Well done. Go home. I'll call you later."

That speech again. Where had she heard it before?

KEVIN CUSACK HAD WATCHED it all from behind a pillar. He would've asked the museum guards to detain Harold Kellogg, but that pair of retired cops didn't look like they could handle an unruly school group. And what about the other two? The lady in the blue coat from the Washington Monument and the man who'd followed Kevin into Georgetown? Were they friends? Business acquaintances? Accomplices? If so, in what?

Besides, Harry Kellogg wasn't the suspected murderer. Kevin was.

So he decided that Vivian was the weak link. Best to keep following her, confront her alone, then give Carter all the info he gathered.

While Kellogg and the Stauers went out the south exit onto Madison, Kevin tailed Vivian through the building to the north exit, then across Constitution and up Tenth Street. He expected her to go back to Union Station, but she kept heading north, across Pennsylvania, past Ford's Theatre to F Street. Then she turned west.

Where in hell was she going? All he could do was follow. They were long blocks, so he could keep his distance. At Fifteenth, she picked up her pace and crossed before the cop in the traffic box put up the stop signal, stranding Kevin on the east side. And he watched her go into Garfinckel's department store. He would've jaywalked after her, but murder suspects shouldn't be tempting traffic cops.

By the time he came in on Garfinckel's street floor, she'd disappeared. He looked toward the escalator, then toward the elevator. Nothing. He'd lost her.

A saleslady in heavy makeup stepped in front of him, squirted a spray of Shalimar on her wrist, and held it to his nose, saying, "The best Christmas present you can buy for a lady friend."

Kevin sneezed.

SOMETIMES, FATE INTERVENED. AND fate never rested in Washington, D.C. Everybody in all the circles of power knew everybody else. And everybody in all the circles seemed to cross paths regularly on the diagonal boulevards and gridwork streets that connected the circles and the squares, too.

But Frank Carter was an outsider. When he left the White House, with his .357 Magnum back in his shoulder holster, he wasn't thinking about circles of power. He was thinking about all the faces in that suspect book, none of which were the shooter. He came out at Treasury Place and waited for the light so that he could cross Fifteenth.

At the same moment, on the other side of Fifteenth, a man in a navy-blue overcoat was walking north. Blue overcoat, owlish eyeglasses, straight-back hair.

Carter barely noticed him. Then he looked again, and thought, *What am I seeing?* The guy from the Bradbury Building walking the streets of Washington, D.C.?

It couldn't be. Or could it? Carter decided to follow, if only to get a closer look. So up Fifteenth they went, then left onto Pennsylvania in front of the White House, then across Lafayette Square to H Street. That's where it got complicated, because the guy in the blue overcoat hailed a cab.

Carter had to decide: Keep following or chalk it up to mistaken identity?

Once more, fate intervened. Another taxi came around the corner, and the driver shouted, "Need a ride, mister?"

Carter jumped in and said, "Follow that cab," just like in the movies . . . through the Georgetown business district on M Street, then onto the Key Bridge.

"Other side of the river is a new fare zone," said the driver. "Keep goin'?"

Carter was trying to decide how far to follow when the first cab pulled over on the Arlington end of the bridge. The man in the blue overcoat jumped out, hurried across the street, and disappeared down an embankment.

"Looks like he's headed for the Mount Vernon Trail," said the cabbie.

"Where does that lead?"

"All the way to George Washington's house, if you can walk six miles. A nice path along the river. Teddy Roosevelt Island is down there, too. I'm droppin' tourists and lover's lane kids in the parkin' lot all the time."

Carter paid, jumped out, and down the Mount Vernon Trail he went. It was a paved walkway though the trees and across busy George Washington Parkway, then down to the Potomac riverbank, and it was deserted, which wasn't surprising. Midafternoon, on a chilly Monday in December, a cold mist drizzling down . . . not a day to bring out baby strollers and hand-holders.

So Carter hurried along, expecting to round a bend and find himself directly behind the blue overcoat. But the guy moved fast or hid well, because he was nowhere ahead, not on the path, not on the grass sloping down to the river, not in any of the little stands of brush along the way. But people didn't just disappear. And the farther he went, the more curious Frank Carter became.

The path took him nearly a half mile south to the parking lot for Theodore Roosevelt Island. He counted three cars, and hunched over one of them, the blue overcoat. The guy was trying to jimmy a car door. When he saw Carter, he started walking again, like he hadn't been caught in the act. Then he was jogging, then running over the wooden footbridge that led across an inlet onto the island.

Carter reached under his coat and loosened his .357. Then he crossed the footbridge, too. On the island, he stopped to read the map at the trailhead. This was one of the first projects of FDR's Civilian Conservation Corps, and a TR memorial was planned, but as yet, the island was no more than a maze of dirt paths and boardwalks winding through old-growth woods and new plantings, with a wide, swampy marshland around the edges.

A young couple came from the trail on his right.

Carter asked if they'd seen a man in a blue overcoat. No, they hadn't.

So he went east through the woods, toward the perimeter trail on the other side of the island. Soon he came to a boardwalk over the marsh, with the river another fifty yards beyond. Before deciding which way to go, he stopped and listened for footfalls on the wooden planking. And he heard them, moving south.

So south he went. After a short distance, he approached a place where the shrubs grew thick. He put his hand on his gun and went more carefully.

But no one popped out. And the footfalls seemed to have stopped.

In this odd corner of Washington, with the Potomac flowing nearby and the gray light dim and depressing, Frank Carter suddenly felt like the only man in the world. The wind rattled the marsh grass. A flock of Canada geese came flapping overhead. Traffic hummed in the distance. Then something rustled under his feet. Through the spaces in the boards, he saw movement. He pulled the Magnum and said, "Stay right there."

The movement continued. He followed it. How could a man move that fast under a boardwalk? But . . . not a man, a muskrat. The black streak of fur shot out and ran off.

Carter lowered the gun, feeling stupid for trying to arrest a river rodent. The nervous excitement drained out of him. But what had flushed it?

That's when he heard a noise behind him. He turned and saw the owlish glasses, the blue overcoat, and the Mauser C96 pointed right at him. The guy was kneeling in the marsh grass, his hand balanced on the edge of the boardwalk.

After two weeks and three thousand miles, Frank Carter had found his man.

And the guy wanted . . . to *talk*. He said, "Why are you following me?"

Carter knew that the guy did things against the grain and always thought he was outthinking you. But Carter didn't let anyone outthink him. *Talk* instead of *shoot*? Just a diversion. So he cocked the Magnum and said, "I've heard that you're a Nazi killer."

"Who told you that?" The guy behind the Mauser had the drop on him, so . . .

. . . Carter decided to go against the grain himself and take the first shot. He raised his Magnum, but as he did, he knew he was a dead man. The guy had anticipated and wasn't surprised by Carter's sudden move. Carter heard the shot and felt the bullet hit his chest at the same instant.

And that was the end of whatever thoughts were left to Frank Carter. He didn't feel the ground when his knees struck it. He didn't hear the blast when his finger reflexively pulled the trigger and the Magnum discharged into the swamp. When Martin Browning stuffed him under the boardwalk, he may have been alive in some technical sense, but he felt nothing, not the cold of the air, not the dank of the tidewater, not the oblivion fading to nothing.

BACK IN THE HOTEL, Martin Browning called for a bellhop. He needed his trousers cleaned. Then he ordered room service and showered. He stayed under the hot water for ten minutes, to rid himself of the marsh stink and the death stink, too.

When he'd picked up the tail in front of the White House, he didn't believe it. By the time he'd crossed Lafayette Square, he was certain. The FBI agent who'd chased him in L.A. had found him in Washington. If he'd only been able to jimmy that car door, there'd have been no need to retreat onto the island. He'd have sped off like a common car thief.

Now, Frank Carter's FBI badge, ID, and revolver lay on Martin Browning's nightstand. They'd be helpful, at least.

He picked up the phone. He should have called Helen Stauer. But he wanted to hear Vivian's voice. He surprised himself by turning to a woman for comfort.

And she offered it. She chattered on about meeting his friends that afternoon and how nice they were. Then she said that she'd try to get both tickets to the tree lighting.

He hoped that she'd succeed, because it was the safest way to get close enough to take the shot with the Mauser C96. At the same time he hoped that she'd fail, because if he made that shot, he'd die right there, and if she was with him, so would she.

And now another worry nagged him. If he'd been able to talk longer with Carter, he might have figured out what that G-man knew. Had Schwinn or someone else in the Bund revealed enough that the feds had figured out the plan? Was it a trap? Should the mission be canceled? A new set of second thoughts afflicted Martin Browning.

AT 5:00 P.M., KEVIN Cusack approached the Willard. He peered in the window to make sure there were no Washington Metros lurking about. Then he went into the lobby. He was supposed to meet Carter. But no Carter. So he grabbed the house phone and called Carter's room.

Stella answered, "Are you with Frank?"

"Me? No. I need to see him."

She said Carter hadn't come back. Last seen at the White House. "He was planning to bring you over to the FBI and straighten things out. Where are you?"

"I'm on the run, remember? I don't come in until Frank smooths the way. Tell him I need his help. Tell him I have information." *Click.*

Ten minutes later, as Kevin approached his own hotel, he saw the unmarked car that had parked in front of the Willard that morning. And at the concierge's desk he saw the two Washington detectives. One was showing a photograph.

A photo of the Hollywood Nazi? Kevin wasn't hanging around to find out. He turned and walked right out and disappeared into the night.

TUESDAY,
DECEMBER 23

MARTIN BROWNING'S FIRST WORDS that morning were "My God." He picked up the paper, saw the photo on the front page, said it in English, and thought it in German. *Mein Gott.*

The prime minister of Great Britain was standing beside the president of the United States, above this headline: CHURCHILL IN UNITY TALKS AT WHITE HOUSE.

In an amazing act of secrecy and bravery, Winston Churchill and his staff had crossed the Atlantic—they weren't saying how—to confer with Franklin Roosevelt over the conduct of the war.

Martin Browning didn't believe in God, but he believed in fate. And fate had now offered him an even greater moment on the stage of history. It had also given him a new surge of confidence. He would kill them both. Fate demanded it, no matter what the FBI might know, no matter the repercussions of Agent Carter's death.

He gazed across Lafayette Square and imagined them enjoying breakfast in the White House, the two greatest enemies of the German people, both planning to give speeches on Christmas Eve, both making targets of themselves. And he would kill them both. . . .

STELLA MADDEN HAD BEEN through a lot in her thirty-four years. She'd been born to money, but also to booze, or the smell of it on her father's breath . . . even at eight o'clock in the morning. He'd been a genius when it came to San Fernando Valley real estate, but he gargled with Canadian rye, which made him mean and unpredictable.

So Stella grew up tougher than any kid in Pasadena. When the little princesses in her all-girls school ostracized her, she smacked the ringleader in the chops and got herself expelled. When her father insisted she go to a finishing school, she got a detective's license instead. But here she was, at eight in the morning, wondering if she should order a beer and a shot to calm her nerves, just like Dad . . .

. . . because Frank hadn't come back.

Did he have some old girlfriend in Washington? Was he a closet drinker himself, gone on an all-night drunk? Had he gotten into a fight? Had he and that Kevin Cusack quarreled, leading to who the hell knew *what*?

She'd decided not to panic but to wait out the night in the hotel.

Now the night was over. And she had two phone numbers: Detective Mills at Washington Metro and Agent Dan Jones at the FBI. She called Jones.

He was right at his desk, a good early-morning man. His first question: "Who was the last person to see Frank?"

"He was supposed to see Kevin Cusack at five last evening."

"Our so-called Hollywood Nazi?" said Jones. "Do we know where he's staying?"

"No. They were going to meet in the Willard lobby."

"We need to bring him in." Jones told her to set up a meeting if Kevin called.

"Do I file a missing person on Frank?" she asked.

"We're the goddamn FBI. We find our own people. And if this Cusack was the last guy to see Frank, well, he might've . . ." Dan Jones's voice trailed off.

"What?" said Stella. "He might've what?"

"Hard to believe some Hollywood guy could take down Frank Carter."

"Don't even talk like that," said Stella.

"Call if you hear anything."

"You, too."

"Better yet," said Jones, "come over. We can talk face-to-face. I'm in meetings till ten thirty, then I'm yours."

At eight thirty, a dog walker stopped on the Roosevelt Island board-walk to let his terrier sniff at a reddish stain. Around 9:15, a young mother pushed a stroller over the planking and through the marsh that was smelling very strong that day. Then, about ten o'clock, an old couple clumped their canes along the planking until the wife stopped clumping.

The husband turned. "What?"

She pointed her cane into the swamp. "Is that a muskrat? And . . . and, oh, dear, he has a coat cuff, and . . . is that a hand?"

As Stella Madden headed out to the FBI, the phone rang. Her heart flipped. Was it Frank or bad news about him?

Neither. It was Cusack. "I need to talk to Frank."

She sank onto the edge of the bed. "He hasn't come back."

"Not since yesterday?"

"Not since he was supposed to meet you. The FBI wants *me* to bring you in. Meet me in front of the Justice Department on Pennsylvania and—"

"Is this another setup? Frank's been setting me up for a week."

Stella said, "Frank couldn't trail Kellogg himself. They wouldn't let him. So he kept you out there, doing his work for him while he let you run."

"Running isn't much fun." Kevin had spent the night on Mary Benning's couch. He'd been walking the streets since seven o'clock, when she sent him on his way. And he'd had plenty of time to think. "But I'm getting used to it. I may learn to like it."

"Turn yourself in," said Stella. "Trust Frank and Agent Dan Jones. Give them your information. Then leave it to the FBI."

Kevin said, "Give me the FBI number. I'll call Jones when I know more. I'll call you, too."

"What are you going to do?"

"Frank's work, like you said, and get myself in the clear, too. I'm the only one I can trust now." *Click.*

TWO ASSASSINS SAT ON a bench. The bench sat on the avenue named for the document that defined the government that they planned to decapitate. Behind them rose the Washington Monument. Before them, some six hundred meters away, the South Portico of the White House offered itself to the world.

The woman in the Prussian-blue overcoat had brought two bagged lunches.

The man in the navy-blue overcoat asked, "Where's your husband?"

"He's tracking Johnny Beevers. It was a good idea to let us meet the girl. Good to get a fix on what she looks like. Perhaps we can use her to get at her old boyfriend." She handed Martin a bag. "Your lunch. Ham. With mustard, I assume?"

"Why do you assume?"

"The way the girl touched her chin so you'd wipe off the mustard yesterday . . . Very sweet. But not as sweet as the front-page picture of Churchill and Roosevelt together."

"An amazing turn of luck," said Martin.

"We can kill them both." She bit into her sandwich.

"But we can't do anything stupid," he said.

She chewed and swallowed. "Such as?"

Two mounted Park Police clip-clopped across Constitution from the Ellipse and went up the slope toward the monument.

Martin waited until they were gone, then said, "I killed an FBI agent."

She fixed her eyes on the White House.

"He chased me in L.A. He found me in Lafayette Square. I can't imagine how."

"Is it in the news, this killing?"

"I expect they haven't found the body." Martin took a bite of sandwich.

"At least now," she said, "only one man in Washington knows what you look like."

"I should have killed him, too."

"Better to determine what he knows, *then* kill him," she said.

"Or assume he knows nothing and stop looking for him."

Helen Stauer turned. "Whatever he knows, Martin, it cannot deter us. With this news about Churchill, we can win the war in one night."

It was the first time she'd used his Christian name. It was as if she said it to emphasize the importance of her words. And he knew she was right. Even if they all died, this was a world-historical moment. Those he'd already killed were martyrs. The deaths of the three assassins would be martyrdom, too.

As if she could read his mind, she said, "We must be prepared to die."

Yes, but that was the hard part, he thought: preparing to die on such a beautiful day.

They sat in silence for a time. The traffic sped by. The sun warmed their backs.

Then she said, "My husband and I have no children to remember us. But the Reich will remember. The world will remember." Then she got back to business. "Now, this FBI agent . . . did you get his ID?"

He pulled out the leather wallet, flipped it open, and showed the FBI identity card, including Carter's headshot and signature.

She said, "Good. I can work with that."

Then he handed her the badge.

She examined it like an appraiser with a piece of jewelry: the shiny brass, the eagle, the words "Federal Bureau of Investigation, U.S. Department of Justice," the blindfolded lady holding the scales. She said, "This could be a great help, too."

Martin said, "Can your husband handle the K 98k?"

"He's better with a pistol," she said, "but put him here, with the K 98k, or on the slope behind us—"

"There will be Park Police on the slope. Besides, it's too far. The best shot is from those branches"—Martin pointed to the tree he'd climbed in the middle of the night—"if he's nimble enough."

"He's clumsy but deadly. With this"—she held up the badge—"he can move freely, even carry a rifle under his raincoat. Then we position you on the South Lawn—"

"If we can get the tickets," he said, "and if the tickets mean we don't have to go through their electrical searcher."

"Two electrical searchers, but three entrances," she said. "That's what's in the paper. That's what you saw. So my husband will shoot Churchill. You will shoot FDR. Both shots at the instant the tree is lit. Then you will change targets."

"A crossfire." Martin knew it would be a beautiful thing. But he was a soldier, and a real soldier wanted to live for his country . . . not die.

VIVIAN WALKED INTO THE G&J Grill and Soda Fountain in Annapolis. And it was as if nothing had changed. . . . the smell of hamburger grease overlaying French fries and coffee . . . the quiet conversation before the lunch crowd came in . . . the fog of cigarette smoke that seemed to flutter with the flap of every newspaper page.

At first, no one noticed her except Johnny Beevers. He'd saved her a spot at the counter, as if to show her off. And he beamed at the sight of her. She could feel the warmth of his gaze from across the room.

Then, one by one, the old regulars looked up, recognized the girl beneath the blond dye job, and called her name or threw her a wave or came over to give her a hi-how-ya-doin' . . . all except for a lone coffee drinker who sat and watched and listened: Will Stauer.

One way or the other, Will was going to get those passes to the South Lawn. He'd already broken into Johnny Beevers's apartment but hadn't found them. So he'd found Johnny himself at the statehouse and tracked him here. And it didn't take long to find out what he needed to know, because he heard Vivian say:

"Do you really have tickets to the tree lighting?"

Johnny pulled them from his pocket and read, "'National Tree Lighting, December 24, 1941. Gates open at 4:00 P.M. Cardholders enter at Northeast Appointment Gate.'" Then he grinned the same boyish grin she remembered from high school.

She reached for the tickets.

He pulled them back. "You have to say, 'Yes, Johnny, I'll go with you.' Then you can hold them both."

Will Stauer was hoping she'd say yes. It would make things much easier.

But she said, "I don't want to lead you on, Johnny."

He said, "Aw, c'mon, we'll drive to Washington in my brand-new Buick Special. We'll get seats down front. We won't even have to stand in line."

Seats down front . . . Will Stauer *had* to get his hands on those tickets.

Vivian said, "Take some new girl you're sweet on, Johnny. A big political deal like you, in your fancy suit with your hair all slicked and your cheeks all shiny and smooth from your barbershop shave . . . you must have a lot of girls chasing you."

"Only one girl I carry a torch for," said Johnny.

Vivian felt her face getting hot. She hadn't blushed in a long time. But Johnny made her blush because he'd always been too honest. And he hadn't changed at all.

Will Stauer wanted to keep watching this little scene, but he was lowering his head into his newspaper, because the door was opening, and the man he'd followed on Sunday was stepping into the G&J Grill.

KEVIN CUSACK HAD WORKED his way up Main Street, restaurant to restaurant, asking for the waitress who went to Hollywood. He'd found her at his third stop. He dropped into a booth, pulled down the scally cap, and watched her talking with a young man at the counter. Then she stood, gave the young man a peck on the cheek, like a sister or an old friend, and left. She never even glanced in Kevin's direction.

But Kevin was out the door right after her, following her down Main Street to Conduit, then over to Duke of Gloucester and down to Spa Creek. He was getting good at the follow. He'd read enough Raymond Chandler novels, with Philip Marlowe on a tail, that he knew just how far to hang back and just how to look casual if someone spotted him.

By the time she reached the neighborhood called Eastport, he'd concluded that whatever was going on, she was an innocent, because she never picked up her pace or acted suspicious. No worry in the walk. Just a simple gal strolling through the old hometown. When she opened the gate to the little corner lot, Kevin decided he knew enough. Best to confront her out here.

He called, "Mrs. Kellogg!"

She turned abruptly. Who could know that name around here?

Kevin stepped closer. "He's not your husband, is he?"

Her face passed through a range of emotions, like an actress showing her wares. Shock to puzzlement to curiosity, then back to shock. "*You.* What are you doing here?"

"Rescuing you." Kevin surprised himself by that answer.

It surprised Vivian, too. She closed the gate between them. "You killed that Sally Drake."

"It was your Harold who killed her."

"My Harold? My husband?"

"Come on, sister. I wasn't born yesterday. He's not your husband. He was using you on that train, just like you were using him to get home from California, just like you used Sinclair Cook to get out there."

"Cook? Mr. Brylcreem? How do you know about him?"

"I know a lot. But do you know what you've gotten yourself into?"

The front door opened and Les Schortmann peered out. "Who's that, honey?"

"Go get your gun, Pa. And tell Ma to call the police."

The old man stepped back into the house.

Kevin said, "You need to ask that Harold some tough questions, Vivian. About himself and about his friends, too, the ones you met in the cafeteria yesterday. Who are they?"

"How did you know about them?"

Kevin didn't respond to that. He pulled a slip of paper from his pocket. "Here's my phone number. If you find any answers, call me. I'll be by the phone at eight and eight, tonight and tomorrow morning."

She took the paper. "You can't keep running, mister."

"I've been running since last Sunday, thanks to you and your friend."

"I had nothing to do with killing that girl."

"No one will believe you if you don't do the right thing now." He started backing away, because he sensed movement in the house. "Just ask yourself, what would Jean Arthur do?"

Les Schortmann burst out the door with his shotgun, tripped on the top step, fell forward, and fired into the lawn.

Vivian shouted, "Oh, damn it, Pa." She helped him up, then turned again, but Kevin was gone. Up the street or down? She couldn't tell. She thought about running after him. But the pumps. The damn pumps. She couldn't run in them. She hated them.

She went back and asked her father if Mom had called the police.

"Not yet," he said. "Never told her. Grabbed my shotgun instead. Had to find the shells."

Vivian decided she'd wait to hear from Harold. Whatever was going on, Harold owed her an explanation.

KEVIN FOUND STANLEY SMITH's car on the waterfront and jumped in the back seat.

Stanley looked over his shoulder. "Hey, man, I said I'd drive you around for a day, but I ain't your damn chauffeur. Get in the front."

"Just go." Kevin slunk down.

Stanley put the car in gear. "Somethin' tells me you found somethin'."

"Somethin's right."

"All I found was white navy boys in blue uniforms struttin' around like they already won the damn war." Stanley drove up Main Street and swung around Church Circle onto West Street. Then he said, "Now what?"

"I need a phone booth."

After a mile, Stanley pulled over by a gas station.

Kevin told him to keep an eye out for the cops; then he went into the booth and dialed Dan Jones at the FBI. He was amazed that the call went straight through. Jones answered, and Kevin said, "Stella Madden tells me you want to talk to me."

"Where are you?" asked Jones.

"I found the woman traveling with Kellogg. She lives in a house on the corner of Chesapeake and Second, in Annapolis. Tell Carter."

Jones said, "Carter's dead."

Kevin thought he'd misheard. He put a finger in his ear to keep down the noise of the traffic. "What did you say?"

"Dead," answered Jones. "Now, what do you know?"

Kevin slumped against the phone booth wall. "Dead? Jesus. How?"

"Why don't you come in? We'll talk about it."

Kevin gasped, then gasped again, then all but lost his breath. If Carter was dead, who'd clear him now? And Carter was his friend, even if he'd used Kevin like a ten-cent mackerel spoon. Kevin took two or three deep breaths and said, "If I come in, do I need a lawyer?"

"I don't know. *Do you?*"

Kevin regained some of his sarcasm along with his breath. "If I was writing this scene, that's the answer I'd put in the FBI guy's mouth."

"Don't be a smartass," said Jones. "The D.C. Metros don't like smartasses, and they have jurisdiction. As for Stella Madden—"

"Does she know?"

"She ID'd the body. She told the Metros you were the last guy on Carter's schedule." Jones paused, as if to let that sink in. Then he said, "Give it up, Hollywood. I can't protect you from the Metros *or* from the Bureau guys who knew Frank Carter."

"Before I turn myself in," said Kevin, "I want you to call Leon Lewis—"

Stanley tapped his horn to warn Kevin that a police car was coming along.

"—or better yet, call the chief agent in the L.A. field office. His name is Hood. Have him call Lewis and tell Lewis to call you. He'll vouch."

"What's to say you're not playing Lewis, too? Maybe you're a Nazi spying on the Jews, not the other way around? We know about your grandfather, one of those Irish troublemakers from '16. They used the Germans and the Germans used them."

"I have two grandfathers. One's Irish. The other's a Jew. Forget them both and find this Kellogg guy and his friends. Start with his girlfriend."

"What's her real name?"

Kevin saw the "stupid" light flashing again. He had to admit, "I never got it."

"For a guy playing all the angles, that's—"

"Hey, listen. I found where she lives. You bring her in." *Click.* Kevin was done with the FBI. Anybody who'd even entertain the possibility that he was some kind of Bund double agent was too dangerous to talk to.

Martin Browning called Vivian at her mother's house.

Before he got a word out, she demanded, "Harry, what the hell is going on? The guy on the train came to see me. The Hollywood Nazi."

Martin couldn't believe it. The guy was everywhere. He told Vivian, "Get on the three o'clock train. Bring an overnight bag. I'll meet you at Union Station. We're invited to a dinner party in Washington." That was a lie. But maybe he could turn it into truth.

Vivian said, "That Cusack guy told me you killed Sally Drake. Did you?"

"My God, what a liar. Just come to Washington. I'll explain everything."

And Vivian agreed. An explanation, a dinner party, a night in a nice hotel . . . maybe she was cheap after all, just a cheap date.

Next he called Helen Stauer and said they had to use one of the other safe houses. Vivian was attracting too much attention in Annapolis, so he was bringing her into town. And he needed a more secure place to hide out because of the FBI killing.

Helen said, "We have Mrs. Colbert. She lives in the Kalorama district."

"Pronounced Col-bair?" said Martin. "That's French, not German."

"She's American. Her late husband was a Swiss commodities broker working with Spanish fascists. He made a fortune brokering Spanish tungsten to the Reich armament industry. Along the way, the Colberts absorbed a great deal of German ideology *and* became leading America Firsters."

"Can she be trusted?"

"Section Six trusts her. But about this Johnny Beevers. My husband has tracked him all day, even stayed with him when Cusack appeared. He thinks we should kill Cusack, too, but he needs to know what to do about Beevers."

"Tell him to come back. We'll lure Beevers to D.C. and deal with him here. Cusack, too."

A PAIR OF FBI agents arrived in Annapolis about three o'clock. They didn't have a full address, just a location: the corner of Chesapeake and Second Street. And they didn't know what they were waiting for. So for a time, they waited and watched.

When the lights came on in the little bungalow with asbestos shingles, they went up and knocked. Mrs. Schortmann answered. She was sucking on a breath mint but the air around her had the sweet aroma of a late-afternoon highball.

They showed their badges and asked for Vivian. Kellogg. That was the only name they had.

Mrs. Schortmann said that they must be looking for her daughter. But her daughter had gone into Washington and wouldn't be home until Christmas Eve. "Got all dolled up in her new polka-dot outfit and headed off to spend an evening in sin. At least the man she's sinning with looks like a movie star."

"What star would that be, ma'am?"

"Leslie Howard."

They left a card and a phone number and asked that the daughter call them. When they got back to the car, one agent said to the other, "Jeesh. Leslie Fuckin' Howard. Why couldn't she pick Clark Gable or somebody?"

MARTIN MET VIVIAN AT Union Station and led her to a taxi. "I hereby admit that I'm lost without you," he said, and he remembered to smile. He knew that she liked it when he smiled. "It must have been quite a shock seeing our Hollywood friend."

"He told me things, Harold. You have to explain. You promised to explain."

Martin gave the driver an address on Kalorama Circle, two miles from the White House. Then he patted Vivian's knee. "Don't worry about anything. Trust me."

Vivian looked out the window. He'd been telling her to trust him for two weeks. On the train ride in, she'd decided that trusting him was still the best path to the life she imagined, instead of what she'd been revisiting in the last few days. He might be less conventional than Johnny Beevers, but he delivered excitement.

And he was about to make it easier to contrast himself with Johnny, because he asked her to call him and invite him for dinner.

"Why? You want to beat him up for moving in on your girlfriend or something?"

Martin gave her a gentle Harold Kellogg laugh. "My dear, you need to calm your speculations. I didn't kill Sally Drake, and I don't want to beat up anyone. But I do want to buy the tickets from Johnny Beevers. Did they have his name on them?"

"No name. They say, 'Admit One, enter by the Northeast Appointment Gate.'"

Perfect, thought Martin Browning. The gate without the "electrical searcher." In America, VIPs didn't submit to such indignities.

Soon the cab was turning onto a one-way circle lined with big houses, the kind where lawyers and lobbyists and diplomats lived, behind hedges, shielded by evergreens, bathed in the fragrance of boxwoods on a rainy night. Across from the Colbert house, a wooded hillside dropped toward Rock Creek. Through the bare trees, headlights were flickering as cars sped along the parkway below.

Martin said, "A long way from Hollywood Boulevard."

"Even longer from San Fernando Road," said Vivian. "But . . . I thought you were staying in a hotel."

"Mrs. Colbert is an old friend." That was a lie. "She just got back into town and invited us to stay." That was another.

The doorbell didn't buzz. It chimed, just like in the movies. The butler, tall and dour, led them across the huge foyer, past a grandfather clock and a twelve-foot-tall Christmas tree, into the sitting room.

Vivian had heard of places like this, where you smelled furniture polish instead of onions and garlic, where the draperies swallowed the outside noise, and you couldn't feel your footsteps because the Oriental carpets were so thick. Then Mrs. Colbert glided from the shadows. "Ah, Harold, is this your lovely wife?"

"Dear Elizabeth!" Martin embraced her like an old friend, though he'd only met her an hour before.

The portrait above the fireplace flattered her, a big woman, buxom, double-chinned, and pretty damn satisfied with how she'd gotten there.

Martin said, "I wanted you two to meet. So I brought Vivian in from Annapolis to keep me company during the conference."

"And for the tree lighting." Mrs. Colbert beamed at the thought of it. "Always such a festive night, even two weeks after what those dreadful Japanese did."

Martin said, "We're hoping to get tickets from the young man you've so graciously consented to entertain at dinner."

Mrs. Colbert clapped her hands. "Oh, yes. I'm setting an extra place. And Vivian, darling, I know you'd like to freshen up. My man, Caesar, will show you to your room."

"Telephone first," said Martin.

"In the library," said Mrs. Colbert.

"Library?" said Vivian, feeling overwhelmed by the opulence of the house and the warmth of the hostess. "Do I need a card?"

Mrs. Colbert gave a little laugh. "No, dear, you don't need a library card. There's another phone by your bed, if you prefer."

Martin called after her, "Be sure to tell Johnny we'll offer him something special in exchange for those tickets."

"And remind him, dear, the porch lights will be out," said Mrs. Colbert. "We're observing the blackout, even if our neighbors aren't."

As Vivian followed the butler through the enormous house, she heard Mrs. Colbert say, "Lovely girl. Just lovely." She also heard Martin say, "I am very lucky."

She didn't hear Mrs. Colbert whisper, "Lucky for you that she has an old boyfriend . . . and a gullible one at that. Are you using Gestapo money to buy his tickets?"

"I don't intend to buy them at all."

AT ABOUT THE SAME time, Stanley Smith was pulling up in front of the Willard Hotel. He left the engine running and said to Kevin, "Considerin' that the heat's on, you sure you want to walk in there?"

"I need to talk to Carter's girlfriend. She's my only—"

"That black Ford in the valet spot, that's unmarked Metro."

"I know," said Kevin. "It's the same car from yesterday morning."

"So the cops must be talkin' to her again, probably about you, and—Oh, shit." Stanley threw the car in gear and pulled into traffic.

The two detectives were coming out of the hotel. Stanley shot up to Fifteenth,

U-turned around the traffic box in the intersection, and swung back to park on the other side of Pennsylvania.

Kevin waited until the plainclothes Metros drove off. Then he opened his door.

Stanley said, "What the hell you doin'?"

"Going in to find her. I have to talk to her. I have to do *something*."

"You have to sit your ass down and *think*. Those cops probably give everybody in there a picture of you, from the manager right down to the newest black bellhop."

"So what do I do?"

Stanley opened his door. "I don't know why I'm helpin' you, man, but . . . let me handle it."

"Hey, Stanley, a Negro can't just walk into the lobby of the Willard Hotel, unless he's wearing a uniform."

"Give me somethin' she'll know you by . . . and give me five bucks."

A few minutes later, Stanley came along the sidewalk, stopped in front of the hotel, and said to the doorman, "Well, if it ain't Cousin Jimmy."

"Keep walkin', Stanley. I ain't talkin' to no-accounts while I'm workin'."

Stanley stepped a little closer. "I need a favor, Jimmy."

"I ain't gettin' you a job. Not after y'all got thrown off your own damn train."

"The cops who just left, the ones who didn't give you a tip—"

"Cops never tip."

"—they was lookin' for a lady guest by the name Stella Madden. I got a friend, sure would like to talk to her." Stanley offered his hand. "Tell her Sam Spade's outside—"

"Sam Spade?" Jimmy looked suspiciously at the hand. "He's a movie actor."

Stanley said, "He's a friend of mine. And he's right generous."

Jimmy shook the hand and palmed the five, which softened him considerably.

TEN MINUTES LATER, STANLEY parked on F Street across from the Peacock Alley door, just as Cousin Jimmy had instructed.

Stella hurried out, looked around, and got into the back seat. Her mascara had streaked. Her lipstick had faded. She said to Kevin, "*Sam Spade*. Very funny. If I was in the mood for comedy, I'd laugh."

Kevin said, "I can't believe what's happened. I'm really sorry."

"Yeah, you and me both," she said bitterly.

"How . . . ?"

"They shot him on Roosevelt Island."

"A robbery?" asked Kevin.

"Not a chance. He had to be tailing someone. The cops think it was you."

Stella sounded shocked and angry. "But you don't look like you ever fired a gun."

"I haven't."

"I'm carrying a Beretta. And I'm in the mood to use it. Any funny stuff, and I might use it on you."

"No more comedy from me," said Kevin. "But maybe we can team up."

She said, "I'm not a team player."

"Neither am I."

"Well, on that basis, maybe we can." She blew her nose and looked out as they drove by the White House. "Do either of you know exactly where they're lighting the Christmas tree tomorrow night?"

Stanley said, "Around the other side, on the South Lawn."

"Could we see it?" asked Stella.

Stanley looked at Kevin, who shrugged. Why not? So Stanley turned south onto Seventeenth, then east onto E Street. A sign on the corner of E Street: WARNING: THIS STREET WILL BE CLOSED TO AUTO TRAFFIC, DECEMBER 24, AT 2 PM.

Stanley said, "My mama loves the tree lightin'. You plannin' to go?"

Stella said, "If I want to find that Nazi bastard, yeah."

"At the tree lighting?" asked Kevin.

"He's going to shoot Roosevelt. Churchill, too, I'm guessing. They'll both be on the South Portico. They'll both make speeches."

And the enormity of it all struck Kevin Cusack. For over a week, he'd been chasing this guy alone, never wondering about the bigger picture, never thinking beyond the personal, never seeing his place in a much larger scheme.

But now? What he did in the next twenty-four hours could mean the whole world.

Stella said, "Carter started putting it together right after they raided the Murphy Ranch. The Nazi was shooting targets there, with a gun that's easy to hide and has a shoulder stock for steadying and a brutal wallop from a hundred yards. He killed three people in L.A., then he killed your girlfriend on the train, then—"

"—a trail of bodies," said Kevin. "But how do you know he's here to kill FDR?"

"A hunch. But why the hell else would he be here? Frank told his FBI pal, Dan Jones, and Jones sent Frank to see the Secret Service."

"So, they'll be looking for him, too," said Kevin.

"Unless they're wasting time looking for you." She told Stanley to pull over.

Stanley said, "Ain't supposed to park here."

"Pull over," demanded Stella. Then she popped out.

Kevin told Stanley, "Go park on Fifteenth." He scrambled after Stella. "Why me? Why are they after me?"

"Because some of them agree with the Metro cops. They think you're the Nazi."

They crossed E Street and went up to the fence. The tourists had all gone home, so Stella and Kevin were alone. The White House shimmered in the silvery mist. Close to the fence, two thirty-five-foot spruce trees framed the view. A crew was just finishing hanging lights and building a low wooden railing around the tree on the right.

Stella blew her nose again. She seemed to be sharpening, layering a professional veneer over her shock and grief. "There'll be twenty thousand people on this lawn tomorrow. And they'll line this fence ten or twenty deep. I don't see how a guy could flash a gun in a crowd like this, especially a pistol with a shoulder stock, and not be noticed."

Kevin pointed to a row of chairs that had been set up about two hundred feet from the portico. "Do you think he could get in there? They look like the VIP seats."

"With a pass, maybe. But security will be tight. Metal detectors. No packages." She looked behind her, at the flat, open fifty acres of the Ellipse. "Too exposed from back there. No pistol would have that range, anyway."

"What if he had a rifle?"

"With a rifle and a scope, he could make the shot from the goddamn Washington Monument."

Just then, two police walked by. One of them gave Kevin a second look, a real silent-movie double take. Did he recognize the Hollywood Nazi?

Kevin took Stella's arm and said, "Let's go, honey. We'll come back tomorrow for the big show. Damn shame that all these monuments are all blacked out."

She got the picture and said, "Yeah. Damn shame. Let's go get a drink."

And together they walked toward Fifteenth.

After a few paces, Kevin whispered, "Are they watching?"

She looked over her shoulder and smoothed the back of her coat. "We're clear."

Then they heard the *boom* of the evening gun from Fort Myer. The sun had set.

Stella said, "We need to stop this. We owe it to Frank."

"We owe it to America," said Kevin. "But first, we need to get off the street."

At seven thirty, a new Buick Special rolled onto Kalorama Circle. The wet pavement glistened. The neighborhood was quiet. Most porch lights were out.

Johnny Beevers drove slowly. He was looking for a big house, tan sandstone with white shutters, just as Kathy Schortmann had described it. He'd spent the drive asking himself why he was coming. She'd said only that there were people she wanted him to meet. And he never turned down invitations to fancy dinners in the District. A young man with political ambition was always looking for another leg up the ladder.

He found a parking spot right across from the house. He didn't even glance into the woods that rolled down to Rock Creek. If he had, he wouldn't have noticed Will Stauer lurking there because Will knew how to lurk. But as he was stepping up onto the sidewalk, he saw a woman coming toward him, her high heels echoing in the dark. He tipped his hat and let her pass.

She said, "Good evening, Mr. Beevers."

He began to say, "Good eve—" *But how did she know his name?*

She whirled around and her hand flashed toward his neck.

He felt the prick of the needle. He was more shocked than anything else. What was happening? He tried to pull away. "Hey—"

"Shh . . . shh. . . ."

And he felt his legs go to rubber. He shook his head. He grabbed for her arm. But stronger arms came from behind and held him.

The woman whispered, "Wait, Johnny, wait. It will be over in a moment." She was smiling, as if they were sharing an intimacy on the darkened, rain-soaked sidewalk, as if she might even kiss him.

Her red lipstick stained her teeth. And . . . it was the last thing he thought.

Somewhere up the street, a light came on, a door opened, and an elderly man came down his front steps with two Scotties on leashes.

Will caught the dead weight of Johnny Beevers as the legs collapsed, and he said in a loud voice, "Come on, now, Charlie, you're too drunk to drive. Give me your keys. There's a good fellow."

Meanwhile, Helen was opening the back door of Johnny's car.

Whoever the dog walker was, he didn't pay them much attention.

Will Stauer stuffed Johnny's body into the back seat and got behind the wheel. Helen climbed in next to Johnny, fished his pockets for the keys, and dropped them on the front seat.

"Is he dead?" Will started the engine.

"Five grams sodium thiopental. Induces coma in seconds. Death in minutes."

Will swung down Belmont Street, heading for Rock Creek Parkway. "What about the tickets? Does he have the tickets?"

Helen pulled them out of Johnny's breast pocket and held them up. "Roosevelt is a dead man. Churchill, too."

VIVIAN SAT BESIDE A roaring fireplace and sipped a Spanish bubbly called Llopart brut cava. If she'd learned anything in the last few weeks, it was that she was susceptible to the lure of luxury, which enhanced Harold's reassurances.

So she'd put concerns about her fake "husband" out of her head. She'd put the nation's wartime worries out of her head, too. She didn't know if it was the cava or the fire or the glow in her "husband's" eyes that did it, but here she was, forty-five minutes from the tiny Schortmann living room, and in Harold's company, she was feeling rich, luxurious, pampered, and a bit apprehensive, too . . .

. . . because she hated hurting Johnny's feelings. But the house was a terrific prop to convince him that his old girlfriend was now living in a world that was too far above him. She was going to tell him that she and Harold had been secretly married in Los Angeles and were saving the news for Christmas Day and—

At the sound of the door chime, Mrs. Colbert rose and glided out. "You two stay. I'll greet our guest."

Harold toasted Vivian. "You look beautiful in the firelight. So relax. You'll do fine. If you feel uncomfortable, just look at me."

She finished her drink, which gave her a little more courage to disappoint such a sweet guy.

But Mrs. Colbert came back with an envelope. "It wasn't your friend. It was a messenger. He brought this." She handed it to Vivian. "I assume that's your maiden name, dear."

Vivian took the envelope. The name was "Kathy Schortmann." And inside, wrapped in a note, were two tickets to the tree lighting, VIP seats on the South Lawn of the White House.

"May I?" Harold took the note and read: "'Dear Kathy, My only hope is for your happiness. Enjoy these tickets with my compliments. Love, Johnny.' What a gentleman."

Vivian thought it odd that he typed the note, but the signature was his. She'd seen it often enough in love letters. She couldn't have known that Helen Stauer had copied it from Johnny's Maryland driver's license.

Martin caught Mrs. Colbert's eye, and she said, "Oh, such a pity, but I have a marvelous meal planned. I'm glad the Stauers are joining us even if Mr. Beevers isn't."

Harold refilled everyone's glass, and Vivian put Johnny Beevers and his hurt feelings out of her mind.

But Johnny's feelings were as nothing now. His body was somewhere in the middle of the Potomac, floating toward the Chesapeake. His new Buick was parked in Mrs. Colbert's garage, off the alley behind the house. And the Stauers were coming up the front walk.

FOUR PEOPLE SAT BY a phone in a tiny Georgetown apartment and waited.

Kevin Cusack looked at his watch. "I said eight and eight, P.M. and A.M."

Stanley said, "Well, it's eight thirty. I ain't waitin' around till morning."

"You're not invited." Mary Benning sat in a corner, knitting the hell out of a scarf. The first thing she'd said when Kevin showed up with a Negro and a scowling female detective from L.A.: "Just what I need. More trouble."

Stanley said, "I don't know why y'all think it's your job to save the president. There's plenty of people takin' care of him without us gettin' in the way."

"We have to do what we can," said Stella. "It's up to all of us."

Kevin was thinking the same thing.

Stella told Stanley, "I'll take a ride back to the Willard if you're offering." She told Kevin, "I'll call the FBI from my hotel."

"Tell them I'll turn myself in tomorrow," said Kevin. "But I need to stay by the phone tonight. I owe it to that girl."

"I think the girl's in on it," said Stella.

"I don't," answered Kevin. "I think he's using her. Like he used me."

"Nah," said Stanley. "That ain't how he used her."

After they left, Kevin apologized to Mary Benning for getting her involved. She just kept clanging away at those knitting needles.

AT MRS. COLBERT'S TABLE, the candlelight glimmered, the silverware flashed, the china tinkled and chimed, and the talk was all about tree lighting and speeches from famous men. Vivian would be there, right in the heart of it all. She'd see them both in the flesh, Churchill and Roosevelt, right on the South Portico. It would all be so exciting. Imagining it almost dispelled the tension that she felt at the table with the scowling Stauers and the overweening Mrs. Colbert.

Oh, there was more cava, and a delicious paella filled with fish and shellfish and a Spanish sausage called chorizo, and a second roaring fire—only rich people had a fireplace in the dining room—to keep them all warm.

But Will Stauer drank twice as much cava as anyone else and said very little.

Helen Stauer picked at her paella and kept stealing side-eye looks at Vivian.

And Mrs. Colbert filled every silence with chatter.

Through it all, Vivian did what Harold told her and just kept looking at him. Staring past the candles and into his eyes, she still felt that she was living a dream.

And his smile reassured her. When his cuff links flashed in the candlelight, they reminded her only of how far they'd come together and how much farther they had to go in the weeks and months and maybe the years ahead. She didn't know he was smiling because he'd figured out a way to live through the next twenty-four hours.

Then, between the main course and dessert, she excused herself because she needed the ladies' room. She bypassed the downstairs powder room and hurried up the grand staircase. A girl who'd shared one bathroom with half a dozen housemates enjoyed having a bit of extra privacy.

WHILE SHE WAS GONE, the talk turned darker in the dining room.

Mrs. Colbert looked from face to face and said, "Courage, my friends. Tomorrow will be a day for the history books. By Christmas morning, you'll all have disappeared again into the vastness of America, but your service to the Reich will never be forgotten."

"Whether we disappear or die," said Helen Stauer, "tomorrow is *der Tag*."

"But our plan needs refinement," said Martin.

Helen Stauer dabbed a napkin at her lips. "You now have tickets to the lawn. You will shoot from there. We will shoot from the Ellipse. Any further refinement must build upon that plan."

"If Cusack has talked to the feds, the feds will be watching the White House gates. They may even ask him to scan the crowd. He knows what I look like, so—"

"You want *us* to take the shot from the VIP seats?" said Helen.

"No. I take both shots with the K 98k, from the tree near Constitution," answered Martin. "You park on Fifteenth. At the sound of the evening gun, you start your engine. When they announce the president, you start driving. By the time you reach me, Roosevelt will be dead."

"Churchill, too?" asked Helen.

"That is my hope," said Martin.

"I've told you, hope is not a strategy," answered Helen.

Martin leaned across the table. "The muzzle velocity of the K 98k is twenty-four hundred feet per second. I'll be no more than eighteen hundred feet away, five hundred and fifty meters. Roosevelt won't even hear the shot before it hits him. Churchill and the others will freeze when Roosevelt's head explodes, then—"

Will Stauer looked up. "You will aim for the head? Not the center mass?"

"I'll aim as low as I can. But the podium will cover most of his body. And it's probably armored, so—"

"The K 98k is a bolt-action," said Will. "How quickly can you get off two shots?"

"I had top scores in training," answered Martin. "I'll get off four shots if I must."

Will took another sip of cava. "Well, I didn't come here to drive a getaway car."

"I didn't come here to die," said Martin.

"Because of her?" Helen pointed her eyes toward the ceiling.

"Because I don't want to die." Martin stood.

Helen said, "If you hadn't left a trail of murder from Los Angeles to Washington, our jobs might be easier—"

"No recriminations, please," said Mrs. Colbert.

Martin headed for the door. "This is dirty business. Murder happens. Now, excuse me for a moment. I need to check on Vivian."

"Yes," said Mrs. Colbert. "Your lady friend is gone a rather long time."

As Martin reached the doorway, Will Stauer said, "Herr Bruning—"

Martin turned.

"A crossfire doubles our chances of success. Since the tickets allow us access without going through the 'electrical searchers,' I will take the shots from the VIP seats. My wife will be at my side, to shield the gun from view. Someone else will have to drive you."

It was what Martin had been hoping. But he wanted the Stauers to come to the decision themselves. He shifted his eyes to Helen.

Will said, "Don't look at her. My mind is made up. We have the tickets. We'll use them. But my Walther has a range of only a hundred feet. I will need your Mauser."

"You know you're likely to die," said Martin. "Both of you."

"So are you," said Helen, "even if you make the shot from the tree."

In her private bathroom, Vivian was taking a few minutes to fix her makeup.

She leaned close to the mirror, and from the corner of her eye she noticed Harold's leather toiletries kit on top of the tank. It gave her an idea. Sometimes, fancy stores packaged their treasures in fancy boxes. And sometimes, a fancy box had the name and address of the store.

With two fingers, she opened the top of the kit and moved things around. She found breath mints, razor, a stick of Colgate shaving soap, toothbrush, and the cuff link box, small and square, spring-loaded and covered in velvet.

She popped it open. In the satin lining were two little molded receptacles for the jewelry, and—yes—the name of the store. She expected an address in D.C., where she could go to buy him that nice Christmas tie clip. Instead, she saw the words "Mr. Fountain's Men's Shop, Burbank, California." She read it once, then read it again.

And in her mind's eye, she saw the salesman that day she went looking for work. She'd barely glanced at him. He'd barely glanced at her. But . . . hair swept back, owlish glasses, and—Vivian could see it now—a vague resemblance to Leslie Howard. Then she heard the talk on the train that Saturday night . . . Sally Drake remembering Harold from *somewhere* because of the cuff links . . . saying how much he looked like Leslie Howard. Could Harold have been that salesman? Could Sally have died because of what she said on the train?

Vivian put the box back and went into the bedroom. She looked around at the heavy drapes, the thick carpet, the deep bed where she expected to be making love to Harold—or whoever he was—that night. It all felt so warm, so rich, so enveloping, but suddenly so smothering. She tried to shake off the effect of the cava and the sudden fear. Could Harold really be a murderer, as that Kevin Cusack had said? And could these Stauers be accomplices rather than business associates?

In her purse, she had the phone number from Kevin Cusack. And she needed to talk to someone. And there . . . the telephone. She sat and dialed.

Kevin Cusack answered on the first ring.

But Vivian didn't speak, because Harold was appearing in the doorway. She hung up and stood up, and the slip with the phone number fluttered to the floor.

He came toward her, smiling as he always did. "Is anything wrong?"

She said, "The curse."

"Curse?"

"You know . . . lady stuff." It was the best lie she could come up with.

"Which means what?" Martin could sense that she was trembling.

"The good news is I'm not pregnant. The bad news is—"

"Why were you on the telephone?"

She looked into his eyes and saw nothing. They'd lost all luster, like a snake's. She stammered that she'd been calling Johnny Beevers. "To thank him."

"And what did he say?"

"She angled her eyes to the floor but saw no slip. "He . . . he didn't answer."

Martin knew that was the truth. He said, "Mrs. Colbert's cook has prepared a lovely flan for dessert. So please—" He gestured to the door.

"I'll be right along."

"No, dear. Now," he ordered. "Go."

She had no choice. She retreated from the room and down the hall.

Then he noticed the slip of paper under the night table. He picked it up.

IN THE LITTLE APARTMENT on the Georgetown canal, Kevin Cusack was puzzling over the hang-up when the phone rang again. He picked up the receiver but said nothing. He could hear someone breathing on the other side.

Then a cultured voice and a British accent said, "Is Richard there?"

Kevin said, "There's no Richard here. Wrong number."

Click.

"What?" asked Mary Benning. "What was that?"

"He's close," said Kevin.

"Who?"

"The man I'm chasing. The man who killed Sally. He's in some hotel room or fancy house or dumpy apartment, and he has the girl with him, and he's planning a double assassination."

Mary got up and fetched a bottle of bourbon from under a cabinet. "I need a drink. You want one?"

"No," said Kevin. "If I hadn't been drunk on the train, Sally might still be alive. If we're all alive on Christmas morning, I'll drink champagne."

MARTIN BROWNING HUNG UP the phone and looked around. To see if anything else had been disturbed. He examined the satchel and opened the inner pocket that contained his many identifications. They appeared untouched, but he should never have left her alone with all this material.

Here he was, planning to escape with her after shocking the world, and she was betraying him.

His anger flared, but he replaced it with the cold calm that was always his best emotion in the worst situations. He still planned to have sex with her. He wouldn't deny himself that. If this was his last night on earth, he wouldn't let his anger or her personal biological calendar interfere with his pleasure. And if this was the beginning of his new life with her, he would have to find it in himself to forgive her . . . or turn her to his purpose.

Then he heard voices down in the foyer.

VIVIAN HAD DECIDED TO leave. She'd found her coat and hat in the closet, and she was now walking out as brazenly as she could. She didn't know what was going on, but she had to get away, if only for a while, to take a walk or jump in a cab for Union Station.

As she crossed the foyer, the big Spanish butler stepped in front of her. "Excuse me, madame, but you are expected for dessert."

"Excuse me," said Vivian, "but I feel ill. I need to leave."

"I am sorry." The butler had a look that suggested he was more than a butler.

Mrs. Colbert came out of the dining room, all smiles and motherly warmth. "My dear, what's wrong? Did something we say offend you?"

"No," said Vivian. No more talk. No more strained smiles. Just get out of here.

And now her "husband" was hurrying down the steps.

He said, "Vivian, where are you going?"

"Back to Annapolis. I don't belong here."

Mrs. Colbert said, "Take off your coat, dear. Please."

"It's just that, it's just that . . ." Vivian fumbled for an excuse.

"What, dear?" said Mrs. Colbert.

"It would be impolite for us to sleep together under your roof because, well, we're not married."

"We know, dear."

"You know?"

And over Mrs. Colbert's shoulder, Vivian saw Helen Stauer approaching, followed by her husband.

Vivian turned to Harry. "I don't think I know you . . . or any of these people."

"But we are so nice," said Helen Stauer. Then her hand shot toward Vivian's neck.

Martin Browning was seldom startled by anything, but for an instant, he was shocked. He would have grabbed for Helen, but Will held him back, just long enough for Vivian's knees to buckle and bring her to the floor.

"What are you doing?" demanded Martin.

"It's not a killing dose," said Will. "Helen knows exactly how much to use."

"Milligrams instead of grams," said Helen. "She will sleep until morning. Then she will be your problem. But for tonight, we must continue our work on our weapons, our tailoring, our false identifications. As you say, our plan needs refinement."

WEDNESDAY, DECEMBER 24

ON THE GROUND FLOOR of the White House, cigarette smoke and tension fogged the windowless Secret Service conference room. This was the day. The newspapers had printed the schedule. The radio people had gotten their passes to set up their microphones. British Pathé News had requested a spot on the portico to film the event. And Washingtonians were already lining up on Fifteenth and Seventeenth Streets.

Mike Reilly had convened a meeting with the leaders of the overlapping agencies running security details: the White House Police; the Washington Metropolitan Police, who'd be covering the surrounding streets; the Capitol Police, who had jurisdiction on all federal property in D.C.; the National Park Service; and the U.S. Army. Dan Jones represented the FBI. And Reilly's boss, Frank J. Wilson, chief of the Secret Service, had come over from his office in the Treasury Building.

Reilly glanced at Wilson, who looked more like an English professor than the man who'd outsmarted Al Capone by outsmarting Capone's tax accountants. Bald, slight, perfectly tailored, but with eight quarts of ice water in his veins, according to Reilly. He nodded and said, "The meeting's yours, Mike."

"Sorry to convene so early," said Reilly. "If it was my choice, the president and the prime minister would sit down to a quiet Christmas Eve dinner, sing some carols, and wait for Santa Claus. But here we are." With a pointer, he directed their attention to the wall map of the White House grounds. "First off, we have seating for two hundred VIPs, along with the choir and band here"—*tap, tap,* pointer on map—"and here, behind the rope fence."

"How far away?" asked Frank Wilson.

"Two hundred feet, as agreed in the original National Park Service plan issued before Pearl Harbor, which also put U.S. Army privates inside the rope, every twenty-five feet," said Reilly. "I want a private every five feet."

"Done," said the army captain. "We'll also add another sergeant and lieutenant."

"We have rope barriers along South Drive, connecting Treasury Place on the east and State Place on the west." *Tap* and *tap,* halfway across the lawn, just north of the fountain. "The public will be allowed behind the ropes, back to the south fence. I want two dozen more privates along the fence, with all eyes on E Street."

"Done," said the army captain.

"We'll also have agents undercover on the lawn and crawling all over E Street between the Ellipse and the south fence," added Reilly.

Jones, who'd been alternately looking at his watch and puffing a cigarette, looking and puffing, looking and puffing, as if he was late for something really important, asked, "Does the president know that an FBI agent was murdered on Monday while investigating a Nazi assassination plot?"

"Yes," said Reilly. "But he's adamant, and so are we."

Frank Wilson said, "*He's* adamant that we keep the news out of the papers, because he wants this show to go on with a smile. *We're* adamant that anyone who gets onto the South Lawn goes through an Alnor Door."

"Including the VIPs?" asked Jones.

"Even the Marine Band," said Reilly. "It'll cause a stink. The VIPs think they're going through the Northeast Appointment Gate. But they'll be directed to the Southeast Gate along with everybody else. We'll set up a separate lane so they can jump the line and get to the Alnor Door."

"That should smooth a few ruffled feathers," said Wilson.

"It doesn't catch the shooter," said Jones. "Or potential accomplices."

"Accomplices?" said Reilly. "Hell, we've only known about the shooter for forty-eight hours. The FBI's been chasing him for *two weeks*. The papers even gave him a name. 'The Hollywood Nazi.'"

Jones lit a second cigarette from the one in his mouth. "We think the Hollywood Nazi is just a stalking horse for the real shooter. But we're not certain."

"One way to find out would be to find *him*," said Reilly.

"The Washington Metros are on it," said the D.C. chief of police.

"I hope the FBI is, too," said Reilly.

And for a moment, Reilly and Jones, the two big dogs at the table, gave each other the big dog stare.

Then the old dog, Frank Wilson, spoke up: "Whoever he is, if he can't get a gun onto the lawn, the president and prime minister will be safe behind the podium."

"Is the podium armored?" asked Jones.

"Steel reinforced," said Reilly.

"Are you closing E Street?" asked Jones.

"To traffic," said the Capitol Police captain. "We'd close it to pedestrians, but—"

"The president won't hear of it," said Reilly.

Jones got up and went over to the map. "What about the Ellipse?"

"Closed to pedestrians. We'll have police at fifty-foot intervals along the sidewalks."

"And Constitution Avenue?"

"Open to traffic," said Reilly. "But it's six hundred and fifty yards away."

Jones spaced two fingers on the map and stretched them from Constitution to the South Portico. "It would be one hell of a shot from back there."

"And nobody hits a potshot from that distance." Reilly dragged the pointer over the map. "He'd need to balance the weapon, take his time aiming, probably walk in the shot with three or four misses—"

"Not happening," said the D.C. chief, "not with our guys patrolling."

Jones studied the map a bit longer. "I've seen intel reports on German snipers in Russia. They use the K 98k with a Zeiss scope. Theoretical range, a thousand meters. But in the field, they say they can hit a kill shot out to about four hundred meters, a stationary target to five hundred. What's the distance from here to Constitution in meters?"

"About six hundred," said Mike Reilly.

Jones nodded. "Like I said, a helluva shot."

"Well outside the range of German snipers," said Reilly. "Besides, our guy seems to favor the pistol."

Dan Jones thought it over and went back to his seat, as if he was satisfied.

"All right. If there are no other questions, here's the schedule." Reilly handed out a mimeographed sheet. "Gates open at four o'clock. Marine Band at four thirty. Evening gun at four fifty-two. That cues the band to play 'Joy to the World,' which cues the Boss. CBS broadcast goes live at five P.M. That's when we lock the gates. 'Hail to the Chief' brings out the president and prime minister at five oh three. Father Corrigan gives the invocation. The leaders of the Boy Scouts and Girl Scouts give remarks. Then the D.C. district commissioner intros the Boss, who lights the tree."

"Where will you be?" asked Jones.

"Right where I always am, three feet from the Boss's elbow. If I sense anything going wrong, I move."

"And don't forget the lights," said Frank Wilson. "The last line of defense."

"Right, the lights," said Jones. "Appropriate in the season of light."

"Glad you approve. Any other questions?" Reilly looked around, glanced at his watch, and said, "All right, then. Seven hours till the curtain goes up."

Jones stood and shook Reilly's hand. They were all professionals, despite the tension. He said, "The FBI will do whatever it can to help the Secret Service."

"Just find the Hollywood Nazi," said Reilly. "If he *isn't* the guy, he's *seen* the guy. And now that your agent is dead, he's the only one who has."

IN THE BIG HOUSE on Kalorama Circle, Martin Browning lay awake. He took comfort in the steady breathing of the woman beside him, even if it was drug induced. He'd slept next to her because he liked her physical presence, whether the possibility of sex existed or not. He also wanted to protect her . . . from the Stauers and Mrs. Colbert, too.

He knew that he had to act with common sense and uncommon intelligence in the hours ahead, or he and Vivian would both be dead by dark. He was likely to die anyway. Even if he escaped Washington, the Americans would never stop looking for him. If he wanted to live, the best plan would be to run with Vivian right now, not for a U-boat off the Maryland shore but for Mexico, and from there South America. Leave now and leave the Stauers to do the job.

He went to the window and looked down through the woods at the cars speeding along Rock Creek Parkway. He longed to ride the smooth concrete strip away to some private happiness, some world without war. But that made him no different from human beings everywhere in the terrible December of 1941.

And he wasn't just any human being. History had placed him here for a reason. He had come too far to shirk his task now.

Vivian stirred. He went to the bed, sat on the edge, reached out and stroked her leg. But she slept on. The drug was powerful.

"Herr Bruning." A voice whispered from the hallway.

He tightened his robe and opened the door.

Helen Stauer wore a silk dressing gown, but no makeup and no heels. Her severe features were softened, her formidable presence lessened. She handed him a mug of coffee and peered over his shoulder at Vivian. "She looks dead to the world."

"If I thought you had a sense of humor, I'd tell you that remark wasn't funny."

"She'll sleep another hour." Helen gave a jerk of the head. *Follow me.*

Martin closed the bedroom door and locked it, so that Vivian couldn't get out and no one else could get in. He dropped the key into his bathrobe pocket.

Helen led him to her room, then pivoted and looked up at him from under that dark brow. "Have you decided what to do with her?"

Martin sipped his coffee. "Where's your husband?"

"He's gone to kill Cusack. We know the phone number. We think we know the street. And we need him out of the way. My husband wants to make it up to me for losing Cusack on Sunday."

"Such a romantic." Martin looked at the rumpled bedclothes.

"No more jokes from you, either." Helen put down her coffee cup and lit a cigarette. "Now . . . the girl. I have two syringes. Give her one, and she'll sleep all day. Give her the other, and she'll sleep forever."

"I still need her," said Martin.

"For the job or yourself? Mrs. Colbert is worried that she will reveal this house if she lives. She says they can dispose of the body." Helen stepped closer. "Perhaps it is time to screw your courage to the sticking place."

"Lady Macbeth informs your thinking?"

"And my actions." Helen Stauer took a drag of her cigarette, then looked into his eyes as if challenging him to test his courage on her.

For a moment, there was quiet between them. But it wasn't gentle. It was like them, a hard, a cold passion.

She stubbed out her cigarette, put a hand behind his neck, and pulled his face to hers. And two assassins kissed, as if to seal their murderous pact.

And the kiss went on. And his hands roamed. He stroked her back, her bottom, made fingertip tracks toward the sable patch he imagined between her legs.

She caressed his neck, his face, his chest. She brushed lower and lightly and pressed the palm of her right hand against him, while sliding her left hand around his back.

Through the soft satin of her nightgown, he caressed her breast.

She pressed herself into him, stroked, embraced.

And with his right hand he grabbed her left wrist. Then he twisted it and pulled her left hand from his bathrobe pocket. In her fingers was the key to his bedroom. He took it and said, "Remember, Lady Macbeth ends up dead. So does her husband."

"But she kills the king."

He backed out and went down the hallway. "I need more coffee."

She called after him, "Make your decision, Herr Bruning. It is *der Tag*."

As he passed his bedroom, he gave the door a try to be sure it was locked.

STELLA MADDEN HAD SLEPT well. The house doctor had given her a couple of Seconals, and the exhaustion of grief had finally driven her into unconsciousness.

She'd awakened to a moment of peace, her mind empty, her thoughts in shadow. Then she'd popped up and thrown off the covers and jumped out of bed with the resolve that she was going to get that Nazi bastard, even if she had to do it herself.

Now, she was on the phone with Cusack, hearing his tale of nighttime hang-ups.

"So," she said. "He's nearby. He knows who you are. He may even know where you are."

"Can he look up an address from a phone number?"

"Only the cops can do that. What's the exchange?"

"Canal. Canal 2323," said Kevin.

"Canal for the office near the Georgetown canal," said Stella. "That will help him to locate. You'd better get out. And take Mary Benning with you."

"She's gone to work."

"Call her and tell her to stay put until this is over."

A knock on Stella's door. Her first thought: somehow, that Nazi bastard had found her. She reached for her Beretta. But through the peephole, she saw an FBI badge. Then she heard a familiar voice: Dan Jones. He needed to talk.

"Give me ten minutes," she said. "I'll meet you in the lobby."

"Make it five, and don't try sneaking out. The house detective is watching."

She waited until his footfalls receded. Then she turned back to the phone. "Time to turn yourself in, Sam Spade. Come to the Willard now. I'll be in the lobby with Jones."

"But I'm worried about the girl."

"Worry about yourself," said Stella. "Worry about the president." She heard a long pause, as if he was thinking. She said, "If I don't see you here in half an hour, meet me on Dupont Circle at one o'clock. We'll figure something out. We have to."

KEVIN CUSACK HUNG UP. Maybe she was right. Maybe it was time. How much more could he do out here? He went to the window just as a shadow flicked by. People used the towpath as a shortcut to avoid M Street. That meant nosy pedestrians could look right in the windows of the little ground-level apartments. That's why Mary Benning kept the blinds down.

Kevin flipped them up. A shaft of sun fell across the floor, the only winter light that reached into the apartment all day. He angled his head west. A guy in a dirty raincoat and sweat-stained fedora had just walked by.

Jesus Christ.

Kevin flipped the blinds down and stepped back.

What had he just seen? The raincoat and hat. The potbelly. The guy who'd tracked him into Georgetown on Sunday? The guy he'd seen in the museum on Monday?

The apartment had a rear exit, up the stairs and through the bedroom. Kevin could go that way and follow the alleys over to M Street. But he had to get another look at that guy, just to be sure. So he put on his raincoat and Dilly's button-covered cap, grabbed his leather overnight bag, and reached for the door.

And the phone rang. Answer it . . . or go? It might be Stella.

He picked it up, put the receiver to his ear, heard breathing, held his own breath, felt his stomach clench like a fist.

Then the voice said, "Hey, man, you there?"

The fist relaxed. Kevin said, "Stanley?"

"Your line been busy. Who you talkin' to?"

"Stella. I'm heading to the Willard now. I'm turning myself in to the feds."

"Good," said Stanley. "Go fast."

"Why?"

"Those plainclothes Metros just came by, askin' all about you, askin' did I ever talk to you on the train and did I think you were in Washington and—"

"Did they ask about Kellogg?"

"They're after *you*, man, not Kellogg. They said you fled L.A. jurisdiction. They said finding you was a matter of what they called 'national security.'"

Kevin said, "I hope you didn't lie to them. Lying to the cops is—"

"I ain't lyin' to no one. I told them right where you are."

"You didn't have to be *that* honest, but—"

"I'm sorry, man, but you should go."

Kevin agreed. He was done running. He couldn't do any more good for himself or the country by running. But he was certain of one thing: if the local cops were in cahoots with Bobby O'Hara of the LAPD, he wasn't running to them. He needed the feds.

He said goodbye to Stanley and hung up. He was fishing for the keys to lock up when the phone rang again, twice. Before he could grab it, the ringing stopped. *What the hell?* Then it rang again, loud, piercing. He grabbed it, and said, "Hey, Stanley, if—"

Nothing. Just breathing.

"Hello?"

Nothing. Nothing. Nothing. *Click.*

Time to get out of there. Up the stairs or out the front door? The front door was faster. So he stepped onto the towpath. He looked west toward Thirty-First. He didn't see the guy in the dirty raincoat or anyone else. He turned left, east toward Jefferson, just a hundred feet away, and he started to move. But halfway there, he stopped. Had he locked the door? He'd been so distracted by the phone calls . . .

Then a black Ford screeched onto the little bridge where Jefferson crossed the canal. *Cops.* Kevin was getting good at picking out cops, even in unmarked cars. This one ran up on the sidewalk and parked illegally. Only cops did that. One of them said something into a hand microphone, then they both jumped out—the two detectives from the Willard Hotel.

And they'd already seen him, so they were coming fast along the towpath, one pulling his badge while the other pulled his pistol.

"Hey! Hey, you!" The skinny one took the lead. "Are you Cusack?"

Before he could answer, Kevin heard a *pop* from just over his shoulder.

The detective's head flew back, he staggered, then he tumbled into the canal. The second cop looked at his partner in shock, then pointed his pistol. But a second *pop* brought a burst of blood squirting from the side of his neck. A third hit him just above the nose and he dropped where he stood.

Kevin turned to see the guy in the raincoat and fedora, coming fast from the other direction, swinging the silenced pistol at him.

But Kevin was swinging, too, with his new leather overnight bag, right into the guy's belly. The gun went skittering away, but from somewhere, the guy snapped a knife and slashed upward. Kevin jumped aside, swung his leather bag again, then stumbled back through the unlocked door, slammed it, bolted it, and chained it.

Kevin guessed that the guy must have gotten the number from Vivian. By force or willingly? Kevin couldn't worry about that now. But someone in some safe location had called that number while this bastard hid in the shrubbery and listened for the ring signals.

Kevin retreated to the kitchenette and turned off the little light over the sink.

The guy outside tapped the silencer on the glass in the door, like a polite guest.

Then, with an earsplitting shatter, he smashed the glass and thrust the pistol into the little apartment. *Pop. Pop. Pop.* Three shots ricocheted around, all misses. Then a hand reached through the broken glass to unlock the bolt.

Kevin took the chance. He sprang for the stairs to the left of the door. As he did, he grabbed the knitting needles on the end table and jabbed down onto the forearm that was poking through the broken window. He heard a cry of pain. *Good.* He leaped up the stairs and tore open the back door, which led out onto a little rickety porch overlooking an alley.

In the distance, he heard police sirens. The detectives must have radioed for backup. He could've written their report: "Arriving at Jefferson, arresting Kevin Cusack, so-called Hollywood Nazi." And now the arresting cops were dead, and he was running—again—this time through the alley maze behind M Street. Destination, the Willard Hotel.

At ten thirty, Vivian awoke . . . alone. She got up, and the room began to spin. She sat back and waited for her head to clear. She was still wearing the blue polka-dot dress. She'd slept in it all night. Ten hours she'd slept. But she didn't feel rested.

Now that her head was clearing, all she felt was . . . terrified. The last thing she remembered was trying to leave. She'd been in the foyer, and they'd all closed in on her.

She stood again, wobbled some more, then wobbled into the bathroom. She splashed cold water on her face. Then she swallowed down a glass of it that worked through her like a potion, waking her up and sharpening her up, too. She looked into the mirror, at her smeared makeup, and wiped it off.

She studied her reflection and tried to make sense of all that had happened, starting with the men's shop and the cuff links that somehow led to the murder of Sally Drake. And the Diebolds? Two strange little men in the middle of nowhere, just *giving* them a car? And then the circle closed from Mr. Fountain's to that Ford Deluxe to the cafeteria at the National History Museum, where she'd met the Stauers and heard a speech she'd heard twice before, first from a Lockheed executive in Mr. Fountain's, then from Harold in that Ford.

Her "husband" was no seed salesman. No suit salesman either. Whatever he was selling, she wouldn't shill for him any longer. She wouldn't play the beard. She wouldn't act the role he'd cast her in. But she agreed with that Lockheed exec: they all had a part to play.

She put her ear to the door: distant voices. She turned the knob: locked. And no key. She went to the nightstand: no telephone, just a screw connector by the baseboard.

They'd turned that luxurious bedroom into a cell. Not for long. She was getting out. She put on her shoes. But not the pumps. To hell with them. She grabbed the flats. She went to the front window. If she could get over to the woods, she could get to the parkway below. Then she could flag a car and get away.

She slid the sash lock and gently raised the window. The day was sunny and mild for December. That was good, because her overcoat was in the foyer. She looked up the street and down. The road curved away in each direction. Not surprising on a circle. And no one was about in midmorning, so screaming wouldn't do any good.

But the little roof over the front door was within reach, just a few feet away. A decorative railing ran around the top. She could grab it, balance, then drop into that big cushiony yew hedge below. If she was lucky, she wouldn't get hurt.

She gave another look into the room, heard the sound of footfalls coming down the hall, and decided to do it. With a deep breath, she swung a leg, then reached toward the little roof, reached and pushed and reached . . . and missed.

She fell but turned in the air so she landed on her back, right in the middle of the giant yew. And she bounced. The soft evergreen branches absorbed her fall, scratching her and poking her but enveloping her, too. And she was all in one piece. So she rolled and rolled again, tore her dress on a branch, and dropped out on the lawn.

Then she popped up and ran. In an instant, she was across the street, past the Ford Deluxe, down into the woods, and running like hell.

She was halfway to Rock Creek when she heard him calling: "Vivian! Vivian!"

She went even harder, plunging through the underbrush, stumbling head-long toward the parkway and the speeding cars.

And he was plunging, thumping, thundering right after her.

She tripped and tumbled. She didn't feel the scratches and bumps. She rolled back to her feet and started waving and shouting.

But she could sense him swooping toward her, like a ghost or bird of prey.

Twenty feet from the grass strip along the roadside, he caught her and pinned her against a tree. "Vivian, what are you doing?"

She pushed him away. "You're not who you say you are. None of you are."

"Please, Vivian." Martin glanced at the cars on the parkway. No one was pulling over or slowing. That was good. Then he looked over his shoulder and saw Helen Stauer gazing down from above. That was bad. "Please, Vivian."

"Please, my ass." Vivian struggled against him. She knew he was strong. She'd felt his strength. She'd taken comfort in it. In bed, she'd liked it.

But he held her against the tree and said, "Stop."

"Who *are* you?" she demanded.

"Not who I've said." He kept one hand on her and reached into his pocket and pulled out the FBI badge. "This. This is who I am."

She looked and said, "FBI? You?"

He jerked his head toward the wraithlike figure marching down the hill. "Don't let her see it. I'm undercover, tracking assassins."

She stopped struggling. "Assassins?"

He jammed the badge back into his breast pocket. "I've been chasing them all the way across the country. You've been giving me cover."

Vivian looked up the hill at Helen. "Her? You've been chasing her?"

"Both of them. I almost caught them in Illinois. They passed through Die-bold's just hours before we did. I was putting the squeeze on Max when Eric—"

"Are the Diebolds really dead?"

"Max was going to finger us. I had to kill him, and you have to trust me, Vivian. For the good of the country."

"What about the cuff links? What about Mr. Fountain's Men's Shop?"

"Where do you think this all started? We infiltrated a Nazi cell right there. Will Stauer probably has Mr. Fountain cuff links, too. It's a way of identifica-tion." Martin was thinking quickly and lying about as well as he could. Good lies, with perfect syntax.

Helen Stauer was close now. She had her hand in her pocket. "Remember what I said, Herr Bruning. Tell her to come quietly, or she'll die right in these woods."

Vivian looked into Martin's eyes. Should she believe any of this? She'd go along to survive. But believe?

He gave her the kind of smile she'd come to trust. In a loud voice, as if putting on a show for Helen Stauer, he said, "Yes, come along, Vivian. We need your help."

Kevin Cusack couldn't get a cab on M Street. So he hurry-walked, a little fast but not too fast, head down but not too down, until he came to the intersection of M and Pennsylvania, where he stopped. He couldn't be caught in the open on the overpass. Until he had FBI cover, he wore a target on his back, especially now that he'd taken it on the lam to escape the cop killer who wanted to kill *him*. What uniformed beat cop would believe that?

So he followed M Street to the Rock Creek trail gate, hurried down the path, kicked his way through the underbrush on the embankment, and came out right on the edge of the four-lane parkway. When the moment was right, he sprinted across and plunged into the bushes on the other side.

If any do-gooding driver had heard the news reports and noticed him, they'd be pulling over at the next phone booth. But it was a chance he had to take if he was going to save himself, or the girl named Vivian, or the president of the United States.

The next obstacle was the creek. Kevin wasn't much for running around with wet feet. So he picked a spot where the rocks made a little bridge, and he went rock to rock across, then up through the trees and brush, to Twenty-Third Street.

It was too late to head for the Willard. It might even be dangerous. So he aimed for Dupont Circle instead.

Mike Reilly learned of the Georgetown shooting around eleven thirty. He told an agent to monitor the Washington police scanner.

Soon, he was getting reports:

"Two detectives dead. Suspect identified as Kevin Cusack, of Hollywood, California, a.k.a. the Hollywood Nazi. Detectives Mills and Conway were on their way to arrest when they were gunned down. Be on the lookout. . . ."

And the reports kept crackling:

"A man matching the description of Kevin Cusack observed on far end of Key Bridge, walking into Arlington. Units dispatched . . ."

"Attention all units. Possible sighting near Mayflower Hotel on Pennsylvania . . ."

"Shooting suspect seen in tourist line at Washington Monument . . ."

"Possible shooting suspect . . . possible sighting . . . possible Kevin Cusack . . ."

Then another bit of news caught Reilly's attention:

"Drivers on Rock Creek Parkway report altercation in woods near Waterside Drive. Possible abduction. Male approximately six feet, female wearing blue polka-dot dress."

Local abductions didn't interest Mike Reilly. But this whole package, just a few hours from the big show? He called Dan Jones at the FBI. "What do you know about that Kevin Cusack and the cop shooting?"

"I know he's a dead man if the Metros get to him before we do. Cops don't take kindly to cop killers," said Jones. "Neither do FBI agents."

"Are we certain that he did it?" asked Reilly.

"Of course not," said Jones. "But he was supposed to turn himself in at the Willard this morning, and he didn't show."

"Do you have a D.C. Metro police scanner?"

"We're the goddamn FBI. We don't listen to police scanners."

"Well, do you have a District map handy?"

Jones looked up. "Right on my wall."

"There's a report of an attempted abduction by Rock Creek near Waterside. A guy grabbing a woman in a polka-dot dress. What do you know about the neighborhood above the parkway? Anybody of interest to your Espionage Unit, maybe?"

"That's the Kalorama district. Lawyers, diplomats, businessmen . . ." Jones thought a bit. "The only person up there we ever looked at closely was a Swiss national, a commodities broker. Did a lot of business with Franco."

"So he liked fascist money?"

"Money is money to guys like that," said Jones. "When he died, his widow gave a big donation to America First but—" Jones was looking at something else on his desk, the report from the agents he'd sent to Annapolis the day before. "Did you say *polka-dot* dress?"

"That's what the scanner said. Why?"

"Keep somebody by the telephone."

"Are you calling the Metros?" asked Reilly.

"Hell, no. Kidnapping is a *federal* crime." Jones hung up and called Stella.

BY ONE O'CLOCK, THE sun was warm on Dupont Circle. So workers from the surrounding offices were enjoying lunch and fifty-degree temperatures.

Kevin Cusack sat behind a newspaper on the great bench encircling the fountain, and he wondered: Why in hell was he here, scared to death? He should be in Boston with the family, or back in L.A., quaffing a double martini in Musso & Frank's, reading the next *Gentleman Jim* or *Everybody Comes to Rick's,* reading anything but the news of the day, which was all bad. . . . Fighting in the Philippines, prognosis grim . . . a freighter torpedoed off Long Beach, no survivors . . . Churchill calling for U.S. "sacrifice" . . .

And "sacrifice" was the word . . .

. . . for everyone, here in the capital of freedom and everywhere else in the whole broad country he'd seen in the last two weeks, seen as if for the first time, with all its strengths and weaknesses and dreams and nightmares. To defeat the forces of fascism and evil, everybody would have to use their own strengths and defer their dreams, overcome their own weaknesses and ignore their nightmares. And they had to start today.

He'd already called Mary Benning and warned her. But he wasn't calling the FBI until he met with Stella. He'd only known her for a day or so, but he sensed that when she talked, she knew what she was talking about. He liked that. He liked her.

And as if from thin air, she appeared beside him, sat down, held a finger to her lips, and said, "I've negotiated your safety."

"What's to negotiate?"

"Your life. Certain elements of law enforcement want to kill you on sight, no matter what Leon Lewis told Jones this morning on the long-distance."

"I knew Lewis would vouch for me."

"If he was here he'd give you the choice I'm offering. Sit and wait for the Washington Metros, who'll drag you to headquarters and beat the shit out of you before they decide you're innocent . . . or decide you're not and shoot you while escaping."

"Or?"

"You can stand up right now and raise your hands so that the FBI agents on the other side of the fountain can come over and frisk you."

Kevin hopped to his feet and went palms-out.

Stella said, "Smart boy."

As the agents flashed their badges, Kevin said, "Am I glad to see you."

AT 2:00 P.M. ON Kalorama Circle: four cars, eight FBI agents. Two cars blocked the exits, one at the top of the circle, the other on Belmont Street. A third rolled down the alley that bisected the circle and parked behind the Colbert house. The fourth—with Agent Dan Jones and a field agent in the front, Kevin and Stella in the back—stopped in front of the Colbert house.

They'd brought Kevin to identify Kellogg. The only other man in Washington who knew what Kellogg looked like, Stanley Smith, was sitting in the car in the alley.

Jones was convinced that Cusack was just who he said he was: Agent 29 of the LAJCC, framed on the Super Chief, set on the run by Frank Carter, and innocent of the shooting on the Georgetown canal. He'd broadcast this conclusion to all units involved. But until he had the actual suspects in custody, he was keeping a protective eye on Kevin.

So Kevin was glad to stay in the back seat.

Stella said to Jones, "Be careful. That Nazi bastard is a killer."

"Sometimes, you just go up and ring the bell," said Jones. "It throws the killers off their game."

"Especially when you have backup." By which Stella meant the agent who'd gotten out at the corner of Belmont and was holding a tommy gun, a totally incongruous sight in one of the richest, quietest neighborhoods in Washington.

Jones said to the other agent, "I suspect this Mrs. Colbert is harmless, but let's be careful." Then he said to the back seat, "If you hear gunfire, duck."

Stella reached into her skirt and pulled out the Beretta.

Kevin slumped down a bit more.

They watched Jones and the agent go up onto the porch. Jones stood to one side with his .357 in his hand, and the agent rang the bell.

Nothing.

Jones nodded, and the agent rang again.

In the car, Kevin whispered to Stella, "You notice anything odd about that house?"

"What?" asked Stella.

"Window, second floor, open wide, as if somebody jumped into that big bush."

"Yeah. And snagged her dress. See the polka-dot fabric in the shrub?"

On the porch, the agent was peering in the sidelight. "Hey, boss, I think we got probable cause."

"So break the window," said Jones.

Smash! The agent reached through the shattered sidelight and unlocked the door. Then the FBI entered the premises.

Stella couldn't contain herself. She popped out, and gave Kevin a wave to follow. As they went up the steps, she told him not to touch anything. "Sounds like we got a crime scene."

Kevin said a silent prayer that they didn't find the girl in the polka-dot dress.

First, they found the butler. He lay on the carpet in the middle of the foyer, close by the Christmas tree, a pool of blood under him.

"Hope they have stain remover," said Stella.

Kevin didn't laugh. He'd seen enough death for one day. But he supposed that she'd seen enough over the years that a joke was a good defense.

Jones turned to them. "You two, stop right there."

Stella and Kevin froze in the foyer and watched Jones go with gun drawn into the dining room. The sunlight streamed through the French doors and fell on a heavyset woman sitting at the table, her unfinished breakfast before her, a single red hole in the middle of her forehead, blood and brain matter on the curtains behind her. The late Mrs. Colbert.

Then the kitchen door swung open, and the agent said, "Another one in here. Female. Probably the cook."

Jones gestured for Stella and Kevin to follow him outside, where he radioed for a crime scene unit. Kevin took a few deep breaths of fresh air. Stella grabbed the piece of fabric from the bush.

Meanwhile, a neighbor came out with his two Scotties. He was old, dressed impeccably in a three-piece tweed suit, and while he talked as if he was used to being listened to, he was just as nosy as anyone. In an accent like Roosevelt's, he demanded, "*What* is going on? You people have brought more commotion into this neighborhood than we've ever had. Last night, we had a drunk coming out of that house and—"

"Did you notice anything strange this morning?" asked Jones.

The old man said the police had circled twice. Then, shortly after they left, a car pulled out of Colbert's garage and sped down the alley.

"What make?" asked Jones.

"A Buick, I think. But then I heard Mrs. Colbert's front door slam. A man and a woman crossed the street and got into a car parked right where you're parked now. Black Ford, Ohio plates. They hurried, as if they were getting away from something."

Jones nodded to Stella, who showed him the fabric. "Do you recognize this?"

"Come to think of it . . . yes, her topcoat was open and—yes—blue polka dot."

Jones said to Kevin, "So she's with him. You know what she looks like, right?"

"I had three meals with her on the train," answered Kevin.

The neighbor kept talking. "The man was dressed rather well. Nice blue suit, hair combed back, owlish eyeglasses. Looked rather like . . . like Leslie Howard."

Kevin and Stella turned to Dan Jones at the same time and said, "It's him."

MARTIN BROWNING WAS DRIVING north on Rock Creek Parkway. How easy it would be to keep going, up into Pennsylvania, or even Vermont or the wilds of Maine. But how many more lies could he invent for Vivian? And how long could he really run? The best path would be to do what he had come for, then run. He owed it to all the people he'd killed and all those who would die if he failed.

While he'd been lying to her all morning, what he said next was the truth: "Mrs. Colbert wanted to kill you. She feared you'd expose her. They were all part of this."

"But how could you just shoot them—Mrs. Colbert, her butler, her cook— all in cold blood?" Those were the first words Vivian had spoken since they'd left the house.

"I was saving you, even though the Bureau wanted them alive," he said. "Besides, the Stauers are the big fish. We want them taken in the act."

"Of assassination?" she said. "You're using the president as bait?"

"We want to draw out any other accomplices." He found this line of lying easy to follow. "An army of agents will join us. I called the Bureau from Colbert's. The president will be perfectly safe."

She just looked at him blankly, as if she couldn't absorb it all, as if her mind were not working . . . or perhaps wouldn't accept it.

He knew she was trying to shake off the shock. So he did his best to soothe her. He wanted her sharp and ready in the hours ahead. She didn't know it, but she'd be driving.

A little peace and quiet might help. So he drove deep into Rock Creek Park, a two-thousand-acre preserve at the northern tip of the District, five miles from the White House. He followed Ridge Road, a country lane winding through the woods, until he came to a parking lot, secluded and deserted. When he turned off the engine, the silence embraced them.

He took two cigarettes from the pack of Camels on the dash and lit them. Then he offered one to her. "If Mrs. Kellogg would like a smoke, she should have one."

She looked at the cigarette, then at him, and realized that she craved a smoke. So she took it and took a long drag.

"There," he said. "Feel better?"

Vivian didn't know what she felt, but the smoke stopped her hands from shaking. She took another drag and looked out into the gray winter woods rolling off in every direction.

He whispered, "I almost blew my cover for you, Vivian. I almost blew it because—"

She turned to him. "This better be good."

"Because I love you." And in that moment, he believed it.

She was too confused to know what to believe. So she took another drag. She couldn't think of anything else to do. She exhaled . . .

. . . and he kissed her. As he did, he felt the turning of the earth around them. He felt the world-historical importance of what he was about to do. And he felt that the two of them, there in those deserted woods, were at the pivot point, the only place that was still.

She didn't feel any of that. And she didn't really kiss him back. She simply let him do what he did. Then she took another drag.

For the moment, he thought, it was enough. Let her work through her emotions however she could.

He got out and went to the trunk and found the Indiana plates under the spare tire. He changed them, front and back. Then he took the K 98k, which he'd wrapped in the blue overcoat, and tapped on her window. "Come on. I need to practice."

She rolled down the window. "Practice? With that? Why?"

"My job is to watch for the Stauers on the Ellipse and stop them with this if I must." Then he thought of something else. "I'm also watching for that Cusack."

"Cusack, too? He's in on this?"

"You heard his lies. You saw his cuff links. The cuff links identify them." He thought it was a good embellishment to his own lie.

"Fine. Just let me stay in the car," she said.

He pulled the door open and said coldly, "You'll come with me."

"Please, just let me sit here, Harold . . . or Herr Bruning . . . or whatever your name is."

"It's Special Agent Frank Carter. That's my real name. Now come on."

She'd learned to read his face. She knew when to argue and when to do as she was told. She threw the cigarette on the ground and stepped on it as she got out. "So what now? You want to deputize me?" The nicotine was sharpening her.

He grinned like Harold Kellogg. "Raise your right hand and repeat after me."

"Ha. Ha." She took the trail into the woods. He told her to keep going until they could no longer be seen from the road. She never considered that this might be another perfect moment for him to be free of her, permanently.

And he only considered it briefly. Once he'd found a clearing that offered distant targets with no houses or trails, he stopped and looked up into the trees.

She sensed that he was feeling something he wasn't telling her. She looked up, too, up through the bare branches of maple and oak and sycamore, up at the sky that had lost its midday blue and was taking on the silver shimmer of Christmas Eve.

He didn't admit it, but he was looking toward eternity.

He was also looking for motion in the trees. But the afternoon was dead calm. So he wouldn't need to calculate windage. The Zeiss scope didn't provide for it anyway. As for elevation, he'd do what German snipers were trained to do in the field: zero the scope at three hundred meters, then compensate for further bullet drop by instinct. But he wouldn't have time to "walk in" the shot. He'd have to hit the targets on the first try.

So here in the woods, he took his time to develop a feel for the scope, the bolt, the trigger, the recoil. In the fading light, it was hard to see if he hit all his targets.

He knew that the lighting at the White House would be much better when he peered through that scope in a little more than an hour.

HELEN STAUER HEARD THE shots echoing. She said, "Herr Bruning is practicing."

They were sitting in Johnny Beevers's Buick, in a lot about a quarter mile away, where they were spending what might be their final quiet moments together. They'd left the Colbert house in a hurry after the police circled a second time. They'd left their luggage, they'd left their fingerprints, and they'd left three dead German agents.

Helen said, "Foolish of Mrs. Colbert to insist that Bruning turn over the girl. She didn't understand that he loves her."

"Foolish of her to tell the butler to pull a gun on him. She didn't understand how quick he is. For a moment, I thought he might shoot us, too."

"Love will make people do crazy things," she said.

"Yes," he said. "Look at us." And he kissed her.

Suddenly they were ravenous for each other, kissing, touching, stroking until Will stopped and looked into her eyes. "Do we really have to kill Roosevelt first?"

She shook her head and pulled him out of his trousers. Then she reached under her skirt, slipped her underpants aside. His stomach was an impediment in a sitting position. But they persisted, perhaps because the last pleasures were the sweetest.

Afterward, they straightened quickly and went right back to business. She said, "I'm afraid, Wilhelm, that killing those detectives on the canal seals our fate."

"They would have arrested Cusack. They would have protected him and used him to identify us. I went to kill Cusack. But I had to kill them first. And I almost got Cusack, but he was quick." He flexed his arm. "Quick with his knitting needles, too."

"Roosevelt will not be quick. And Churchill, most likely, will be drunk."

"Do you really think we can kill them both?" he asked.

"I promise." She kissed him again. "And we will live forever."

Then he reached into the back, took the wooden holster, and pulled out the Mauser C96. He'd exchanged it with Martin Browning for his Walther P38. He slid the grip into the connector on the holster and held it up. "A powerful pistol with a shoulder stock. Superb German design."

Martin Browning had stayed up half the night sewing a harness into Will's dirty raincoat to hold the gun. Great to have an accomplice who was the son of a tailor. Now they walked up into the woods so that Will could practice. Open the raincoat, pull, and aim. Pull and aim. Pull and aim with Helen on his right, covering his movement, protecting him from do-gooders. Pull and aim and fire . . . six practice shots. Six hits on six trees about two hundred feet away.

She said, "Very good, my dear. Franklin Roosevelt is a dead man. Churchill, too."

AN HOUR TO GO till the evening gun. Mike Reilly stood behind the president's armored podium and looked across the South Lawn. The Washington Monument and the Jefferson Memorial loomed like dark sentinels in the distance. U.S. Army privates, real sentinels, had moved into position directly below, one every five feet, facing out toward the VIP seats. The bandstand was filling with crisply uniformed U.S. Marine musicians. Brass trumpets and drums were already tuning and tootling and thrumming.

And the excitement of Christmas Eve was building. Thousands of Washingtonians were now lining up on the streets around the executive grounds. In a few minutes, Reilly would give the word, and they would come pouring through the Alnor Doors at the southeast and southwest entry points.

He watched the cars moving on Constitution Avenue. He felt confident about leaving it open. And closing E Street had been an easy decision, too. The roadblocks had gone up. The traffic had stopped. The pedestrians were already crowding the fence. They were actually closer to the Christmas tree than the people who'd get onto the lawn itself. But agents were circulating out there, and soldiers lined the fence. Once the crowd filled in on the lawn, it would be impossible for anyone outside the fence to take aim from ground level.

Reilly stepped into the East Room, into a holiday burst of evergreen, poinsettias, ribbons, and bows. Two hundred household staff were buzzing about the buffet table, downing punch and Christmas cookies and filling the great space with their high spirits. Over in the corner, their token gifts were piled around the tree. And the piano player was delivering one carol after another.

Reilly wished he could feel as festive as the room, but that wasn't his job. He put his hand in his pocket and ran his thumb over the neck of the headless Hummel angel. He'd be vigilant so that no other angels lost their heads.

An usher approached and said, "Agent Jones is at the Northeast Appointment Gate with three people. He says you should talk to them."

"Why?"

"One of them is the Hollywood Nazi."

Just then, the piano player gave a flourish, and everyone applauded because a butler was wheeling the president into the room.

Christmas Eve in the White House had officially begun.

AT 4:10, THE FORD Deluxe with Indiana plates turned off Rock Creek Parkway onto Virginia Avenue. Martin had given Vivian the wheel. He wanted to engage her in the "mission" and see how well she drove. She negotiated the

stop-and-go traffic down the diagonal avenue, and took a left onto Constitution eastbound, just as a parking spot opened up in front of them.

He said, "We must be living right," and told her to pull in. Then he triangulated. About fifty feet east was the stone Lockkeeper's House, the public
bathroom. Beyond that, on the other side of Seventeenth, the land rose to the
Washington Monument. And from where he sat, he could see through the
trees rimming the Ellipse, all the way to the corner of the South Lawn, where
an evergreen waited for Roosevelt to throw the switch. . . .

Vivian turned off the engine and said, "Now what?"

"No sense in exposing ourselves yet."

"Exposing ourselves? But you said there are other agents around."

"Agents and police everywhere." He pointed to the monument, where four
Capitol Police sat on their horses, then to a police car on the southwest corner
of the Ellipse and another halfway up Seventeenth, where officers were turning
the northbound traffic onto D Street. And there were plenty of foot patrolmen,
too. "But we're the only people in Washington law enforcement who know
what Cusack looks like."

She'd heard a lot since morning that she questioned. But this struck her as
truth. She said, "Hard to believe that he's in on it, too."

"Why do you think we were on that train? Why do you think we enter-
tained him? We think he'll be working from back here while the Stauers work
on the South Lawn."

"Working? You mean shooting?"

He nodded. He'd been refining his lies. They were working well.

She said, "So why were you so hot to get VIP tickets? They don't do us any
good way back here."

"I promised the Stauers I'd get tickets for *them*. I had to deliver."

"But they're *real* tickets. What if the Stauers get close?"

"They'll be stopped at the VIP gate," he lied. "It's all arranged."

She thought about that, then snatched cigarettes from the dash and lit another one.

At four thirty, the Marine Band launched into "Deck the Halls." Kevin
Cusack heard it because—though he couldn't believe it—he was walking into
the White House itself.

Stella whispered, "You're not in Kansas anymore."

"Or Kansas *City*," said Kevin. "Or even Hollywood."

"If Mama could see this," said Stanley, "she'd just—"

They were following Agent Dan Jones and two uniformed Secret Service
officers down the long center hallway on the ground floor, passing one room

after another that Kevin had read about but never thought he'd see: the Library, the Vermeil Room, the Diplomatic Reception Room, and a hand-lettered sign that read PRESIDENT'S MAP ROOM. Then they came to the Secret Service room.

Mike Reilly was standing by the conference table, hands on hips and the sound of the Marine Band rattling in a tinny intercom. He looked at the three strangers, then at Jones. "The show's started. The crowd's coming in. What do you know?"

Stanley looked at Kevin. Kevin looked at Stella. Stella looked at the carpet. They were all struck dumb by where they were.

Jones said, "These people think the assassin and his pals are in that crowd."

"Yeah." Kevin overcame his awe first. He figured that after all he'd been through, he'd earned the right to speak up. "The same guy I've been chasing since Kansas City."

"And a married couple, too," said Stella.

"Accomplices?" said Reilly. "I'm not surprised."

"I wasn't sure until this morning," said Kevin, "when the husband came after me and ended up killing those Metro detectives."

"Do you know what they look like?" asked Reilly.

Kevin said, "I know Kellogg. The others I could pick out of a crowd. The husband wears a dirty raincoat, the wife wears a fancy blue overcoat, not navy blue, not light blue, but something in between."

"That'd be *Prussian* blue," said Stanley Smith.

And four sets of white eyes turned in surprise.

"What?" said Stanley. "You think a porter's dumb? I run the best car on the Super Chief, decorated in colors that folks always want the name of. I can talk about turquoise and burnt umber all day. And I damn well know what Prussian blue is."

"Right," said Kevin. "*Prussian* blue. Good choice for a German."

"And they mean business," said Stella.

"So do I," said Mike Reilly.

"So where do you want these folks?" asked Jones. "At the gates, watching faces?"

"We have enough security at the gates to stop an SS division," said Reilly. "We didn't spend a fortune on those Alnor Doors for nothing. Women can't even get hatpins through."

"Where, then? It's your call," said Jones.

Reilly said, "Circle the perimeter. Move through the crowd on the streets. Look for familiar faces—and *Prussian* blue—especially on E Street, near the fence—"

"What about the Ellipse?" asked Stella.

"The grassy area is closed. And the surrounding streets are too far, or else they don't have an angle on the portico."

Stella pointed to the map on the wall. "Somebody with a rifle could take a shot from back on Constitution."

"That's six hundred and fifty yards away," said Reilly. "And the cops are watching, every fifty feet. Concentrate on E Street."

"And if we see something?" asked Kevin.

"Sing out," said Reilly. "We have men everywhere."

"Even me?" said Stanley Smith. "I sing out, somebody's likely to shoot *me*."

"You stick with the FBI," said Jones. "And sing out if you see Prussian blue."

"You're going out, too?" Reilly said to Jones.

"Like I said this morning, the FBI will do whatever it can."

Another agent popped his head in and said, "The Boss is on deck."

Reilly told them all to stay right where they were until the president went by.

But Kevin couldn't resist. He had to see this. He slipped over to the door and glanced down the hallway. In the shadowy distance, by the elevator, he saw commotion, then the president's bobbing head and a butler pushing him along. Then a short, balding man stepped out of another office diagonally across the hall. And Kevin realized he was looking right at Winston Churchill, who glanced at him, then turned toward the rolling wheelchair.

"Ah, Mr. President." Churchill puffed up his cigar. "I must say, sir, that your people have put together a fine map room for you."

"Well, Winston, if you have one upstairs, I should have one, too. I can't have you one-upping me in my own house, can I?"

"Just so long as you let me one-up you this evening," said Churchill.

"I'm letting you close the show. So you'll have your chance." Roosevelt threw his head back and gave a big laugh. "Now, my doctor checks my blood pressure every day around this time, Winston, so excuse me for a few minutes."

As Churchill and his entourage headed for the elevators, Roosevelt kept rolling toward the door directly opposite the Secret Service room.

And for a moment, the president of the United States glanced at the people gathered around Reilly's conference table. Kevin Cusack felt a chill run right up the back of his neck. He'd been in Hollywood. He'd crossed paths with movie stars. But he'd never seen a man with more presence, all of it compacted into his upper body. It was as if FDR were a larger-than-life caricature of himself, all chin and grin, cigarette holder and energy radiating like light.

Roosevelt looked at the faces peering out at him and said, "Merry Christmas, folks. Best get outside and get good spots for the viewing."

Kevin Cusack couldn't think of anything to say but "And a Merry Christmas to you, too, Mr. President."

Then Stella said, "God bless us every one."

"Indeed," said the president, and he disappeared into his doctor's office.

HELEN AND WILL STAUER parked the Buick Special on K Street and started walking. It was 4:35, and they were late. They'd been hoping to get onto the grounds as soon as the gates opened, so as to grab the best seats, so as to get the best shot. But they'd been stuck in traffic. Now, all they hoped was to get through the VIP gate.

They joined with the crowd flowing down Sixteenth and across Lafayette Square, young couples, families, patriarchs with trains of children and grand-children, all drawn by the sound of Christmas music from somewhere on the other side of the White House. And none of them could imagine the horror that the Stauers were bringing as their gift.

Helen looked up at the illuminated north front and said, "They're ignoring the blackout tonight."

"They think the Reich won't attack on Christmas Eve," said Will.

"Do you have the tickets?" she asked.

He patted his breast pocket. "And the train tickets. Seven o'clock express to Penn Station. Let's hope we get to use them."

"Hope is not a strategy." She clutched her husband's arm. "Tonight, we sleep in our own Brooklyn bed. That's our objective, not our hope."

They were approaching the Northeast Appointment Gate on Pennsylvania, which guarded the entrance to the White House circular driveway. But the crowd here was surprisingly thin. Where were all the VIPs? The big deals? The cardholders? Two U.S. Army privates and a sergeant were standing by the guardhouse, turning people away.

"I don't see Cusack," whispered Helen. "I didn't think he'd be watching the VIP entrance. But keep your head down just the same. Let me do the talking."

They walked up to the gate and offered their tickets.

The soldier said, "Sorry, folks. You need to go around to the Southeast Gate."

"But we have tickets," said Helen. "And it says right here, 'Enter by the Northeast Appointment Gate.' Isn't this—"

"There's been a change, ma'am. You'll see the crowd lining up along the fence beside the statue of General Sherman. But you don't have to stand in that line. Just show these tickets and you'll get right in."

"Why is this happening?" asked Will.

"They don't tell us privates much, sir, so . . . Merry Christmas."

Harriet pivoted her husband toward Fifteenth.

Will said, "They're onto us. If I see that Cusack anywhere—at the gate, in the guardhouse, anywhere—we're heading straight for Union Station."

"No, we are not. And no panic, please," said Helen. "We came here to kill the Reich's two greatest enemies. That's what we are going to do."

They didn't speak again until they were approaching the Southeast Gate on Fifteenth. Hundreds of people were arriving, by foot, by car, by taxi. Off to their left, Pennsylvania Avenue angled down from the Capitol. At the entrance to Treasury Place, soldiers were shouting orders and directing people into line.

Will glanced beyond the little wooden guardhouse, stopped, and said, "There it is." A large metal archway was wrapped in evergreens and red ribbons to make it look as festive as the Christmas music echoing between the buildings: the "electrical searcher."

Helen squeezed her husband's hand. "Patience, dear . . . and courage. It is *der Tag.*"

"I don't see Cusack." He wiped the sweat from his forehead. "That's good."

A special line had been set up on the right side of the gate with a sign: CARDHOLDER VIP. The Stauers got into line. Two uniformed Secret Service were giving instructions and checking names on a clipboard.

"Checking names?" whispered Will. "I didn't expect that. Do we say 'Beevers'?"

They watched one couple go through the archway without incident.

The next couple were laden down with bundles. *All packages in the tent, folks. No exceptions. And no ma'am, we can't guarantee they'll be here when you get back.* That couple stepped out of line.

Then came two young people dressed in their best. They gave their names and were directed to go one by one through the decorated archway.

The young woman: no problem.

The young man: a harsh electrical noise and a flashing light.

Will whispered, "Oh, good Lord," as if all his nerve were dribbling right down his trouser leg.

Helen squeezed his hand and pressed herself against the gun under his coat.

The officer ordered the man to step back, asked what he was carrying.

The man flashed a metal flask.

"Either whiskey or Christmas," said the girl. "So ditch the damn flask, Charlie."

Charlie did as he was told and stepped through.

Then the officer with the clipboard asked Will Stauer, "Name, sir."

Will started fishing his pockets and patting his clothes. "I . . . I forgot my ticket. We'd better run back to the car." He grabbed Helen and they hurried down Fifteenth Street.

KEVIN CUSACK HAS JUST missed them. He and Stella had already headed south on Fifteenth. They were looking into the faces lined up along the fence.

But in a mob of people four deep, stretching past the statue of General Sherman and across E Street, it was hard to see much of anything, especially as the afternoon light faded.

"Half these people aren't even getting in," said Kevin. "They'll be locked out."

As they rounded the corner onto E Street, the Marine Band grew louder, the brass echoing joyously, traditionally, reassuringly over the White House grounds. "O Come, All Ye Faithful" was the tune.

Kevin and Stella kept looking . . . into hundreds, perhaps thousands of faces, happy faces and solemn faces, fathers and sons, mothers and children, lovers and friends, all coming for that magic moment of communal hope. They saw plenty of police, too, of every uniform, and U.S. Army privates with shouldered rifles staring stone-faced from behind the fence.

Kevin and Stella pushed and sidestepped along, working their way through the crowd. When they got far enough west that the trees thickened and blocked the view of the White House again, Kevin said, "I don't see any of them. Do we go back along the fence?"

"Hell, no," said Stella. "The Secret Service geniuses wouldn't listen to me, but I want you to listen right now. This guy is working with a rifle. He has to be. He's a safe distance away. But he's within his range. He's back there." She pointed across the Ellipse to the trees lining Constitution Avenue. "I say we go back there and look."

Kevin hesitated. They were planning to meet Stanley and Dan Jones, who were inspecting the crowd going in the Southwest Gate, along Seventeenth.

Then the music stopped. The band leader paused and looked at his watch. The sun had just gone down. A moment later, the evening gun boomed across the Potomac.

"Did you hear that?" said Stella. "We don't have any more time to waste."

And the band began "Joy to the World."

Stella grabbed Kevin by the elbow and pulled him toward the Ellipse. They tried to cut across the open grass, but a Metro cop told them to use one of the streets, Fifteenth or Seventeenth. "Ellipse is closed, folks, per order of the Secret Service."

"Goddamn fools," said Stella to Kevin.

"Beat it, sister," said the cop. "You're spoilin' my Christmas spirit."

Kevin pulled her along E Street, whispering, "No trouble. You don't want them frisking you and finding that Beretta."

So they went west, closely watched by police every fifty feet along the low fence. At Seventeenth, they turned south toward Constitution, with the wide, tree-rimmed Ellipse on their left and along the other side of the street, the beautiful white buildings of the American Red Cross, the Daughters of the American

Revolution, and all the other institutions smart enough to grab that good Washington real estate.

Kevin looked over his left shoulder to try to see the White House, but the trees were so thick that there was no view of it at all.

At the sound of the evening gun, Martin Browning knew it was time. If the crossfire was to work—two shots as the tree was lit, two more an instant later—he had to get into position. He gauged that there were more police watching the north side of Constitution, so he'd move along the south side and take the crosswalk in front of the Washington Monument, where the cops were busiest, then talk his way onto the Ellipse.

But in all his imaginings of this moment, while selling shirts in Mr. Fountain's, or shooting targets at the Murphy Ranch, or watching the desert go by from the Super Chief, he never thought that he'd have a woman beside him, complicating everything.

He touched her knee and thanked her. He should have apologized for using her, but that would come later . . . if there was a later.

She looked at his hand and smiled, a strained little expression.

He said, "If I'm not back in ten minutes, drive to the middle of the next block. But if you hear gunfire, drive there immediately."

"Gunfire?"

"Gunfire means I need you your help. Right away, do you understand?"

"I understand," she said flatly.

He grabbed for the door handle, then turned back to her. "You are a wonderful actress. But right now, your performance betrays you."

"I think you're lying to me, Harry . . . or Bruning . . . or Frank . . . whatever your name is. I think you've been lying for three thousand miles. I just don't know which lie to believe."

Could he have come this far to have it fall apart now? After all his planning and all his adjusting to accommodate her? He reached into his pocket and pulled out the leather wallet with the FBI ID. His picture had been perfectly fitted into the spot where Carter's had been. Helen Stauer was an excellent forger.

He let Vivian look at it but not long enough to study it or question it. Then he snapped it shut. "Now do you believe me?"

She looked up Constitution. "Go do what you have to do. I'll sit here and figure it out."

He took the key from the ignition, got out, unlocked the trunk, pulled out his navy-blue cashmere overcoat, now fitted with the K 98k, and put it on. Then he came back to the driver's side to give her the key.

She rolled down the window and put her hand out.

But he hesitated. He knew this was his last chance to leave the war behind. For a few final moments, he imagined all that might be theirs if he just told her to slide over and let him drive.

She said, "What? Get going."

And he knew there was no escaping. He could not evade the responsibility of history. This war had to be fought here and now. So he gave her the key, straightened himself, and said, "Be ready." Then he headed east on Constitution.

Vivian watched him and wondered: Why did he need her to drive? Where would they be driving to? And . . . why was he walking like that? For a guy who usually moved like a cat, he seemed to be having a hard time, as if something was in his way. Then, in front of the Lockkeeper's House, he stopped, twitched a bit, and stepped into the public bathroom. Did he really need to go that badly?

WILL STAUER AND HELEN were moving along E Street, trying to get close to the south fence, to find an angle for the shot. Then Will noticed a black man about two hundred feet away. He didn't see many blacks in the crowd, and when this one pointed at him, it got his attention.

Worse, the black man was talking to a white man, whose face now turned to them.

Will grabbed Helen's arm and pivoted away. "They've seen us. We can't stay."

She pulled away. "We came here to complete a mission."

"Mission canceled." He dragged her along, panicked and with good reason. But in addition to murder, Will Stauer was good at disappearing into a crowd. He commandeered a taxi that was dropping off revelers at the intersection of Pennsylvania and Fifteenth, pushed his wife into the back seat, and told the cabbie to take them to Union Station.

Helen cursed her husband, called him a coward, but he was unmoved.

He whispered, "We shall live to fight another day. And the Reich will thank us."

"So Martin Browning is on his own?" she asked.

"That's how he likes it. And he has the girl to help him. Now we'll see if she really loves him."

IN THE OVAL-SHAPED BLUE Room, Mike Reilly glanced at his watch. *Almost time.* Father Corrigan from Catholic University was rereading his invocation. Mr. Mason, D.C. commissioner and master of ceremonies, was taking deep breaths to calm himself. Mrs. Roosevelt was chatting with the Crown Princess of Norway and her family and a few other guests.

Winston Churchill stood at the door and peered out.

Press Secretary Joseph Early said to Roosevelt, "Mr. President, they're play-ing 'Joy to the World.' That's our cue."

Roosevelt turned to his naval aide, Captain Beardall. "I'll take my cane."

Mike Reilly locked the wheelchair and the president's leg braces, then helped him to stand. Roosevelt wobbled a bit, put some weight on the cane, but never stopped smiling, because he never showed stress over the braces.

Early said, "After the CBS radio intro, I'll signal the bandleader. The doors will open on 'Ruffles and Flourishes.'"

Roosevelt looked at Churchill. "Remember, Winston, the president gets four ruffles and four flourishes. Then out we go on 'Hail to the Chief,' which is known in certain Republican circles as 'Hail to the Class Traitor.'"

"I'd wager that the happy assemblage out there this evening think much differently, sir."

Joseph Early glanced at his watch. "Two minutes, Mr. President."

IN THE COLD LITTLE men's room in the Lockkeeper's House, Martin Browning stood in a stall. He was trying to rearrange the rifle so that he could walk normally but not drop the gun. Something had torn on the lining. The eight-pound rifle was much heavier than the C96 and his stitching had failed. He'd worked on it the night before. He'd practiced moving with it. He thought he had it. But perhaps a few more adjustments and he could move naturally. As he fidgeted, the gun slipped, so that the barrel struck the stone floor with a loud echo, right by his shoes.

At the same moment, someone came into the bathroom and stepped to the urinal.

Martin stopped moving.

A grunt, a piss, a flush. Then a pair of shiny black shoes and blue trousers appeared at the bottom of Martin's stall. A policeman's hat appeared above. "You havin' a problem in there, fella?"

"Just straightening up, Officer, and—" Had the cop seen the rifle? Now was not the time to gamble. So he reached toward his shoe.

"Come on, come on," said the cop. "Open up. No weirdos in the men's rooms on the National Mall. Not on Christmas Eve."

"But . . . Officer," said Martin like a befuddled old man, and he opened the door.

The red-faced cop said, "So what the—"

And Martin Browning exploded upward with the punching knife, up into the officer's throat, right above the Adam's apple. The cop was a big man. But the blow shocked him. He jerked; then he shook himself violently, like a speared fish. Did he feel his own tongue cut loose in his mouth? Maybe. And he must also have felt the life going out of him, because he slammed himself into the stall, slamming Martin's legs against the toilet and his head against the wall. Then, with a great expulsion of gas and air, the cop died on top of his killer.

And another voice echoed, "Fred? C'mon. We got a beat to walk. And we don't want to miss when the tree lights . . . Fred?" Then, *tap tap* on one stall. "You in there, Fred?" *Tap tap* on another. Then, push open a third.

The first thing the officer saw was his partner, splayed over another man, as if they'd been caught in some lewd sex act. The next thing he saw was the last: a hand pointing a pistol with a silencer. The shot hit him square in the chest and he fell back.

Martin Browning shoved the body off himself and crawled out.

The second officer was a bloody mess. The first, a clean kill. Very little blood on Martin Browning or the blue overcoat. But the knife was stuck in the officer's throat. And there was no time to free it. If he had to do any more close killing, he'd use the pistol. He put it in his outer pocket, easy to reach.

Then he stepped out onto the sidewalk, glanced toward his car and Vivian, and headed east. But something had happened. The big cop had driven him so hard against the toilet, he'd bent his right knee backward. Now the knee felt as if it wanted to give out altogether. And it hurt so badly, he could barely move it. But he couldn't admit to pain. He had to keep going.

IN ALL THE PLACES where they'd listened to the president declare war sixteen days earlier, they were listening now. Of course, if they'd tuned in for *The Story of Mary Marlin* at 5:00 P.M., presented by Ivory Snow, or *The Goldbergs*, brought to you by Duz detergent at five fifteen, they were disappointed. Instead they heard the CBS Radio Network announcer: "Columbia brings you the following special broadcast."

Then the on-scene correspondent said, "The White House Grounds, Washington, D.C., December 24, 1941. The United States begins the celebration of one of the most solemn Christmases it has ever observed . . ."

Joseph Early signaled to the band: "Ruffles and Flourishes."

VIVIAN HAD DECIDED TO call him Harold. That's how she knew him: Harold. And she'd just watched him go into the bathroom, followed by two cops. He'd come out first and was now moving along Constitution. But the cops were still inside and . . .

Was that "Hail to the Chief" she heard? The brass echoes bounced off themselves as the amplified music traveled across the open space of the Ellipse.

The president of the United States and the prime minister of Great Britain, two of the three most famous men in the world, were coming into view, and she couldn't see them because she was sitting in this goddamn car? She should have been right there on the South Lawn, but she was here, because of all the hooey that this guy, so attractive and so frightening, so calm yet so dangerous, who'd pampered and imprisoned her, and now appeared to be relying on her or lying to her or both, had been feeding her for three thousand miles and sixteen days.

Well . . . she'd earned a look at that Christmas tree, even if it took a little longer to get the car to him. She'd earned a look and she'd have it. So she got out, locked the car, and started walking.

She could see his blue overcoat half a block ahead of her. He was moving quickly, but . . . was he limping? He'd never limped before. Something was wrong. She picked up her pace and hurried east toward the intersection of Constitution and Seventeenth. Maybe she could catch up to him.

KEVIN CUSACK AND STELLA Madden were approaching the same intersection from the north. They had the Ellipse on their left and the traffic on their right. Kevin scanned the intersection. Stella looked along the trees on the north side of Constitution. They didn't see the man in the blue overcoat. But they did see a lot of police.

Then Stella said, "Look at that gal crossing Seventeenth. She's going like her pants are on fire. Her coat's open. Polka dots?"

"It's her. But . . . where the hell is she going?"

At that moment, a father and his little boy stumbled out of the Lockkeeper's House, diagonally across the intersection, and the father cried, "Help! Police! Murder!"

"Uh-oh," said Stella. "Diversion time."

Suddenly, cops were running from everywhere.

Stella said, "Get across Constitution and grab that girl if you can. See what she knows. I'll go down this side and look for Leslie Howard. He might be in the trees."

"Be careful," Kevin called after Stella as she took off on the north side of Constitution. Then he called across to the south side, "Vivian! Hey! Vivian!"

MARTIN BROWNING SAW THE commotion half a block behind him. That meant they'd found the two dead cops, and other cops were running from everywhere. And a set of flashing blues was speeding by. And down from the monument two mounted police came galloping. This thing was getting messy, which was good.

He could also hear "Hail to the Chief." FDR was coming out. So he had only minutes to get into position. He ignored the pain in his knee and picked up the pace, limping hard because he was afraid to flex the leg. He crossed Constitution with the light and headed for the two cops at the corner of Sixteenth, which, in this area, was no more than a stretch of driveway leading onto the Ellipse from the south. As he went, he adjusted the rifle under his coat and fingered the Walther P38 in his pocket.

"Sorry sir." One of the cops stepped in front of him.

Martin flipped the badge on his lapel and pulled the FBI ID out of his pocket. "I'm supposed to be over on E Street. But I twisted my leg. If I can cross the Ellipse, it sure would save me time." He hoped that they hadn't been prepped to look for a fake FBI ID, because if they had, he'd have to kill them.

But they were distracted by the cries and commotion back at the corner of Seventeenth. One of them gave the ID a look, then gave Martin a jerk of the head and let him go.

Perfect, thought Martin. Just fifty feet to reach the inner ring of trees, but an echoing voice carried out over the lawn: "In the Name of the Father, and of the Son, and of the Holy Ghost, Amen. . . . amen . . . amen."

The invocation had begun, from a Catholic priest. Martin had been raised Catholic. He expected to be damned or beatified for what he was about to do. He limped toward the tree that he'd climbed three nights before. He put the tree between himself and the street. Then he looked around it to see if the cops were watching and . . . was that Vivian hurrying along Constitution? *Goddamn her.*

She'd ignored his instructions. She was out of the car. She was ruining his plan within the plan.

But he couldn't worry about her now. This was the moment. He had to hold himself together, despite his anger at her and the pain in his leg.

He was deep in shadow now. No one was watching. Most eyes were on the confusion at the corner of Seventeenth or on the White House, so tiny in the distance. And his first task was to get into that tree.

The voice echoed, "Almighty God, Father of us all, keep us in thy providence as war and Christmas meet in the fatherland, here, of a united people . . . ple . . . ple."

Martin pulled a piece of rope from a pocket and flipped it up over the lower branch. Then he wrapped his hands in the rope and lifted. But when he put pressure on the leg to climb, it buckled, and the pain felt like an explosion under his kneecap. He'd torn something, he knew. His knee wouldn't work. He'd never get into that tree on one leg. Never. Time for a new plan.

OUT ON THE SIDEWALK, Vivian stopped. Where had he gone? Her "husband," the man who told her he loved her and lied to her and told her truths she didn't believe, the man she'd loved or tried to love, her central-casting FBI agent husband . . . he'd disappeared. She'd watched him cross the street to Sixteenth and just . . . disappear.

She wanted to scream out, but she didn't know what to scream. There were still people shouting around the Lockkeeper's House. Cops were still hurrying. Others looked confused. And the people driving home for Christmas Eve were speeding along Constitution with no interest at all in what was going on here.

She could hear the distant, amplified voice of a woman saying something about Mrs. Roosevelt and the Girl Scouts. Then she heard her own name. She spun round and was looking at Kevin Cusack. "You! You're here to kill the president. That's—"

"*He's* here to kill the president," said Kevin. "Your husband is. You know he is."

"That's baloney." Vivian still didn't want to believe it. She turned and sprinted into the middle of Constitution Avenue. Horns blared. Tires screeched. But she dodged and jumped and got across.

On the other side, a cop said, "Lady, stop!"

But she kept running.

The cop who'd just checked Martin's ID grabbed her. She pointed at Kevin. "That guy's chasing me. He wants to kill the president. He's the Hollywood Nazi."

A distant voice echoed. "The Boy Scouts salute the president . . . sident . . . sident . . ."

The cop turned to Kevin Cusack, who was dodging traffic to get across the six-lane avenue. He pulled his gun and said, "Just come up onto the sidewalk nice and easy, Mr. Hollywood Nazi."

"Oh, Jesus," said Kevin. "Not that again. You just let the Nazi onto the Ellipse . . . *and* his girlfriend."

The cop's partner was working a big walkie-talkie, calling his command post. "Hey, Sarge, are we still lookin' for that Hollywood Nazi?"

Kevin slapped his arms against his sides. "For Chrissakes." Then he looked along the north side of Constitution, but he couldn't see Stella anywhere in the thickening darkness.

VIVIAN RAN INTO THE shadows beneath the elms and evergreens. And the deeper she went, the darker it got.

Another voice was echoing across the Ellipse, a man's voice: "Mr. President, I speak both for the Boy Scouts and the youth of the nation . . . nation . . . nation . . ."

And Vivian saw movement, off to her left: a figure in a long coat was limping from an elm toward an evergreen, a tree about twelve feet tall with a wide bottom. When he reached it, he leaned into it, almost as if he was trying to disappear. And . . . now he was opening his coat pulling out the rifle.

She watched him raise it and point it, and she followed its trajectory across the open Ellipse toward the glow of the White House. And it all came clear to her in the darkness. He wasn't protecting anyone. He wasn't watching anyone.

Kevin Cusack was right. Her "husband" was the one who'd come to kill the president.

She cried, "No. Harold. No."

MARTIN BROWNING WAS SO focused, he didn't even hear her. He had them. He had both of them. He was certain. He worked the bolt and felt a cartridge slide into place. The angle wasn't as good here. But he steadied the K 98k level on a branch and calculated that he was about five hundred and forty meters away now. It would be a long shot but he could do it.

And he thanked the darkness. On the shortest afternoons of the year, twilight didn't linger once the sun set. And the sun was about to set on the United States and Great Britain, too, so long as the Stauers were in position.

Then he heard Vivian shout. "Harold! What are you doing? Stop!"

He ignored her and put his eye to the scope. The White House suddenly leaped into his view, clear and close. He could see the speaker, an overgrown Boy Scout. He could also see Roosevelt, standing in profile, and farther back, the bald head of Winston Churchill.

Deep breath. Focus. Deep breath. Adjust the scope for another two hundred and fifty meters. Five clicks on the turret. Deep breath. Trust your instincts. Deep breath. They were both dead men.

The Boy Scout finished. The district commissioner stepped back to the microphone. "And now, the National Community Christmas Tree will be lighted. . . ."

VIVIAN SCREAMED, "HAROLD! HAROLD, no!" She ran toward him, ran up to him, stood beside him. "Stop, Harold! Don't do it."

Without taking his eye from the gun, he said calmly, "Go and get the car, Vivian."

"You son of a bitch. Why didn't I see it? You're here to kill the president."

Martin wanted to say it wasn't like that. But it was. So he looked at her, his face drained of all emotion, and said calmly, "Vivian, just go and get the car . . . please, dear."

". . . by the president of the United States . . . States . . . States . . ."

Then Martin put his eye to the scope again. Roosevelt was swinging himself toward the microphone. In the viewing field, the president of the United States looked like a puppet on a little Punch and Judy stage.

Martin watched Roosevelt steady himself. He needed a stationary target because at this distance, the slightest movement would cause him to miss. But it was almost time.

And Vivian decided she couldn't let this happen. All the lies he'd told her, all the coincidences, all the easy answers that turned out to be inventions—it had all come to this. And . . . she couldn't let it happen. She threw herself at him.

He pushed her away, pushed her so hard that she slammed to the ground, stunned. But she staggered to her feet, turned toward Constitution, dug deep into her own core to bring up the biggest voice she could, and she screamed for help.

OUT ON CONSTITUTION AND Sixteenth, the cop with the walkie-talkie told his partner, "The sarge says this Hollywood guy is jake. But there's a bulletin out from the FBI. We're supposed to watch for a fake FBI ID with the name Carter."

In overlapping jurisdictions, overlooking sometimes happened.

Then a woman's voice reached them from the darkness. "Help! Help!"

The two cops looked at each other, then at Kevin, who said, "What did I tell you?"

The cops pulled their guns and ran toward the screams.

MARTIN BROWNING HAD TO shut her up. If he didn't, he'd never get this job done. And the job was all. It was why he was here. It was why she was here. It was why he'd killed so many already. And even if he really did love her, it was why he'd opened himself up to the woman now screaming beside him.

She was still turned to the street, sending her screams into the darkness. *Knock her out. Shut her up. Finish the job.* That was what he had to do. So he hit her a single hard blow on the back of the head with the rifle butt.

She dropped like a stone. He wanted to drop the rifle and help her. But not now, because the cops were coming, a pair of running shadows, with a third shadow behind. It was all falling apart.

He pulled the silenced Walther P38 and fired two shots. *Pop. Pop.* Both cops went down.

The third shadow jumped behind a tree. No time to worry about him. Some would-be hero too scared to act the part.

Martin glanced again at Vivian. She wasn't moving and didn't seem to be breathing. He'd killed her. He could tell from the way she lay that he'd broken her neck. And he'd broken himself in the process. For a moment, he didn't think he could go on. But he had nothing more to hope for than this, the shot that would lead to lasting historical fame, the shot that would also end his life.

Roosevelt's voice echoed. "And now, for the ninth time . . . time . . . time . . ."

Martin Browning, raised in the United States of German parents, friend of the New Germany, educated into the history and culture and, ultimately, the perversions of a great people, balanced the rifle again on the branch.

Roosevelt's steady voice rolled out, "I light the living National Community Christmas Tree . . . Tree . . . Tree . . ."

Martin Browning repeated to himself, "He's a dead man." Then he put his cheek to the gun and peered through the scope once more.

But . . .

Where the hell was Roosevelt?

The president of the United States had disappeared.

Martin couldn't see him. Neither could the twenty thousand people in the audience. None of them could see either of the men they'd come to see . . .

. . . because the lights in front of the podium weren't pointing at the White House. They were aimed out at the crowd, and at the critical moment, the Secret Service had turned them on, raising a wall of light like a last line of defense to protect Franklin Roosevelt and Winston Churchill!

Goddamn them, thought Martin Browning. Goddamn smart of them, too.

Then, the Christmas tree on the South Lawn burst into life, into red, white, and blue light that shone out into the Washington night like a beacon of patriotic hope. And from somewhere, solemnly, a bell began to ring as a marker of the moment.

To hell with the bell, thought Martin Browning, and to hell with the lights. He didn't know what to shoot at. But he wasn't done. He raised the rifle higher and pointed at the South Portico, then slowly lowered it. The shot would be wild but a rifle slug traveling at that speed could kill a man if it even winged him.

He took a deep breath. He squeezed the trigger.

AND THAT WAS WHEN Kevin Cusack decided he couldn't cower behind the tree any longer. He'd come too far. Saving Roosevelt was his job now and his alone. He jumped up and started to run toward the shadowed figure in the shadow of the evergreen.

He barreled into the tree and slammed into Martin Browning. The K 98k went flying, but it never went off.

Martin spun and pulled the pistol and saw the face. "You!"

"You son of a bitch." Kevin decided not to fall back from the gun but to go right at it. He launched himself shoulder-first into the killer's midsection.

The Walther went off and the bullet pinged past Kevin's ear.

And now they were grappling, first on foot, where Kevin could pummel Martin with jabs and left hooks.

Then Martin Browning found an angle, grabbed, and body-slammed Kevin Cusack into the ground. He had to get off that ruined leg. He'd be much better on the ground, and he was, once they were rolling and struggling. Hands, fists, fingers, eyes, noses, ears . . . all grabbing and gouging and ripping.

Kevin Cusack was a Boston boxer, and he went for the kidneys, but he couldn't drive through the heavy layers of cashmere.

Martin Browning was a Reich-trained killer, but he didn't have his favorite tool, the punching knife. What he had were his hands and those steel-cable arms, and if he could just . . . get them . . . around Cusack's neck.

Yes.

He had him. Now . . . snap . . . that's all it would take, a quick twist and this Hollywood nuisance, this Irish American friend of the Jews, would die like a Spanish widow or a girl in a train compartment—

Kevin Cusack knew that Browning had him in a death grip, one hand on the neck, one on the throat, strangling, maybe breaking.

Martin said, "Just like Sally. Another martyr."

Kevin spit blood and said, "Fuck you," as the world went dark. He didn't want this face to be the last thing he ever saw, so he thrashed to get loose, but he was caught, so he thrashed again, throwing his whole body upward, but it was no use until . . .

. . . he heard a gunshot, and the hand on his neck let go.

Then he heard another. A spray of blood hit him in the face. The hand at his throat released, and Martin Browning fell over.

And Franklin Roosevelt's voice was echoing again: "Fellow workers for freedom, there are many men and women in America—sincere and faithful men and women—who are asking themselves this Christmas, how can we light our tree . . . tree . . . tree . . ."

Then Stella was standing over Kevin, the Beretta in her hand. Two police came running up behind them. Two more ran to the downed officers nearby.

Kevin pushed the body off and sat up and gasped for breath. "What kept you?"

Stella was gasping, too, as if she'd run a long way. "Do you know how many goddamn trees there are along this goddamn street?"

Kevin looked at Martin Browning. "Nice shooting . . . for a girl."

She glanced at Browning and said, "Wow."

"Wow what?"

"That son of a bitch really does look like Leslie Howard."

WHATEVER WAS HAPPENING ON the Ellipse did not affect the events on the South Portico. History would record that this was one of the most unusual and inspiring Christmas Eves in American history.

Roosevelt delivered a solemn speech, then turned to "my associate, my old and good friend, to say a word to the people of America tonight, Winston Churchill, Prime Minister of Great Britain."

Churchill, orator and stylist, great communicator and great rhetorical navigator, gave a speech that would conclude with what amounted to a Christmas prayer for all humankind. "Here, in the midst of war, raging and roaring over all the lands and seas, creeping nearer to our hearts and homes, here, amid all the tumult, we have tonight the peace of the spirit in each cottage home and in every generous heart. Therefore we may cast aside for this night at least the cares and dangers which beset us, and make for the children an evening of happiness in a world of storm. Here, then, for one night only, each home throughout the English-speaking world should be a brightly lighted island of happiness and peace."

THURSDAY,
DECEMBER 25

EARLY THAT MORNING, KEVIN Cusack stepped off a train in Boston's South Station. He gave the cabbie an address in Savin Hill, and they headed out through the old, familiar, Christmas-quiet streets. The cabbie chatted the whole way about the war, about the weather, and about the excitement down in Washington at the tree lighting. Little did he know . . .

The Cusacks lived in a triple-decker—Kevin's parents on the first floor, his brother and family on the second, his sister and her husband on the third—and a candle glowed in every window on that mild Christmas morning.

Kevin still had a key, so he let himself in. He could hear the kids jumping and shouting upstairs. Christmas morning had come in big, as always. He hoped they liked the Erector Set he'd sent them. He'd heard they were getting American Flyer trains, too.

But he'd see them later. He wanted to see Mom, so he went into the first-floor apartment. He worried about what he might find. The reports hadn't been good. But the moment he stepped in, he smelled turkey in the oven and followed his nose to the kitchen.

His mother, in bathrobe and curlers, was peeling potatoes at the sink. Without looking up, she said, "It sounds like the kids were up awful early, Tommy. Next year, take them with you to midnight Mass. Then they'll sleep late."

"It's not Tommy, Ma. It's Kevin."

She turned slowly. And the look on his mother's face in that moment made all that he'd been through worth it. Then her expression darkened. "Kevvy, are you still running? The FBI—"

"In the clear, Mom. Squared away. It's all ahead of me now."

AT ABOUT THE SAME time, agents from the FBI New York field office were acting on a tip. An old lady named Ina Schwartz had read in the *Daily News* about a husband-and-wife assassination team, a husband in a dirty raincoat, a wife in a Prussian-blue overcoat, seen near the White House the night before. And . . . well . . . she had neighbors who fit the description, and they had a German name, and they'd left with suitcases the previous Sunday, but they'd come home late on Christmas Eve without them.

The agents expected they were wasting their time, until they found Helen Stauer sitting in her chair by the window, in her white slip, with a syringe in her arm. She was dead. Will Stauer lay in bed, naked, a sheet covering his big belly and a puncture wound in his neck.

The bodies were still warm. The agents surmised that Helen Stauer had seen them get out of the car, and she'd decided that the jig was up. So she'd chosen what she considered an honorable way out and the best way to avoid interrogation.

FRANKLIN AND ELEANOR ROOSEVELT, Winston Churchill, and their entourage worshiped that Christmas morning at Foundry Methodist. They traveled by motorcade to the church just a mile up Sixteenth Street, surrounded by Secret Service men bristling with tommy guns and revolvers. The facts of the night before were still sketchy. But one thing was certain to Mike Reilly: they could never let their guard down again, even in Washington.

FDR took some pleasure in tweaking the prime minister, who was not known for his churchgoing. "It's good for Winston to sing hymns with the Methodies."

At the service, Churchill heard a carol for the first time, an old American tune called "O Little Town of Bethlehem." It became one of his favorites.

The afternoon brought all business between the world leaders and their staffs. The situation in the far Pacific was bad for the Americans, worse for the British.

But at eight o'clock, sixty Americans and their British cousins gathered in the White House for a sumptuous Christmas dinner of turkey, oysters, sausage dressing, and, for dessert, a magnificent plum pudding, straight out of a Dickens novel. It came to the table beneath a blue flame that shimmered with Christmas magic and the promise of victory, even in the darkest days of the Second World War.

AT CUSACK'S, MOM'S RECOVERY and Kevin's return made for a day of Christmas joy.

But after his third glass of Christmas champagne, Kevin announced that he had to go right back.

His mother was disappointed. She was getting stronger, she said, and the arrival of her youngest son was a true tonic to her, better than the champagne.

"An even better tonic," he said, "is knowing that I'm doing something to help the country."

"And what is that?" asked his brother, the son who'd stayed home and gone to law school.

"I just read a play about wartime Casablanca," answered Kevin. "It's about people figuring out how to do their best, finding love, losing it, finding it again, about doing right when it goes against what you want to do. Stories like that help a country win a war. I expect to be drafted, but maybe I can write something that'll help. So I have to go back. I have to try again."

And his father, the bricklayer, said, "If you think you were put here to do something, Kev, do it, or keep trying until you do."

So fourteen hours after he arrived, Kevin Cusack was back at South Station. The night train was crowded, even on Christmas.

America was on the move.

AT HIS HEADQUARTERS IN East Prussia, Adolf Hitler sat up late, as usual. He picked at a bland vegetarian concoction that did nothing for his pallid complexion or his chronic flatulence. He grumbled about his generals, who were not up to the "winter crisis" on the Eastern Front, but he took pleasure in a report that Joseph Goebbels had prepared about the Washington, D.C., meeting of Roosevelt and Churchill.

Hitler called them "the Cripple" and "the Drunk." He said they believed they could "magically make the Pacific Fleet reappear" at Pearl Harbor, and he repeated Goebbels's contention that their meeting in Washington was no more than a "media circus." He called them two trained monkeys performing for the microphones. "But that is what we get when Jews are running the press."

Everyone agreed. At Hitler's table, they always agreed.

Then Hitler wondered how Roosevelt and Churchill could have deceived so many Americans so easily. "They must truly be the dumbest people that one can imagine."

He knew nothing of the assassination plot hatched in Section 6 of the Reich Security Office. For that matter, neither did the Abwehr, German military intelligence. In a bureaucracy like Nazi Germany's, agencies competed, and when one agency failed, others relished the failures. So no news of this plot ever reached the top of the German chain of command.

It would have disappointed Adolf Hitler too much to learn of its failure. He might have gotten angry.

Far more concerning to Hitler should have been the truth behind it, that Americans from many walks of life, from many races and faiths and ancestries, had done their small part to run down a trained Nazi killer, and they had put Hitler's belief to the lie. Americans were surely not a stupid people. As he would come to learn, underestimating them was a bad idea.

FRIDAY, DECEMBER 26

THE TRAIN DELIVERED KEVIN to Union Station at nine o'clock that morning. He had just enough time to get over to Arlington National Cemetery for a burial ceremony.

Frank Carter's service in the army had made him eligible for a plot. The manner of his death had made him a hero. If not for his persistence, that Nazi killer might have put three or four shots into the South Portico on Christmas Eve.

A small group bid him farewell, heard the rifle salute, and bowed their heads for the Lord's Prayer—Kevin Cusack, Stella Madden, Agent Dan Jones, and Carter's sister, who came down from New York.

Then Stella announced that she had to get to Union Station. "Milk run to Chicago, Super Chief home."

Kevin went along to keep her company until departure time. They had lunch beneath the great vaulted ceiling of Union Station. They chatted a lot and laughed a bit, and when the PA called her train, she took out her compact and powdered her nose.

Kevin watched her and couldn't help but admire her.

She lowered the compact. "What?"

"You saved my life, you know. That guy would've killed me."

"He needed killing. I'm just surprised they didn't name him in the papers."

"The papers called the whole thing a 'disturbance near the Lockkeeper's House.' They want to minimize what almost happened," said Kevin. "They already buried him in an unmarked grave."

"We'll bury all of them before it's over." She took out her lipstick.

"It won't be easy. I saw a true believer when I looked into those eyes." More than that, he'd seen a dangerous, relentless adversary, who'd say anything, become anything, do anything to gain his goal. "Scared the hell out of me."

"I'm glad he didn't scare that Vivian," said Stella. "He might have pulled it off if he hadn't fallen for her."

"Do you think he was capable of falling?" asked Kevin.

"Beauty kills a lot of beasts in books and movies. But the rest of us had to step up, too." Then she put on the lipstick.

Kevin said, "A good color, that red."

She said, "I wear it to distract from my broken nose."

"I think your nose looks just fine."

She snapped the compact shut. "You know, I could use a new partner. If the Hollywood stuff doesn't work out, come see me. I'm at the corner of Wilshire and Alvarado."

As he watched her heading toward the platform, he thought about going with her. But train tickets in wartime America were getting harder to come by. And putting dreams on hold was now part of life. And he had other stops to make. A man fulfilled his responsibilities . . . to himself and to others.

THAT AFTERNOON, HE BROUGHT Mary Benning together with Sally Drake's father on a bench at the base of the Washington Monument. So much had happened there, it seemed like the right place for them to talk about the person they both loved, the person he'd loved, too.

Then he left them to their conversation.

He had to find a post office, so that he could mail a button-covered cap back to Dilly Kramer in Kansas City.

AND THAT EVENING, HE rode with Stanley Smith out to Annapolis, to the funeral home where Kathy Schortmann's bereft parents mourned their only child.

They dressed her in a skirt and blouse she'd worn in high school, something homey and girlish, not the kind of fashion she'd come to prefer in the company of Martin Browning. There was no hint of the movie star, just the daughter of simple people, surrounded now by sweet-smelling flowers and a few old friends.

The parents treated Kevin with suspicion until he explained that he'd tried to save their daughter.

"She had too many dreams," said the mother.

"Dreams can kill you," said the father.

"Or keep you going," said Kevin Cusack.

He knew that they had no real sense of what their daughter had been through, what she'd done in that final half hour of her life, of how she'd raised the alarm that helped to stop what would have been the most spectacular assassination in history.

In all her dreams of silver-screen glory, Kathy Schortmann, a.k.a. Vivian Hopewell, could never have imagined the role she finally got to play.

He didn't bother to tell them any of that. He didn't think they'd appreciate it, not until later, when Marlene Dietrich played Kathy in the movie . . . or maybe Jean Arthur.

On the ride back to the Mayflower Hotel, Kevin and Stanley had a final talk.

Stanley had been offered his job back, but he wasn't going back. He was en-listing. "We all got to fight for freedom in Europe and everywhere else, 'cause where one man ain't free, none of us are."

"Stanley, I do believe you are a philosopher."

"Don't know about that, but I know the difference between navy blue and Prussian."

In front of the hotel, Kevin shook Stanley's hand.

Stanley said, "If you get called up, look for me in a tank. That's where I plan to be. Fightin' for freedom in a big, fat, motherfuckin' steel monster, with my fingers on a .30-cal machine gun, and nobody callin' me nigger—or George—ever again."

"If they do," said Kevin, "they'll have to answer to me."

As Stanley drove off, Kevin realized that he was exhausted. Two nights riding on the Penn Central could do that. Exhausted but wide awake.

So he went for a walk, down Connecticut, across Lafayette Square, and straight toward the White House. It wasn't lit up and wouldn't be for a long time. So he kept walking, unconsciously following the path that Martin Browning had taken on his midnight scouting trip.

He went down Fifteenth, across the Ellipse, past the spot where Stella had killed Browning. He crossed Constitution and climbed the knoll to the Wash-ington Monument.

The wind was blowing out of the northwest, bringing snow, bringing real winter. Forty-eight flagpoles, symbolizing the forty-eight states, surrounded the monument. The hardware on every flag line clanged in the wind, playing a strange metallic symphony.

Kevin looked up at the stone obelisk, a giant shadow with a flashing red light at the top, a light warning of danger, a light reminding of vigilance.

Then he looked east toward the Capitol. He could just make out the dome, a darkened silhouette against the sky. And he looked at it for a long time. He liked looking at it. It comforted him somehow.

THE WORLD WOULD TURN on its axis nearly fifteen hundred times before another tree lighting on the South Lawn. After 1941, the Secret Service deter-mined that the security risks were too great. Yes, they would allow midafternoon celebrations, with carols and visitors. But no more lights. No more mobs. No more invitations to assassination.

By December of 1945, when Americans gathered again to watch the presi-dent light the National Community Christmas Tree, Franklin Roosevelt would be dead. Some would call him a casualty of war. Winston Churchill would be a private citizen, turned out of office after standing steadfast against Nazi Ger-many when England stood alone.

Berlin and Tokyo would lie in ruins, both capitals bombed "until the rubble jumped," to use one of Churchill's more brutal phrases. A third of the Soviet Union and much of Europe would be laid to waste. And millions would be gone to the slaughter . . . on battlefields, in concentration camps, or under bombs that grew ever more terrible until, at the end, a single explosion could vaporize a whole city.

At no moment in history was it ever more certain that war was the original human fact. But for every death there was a story. For every person, there came a moment that was *der Tag*, the day to decide, the day to live or die, but surely the day to stand and perhaps to hope.

AFTERWORD

This is a work of fiction. The characters, except for those obviously historical, were born in my imagination and have lived, I hope, in yours.

That imagination was inspired first by the story of Churchill's December '41 visit to Washington. Then I came across an obscure memoir called *Reilly of the White House,* written by the agent who led Franklin Roosevelt's Secret Service detail during the war. Mike Reilly tells us that in the days after Pearl Harbor, while some worried about an actual armed assault by paramilitary forces, he worried about the lone assassin, or the small team dispatched to kill the president. Out of that worry sprang this plot.

As for other historical questions, a few answers:

Yes, there was a powerful German presence in Southern California between the wars, and a powerful homegrown fascist presence, too. Of Deutsches Haus you will now find no trace. But if you know where to look, you may find the ruins of supposed Nazi enclaves in the dry hills around Los Angeles.

The Los Angeles Jewish Community Committee, organized by Leon Lewis, kept an eye on Nazi sympathizers during the 1930s and early '40s, when neither the FBI nor the LAPD could be bothered. Lewis called upon people from many walks of life and of many religions to aid the cause. They warned of nefarious doings. They raised the alarm. They were unsung heroes.

The play called *Everybody Comes to Rick's,* by Murray Burnett and Joan Alison, really did arrive at Warner Bros. on the day after Pearl Harbor. A young reader named Stephen Karnot wrote the report, then left to work in the defense industry. But producer Hal Wallis bought the play the week after Christmas. The movie arrived a year later, at the perfect moment in history and the perfect moment at the box office, when the Allies were invading North Africa, liberating Casablanca, and, across multiple fronts, turning history's most destructive war in the right direction.

Leslie Howard, doppelgänger for our antihero, was not only a star but a fierce and committed anti-Nazi. He returned to England after *Gone With the Wind* to make films that would inspire his countrymen. He would die in 1943, when German fighters shot down the civilian airliner carrying him.

And yes, "Chattanooga Choo Choo" went to No. 1 on the *Billboard* charts on December 7, 1941.

All of these facts fed into the writing of the book and the atmosphere around it. And many people helped or inspired me to write it. My thanks to all of them. Let me single out, as always, my longtime editor, Bob Gleason, and my even longer-time agent, Robert Gottlieb. They have helped to keep me in the business of storytelling for decades, which means they've helped me to spend my life dreaming up plots and characters, which has made for a very satisfying career. They are good and loyal friends.

But most important, I thank my wife, Chris. She *really* makes it all possible. She's downstairs reading the first draft as I write this. I hope she's enjoying it.

William Martin
January 2021